## PARADISE PROMISED

What would he look like, this god of the volcano? As repugnant as the pearl-eyed statues that lined his temple, the fiery flames of his hair flying all around him? Malana could only hope that whatever Te Tuma planned to do with her, it would be merciful and swift.

Then he entered. Feet braced wide apart, the fear-evoking god paused in the doorway. The first thing she noticed about him were his eyes, as blue as the ocean, yet with none of the pristine sparkle. Instead, sharp and dangerous as a coral reef, they raked over her. But it was his hair that held her fascination. Just as the priests had told her, the flame of fire glinted there.

With the regal pride Malana's mother had ingrained in her, she faced him, this vengeful god of the volcano who, with one mighty swoop, could destroy everything in his path.

"Te Tuma," she said, her eyes meeting his boldly, if briefly, before she fell to her knees before him. "I am yours. Do with me what you please."

To Zeph Westley, captain or not, what he pleased would simply not do.

# PARADISE
# PROMISED

## Terri Valentine

Zebra Books
Kensington Publishing Corp.

*To Zeph.*
*May the path you follow in life be*
*the one of your choosing.*

ZEBRA BOOKS are published by

Kensington Publishing Corp.
850 Third Avenue
New York, NY 10022

First Printing: October, 1996
10  9  8  7  6  5  4  3  2  1

Printed in the United States of America

# Chapter One

*February 1813*
*Hitihiti Island, South Pacific*

The boom-boom-boom of the distant *lali*—huge wooden drums—emulated the pounding of madcap hearts in the darkness. From the deck of the whaling ship, the *Dolphin*, the faraway stream of hand-held torches took on the eerie essence of a snake slowly writhing its way up the side of the volcano. The chanting voices sent chills down the backs of those few still topside.

"What do ya make of it all, Cap'n Zeph?" Youthful awe tinged the excited voice of the boy who leaned as far out over the railing as he could. He craned his neck to take in as much of the island and its pagan ways as his inexperienced eyes could soak up.

"Well, Danny boy . . ." His own pulse an arrhythmia of cautious uncertainty, Captain Zephiran Westley leveled a look on his cabin boy. How well he remembered his own first South Seas adventure—the strange sights, smells, and food. If only he could offer the wide-eyed lad some sort of explanation. But the truth was, he himself didn't know what to make of the islanders' odd behavior of the last few days.

Ever since their arrival the day before, the normally complacent Hitihitians had been acting a bit strange, like a nest of ants stirred to a frenzy. Oh, as expected, they had rowed out en masse to greet the ship the moment it reached harbor, its mission to take on much-needed fresh water and a supply of breadfruit and coconut to stave off scurvy. The exotic, scantily clad women, as friendly as ever, had immediately begun offering the female-deprived sailors favors in exchange for pretty cloth, nails and screws, or any kind of metal building material impossible to obtain except from outsiders.

Wise to the island ways, Zeph had brought along many colorful bolts of material and a kegful of trade goods, divvying out an allotment to each man meant to last the entire voyage. Otherwise, the crew might strip the ship of vital hardware to satisfy their avaricious needs, rendering it unsailable. It had been known to happen to masters much stricter but less prepared than he.

Whatever had the island astir, Zeph suspected it had religious connotations. The name Te Tuma had been bandied about, spoken with reverence and rolled eyes of fear even during the lavish feasting of that first night they had anchored in the lagoon and come ashore.

As usual, he turned a blind eye to the indulgences that invariably followed. What his men did on liberty did not overly concern him unless it put his ship in danger.

Nonetheless, he refused to partake of what was so freely offered, although there had been times he had been sorely tempted by some sloe-eyed island girl determined to seduce him. At such times he conjured up the image of Leatrice, her ash-blond hair framing her pale, gentle face.

Sweet, patient Leatrice, his fiancée. She waited for him back in Mystic. He would not betray her.

Crossing his hands behind his back, Zeph spread his booted feet and returned his attention to the matter at hand. Te Tuma. It was a name with which he wasn't familiar. Must be some kind of god. But god of what? he wondered with mild curiosity, as he rocked back on his heels and once more focused on the crawling line of torchlight inching its way up the mountainside. Could be anything, for it seemed paradise had more gods than the ocean did fish.

"Look there, Cap'n," Danny pointed, even as the watch called out a warning that a small craft approached from the lee side.

The sleek canoe fashioned with an outrigger slid noiselessly toward them like a shadow. Even squinting, Zeph couldn't make out its occupants in the darkness. Islanders, no doubt. Yet the sixth sense of a seasoned sailor counseled him to not let down his guard, even for a moment.

"Whoever they are, Mr. Kennedy," he issued a low command to his second in command, his rich baritone carrying easily across the expanse of the deck, "welcome them aboard, but don't take your eyes off them for a moment."

"Aye, sir," the mate replied, throwing the rope ladder over the side, then swinging a lantern to indicate a friendly reception.

"Danny," Zeph said quietly, bending to speak in the youth's ear, "bring me my pistols."

"Aye, Cap'n Zeph." Staring up at his commander, the cabin boy's eyes glistened with a mixture of fear and excitement. Unquestioning, he turned and scampered away to do his captain's bidding.

The deceptively soft lap of paddles contrasted sharply with the near-frenzy rhythm of the island drums. Zeph's pulse took up the pounding tempo, yet he couldn't say for sure just what caused his alarm. Island mumbo jumbo, no doubt. It had a way of getting under the skin of even the most levelheaded. Nonetheless, he felt much better when the boy returned moments later and slipped the loaded weapons into his hand. Zeph tucked the guns into the sash about his waist with an outward calm he didn't feel.

"Go below, Danny," he ordered.

"Do ya think they plan on attackin' us, sir?" the boy blurted out, loud enough for several of the crew to turn and stare at Zeph in anticipation of his reply.

"We'll take it as it comes." He shot the lad, and then the curious, a look that would wither the toughest ol' salt. At the sound of a feminine voice, he glanced up, surprised to see his man assist an island woman over the railing.

Le'utu. Zeph instantly recognized the Hitihitian princess. A few years older than he and still boasting the figure of a much younger woman, she was almost as beautiful as the first time he has seen her nearly two decades ago.

Like the eyes of a cat, her dark orbs searched the deck, found him, clung, and refused to look away. She didn't smile. Hers was not a social call, he suspected. Had she perchance come to warn him?

"Zephiran." She said his name in her soft Polynesian slur, carefully accenting each syllable. *"E 'olu'olu'oe,"* she pleaded, "you must help me."

When his unyielding face showed no signs of softening, she reached out and touched his arm. He glanced at the tattoos across her knuckles, markings that indicated her royal status among her people.

"For the *hano* of James Kilpatrick," she begged. "We must speak alone. *E 'olu'olu'oe,* do not turn me away. Hear what I have to say."

James Kilpatrick, his mentor and friend. It had been Captain Jim who had taken him, an untried boy, on his very first voyage. James Kilpatrick had taught him everything he knew about the sea and whaling. He had been more of a father to him than his own flesh and blood.

Only mildly concerned about what his gawking crew might think, Zeph claimed the half-clad woman's arm just above the telltale tattoo bracelet and led her toward his cabin.

"Le'utu, you shouldn't have come here like this," he warned as they descended the companionway stairs leading below deck.

"But I had no one else to turn to," she explained, shaking her dark head in denial, once they reached the door to his cabin. She looked up at him with steady eyes as black as a fathomless sea.

Zeph assessed her with the experienced eye of a sailor. Her regal beauty was heart-stopping, especially to a man who had been without female company for so long. Even now, he could see what it was about her that had intrigued James years ago. In deference to his friend, Zeph allowed his unseemly thoughts to stray no further as he led her inside his private domain.

"Very well, Le'utu." The door now closed, he steered her toward a bolted-down chair and urged her to sit. Positioning himself so that he stood above her, he crossed his arms over his chest.

She appraised him then, as any woman might a man, but the islanders had a special way of doing it that made him feel self-conscious. Suddenly aware of how his posture caused his muscles to bulge beneath his green pea coat, Zeph uncrossed his arms and clasped his hands behind his back.

"So what is it? What is so important that you risked coming here alone?"

As quickly and naturally as her perusal had begun, it abruptly ended. She stared up at him with pleading eyes. "Malana, my daughter. *E 'olu'olu'oe.*" Reaching up, she clutched his arm. "You must help me save James's daughter."

"Malana?" he asked, sitting down on the edge of the bolted-down desk that held all of his maps and charts. One brow shot up warily, conjuring up the image of a lithe little creature who had years ago clung to her mother's garments. Rather shy, she had peeped at the strangers with saucer-size eyes the color of coal.

The last time he had seen Malana she could not have been more than ten or eleven. Even then, on that final voyage they had taken together, James had not acknowledged the child as his, even when Le'utu insisted otherwise. Yet, how could a man who could identify a whale a quarter mile away be so blind as not to see the obvious likeness of his own face in the little girl's, nor recognize her mother's fear? Fear. It was what Zeph saw now in the woman's pleading look.

"Is she ill? One of my men is a medic of sorts. *Kauka,*" he added in explanation. "He could take a look at her. . . ."

"No. No. She is not sick, Zephiran. *Ho'olohe.*" Cupping her hand about her ear to indicate he should listen, she spoke to him as if he were a child. Instead, he considered childlike her pristine unawareness of the vastness of the world beyond the horizon. "Do you not hear the message in the drums?"

The drums. Zeph looked up and stared angrily at the ceiling of his cabin. How could he not hear them? Their unrelenting pounding pulsated in his veins, filling his head with their heated rhythm, refusing to give him a moment's peace.

"I hear them, Le'utu, but I do not know what they are saying."

"They speak to Te Tuma," she explained in an awed whisper.

Te Tuma. That name again. He shrugged his shoulders and stared at her in curious expectation.

Again that look of disbelief.

"Te Tuma. The god of the volcano. The most fierce, vengeful god of all. Tonight he receives another virgin bride. *Mankana* from the People. After much *le'ale'a,*" she explained, sliding the finger of one hand in and out of the circle created by the fingers of the other, "then he will continue to slumber. Through many *'ulu* seasons, if we are lucky."

The sexual meaning of her graphic sign language crystal clear, Zeph found it incredible how easily and openly these people spoke of such private matters. He also understood the quaint island measurement of time. In February the *'ulu,* or breadfruit, a large, rather strange fruit with a consistency between bread and sweet potatoes, which constituted the main staple of the Hitihitians' diet, ripened. For the islanders, this annual main harvest signified the start of the new year. But this bit about the god of the volcano given a woman to sate his lust . . . it sounded like more than a little South Seas promiscuity.

A shiver ran down his rigid spine. Surely she wasn't talking about some kind of human sacrifice.

He had heard accounts of such pagan rituals, of young girls tossed alive into a volcano, but had never himself encountered such unthinkable barbarism.

"Malana!" he murmured, suddenly realizing just who the savages planned to throw into the bubbling lava. He shot the woman—her mother—a look of horror. "But why? She's a princess?"

"It does not matter. Mao wants only to be rid of her. He claims her mixed blood is a mockery to the People."

"Mao?" Confronted with an image of the fierce-looking island king, Zeph grimaced. "She's like his own daughter. Surely he doesn't intend—"

"Please, Zephiran, you must take her away. She does not belong here." Le'utu clutched his arm once more, her blunt fingernails digging into his flesh. "You must take her to her real father."

Her real father. James Kilpatrick. What would Captain Jim say if he showed up with a strange, half-caste girl claiming to be his daughter? God knows the seasoned whaler had denied her for so long. And yet, Zeph remembered the last time he had seen his old friend, just before he had departed on his present voyage. With a faraway look, James had spoken of regrets for never marrying and having a family, for not seeing to it that the Kilpatrick name was carried on. Well, now it seemed he had, even if it was not quite in the way he had envisioned. How could the man think now to deny a last opportunity at immortality?

"Where is she?" Zeph asked, uncertain just why he felt an overwhelming need to rescue the child. It was more than the pleading look of helplessness in Le'utu's eyes, or even what might be best for James Kilpatrick.

"In the god-house at the *marae* at the base of the volcano."

He vaguely recalled seeing the open-air temple of which she spoke. It had given him an uneasy feeling, all those pagan icons staring at him as if he were some kind of invader . . . as if *he* were the heathen.

"Hurry, Zephiran. We have little time. Already she has been given much *kava* and sleeps the sleep of the dead."

*Kava.* A drink made from the root of a native tree, its druglike qualities were well known to him. Zeph had seen what even small quantities could do to a full-grown man, rendering him disoriented and confused and often unconscious. What in God's name would a large dose do to a mere slip of a girl?

Prompted by a surge of unexplained protectiveness, he rose on legs long steadied by a life at sea. Then tempered by a cautiousness that had seen him through many a scrape, Zeph began to wonder just how in hell he thought to get away with snatching a guarded prisoner, especially an unconscious one, from beneath the very noses of the island priests. Even if he succeeded—which was doubtful at best—such recklessness could put his ship and crew in danger. And not even he, the captain, had the right to run such a risk.

The drums, the chanting, took up a wild rhythm. Glancing at Le'utu's dark eyes, filled with desperation, Zeph was forced to look away.

"Please, Zephiran."

"I'm sorry. There's nothing I can do."

But the tug on the sleeve of his jacket pulled equally on the strings of his heart. His sense of duty fought valiantly with his sense of honor.

"If you fear that they will catch you, I can make it so they will never know."

How? sprang instantly to his lips, but he clamped his jaw, refusing to give voice to the question. Did he really want to know to what extent she would go to save her daughter's life? If it were his child, he knew no sacrifice would be too great. But it wasn't his child.

Yet he could not dismiss the fact it was the child of James Kilpatrick.

"Very well, Le'utu. I will do it."

Such was the way of Zephiran Westley. When given, his word was as good as gold.


The blackness of the moonless night cloaked the activity on the white sands of the beach. Risking only one other man, a volunteer, Zeph came ashore, leaving explicit instructions with his master's mate. At the first sign of trouble, Mr. Kennedy was to pull up anchor and depart.

As expected, his orders went unchallenged.

Leaving the lone sailor on the beach to guard the jolly boat, Zeph repeated his instructions. At the first sign of trouble, the ol' salt knew to row back to the ship and stop for nothing.

When it came to the *Dolphin* and its crew, Zeph refused to take any chances.

Turning to Le'utu, he waited for her to lead the way. With the grace of a jungle cat, she crossed the open stretch of beach and slipped into the trees, beckoning for him to follow. Zeph stayed close on her heels, marveling at her ability to find her way along what, only after a concentrated effort on his part, appeared to be a faint path through the undergrowth. All a matter of what one was familiar with, he supposed. Her ability was no more remarkable than his own when it came to making his way around his ship in total darkness, never once tripping over the maze of coiled rope and lowered sail.

Just beyond a colossal banyan tree that had to measure at least a hundred feet in circumference, they came upon an overgrown stone wall with a narrow opening. Zeph peered into the cavernous entrance, discovering an open-air clearing terraced and well tended to keep the jungle at bay. This had to be the *marae* of which Le'utu spoke. There was something definitely eerie and unsettling about the place.

Le'utu signaled behind her back for him to come no farther, so Zeph squatted down among the aerial roots of the ancient banyan tree, feeling the raw, untamed power of the place. From his strategic position on the outside, he could see into the clearing beyond. An ominous silence hung over the location, cresting like a wave all around him, and yet it was almost as if he could feel the cries of those who had suffered to satisfy pagan beliefs. All around upright stones were carefully arranged in geometric shapes, altars of some kind, he decided. But it was the icons of every shape and size, glaring at him, that made him shiver.

Their eyes seemed so alive. He realized then why they

glistened with such animation. They were all pearls. The gems glimmered everywhere, enough to make a poor man wealthy beyond his wildest imagination. No doubt, they could as easily be the death of him.

All he wanted was to be back aboard his ship, in command, his only opponents the sea and the giant creatures he hunted. Those adversaries he understood.

Not so the people and the customs of Hitihiti. The hiss of burning torches across the way drew his attention to a small thatched hut—the god-house. Just as he suspected, guards were stationed on either side of the entrance. They rose when Le'utu approached, seemingly agitated by her sudden appearance.

Remembering he still had his pistols tucked in his sash, Zeph curled his hand about the butt of one, taking comfort in its solid familiarity. Easing it out, he took aim, knowing he could pick off both men from where he sat if it became necessary.

If he were willing to attract undue attention. Attention that would likely get him killed, if not worse.

Shaking off the feeling of cold fingers trailing down his exposed back, he reinserted the gun into his sash and resigned himself to wait.

Just what Le'utu said to the guards, Zeph could only imagine. After a moment of intense discussion and waving hands, the two men took off in a hurry, heading into the small stretch of jungle between the rear of the clearing and the base of the volcano. Stooping, Le'utu disappeared into the hut, leaving Zeph crouched in the darkness. He felt anything but alone with those glaring statues all around. High above on the face of the mountain the drums pounded, the voices chanted. Gods, like little imps in his imagination, hid behind every tree just waiting to pounce on him. His pulse, like hot molten lava, responded with equal fervor.

After a few moments Le'utu reemerged, signaling for him to join her.

Somewhat uncertain, Zeph glanced around, looking and listening for signs of the guards' return or perhaps for those imaginary demons to reveal themselves and their sinister intentions. Relieved and yet amazed that a confrontation had thus far been avoided, he eased forward. Ducking to avoid hitting his head on the rock entrance, he hurried across the clearing, ignoring the glaring pearl eyes, and followed Le'utu into the hut.

Inside the sturdy structure, Zeph glanced around. The hut was filled with even more pearl-eyed icons of every shape and size. He marveled at the ingenuity of the island architects. The floors and walls of the building were made of tightly plaited coconut fronds as solid as wood. Even the thatched roof revealed superb construction, made of an intricate latticework over beams lashed with coconut-fiber sennit, a technique from which the most experienced rigger could learn. But it was the prone female figure lying in the far corner that captured and held his attention. He held his breath in awe of the work of the Master Creator.

Malana. Only with extreme effort did Zeph manage to keep his wont-to-roam eyes focused on the girl's face instead of on her lovely, bare bosom, as round and firm as husked coconuts. Even without the strange red and yellow markings that had been painted on her bare torso, he found that difficult to do. So he looked, telling himself it was to ascertain that she was breathing. The rise and fall of those pointed peaks of feminine flesh assured him that she lived long before he found the strength to look elsewhere.

Aided only by his strength of self-discipline, he settled his gaze on a face as lovely as her mother's. No, lovelier, he decided without hesitation, noting the sensuous curve of her slightly parted lips, the long, dusky lashes over closed eyes, and the straight, delicate line of her nose. In contrast to Le'utu's rather broad and flat face, it indicated her true lineage.

"Hurry, Zephiran. We do not have long," Le'utu chided, her coarse nostrils flaring as she squatted down beside the prone figure. Yet the look in her dark eyes indicated only pleasure at seeing his fascination with her daughter. In a motherly gesture, she brushed at a stray lock of hair on one of the girl's high cheekbone. High and prominent like her beautiful, bare . . .

She was only a girl, Zeph reminded himself, forcing his errant gaze to return to her face. Not more than fifteen or sixteen at the most, and much too young for a scrupulous man like himself to lust after.

Above all else, Zephiran Westley had rigid, uncompromising scruples.

Nonetheless, he felt keenly disappointed when Le'utu maneuvered so that her own body blocked his view. Why, if he didn't know better and if the situation wasn't so dire, it would surely seem she teased him with a glimpse here, a peek there, as she quickly stripped first the ornate head-dress from the girl's dark, wavy hair, then the yellow-feathered cape from her slender shoulders. Lastly, she unwound the length of gaily colored cloth that constituted feminine island attire, stripping the girl bare. And then, with no inkling of modesty, Le'utu divested herself of her own clothing.

Unsure what made him look away—it certainly wasn't conscience—Zeph glanced out the doorway of the god-house to the clearing. Something seemed different, missing, a stillness that appeared to have sucked the breath from the earth's body. In fact, it caused the hair on his arms to bristle. But whatever it was . . .

The drums, the chanting voices. When had they grown silent? What did it mean? Did the islanders even now return to claim their sacrificial victim?

"Come on, Le'utu. There's no time to waste." Zeph

whipped around with the intention of grabbing the help-less girl, naked or not, and dragging both mother and daughter to the safety of the jungle, the beach, and the ship beyond. Instead, his mouth went slack, his hands clutching and dropping to his sides. A figure, dressed in colorful cloth, feather cloak, and headdress with lowered veil, stood before him. But how could that be? Just moments before the girl had been unconscious.

The concealing veil lifted, revealing Le'utu's still-beauti-ful face. Her dark eyes, possessed by serene determination, stared up at him.

"Foolish woman, what do you think you're doing?" Zeph demanded, knowing what her answer would be even as he posed the question. "Surely you don't mean to stay here and face those sav—" He caught himself before he said *savages*. "You can't hope to take her place." He grasped her arm, thinking . . .

Thinking what? To shake a little sense into her? But with the veil lowered, she had fooled him. Chances were, in the excitement and confusion, the islanders would come to the same conclusion. Why wouldn't they? They had no reason to suspect deception.

"We both know it is the only way," she said with a calmness Zeph found incomprehensible, considering what she faced. "If they come back and discover the god-house empty, they will search the island. If they discover you have taken Te Tuma's bride, they will avenge their honor and overrun your ship before you can get out of the harbor. Go now, while there is still enough time."

Although he recognized the truth in her words, Zeph could not bring himself to abandon her. Not so callously, so heartlessly, and to such a horrible fate. In his eyes he considered it a cowardly thing to do. But what about his ship and crew? What right did he have to jeopardize their safety any more than he already had?

"Please, Zephiran." Reaching out, she clutched his sleeve. "For James Kilpatrick, you must take her now and not look back."

For James Kilpatrick. The name, the need, the obligation to his mentor, echoed in his mind. James, who wanted a family, who had one but had turned a blind eye to it.

James's daughter lay there so helpless, wrapped in her mother's garment. The ultimate gift he could give his mentor.

The invasive sound of many feet forced Zeph's decision. He looked at the girl, then at her mother, and made up his mind. Such was the way of Zephiran Westley. When he made up his mind, he didn't change it.

Scooping up the slight figure of the girl, he cradled her to his heart as if she were his own flesh and blood. God's truth? She couldn't have been closer. James Kilpatrick was as much his family as anyone else.

Zeph hurried from the hut across the clearing, once more ducking to avoid hitting his head on the rock archway. He didn't look back; he had no regrets, not until he reached the safety of the jolly boat.

The sailor he had left there was nowhere to be seen. Why had the man abandoned his post?

"Ainsworth," Zeph called in a desperate whisper, fearing that something might have happened to the man, one of his best harpooners.

If he didn't return, what would he do? There was no time to search. And yet, he couldn't in good conscience abandon one of his crew. Still, there was the entire ship to consider. Jake Ainsworth had volunteered and had known the risks when he came ashore.

To his left, Zeph heard the rustle of bushes and knew he had no choice but to leave. Placing his human burden in the bottom of the boat, he drew his pistol in anticipation as he set about launching the tiny vessel. To his relief the missing sailor emerged, breathless, as if he'd been running, his pea coat bundled under his arm.

"Jake, where did you go?" Zeph demanded, returning the pistol to its cradle in the waistband of his pants. "And what is that?" He pointed to the balled-up jacket, frowning.

"It's nothin', sir. I swear. I got worried and went lookin' for you." Jake tossed his bundle into the boat, then glanced behind him, a look of fear crossing his face. "I think they're comin'."

With no time to spare or to chide the man for his senseless, if not courageous, act of disobedience, Zeph turned his attention to the task at hand. Together they worked to push the boat into the water.

"Row for your life, man," Zeph commanded the lone sailor.

The boat shot out, straight as an arrow, into the moonless harbor, making its way to the side of the mother ship. Only then did Zeph allow himself to look in the direction from whence he had just come.

The volcano blazed with torchlight, alive with the frenzy of chanting voices and pounding drums. Then he heard the roar of approval and satisfaction, as undoubtedly the hapless victim met her death.

"No, no," Malana cried. She spoke in a childish voice in her native tongue, wrenching his heart as little else had in a long time. "Do not make me. Do not."

"Ssh. Ssh," Zeph soothed, picking the girl up from the floor of the boat and holding her close to his heart. Such a child, yet as beautiful as any woman. Then he thought of the mother who had been willing to make the ultimate sacrifice. Le'utu. Alive and conscious. Knowing her fate. What had been her final thoughts as the scalding lava had consumed her?

"It was not in vain, Le'utu. That I promise you," Zeph whispered, as if he could feel the island princess's restless spirit beside him on the seat of the boat. "I'll protect her, until I can give her over to the safekeeping of her father."

And he would. He had given his word. God knew, he'd never in his life gone back on his word. And he wasn't about to start now.

# Chapter Two

Te Tuma.

Uncertain what she would discover, Malana trembled at the mere thought of opening her eyes. So she lay there, the aftereffects of the *kava* still clouding her reason. Her long, dusky lashes squeezed tightly together; her sensitive nostrils quivered with the strange odors that assaulted them. Although the air smelled of the sea, it was not the tangy aroma of the white beaches she had known all her life.

Instead, a sour stench of rotted seaweed and death filled her offended senses. A queasiness rose in her throat and hung there, even when she valiantly tried to swallow it down.

As if that was not unsettling enough, sounds, both familiar and unfamiliar, startled her. Ocean noises, some of them—sort of. The lap-lap-lap of the waves as they lifted and lowered a world she feared to explore accompanied clanks, squeaks, and moans that could only be attributed to those tortured souls who had already entered the fiery domain of the volcano god.

Te Tuma's world. Where else could she be?

There were other sounds, too, that confirmed her fears. Voices—harsh, unfamiliar voices overhead—saying things she did not fully understand. One rang out especially loud and domineering. Malana swallowed so hard, nearly choking.

It must surely be Te Tuma himself. Fierce and frightening to gaze upon, did the hot fires spew from his mouth as he spoke? Instead of hair, did the scorching flames encircle his monstrous head in the way the priests had described? What would such a vengeful god expect when finally he came for her? The priests hadn't been able to tell her precisely, only that no matter what he wanted or what happened, she must comply and accept her fate, if the rest of the People were to escape his burning wrath.

Uncertain which to consider worse—what she did know or what she didn't—Malana finally garnered enough courage to open her eyes. At first she slit her lashes just enough to take a quick survey of her surroundings, before snapping them shut again. Just what she'd expected to find she couldn't say, but it certainly wasn't the neat, almost tranquil world she had glimpsed.

More confused than ever now, Malana forced her eyes open, wide and searching, her gaze devouring everything she saw, her whirling mind trying to digest it all. She lay on a bed in a structure of some sort. Overhead, not one beam was lashed and the walls—she reached out and touched the one nearest to her—were of solid wood, not the lattice matting to which she was accustomed. Then she realized from whence came the soft moans and creaks.

As if the swells of the sea held the hut in their grasp, the structure gently rose and settled without cease. The ocean beyond. Was it the one she knew of clear blue water, or did it consist of bubbling hot lava?

Unexpectedly, the building pitched like a boat. Thinking to be tossed, Malana clutched at the soft, thick fabric beneath her hands. She looked down, finding it odd that such a harsh god as Te Tuma would possess something so beautiful. Why, it appeared as if someone had gathered up all the colors of the earth, sky, and ocean and cast them on the coverlet.

She hadn't even time to put meaning to this latest discovery when she heard that voice again. Te Tuma. He was closer this time, coming toward her. Malana's heart pounded like her mother's *tapa* mallet.

It no longer mattered what the priest had told her, that it was her sacred duty to bow before the all-powerful god of the volcano and bravely do his every bidding. She, Malana, brave? No, no, Mama forgive her, she was terror-struck.

More than anything, she wanted to run, to hide, to deny her responsibilities. But where could she go? She stared at the door, wondering what lay beyond. Freedom or the culmination of all her nightmares?

As if in answer, the stump of heavy, unseen footsteps grew closer. The thundering tread of a restless, demanding god shook the floor beneath her.

"Mama, help me," Malana pleaded in a choked whisper that quaked with fear. But no one could help her now. In fact, her mother was one of those who depended upon her to appease this unknown beast that advanced steadily toward her. She couldn't let her mother down.

What would he look like, this god of the volcano? As repugnant as the pearl-eyed statues that lined his temple, the fiery flames of his hair flying all around him? She could only hope that whatever Te Tuma planned to do with her, it would be merciful and swift.

With the inborn instinct and grace of her royal breeding, Malana stood to face her fate. From whence came her courage she couldn't say, perhaps from the father she had never known but had been told was the bravest of all men.

The door rattled; the latch twisted. So did her nerves, but she held her ground on shaky legs. Even her fingers trembled as they clutched the front of her simple garment, wondering again what Te Tuma would demand of her.

And then he entered. Feet braced wide apart, the fear-evoking god paused in the doorway. The first thing she noticed about him were his eyes, as blue as the ocean, yet with none of the pristine sparkle. Instead, sharp and dangerous as a coral reef, they raked over her. But it was his hair that held her fascination. Just as the priests had told her, the flame of fire glinted there. But it was not frightening, in fact, she found it fascinating.

It could all be a deception. When he spoke, the hot flames could spew forth, burning her alive.

Somehow she found the strength to remember her duty. In spite of it, her hand fumbled with the tucked fabric beneath her arm. The garment fell away, as did all hope and, strange as it seemed even to her, all desire of escaping. This was her destiny. She must simply endure it.

With the regal pride her mother had ingrained in her, Malana faced him, this vengeful god of the volcano who, with one mighty swoop, could destroy everything in his path. And yet, by the way he looked at her, his eyes at last coming alive as they feasted on her as would any mortal man's, she knew destruction was not his immediate intent.

"Te Tuma," she said, her eyes meeting his boldly, if briefly, before she fell to her knees before him. "I am yours. Do with me what you please."

With head bowed, the girl's ebony hair cascaded like a cape about her slender shoulders, across her bare back to the glistening curve of her buttocks. Concealed or not, Zeph knew what lay beneath. God help him, even if he didn't wish for it, the memory of her womanly beauty, pagan yet pristine, would be forever etched in his brain.

He would remember every detail of her body, even the small, inconspicuous tattoos, one on her right shoulder, another just below her navel, more clearly than the lines and names on the charts and maps stashed away in the desk behind her.

Although his knowledge of Hitihitian was somewhat limited, he still had a fairly good idea of what she had said to him, something along the lines of him doing with her as he pleased.

Frowning, Zeph allowed his gaze to sweep over her, telling himself he had the Godgiven right granted any captain to assess a glaring problem.

Nonetheless, captain or not, what he pleased would simply not do. Not at all. She was just a girl, he told himself, choosing to ignore the anything-but-girllike flawlessness of her sun-kissed skin. Above all else, he must never forget she was a mere child. James Kilpatrick's daughter, no less. No matter what she said or, in her innocence, offered him . . . Like now, with her delicately sculpted face turned up to him expectantly, her gaze guileless, guiltless, her cheeks without the blush an innocent girl's should have at such an intimate moment. And the ruby-red peaks of her breasts . . . they rode high in the water like ships with empty cargo holds, jutting from the cover of her glorious long hair.

Zeph swallowed down the raging fire that flowed through his veins like hot lava, telling himself such overwhelming desire existed only because he had been at sea for too long, and a flesh and blood female had flaunted herself flagrantly. After all, he was only human.

However, to hear Malana tell it, he was much more. He could swear she had called him Te Tuma. Still groggy from the *kava* she had consumed, did she honestly mistake him for that vengeful, heathen god of the volcano? A less honorable man might find her delusion amusing, might even take advantage of what she offered and count himself damn lucky. If she wasn't James's daughter and so young.

No. Only a rogue and a libertine would even consider such a dissolute thing. Besides, there was dear Leatrice, faithfully waiting for him back in Mystic.

Even now she might be braced against the railing of the widow's walk atop her house, one fair hand lifted to fend off the glare of the morning sun. The wind that seemed to eternally sweep the Connecticut coast would be whipping at her skirts, but she would ignore it. Instead, with a steady, never-to-falter certainty that his return was imminent, she would be looking out toward the Sound for a sign of his sails cresting the horizon.

How could he ever forget Leatrice or even think of betraying her loyalty?

Prompted by such self-righteousness, Zeph loved to rake himself over the imaginary hot coals of morality, questioning his integrity, probing to discover his true worth. It always pleased him whenever he lived up to his mental code of honor. Like now, when he snatched the coverlet from the bed and tossed it over the girl's naked form.

"Have you no shame, girl? Get up," he ordered, signaling with his hand, belatedly realizing he spoke in English, and rather brusquely at that. Yet when she clutched at the multicolored quilt and looked at him in fearful indecision, Zeph sensed that she had comprehended, but whether his words or his gesture, he couldn't be certain.

As a way to amend his thoughtlessness—she was only a child after all—he stuck out his hand, wiggling his fingers to encourage her to get up. Truly, that had been his only intention, to assist her to her feet, then retrieve her discarded clothes from the floor and insist she don them again.

Malana looked at his outstretched fingers for the longest time, then, when he offered her a stiff smile meant to allay her fears, she placed her hand in his, willingly accepting his assistance, as expected.

But then, to his utter and complete surprise, she threw

herself upon him. Her brown, willowy arms wrapped around his neck. Her body, naked and sleek and warm as sand on a beach, slammed against his. But it was her mouth, hot and seeking, covering his, open in surprise, that caught him off guard.

It was like trying to disentangle himself from a rapacious octopus, its inexhaustible tentacles impossible to escape or control. They were everywhere, those hands, slipping under his clothing like barnacles, latching on to everything in their path. When finally he reeled her appendages in, amazed to find there were only two of them, Zeph wrapped his arms about her, then turned Malana so that her breasts and hips were not pressed against him. The pleasure had been torturous. Even as he sighed with relief, she began to wiggle like a slippery fish.

"Hold fast, girl," he muttered. He didn't mean to hurt her, only to control her, to put some much-needed space between their bodies.

Needless to say, his order went unheeded. Zeph couldn't decide which contributed more to his rapidly deteriorating willpower—the memory of her firm breasts crushed against his chest, or the current abrasive pressure of her bare buttocks sliding up and down against his groin. Using the quilt like a fisherman's seine, he scooped up a still-squirming and bucking Malana.

"*Lele! Lele!*" she cried in great, heart-wrenching sobs.

The sincerity of her vow struck him with the force of a raw wind. If, indeed, she intended to jump, to throw herself overboard, he couldn't allow it. Having few options, Zeph tossed her back on the bed, just to be rid of her and the feel of her nubile body wreaking havoc with his. He needed space to think, to figure out how best to handle an unfathomable female. Such irony. Neither raging sea, mutinous crew, nor the threat of a wild "Nantucket sleigh ride" could put him in such a state of indecision. How could a woman have such power?

Before Zeph could come to a conclusion, she was up and running like a whale before a harpooner. If she managed to get to the door and out . . .

He had to stop her. His crew, eternally wound up like randy Satyrs, would go berserk at the sight of a naked woman. Zeph would be hard-pressed to stop them from converging on her, doing what sailors long at sea often did to an unfortunate, exposed female. It wouldn't be a pretty sight.

His was a good crew, one of the best, but it was still too much to expect them to uphold his personal moral code. Then, even if he did manage to stop them—and that would be a feat in itself—there would be hell to pay for abandoning their posts. He would have no choice but to give the guilty a taste of the cat.

Zeph shuddered at the thought and the repercussions. Many an attempted mutiny had been provoked by less. He couldn't afford to take such a risk, not when he had a fortune's worth of whale oil in the hold.

Torn between bad and even worse, he leapt into action, managing to block the escape of the fleeing girl just as she reached the door.

"Avast, girl."

"Let me go! Let me go!" she cried, struggling to get away, the blanket falling from her shoulders as she clawed at his restraining hand.

"Steady. Steady there. I'll let no harm come to you." He spoke to her as he would his beloved ship, pulling the coverlet back up and holding it firmly under her determined little chin. Only then with her face so close, her trembling mouth inches from his own, did he realize they conversed in English. "Then you do understand me."

"Why do you speak *haole?*"

"Why would I not?" he replied, answering her suspicious question with one of his own. Uncertain of her reaction, thinking she might again try to bolt, he tightened his grip on her bare arm.

Instead of the struggle he expected to encounter, her legs went limp and she sank to her knees, her hand lifting in supplication.

"Please, Te Tuma, I wish only to please you."

"No, girl." He shook her rather roughly. "Get it through your thick skull. I am not Te Tuma."

"Then who are you?" she asked, a look of bewilderment widening her dark eyes into nearly perfect round orbs. "If you are not Te Tuma, then why am I here?"

Why indeed? How much was she ready to hear? How much did she actually know? Had her mother ever revealed her father's true identity? In all of the confusion, he hadn't thought to ask Le'utu.

"For now, it's enough that you know you are safe." Zeph reached out and placed his open hand atop the girl's dark head, cautiously patting it, hoping she didn't misinterpret this gesture as she had his other ones. Her hair felt like silk against his calloused, scarred palm, soft and vulnerable, untouched. "No one will hurt you, girl. No one is angry."

"Then I do not disappoint you?" Wrapping her arms about his legs, Malana looked up, a glimmer of hope and relief filling her dark eyes.

He stared down at her, wondering how much she actually knew about the way the male psyche worked, wondering, too, how truthful he should be at the moment.

"No," he finally said, realizing there would be time later to better explain. "You don't disappoint me. But you must stay here." With a sweep of his hand, he indicated the small cabin.

She nodded, so eager to please.

"You must promise not to leave and to wait for my return."

Even as her head bobbed again, the scope of her unquestioning acceptance was heartbreaking to witness. It made him feel a cad to be the recipient of hero worship, such an unnatural thing for a man who had no heroes of his own. He of all people didn't deserve such devotion from another. Quite frankly, he didn't quite know how to cope with it.

"By damn, girl, get up and get dressed," Zeph ordered rather gruffly. "And stay that way," he insisted, averting his eyes when the coverlet began to slip from her slender tattooed shoulder. It was such an unworldly gesture on her part, yet one so utterly sensual. "Please," he added.

Without looking back to see if she complied, Zeph exited the room, closing the door firmly behind him. God give him strength. As an afterthought, he decided to lock it. The bolt, rusty from disuse, refused to budge. He struggled with it, cursing softly. As soon as he went topside, he would send someone down to oil it. No, no. The last thing he needed was for one of his men to be confronted by a naked, nimble, uninhibited island girl.

Clank. The bolt slipped into place with the ominous finality of a gaoler's lock. Had she heard it? He stood there, listening quietly for a reaction from the other side. None was forthcoming. Did the naive island girl even know what the sound meant? Did she know what it meant to be a prisoner?

Not until he reached the relative protection of the companionway did the truth of the matter hit him. And it did so with a jolt.

This would be only the first of many seemingly innocent incidents to come. But like an innocuous keg of gunpowder, it took only a spark to ignite it. It was a long way back to the New England coast, many miles of endless sea, many months of a restless crew. Just what had he been thinking when he'd so foolishly accepted responsibility for a lone female, especially one who hadn't the faintest notion of propriety?

His only consolation? As soon as he reached home—

actually, James Kilpatrick's home in New Bedford—Zeph
would be rid of his problem once and for all. His duty
done.

For that was what it was, he assured himself. A duty
returned to someone who had done his duty by him.


Te Tuma didn't want her.

Filled with a confused mixture of relief and disappointment, Malana stared at the closed door. If he didn't want
her, then she would not have to suffer . . . whatever it was
she had been prepared to suffer.

But why didn't he want her?

Tears crested her long, sooty lashes, hanging there suspended, refusing to budge. Had she not been persuasive
enough? Perhaps she wasn't pretty enough? Not endowed
enough?

Through the blur of tears she stared down at her own
body, naked and brown and much too slender. Perhaps
Te Tuma preferred his women with larger *poli*. Feeling
inadequate, Malana cupped her breasts, easily covering
them with her hands. Or maybe he liked lighter-skinned
females.

Hadn't her mother cautioned her to stay out of the sun,
reminding her that a Hitihitian princess should strive to
be as pale as the inside of a ripe coconut? Foolishly, Malana
had ignored the warning, confident she was much fairer
than most of the other girls. She had thought it wouldn't
matter if she was careless. So she had frolicked and swam
and dozed in the warm, wet sand, tossing aside the large
palm fronds Le'utu had insisted she take along for shade.
She had even neglected to anoint herself with the special
preparations her mother had concocted to whiten her
skin.

Ashamed, afraid, and filled with regret, Malana gathered
up the colorful god-cloth—for that is what it must be if it

belonged to him—clutching it to her still-pounding heart.
Never again would she uncover herself, not until the sun
damage had faded.

But by then it might be too late, a nagging little voice
inside her head cried. By then Te Tuma would have forgotten her. No matter what he said, she knew he must indeed
be Te Tuma. The priest had warned her. The god would
try to trick her, confuse her, for he did not wish to be
distracted, seduced from his destructive course. Even now
he might be spewing forth his deadly lava upon the defense-
less People.

Her heart lurched, painful in its sudden stillness. How
could she have failed so miserably in her duty to lull him
into forgetfulness? She should have tried harder. Instead,
she had been fooled into being momentarily relieved to
see him leave.

Wrapping the blanket about her, Malana aimed for the
door, determined to find her deceiver and stop him from
destroying the only world she knew, the island paradise of
Hitihiti. She would use any means available, would throw
herself upon him, impale herself if she must. She wouldn't
fail those who depended upon her.

The impenetrable door thwarted her plans and dashed
her hopes.

"Open. Open," she cried, vigorously shaking the barrier
by the handle, uncertain why it refused to obey. She had
seen Te Tuma both enter and exit this way. What *mana*,
what powerful magic, had he used to prevent her from
following?

No. No. There had to be a way. She would never give
up. Hadn't her mother told her there was always a way to
accomplish any task if only she searched hard enough?

Her back pressed to the door, she lifted her tear-spiked
lashes and studied her surroundings, looking for a solution. This undoubtedly was the volcano god's lair. Eventually, he would return.

Hadn't he promised to return? She pressed her fingers to her temple, trying to recall everything he had said. She couldn't be certain. How unlike her not to be able to remember. What kind of spell had he put her under to make her forget?

Carefully, Malana retraced her impulsive steps, noting every detail, testing her power of memory. By her standards, the room was cluttered. She lifted the heavy metal lid of a trunk and peeked inside. So many clothes. She touched them with awe, running her fingers through an orderly stack of shirts. Were they truly all for one person?

Another trunk revealed an assortment of strange-looking, unfamiliar gadgets. She handled each one with care, turning it over in her hands for closer inspection, committing each item to memory. Then she returned the entire lot to its place, making it appear as if nothing had been disturbed. Undoubtedly, they were the tools of a god, she thought, as she reverently lowered the lid.

It was Malana's discovery in the shallow, legged chest that ultimately captured her fascination. Islanders had no need for paper and writing implements. She had seen them only once before. Her mother had shown them to her and said they were from her father. Le'utu had held them reverently to her heart, as if they contained his spirit.

The key to the spirit of Te Tuma. Malana fingered the scrolls, first gingerly, but when nothing adverse happened, she grew bolder with curiosity. What strong *mana* did they possess? she wondered, unrolling one of the parchments that crinkled at her touch.

She stared at it, frowning, then sat down to study it closer, once again easily committing to memory every detail. The wiggly lines, the straight one, the words—none of them made sense, and yet she knew that somehow they represented a vast knowledge beyond anything she had been taught. They must indeed possess a strong magic, a magic that perhaps she could use to lure the god back to his lair.

Malana thought about that for a moment, her methodical mind envisioning what she had been looking at. Then she smiled and turned to gather up more of the scrolls.

The floor beneath her rolled and groaned suddenly, as if caught in a tremor. Jerking back her hand, she glanced up as the sound echoed in the ceiling. A warning, perhaps, or a protest to her invasion. It frightened Malana, but before the fear overtook her, her whole world shuddered and listed to one side.

She screamed. Clutching at the desk, Malana felt her feet and those of the chair pulled out from beneath her, and she did the only natural thing. Rather than fall, she let go. Grasping at the bedstead as she slid by, she hung there, praying. Praying for mercy and forgiveness. Then the world shifted the other way. The sudden movement tossed her once more like a bit of flotsam in a stormy sea.

She glanced down at the parchment still clutched in her hand, noting the new wrinkles and small tear that had not been there before. Terrified, Malana rolled it back up, grabbing hold of the desk as she bumped into it. Frantically searching for the leather thong that had secured the scroll, she found it, retied it, then stuffed the parchment back into the cubbyhole and closed the lid. She could only hope Te Tuma wouldn't notice the scroll was not rolled as tightly as when she had found it.

Then she dropped to her knees, clung to the nearest desk leg, and began to pray fervently. It seemed the great god's power stretched beyond her wildest imagination.

He had the ability to anticipate her thoughts before she even formulated them.

How was she expected to outsmart him? Oh, why had the priest left her so ill prepared?


The squall hit so suddenly that the crew had little time to prepare. They lowered the main sails, secured the boom, and battened down the hatches. Otherwise, they could do little more than put a shoulder to the parallel rains and howling wind that swept over the decks, rocking the ship like an insignificant cork.

At his self-imposed station near the tryworks—a brick oven used to turn whale blubber into oil—Zeph tried to ignore the steady stream of water rolling off the brim of his slicker hat and into his eyes. He knew he should have seen the storm approaching, should have heeded the telltale ring around the moon. Instead, he had been distracted by a woman. By a mere slip of a girl with nary a brain in her head, he corrected himself. That mistake might yet cost him his ship, if not the lives of his entire crew.

"Pardon, sir. The helmsman expressed concern that you haven't ordered us about, back to the shelter of the leeward islands to wait out this storm."

"Mr. Kennedy." Zephiran critically eyed his first officer through the distracting drip, drip, drip from both of their hats, suspecting that more than just one seasoned sailor had expressed concern. "You tell the helmsman to mind his wheel. If I want his—or any man's opinion," he added rather loudly, "I'll ask for it."

"Aye, sir." The mate snapped Zeph a respectful, if soggy, salute, but a glint of doubtfulness flickered in his intelligent gray eyes before he turned to do his superior's bidding.

Doubt. It was a captain's worst enemy. Left unchecked amidst a crew of superstitious seamen, it could easily run rampant and, like a bad seed, sow unrest.

"Mr. Kennedy," Zeph called quietly to his second in command.

Just as seemingly unemotional, the sailor turned in silence.

"I'd rather face a tempestuous sea than a mob of angry islanders any day. Mercy is an accountable trait rarely found in the savage."

"Perhaps, sir, you should have thought of that before taking that girl aboard."

Zeph had keelhauled men for saying less. At the moment, however, he respected Mr. Kennedy for his courage to speak what he knew to be the truth.

"Aye, perhaps I should have, but there can be no undoing the reckless deed now."

At that, Mr. Kennedy smiled, a rather mirthless expression that gave Zeph great assurance. Everyone knew Captain Westley of the *Dolphin* to be anything but a reckless man. Heartless, perhaps, but never reckless.

But if the crew thought their captain a hard taskmaster, they had only to stand tall on his seaworthy legs for a mere moment to understand that he expected far more from himself than from anyone else.

Perhaps that was why his success had been calculatedly slow, but nonetheless steady, over the years. He never took unnecessary risks, never dabbled in heroics—at least not until today. For if the truth be known, he didn't believe in such nonsense, having nothing but contempt and impatience for men who indulged in conceit or for those who praised such ill-thought-out behavior.

So now, what did that make him? At that, he grimaced. A hypocrite, no doubt, but more likely a fool who deserved to lose everything he had worked so hard for all his life. As for his crew . . .

He had more heart than they gave him credit for, which was something they might all regret.

Zeph stood there with the rain cascading off the brim of his hat, immersed in self-flagellation, damning himself for his stupidity. If they did manage to survive the sudden squall, he didn't even have a bed to sleep in that night. Not that he had grown so soft that he required a bed in order to sleep. But, damn it, he just didn't want to forfeit it so needlessly.

Hours later, Zeph still stood at his self-imposed station,

the nighttime cloak of darkness encompassing him, his ship, and his crew. By the grace of God, the storm blew itself out with the same fury with which it had begun, leaving in its wake a minimal amount of destruction.

But enough, he thought with relief. Over the next few weeks, there would be no idle days for the crew. Not after such a bad storm. The cleanup would take time.

Canvas and rigging needed sorting and repair; pumps had to be manned; barrels stashed in the hold required checking to make sure none had sustained damage and were now leaking precious whale oil. Of course, the decks could always use a good sanding. And if the men ran out of chores, he would simply think of more.

In spite of the scrimshaw—the art of carving trinkets from whale teeth—practical jokes, singing, and other idle amusement the men devised for themselves on the long trip home, idleness invariably led to boredom, the birth-place of trouble.

Already, Zeph had enough trouble of his own creation; he didn't need any more. With that in mind, Zeph ordered all but a skeleton crew to their beds, to rest and prepare for the work ahead. Leaving orders to maintain their course, he then took himself off to face the one he'd made for himself.

Yes, indeed. He'd made himself an uncomfortable bed of thorny spines, as James Kilpatrick would be apt to say to a young seaman under his command. Now Zeph had no choice but to accept responsibility and lie in it.

# Chapter Three

By pure accident, or perhaps by the guiding hand of a more benevolent deity than the one who presently held her in his clutches, Malana discovered the candlesticks stashed in the small drawer on the side of the desk. Oddly enough, she knew their function, as well as that of the light box stored with them.

Her mother had possessed several such aromatic tapers, precious and coveted, hidden deep in the island underbrush along with her equally precious papers. Le'utu had lit the wicks only on special occasions, a ritual of sorts that she had thought had gone unnoticed.

But Malana had known and watched and been fascinated.

When Le'utu discovered her curious daughter lurking in the bushes and spying on her, she had been angry at first, almost frantic in her insistence that no one ever learn of her secret goings-on. It had been then, and only then, that Malana had learned her mother's secret: Le'utu didn't believe in the gods of the People.

"No, not anymore," the woman had whispered, her dark eyes darting about as if she feared being caught in such a confession. "There is a God much more powerful, my daughter. The God of the *haole.*"

Malana had stood there, unblinking, at first unable to comprehend her mother's defection, nor the reason she would take pieces of the paper and put them to the flame.

"Because He is the God of your father's people, Malana. To Him I pray and make civilized sacrifice for James Kilpatrick's return. You see, your father promised that if I gave up my pagan beliefs, he would come back for me someday."

In stunned silence, she had watched the paper burn to a blackened scrap, which had disintegrated into cinders and been carried off by the island breeze. Not long after, James Kilpatrick's ship had anchored in the lagoon.

Even now she wasn't certain what upset her more—to learn that her father was a *haole,* which made her a despised *hapa haole,* or that her mother considered the island ways uncivilized. It wasn't just Le'utu's betrayal of the gods and her own kind, but her unnatural attachment to a mate, especially a *haole,* who had come and gone with the whim of the tide, a man who had never once admitted he had a child.

Malana had been taught that a man and a woman naturally came together, even remained that way for a while. If eventually they drifted apart . . . well, one didn't pine for the other. Always there was another to take his place.

But a father was a different story. Fathers at least acknowledged their children. Hers had looked through her as if she didn't exist. She blinked back a resentful tear, remembering clearly his appearance.

Like the god, Te Tuma. Tall and fair, with eyes the color of an indolent sky. A deceptive blue that had quickly turned into a destructive tempest when challenged.

Suddenly, it all began to make sense. Why Te Tuma had

chosen to present himself to her as a *haole*. Using her greatest fears and anger, using her fascination yet repulsion with her father's identity, the fearsome god tested her. And now she knew, too, the reason she had found the candles and the magic scrolls, why as a child it had been destined that she stumble upon her mother's secrets.

"All things, good and bad, eventually serve their purpose, Malana. Like the *haole* language. Your father insisted that I learn to speak it and I did, and I have passed this knowledge on to you, hoping someday it would be useful. Always remember what you learn and experience." How many times had her mother told her that? Until now, she had never given credence to such words of wisdom.

A long time had passed since that fateful day in the underbrush. With concentrated patience, Malana recalled with remarkable clarity every detail of her mother's private ritual, meant to appeal to the *haole* God.

Making up her mind, she gathered all the candles, along with the light box, from the small drawer. Then she removed the scroll—Te Tuma's paper—tucking it beneath her arm. A twinge of conscience caused her to reconsider such deliberate theft, but it wasn't actually stealing, she assured herself. This was war, a battle of wits she must win in order to prevent those she left behind from losing their homes, their very lives. These, she thought, gripping the candles and the scroll a little tighter, were the weapons she must use to save her people from certain death and destruction.

Using any kind of container she could find—a drinking tankard, a strange-looking shell, even a heavy cylindrical object she found in one of the chests—Malana managed to prop upright all of the tapers.

Her awkwardness with the light box momentarily rattled her confidence. Because her hands shook so, the corked bottle nearly slipped from her fingers as she tried to ignite one of the small splints. When it suddenly flared, it surprised her so much that she dropped it on her bare foot, knocking over several of the candles as she hopped about in pain. Not to be thwarted, she tried again, finally managing to control the stick of fire long enough to touch each wick and set it dancing in place.

Blowing out the splint, she glanced around the illuminated room—her makeshift shrine—and smiled with satisfaction. Then, taking the scroll from beneath her arm, she directed it toward the closest flame. Closer, closer, until the end of it caught fire.

If her mother's beliefs were right, Te Tuma would appear at any moment. Malana waited calmly, knowing what she must do.


Standing in the dark companionway illuminated by only the dim light of a whale oil lantern, Zeph shook himself like a street mongrel. The rivulets of water dripping from his slicker peppered the walls, hissing as they struck the hot glass of the lamp. He lifted it in order to see his way better. The light cast eerie shadows on the still-closed door to his cabin.

By his calculation, it was nearing dawn. The girl? What must she feel? A pang of an as yet unnamed emotion coursed through him as he envisioned her alone and hungry, huddled against a wall, so afraid in her ignorance.

Innocence, he corrected himself. Hers was an innocence, not an ignorance. The subtle distinction made a whale of a difference, at least in his mind.

Nonetheless, she must surely think she had been abandoned, that the end drew near. He expected she would be only too glad to see him ... well, at least to see what he brought her. Zeph glanced down at the trencher of food in his hand.

The rusty bolt made as much noise and offered the same frustrating resistance releasing as it had slamming home

Filled with anger, he turned on her. "Have you any idea what you've done?"

"You have come to me, Te Tuma." Malana smiled and started toward him, her movements sleek and slinking as a jungle cat's, and just as dangerous. Just as unpredictable. "Come," she said, putting out her hand to him. "I will make you happy."

Such a simple statement, yet so filled with the complexities of life that under different circumstances he might have laughed. Instead, he frowned and tried like hell to mean it.

He understood exactly what she offered, and although she'd obeyed his order and remained fully clothed, Zeph knew what lay beneath. He swallowed so hard and loud, he wondered that it did not cause her smile to widen. The knowing, God help him, was as difficult to battle, if not more so, as the seeing.

He could swear he heard drums. No, he didn't actually hear them. It was as if he *felt* their pagan rhythm emanating from her fingertips, then coming to life in the very pulse of his own body. The pounding grew louder and faster, filling his head, wearing down his resistance with every second he stood there unmoving, with every step that brought her closer. Such lack of control made him that much more determined to master it.

Wordlessly, he rolled up the destroyed map and stuck it under his arm, knowing how utterly ridiculous he must look clutching that smoldering bit of uselessness. He flung open the top of the desk and scooped up the contents, fairly certain no other precious charts were missing.

"Te Tuma, where are you going?" Malana demanded, her cry studded with desperation.

"Like I told you before," he replied, allowing the top of the desk to slam shut, "I am not Te Tuma. I am Captain Zephiran Westley, master of the *Dolphin*. Got that, girl? Zeph Westley. I have never been, nor will I ever be, seduced by pagan hogwash, no matter how attractively it is packaged. If you're smart, girl," he added, casting an insolent look at the altarlike cluster of burning candles, "you'll curb your wastefulness. Those candles are all you'll get to last you to the end of this voyage."

It occurred to him only after he walked out the door and locked it behind him that she probably hadn't the foggiest notion of their destination nor of how long it would take them to get there. But he was in no mood to explain it to her. At least not now.

Chaos ruled Malana's world and shattered the already-fragmented uncertainty of her beliefs. Just where was she? She studied her surroundings, seeing them in a different light, and not just because she had snuffed out all but one of the candles. How had she gotten here? But more importantly, where were they going?

Te Tuma had said they were on a voyage. No, he wasn't the god of the volcano, she reminded herself, battling confusion by pressing trembling fingers to her aching temples. Or was he?

If he lied, then why? A trick? What did he hope to gain by such deception? Knowledge of her mission? What would he do if he learned that she was a pawn, an appeasement sent by others, not there by her own choice?

However, if he spoke the truth . . .

Either way, it was in her own best interest, as well as that of her people, to create the appearance of believing him. At that she frowned. The name he had called himself. What was it? "Z—z—z." The vibrating first sound passed through her clenched teeth, tickling her lips. "Zeph Westley," she pronounced after a long struggle to form the strange and unfamiliar words. "Very well, Zeph Westley, if that is what you wish to call yourself." She turned to the food he had left her and began to eat, mindless of the strange taste and texture, wondering if gods found such unpalatable affair enjoyable. She wondered further why she would even feel such hunger if she were truly with a god.

She licked her fingers, wrinkling her nose at the unsavory smell and saltiness that lingered on them. Her eyes lifted and settled on the closed door. More confused than ever, she somehow knew the answer to all her questions lay beyond that unyielding barrier. Somehow, she must find a way past it.

Even as she came to her desperate conclusion, Malana heard the muffled scurry of unidentified activity coming from the other side. One finger remaining in her mouth, she stilled, straining to listen. Those weak-voiced whispers? What did they mean? Some instinct indigenous to the islands warned her not to be fooled.

Pushing aside the remains of her meal, she quickly made her way to the door and pressed her ear to the wooden barrier.

The whispers grew louder, bolder. She heard only bits and pieces, frightening terms like "little savage," "heathen temptress," and others so crude and profane she could not repeat them even in her mind. Nonetheless, she had no doubt as to their meaning.

The *haole* often called her people, especially the women, such unkind names. Still, that did not signal alarm.

So why did her heart insist on hammering with such runaway fear?

The door latch jiggled against her palm. More cursing. Malana jumped back when the door began to swing open.

"Hey there? What do you think you are doing?" she heard someone demand in a childish voice.

She knew then that more than answers awaited her on the other side of that door, something much more dangerous.

                                * * *

"*She* did this you say, Cap'n?" The first mate stood at
Zeph's elbow in the cramped storage room he temporarily
called his quarters, staring down at the destroyed map.
"Little heathen," the sailor murmured, running hemp-
calloused fingers through his unkempt beard. "I knew the
minute I laid eyes on her she'd be the death of us."

"That's enough, Mr. Kennedy."

It didn't matter that he had called Malana names much
worse in his own mind, or that he, too, feared the worse
would happen if his memory of what lay ahead should fail
him. That wasn't the same. He couldn't explain why, but
it simply wasn't.

Zeph straightened, all of his pent-up frustration concentrated in the critical gaze he leveled on his first mate, the
man who had been with him since his maiden voyage as
a captain many years before. The map snapped closed and
rolled to the floor.

He ignored it for the moment, aware only of the power
struggle and the powerful stench that was such a part of
a whaler's existence. The reek of whale oil and gurry,
the offal of the great beasts that gave them their living,
permeated every bulkhead and seam of the ship. Here,
just below the tryworks and so close to the forecastle where
the crew, mindless of it all, resided, it was far worse than
in his own cabin.

Zeph abhorred uncleanliness in others almost as much
as in himself.

"Take a bath, mister," he ordered in way of dismissal,
bending over to retrieve the fallen chart. "You and every
jack-tar aboard. Your smell offends me."

Mr. Kennedy blinked, obviously taken aback. "Can't see
what possible difference a little offense makes now when
we'll all be consigned to Davy Jones's locker soon enough."
He muttered the derogatory comment under his breath.

Nonetheless, Zeph heard it. His heart, heavy with dread, lurched like a ship run aground. Such disgruntlement and lack of confidence in his judgment as captain portended a fate far worse than merely being lost at sea.

"Mr. Kennedy?"

"Aye, Captain," the sailor replied with a crispness that bordered on a challenge.

"Let no man aboard this ship deceive himself." Zeph stood, easily a head taller than his subordinate. "Only I among us has a chance in hell of getting us home. Are you with me or against me?"

A silent battle of wills ensued, one he supposed was inevitable, shattered only by a sudden intrusion.

"Cap'n. Cap'n Westley. Come quick, sir."

"What is it, Danny boy?" By necessity, Zeph tore his gaze from that of his mate's.

"There be trouble abrew in the companionway in front of your quarters." Genuine terror tainted the cabin boy's youthful voice.

Zeph's concern was instant and singular. Malana. She was in trouble, or worse, she was the source of trouble. Again his heart breached like a harpooned whale, only this time with an emotion so irrational, he would have gladly turned his back on his current problem and forfeited to his first officer.

Instead, he forced himself to stand there calmly, focusing his steady, seemingly unshakable attention once more on Mr. Kennedy.

"Well, mister, you have yet to answer my question."

He counted the precious seconds by the beats of his pounding heart.

"Mutiny makes fools out of otherwise smart men, Captain," the sailor declared. He looked down submissively. "I have no quarrel with you or your judgment."

"Ah, Mr. Kennedy." Zeph's lips parted in a rare smile, and he reached out to grasp the man's burly shoulder. "I had hoped my usual keen instincts regarding a man's nature hadn't failed me. It's good to know you're with me."

With that stated, he turned quickly and headed toward the door, confident his first mate would be right behind him. Fortunately, Zeph had had the foresight to keep his pistols with him. He handed one to his officer.

"No, Danny. You stay here," Zeph insisted when the loyal cabin boy tried to follow. He gently pushed him back into the storage room and closed the door.

Enough trouble would probably ensue without senselessly endangering the life of a ten-year-old child.


There were only three of them, but they came through the door, intent glistening in their *haole* eyes. It was at that moment she realized where she was, if not exactly why or how she had gotten there. These men were *haole* sailors. Someone had brought her aboard their ship.

"Make nice, girlie, and we'll give you this sack of pretty buttons." The man in front, his rotten teeth grossly exposed as he grinned at her, lifted his hand. A small leather bag on a thong swung back and forth from his dirty fingers.

The way of sailors with island girls was nothing new to Malana. She had seen many of her friends take such an enticement in exchange for a few moments of intimacy, for the most part a fair exchange as far as her people were concerned. Her mother had shielded her from such encounters, however, hiding her whenever a ship came to the island. Perhaps such protectiveness had to do with Le'utu's attachment to James Kilpatrick. Perhaps she had known all along her daughter's virginal fate.

"Go away. I do not want your trinkets." Steadily, she eyed the unsavory trio. Already her spine pressed against the wall farthest from the door, so she couldn't retreat.

Malana wasn't scared; they weren't threatening, even if, like all dirty, reeking *haole,* somewhat insistent in their demands.

All *haole,* that is, except for Zeph Westley. He had smelled of clean, fresh sea air. But then, he had not wanted her.

Just as she did not want what these men had to offer.

"Whatta ya mean you don't want 'em? Of course, you do. All you island wenches want what Jake Ainsworth has to give 'em," he bragged, thrusting his hips toward her.

The three men guffawed, elbowing and slapping each other on the shoulders. Malana didn't mind gaiety and laughter. Up until the last few days, her life had been filled with it. She took offense at being the brunt of such unkind teasing, however, especially when she had already said no.

"Leave me alone," she cried, striking out at the leather pouch, not wanting it to dangle in her face for another moment. Her wild swing sent the bag flying across the room. The buttons, a rainbow of color, scattered on the floor, pinging and popping as they bounced and rolled in every direction.

"Now look at what you've gone and done, girl. Pick 'em up," Jake ordered. His glistening eyes pinned her mercilessly.

"If you want them, you pick them up," Malana replied in an imperial tone, returning his stare.

Jake Ainsworth's look turned black.

Fear shadowed Malana's regal courage when he focused that anger on her. Suddenly, she realized the reality of the danger she faced.

"Come on, matey. Take it easy," one of the other sailors urged, touching his companion's arm.

Jake shook off the interference. "No uppity little heathen is gonna get away with talkin' to me like that." He grabbed Malana's arm, forcing her to her knees. "Now get down there and pick 'em up, or else—"

"Or else what, Jake?" The welcome voice rang out like that of an avenging god.

"Cap'n Westley." The sailor released Malana so quickly that she nearly fell flat on her face. He laughed nervously; his companions tittered, too. "It ain't what you think, sir."

"Isn't it, Jake?"

Malana looked up. Zeph stood in the doorway, feet braced wide apart, his masterful presence stirring up a terror among her attackers as intense as a tropical storm. In spite of that, she noticed for the first time the very mortal weariness in his gaze as he allowed it to touch on her briefly, then move away.

Why, he had spoken the truth. He wasn't a god, not at all. Nonetheless, her tormentors feared him as such when that same look pinned them with accusation.

"Confine them below, Mr. Kennedy."

"Aye, sir."

"Cap'n, please," Jake pleaded, suddenly no longer the one making demands. "I promise, it weren't nuthin'. It won't happen again."

"It shouldn't have happened in the first place."

Led away in clanking chains, the offenders uttered no further protest.

"Are you all right?" Zeph asked rather gruffly, turning on her when they were alone.

"They did not harm me." Why did he look at her as if she had done something wrong? "Tell me, Zeph Westley, what will become of those men?" Malana asked, returning his look glare for glare.

"Your concern for them is quite touching, if totally unnecessary." His gaze raked her up, down, then up again, settling on her puckered mouth.

Instantly, she relaxed her lips, wondering what it was about them that fascinated him so.

"They will be punished for their disobedience, of course," he continued. "As for yours . . ."

Hers? What did he think? To somehow blame her for what had just happened? The contemptuous curl to his lip offered anything but assurance. If she expected gentleness or compassion, she apparently looked for it from the wrong person.

"Whatever your reasons for taking me against my will aboard your ship, Zeph Westley," Malana protested hotly, "that gives you no right to—"

"No right you say, girl." He laughed, a bitter, threatening sound. "Aboard this ship, I'm the only one with rights." He continued to stare at her for the longest time before turning away. "I see you have wisely decided to forswear the Te Tuma foolishness." He paused at the door and looked back. "I suppose you realized it wasn't getting you anywhere."

"Only a fool would mistake you for a god," she blurted out.

At that, one side of his mouth lifted. If it was meant to be a smile, the expression had a long way to go.

"You'll be safe enough here, as soon as word spreads among my crew as to what happens to anyone who dares to defy my authority."

"Tell me, Zeph Westley, what does happen to anyone foolish enough to defy you?"

"Why do you ask, Malana? Have you planned on taking such an imprudent risk?" At that, he actually smiled. "And for the record, when I brought you aboard my ship, you had no will to speak of. Still, if it hadn't been for your mother's pleading and courage, as well as for the debt I owe James Kilpatrick, you wouldn't even be here."

"James Kilpatrick?" she asked, the name tumbling from her mouth on a great rush of surprise. "You know James Kilpatrick?" Nothing else he said, not the hurtful slurs, the arrogant demands, mattered at that moment.

"Indeed, girl, I know him. I know him very well. In fact, that is where I am taking you—to James Kilpatrick. Once we get there, I will turn you over to his care and quite frankly be done with you.''

Taking her to James Kilpatrick? Her mind could absorb no more of what he said. James Kilpatrick. Her father. After all of this time and lack of acknowledgment, did he finally want her? The prospects whipped up such a jumble of emotions, Malana knew not which to deal with first. One thing struck her as odd, however. Very odd, indeed.

"What of my mother?" She narrowed her eyes, watching him for some reaction that would give her a clue as to what was really going on. "Why didn't she come with us?"

Her mother would have never passed up an opportunity to be with her father. Never. It was all she had lived for for as long as Malana could remember.

"Le'utu chose to stay behind."

"You lie, Zeph Westley," Malana snapped, confident in her accusation. She tossed her chin haughtily. "My mother would never do that. To be with my father is all she ever wanted."

He moved with such speed and direction, she hadn't time to determine his intention. His hand, rough and calloused, shackled her elbows like iron bands, shaking her as if she were of no more substance than a palm frond.

"No one calls me a liar. Do you hear me, girl?" He stopped shaking her, but his angry look terrified her more than his painful grip. "Your mother not only would *choose* to stay behind, but she did."

"Why?" Malana demanded. "Why would she do that?"

"To save—" Zeph clamped his mouth shut. "Because she thought it best, and that is the only reason you need to know."

At the sound of running feet overhead, he looked up.

"There she blows!" One after another, excited voices took up and repeated the call.

"Damn," Zeph muttered, his hands, his concentration on her, growing slack.

"What is it?" Malana asked, certain that something terrible was happening to the ship. Listening to the frantic pace overhead and in the companionway outside the door, she wondered if they might even be about to sink. Suddenly, she wished he would hold her again, only much tighter.

He didn't. Instead, he moved farther away, aiming for the door.

Once again, excited voices took up the frantic call.

"Please, tell me, what does it mean?" she asked.

"It means that King Neptune, in all his infinite wisdom, has chosen this moment to mock me."

The strange, unyielding expression on Zeph's rugged, weather-chiseled face did nothing to alleviate her concern. In fact, it only added to it.

# Chapter Four

"There she bloooows!"

By the time Zeph reached topside, the entire crew was swarming across the deck like a hive of focused bees.

"Where away, mister?" he called up to the lookout perched in one of the topgallant crosstrees, at the same time glancing about for Danny.

Where had that blasted boy disappeared to? He needed his spyglass. Then he remembered he'd left the obedient cabin boy below with strict orders to stay put no matter what he heard. As for the glass, it was stored away in the instrument chest in his cabin. Zeph dared not send anyone after it, not with Malana there.

Damn. The sighting of whale was the last thing he'd expected to happen. And not now, when he had been forced to confine in chains his two best harpooners.

"Off to lee bow, Cap'n," the sailor, braced against the iron hoops high above him on the main mast, shouted down, pointing out to sea.

"Stand by!" Zeph ordered. "Get those boats ready! And

be quick about it!'' He looked out across the eastern sea
line, but from where he stood, he could see nothing.

"Damn!" he muttered aloud his frustration. He needed
the glass.

With the agility of a man half his age—not that he
considered mid-thirties all that old—Zeph took to the rigging, climbing quickly. Securing himself in the lines, the
stiff tropical breeze swinging him back and forth, he lifted
his free hand to block the morning sun's glare, surveying
the horizon again with the keen, naked eye of a seasoned
sailor.

"Ah, yes. I see it," he confirmed, spying a faint, wispy
spray not too far in the distance.

And then another, much stronger, without a doubt a
whale's spout, and yet another and another. So many, in
fact, he lost count.

"Damn me. It must be a whole friggin' school of 'em,
Cap'n. Easily a mile wide," the lookout not too far away
observed, the awe evident in his unlettered speech pattern.

God in heaven. Zeph lowered his hand, shading his brow
furled with abject astonishment. If the seaman and his own
eyes could be trusted, it was every whaler's dream come
true. A streak of "greasy luck" that came maybe once in
a lifetime, and his only thought . . .

That the timing couldn't have been worse if they'd sailed
straight toward the ends of the earth in a leaky boat from
hell.


Malana knew not what to make of the sudden flurry of
excitement and activity.

"There she blooows!"

She understood the words but not their meaning. Had
something terrible happened to the ship? Were they soon
to sink? Why else would the *haole* scramble about as if their
lives depended upon it?

Malana stood there in the confusion on the deck, side-stepping a curl of rope as it uncoiled with a whining whip that could have taken off a person's leg. A crack issued overhead, so loud that she jumped. Looking up, she saw a great white sail billow out as it caught the wind, joining forces with the others.

"Please. What is going on?" she asked those who passed by her, as more canvas was raised, the ship picking up speed.

No one noticed her, or if they did, no one bothered to answer. Even the sailor who backed into her, his heel grinding into her bare foot, merely glared at her repeated question.

"This ain't no place for a woman now," he muttered in place of what should have been an apology. Then he scampered away, leaving her alone again.

What did he expect? Leaning against a stack of barrels, she clutched her throbbing toes, squeezing back unbidden tears of pain and indignation. What did they all expect from her? She turned her terror-laced anger on the man, Zeph Westley, hanging fearlessly high above her in the sails. Why, even he didn't bother to notice her.

Surely they all didn't expect her to go meekly below and wait for the watery will of *Moana*, the ocean, to find her. Or did they?

A debilitating thought struck her. Malana panicked in her perceived helplessness. Somehow, through no fault of her own, she had become stuck between the wills of two opposing forces of nature—the ocean and the volcano, both givers and takers of life. And she had yet to figure out the true tally between the gods that ruled them.

Her mother would tell her to accept the ways of the world, not to question them so much; to submit to her role, as no more than a bit of flotsam bandied about for a purpose greater than she.

"The ocean and the volcano are brothers, my daughter. As are the stars and the sun, the moon and the tide."

That she had always vehemently refused to believe, simply because she couldn't understand it.

But now, perhaps she could see the truth of it. Standing there, she watched these strange *haole* being led by a man who claimed to be of the sea, yet his hair and very presence reflected the heat and fire of the volcano. At his command, they all scurried and raced about, preparing boats, oars, and weapons more wicked than any she had ever seen. The purpose of those deadly spears she couldn't imagine, but it was obvious the men intended to leave the ship.

Did that mean they planned to abandon her as well? Not one of them, not even Zeph Westley—she shot him a wary glance—made a move to include her in their escape.

Cool water or hot lava. Did it really matter? Either way, she faced the certainty of an uncertain fate.

Such dire thoughts spawned an out-of-control shiver that coursed through her body like a jolt of lightning. Without warning, something tapped her on the bare shoulder. With a jump, she turned, coming face to face with a boy much younger than herself.

"Excuse me, miss, but you shouldn't be up here."

She'd heard that before, but at least this *haole* spoke with kindness and a touch of what might actually be genuine concern.

"It ain't safe," he continued in the wake of her startled silence. "Cap'n would prefer you came below with me, miss."

"Below?" she questioned. "I do not want to go below. Are you not afraid? They are all leaving." She waved her hand toward the activity on the deck.

"Aye," he nodded. "But they'll be back soon enough."

"Will they?" she demanded suspiciously, watching as the sailors prepared to lower the small rowboats into the water. "Then where are they going?"

"After the whales." As he spoke, the boy pointed out to sea.

A hulking blackness rolled in the watery distance, a great, misty spew erupting as it did. Malana gasped, instantly recognizing one of the mighty sea creatures her people considered taboo. No warrior alive dared to face the great, spouting fish.

"Once they've harpooned their allotment, the boats return haulin' the catch. Then the cuttin' in and tryin' out begins. Believe me, miss, that ain't no sight meant for delicate eyes like yours."

Cutting in and trying out? Whatever did that mean?

"I do not care." She stared at him, unwavering in both look and determination. "I will stay right here," she insisted, turning away, dismissing both the boy and his warning.

It was at that moment, her chin lifted with stubbornness, that her gaze collided with the sea-depth blue of Zeph Westley's. At first startled, he then frowned, signaling to one of his men to hold the long, wicked-looking weapon he clutched in his hand. With strides that spoke of unquestioned authority, he made his way toward them.

"Oh, no. We're in big trouble now," the youth muttered. He fairly stiffened beneath the challenge of his master's glare.

"What are you doing up here?" Zeph demanded. His icy gaze, void of any discernible emotion, raked first her, then turned on her unwitting companion.

"I—I—I'm sorry, Cap'n Zeph," the boy squeaked, his voice cracking with youthful diffuseness. "It's just that I heard the lookout's call. I—I—I thought only to make myself useful, sir."

"Then do that, Danny boy. Make yourself useful by seeing our—" Zeph paused and eyed her with another dispassionate look, "seeing our passenger safely below."

"No," Malana piped in. "I will stay right here until you

come back." Under Zeph's intense scrutiny, she once again lifted her chin with defiance.

A defiance mirrored in the furl of his brow, the downward curl of his upper lip.

"Then, by damn, stay here and rot, for all that I care," he replied. "Just stay out of the way."

At that moment, when he turned away, she came to a most amazing realization. Why, his crustiness was simply that—a thin crust concealing something much more human . . . and vulnerable.

"Zeph Westley," she called softly, triumphant amusement trifling with some deeper emotion, a new set of feelings she did not quite understand.

With obvious reluctance, he paused, his spine stiffening against what he no doubt perceived as just another attack.

"Be careful," she said with all sincerity.

His only reaction was none at all. He didn't even bother to look back at her, although she sensed his hesitation before he spoke.

"I'm always careful, girl. I don't need you or anyone else to remind me."

His words issued a challenge, one that intrigued her almost as much as did the man himself.

"Launch the boats."

Amidst the scurrying of the crew readying equipment, Zeph took to the prow of the lead whaleboat as soon as it hit the water.

"Are you sure you want to do this, sir?" his second in command shouted over the din, as the next two boats followed the first. The splash they made sent out a cold, salty spray that dotted the clothing of both men—Zeph in his boat, the mate making his way down the rope ladder suspended over the gunwale of the ship. "Wheeler is a fairly decent harpooner, you know," the mate reminded him, feeling out his superior with the caution of a man weaned to it over years of familiarity.

"Aye, and so am I, Mr. Kennedy," Zeph responded in an equally loud, yet much more confident, voice. "Do you doubt me, mister?"

"Not at all, Cap'n," Kennedy replied, much closer now, so he spoke in a softer tone of voice. The sailor's gaze wavered slightly, then steadied beneath Zeph's unrelenting one. The lapse could have been caused by the movement of the boat as the man stepped on the plank seat. More likely, it indicated a momentary battle of wills won by seniority. "Every man here knows your reputation with a harpoon and respects it. What I question are your priorities, sir. If something should happen to you . . ."

"Ah, yes. The burned map." If his first officer had not mustered the courage to speak his mind, Zeph would have thought less of the seasoned sailor, even less of his own ability to pick a good mate. "Your concern is duly noted, Mr. Kennedy. I'll be careful. Now launch the last boat and check to make sure all the tholepins are securely wrapped to muffle the oars, so our prize doesn't gally."

Gallied whales were scared ones, apt to shoot off at full speed without changing their course knot after knot. Such whales on the run, sometimes for days without stopping, were well nigh impossible to keep up with, even in pursuit with a fast ship like the *Dolphin* under full sail.

It took only a few moments for each whaleboat crew to get organized. They made sure the whale line encircled the loggerhead properly from the coil housed in the line tub, leaving sufficient stray line for the harpoon running through the fairlead. Finally, each rower checked the tholepin of his oar as the captain had instructed.

Zeph watched wordlessly. They had all done this so many times before, most of the men could have performed their duties without orders and half asleep—and often that was the case. Soon the small fleet—each manned with four rowers, a harpooner, and a mate at the steering oar—fanned out in the water. Every crew worked independently of the others, each on their own to find game, harpoon it, and bring it back to the ship. It was understood that if any boat got into trouble, however, the others would come to the rescue if at all possible.

At the front of the lead boat, Zeph took to rowing like any other man, pulling with all his might—the unified goal to surpass the still-unalarmed speed of the school of whales. Only when they drew close to the huge bodies would he dock his oar and concentrate on readying the barbed harpoon as he picked his target. Then, if their luck and his aim held true, the kill could take only moments. If not, and he merely stung the beast, the risks were too numerous to count as the wounded whale took off, the harpoon secured to the boat and embedded in his hide, on what was known as a "Nantucket sleigh ride."

Zeph had done this more times than he could remember, and although it had been a long while since he had actually wielded a harpoon . . .

There was no need for the strange, fluttery feelings in the pit of his stomach. Why, he hadn't felt this way since he was a "greenie," a lad of sixteen on his first whale hunt.

He remembered that day long ago only too well. The great beast they had pursued had caught wind of them. With a bellowing snort and a slap of his enormous tail as loud as a thunderclap, the prey had dived for the bottom, leaving the boatful of men to wonder what would happen next.

In the stillness that had followed, broken only by the rhythmic squeak of the oars, Zeph had known real fear. Then unannounced, the giant had resurfaced, breaching so close that the spray from its blowhole had fallen like a pelting rain on them all. His first instinct had been to drop his oar and turn starboard to see what was going on.

"Pick up your oar and keep your eyes on me, boy."
Captain James's stern command brooked no defiance.

So, fearing his captain's wrath more than the whale,
Zeph had obeyed. He had resisted the overwhelming urge
to abandon his station, stand up, scream, jump out of the
boat—anything to alleviate the terror that tightened about
his chest like a band of iron.

Only afterward he learn that had he disobeyed, James
Kilpatrick would not have hesitated to knock him unconscious with the steering oar. Otherwise, the entire boat
would have been in immediate danger. It only took a
moment and a wrong move by one man to cause the small
vessel to swerve off course, or worse, to accidentally bump
the equally terrified whale who swam alongside, so close
the harpooner could have reached out and touched its
slick, oily skin.

But there were no "greenies" in the Dolphin's seasoned
crew. And by damn, he could think of no reason for him
to feel the way he did.

"Be careful." The memory of Malana's warning soughed
in his ear like a soft breeze in a swaying island palm.

Why had she said that to him? What sinister motivation
had led her to say the one thing that might make him
doubt himself?

There was something about her that unnerved him. It
was almost as if, with those slightly slanted eyes of hers,
she could see past the barriers he had so carefully erected
to shield his heart, and perhaps even his soul, from outside
influence. Malana. Something about her beckoned to him
as did pristine, white beaches to a sea-weary sailor. But it
was more than mere idle fantasy, more than arresting eyes
and sleek, slender body.

"Cap'n, we draw near."

Zeph's head snapped up, his gaze locking with that of his
mate's. Wordlessly, without apology or acknowledgment of
the other man's concern, he set about his business, his

heart hammering, pounding like island drums. The harpoon weighed heavily in his hand, feeling strange and unnatural. Standing in the bow, skimming across the water with the velocity four men could row, he shifted the long, barbed spear, adjusting to its balance.

Riding just beneath the surface of the water, the whale looked like a speeding black bullet, its fantail as wide as the whaleboat was long.

"A little more, men, and we'll be upon him," Zeph called out in encouragement. The boat maintained its course and pace, moving alongside the target's body, closer and closer to the head. And then the strangest thing happened. Still submerged, the giant rolled ever so slightly, one tiny eye coming into focus.

Lifting the harpoon, Zeph suddenly found himself staring straight into the monster's eye that wept great, greasy tears, for no reason other than to protect it from the briny water. Momentarily, he wondered at the intelligence behind that eye. Zeph hesitated and began to doubt himself.

What in God's name was the matter with him? It was her fault. Malana. She had done something to him. Damn it, he had to get ahold of himself.

Steeling his emotions, he gripped the harpoon and took careful aim. With all of his strength and renewed determination, he let the weapon fly. The high-pitched whine as the line fed through the loggerhead and past his ear was deafening.

That is, until the harpoon struck true, piercing the vulnerable spot just behind the whale's head, where major blood arteries converged near the lungs. The creature screamed with pain and surprise. The cry sounded almost heartrendingly human. From its blowhole erupted a spout that splattered the whaleboat and crew with a scalding red froth.

"Sakes alive, Cap'n, you've set his chimney afire with

only one try," the rower directly behind him announced
with utter astonishment.

"Congratulations, sir." The felicitations echoed all
around him.

But it had been luck—pure, blind luck, he wanted to
tell them, but said nothing except to order, "Cut loose
and stern all."

Barely in time, the rope was severed, just before, when
with a snap of its mighty jaws that rang in Zeph's ears, the
mortally wounded beast lurched away, its great tail slashing
the water like a razor-sharp blade.

The throes of death took only minutes, but it seemed
more like an eternity as the lumbering leviathan thrashed
about, its plaintive cries for assistance unanswered except
in the heart of Zeph Westley, who until now had never
considered the plight of the whale, only the profits he
made from the slaughter. In spite of his sudden insight,
the sea turned red and foamy with the unstaunched flow
of life's blood. Finally, the whale rolled fin in the air like
a broken mast of an abandoned derelict. Its eye stared
up—tearless, sightless, lifeless, yet rendering silent con-
demnation.

God help him, he would never forget that forlorn look
as long as he lived.

"Let's haul him in, men," Zeph said quietly, glad that
the praise turned to admiring the size of the catch rather
than his prowess with a harpoon.

The crew brought the boat alongside their prize, lashing
ropes with expertise to anything tow-worthy. Within minutes, they were at the oars again, pulling hard to drag the
dead whale back to the ship.

With a sense of foreboding he couldn't quite explain,
Zeph dreaded the return to his own ship, which had nothing at all to do with the monumental task of cutting in
and trying out. Still, he put his shoulder to the task of
rowing like every other man.

As they neared the ship, he caught sight of her and knew from where his anxiety stemmed. Malana. Mysterious island nymph. What was it about her that pierced the thick hide of invincibility he'd prided himself on having developed over the years? Never missing an oar stroke even if his heart missed several, Zeph sized her up, so damn small yet so intimidating, standing on the deck of his ship looking over the rail at him.

Not knowing what else to do, he nodded at her, stiff-necked and formal. She merely lifted her head a little higher, as if staring down her pert, imperial nose at him was the expected thing for her to do. Her head swiveled as she maintained eye contact. Only after a moment did he realize his head turned, too, accommodating what quickly became a war of more than curious stares.

Then, through no fault of his own, the side of the ship came between them as the whaleboat drew alongside the stern, where the cutting-in platform had been lowered by the crew remaining aboard.

With a sigh of relief, Zeph thrust aside the crazy impulse to abandon the prize catch to the discretion of his more than able crew and go topside, with the purpose of shaking a little respect into his haughty passenger. He refused to allow her to get to him. And so he buried, as deep as he could, the disquieting emotions that otherwise refused to be tamed. He had no time for them, nor for their even more annoying cause. There was too much to do, too much at stake.

"Throw down the blubber hook," he ordered.

To the surprise of his crew, Zeph strapped the canvas belt of the "monkey rope" about his own middle and climbed onto the hulking mass of whale, setting about the dangerous task of inserting the hook into the thick rubbery skin.

No one dared openly to oppose his unconventional actions, but he could see the crew's objection written

plainly in their eyes. They thought their captain had lost
his mind.

Maybe they weren't too far off from the mark, either. If
the truth be known, he feared for his sanity as much as
did they.

From the deck of the *Dolphin,* Malana watched what she
considered the most savage ceremony she'd ever witnessed.
One by one the boats returned to the ship, hauling in
their dead trophies. And they called *her* people uncivilized.

What honor had there been in the senseless slaughter
of the regal ocean giants?

"Hook fast. Haul away." Zeph's call was repeated time
and again as he inserted a wicked-looking barb as thick as
a man's thigh into the sides of the dead whales. Over and
over the mutilated bodies flopped.

What purpose could there be in such a ritual? Malana
wondered, as she watched the *haole* meticulously peel the
thick blankets of fat from the carcasses and pull them
aboard, followed by the animals' heads, setting adrift in
the sea any part that might be considered edible for the
sharks.

It made no sense, she thought, as she clung to the rail
of the ship as it rolled and groaned with the effort of
pulling aboard the booty. Yet this was only the beginning.

Not far away from where she stood on the deck, giant
ovens had been stoked. The whale blubber, cut up in
chunks and slabs, was tossed into big black cauldrons that
belched and bubbled. The stench they emitted overwhelmed her senses, used only to the sweet smell of white
beaches, island wildflowers, and small cook fires. Not one
of the *haole* seemed even to notice as they slipped and slid
in the greasy film that quickly built up on the once-spotless
deck. And when one man emerged from the carnage below
carrying a large chunk of waxy substance extracted from

the innards, and all of them clapped and whooped, claiming they were rich . . . well, her stomach churned in disgust.

Yet, perversely, Malana made her way closer to the activity in the rear of the ship, to better observe the goings-on. Surprisingly enough, no one paid her the slightest attention.

Looking down on the frenzy of activity below, she was stunned to see Zeph Westley in the middle of it all. How could she have been so wrong about him? She had thought an affinity had blossomed between them at that moment of enlightenment before he had rowed away. She had thought she knew him. But now, watching him tackle the slaughter as if he might actually enjoy it . . .

It was then that he looked up and spied her, a frown turning his features hard and unreadable. He said something to the sailor next to him, who glanced in her direction with a spine-tingling look. Still gaping, the man accepted the long-handled knife from his still-glowering captain.

What gave any of them, especially Zeph Westley, the right to show such disapproval of her? Why, if she could figure out a way, she would march right down to where he stood and confront him with her own accusations, not only for exhibiting savage, uncivilized behavior, but for cruelly leading her to believe he had intended to abandon her on a sinking ship.

Then she realized his intent. Why . . . why . . . he was coming after her.

All of her previous courage drained from her like sand slipping through her fingers. Malana considered running. But where could she hope to hide on a ship no larger than a small atoll? Suddenly, the little cabin she'd considered a prison not so long ago offered the only possible safe haven. Turning with a purpose of her own, she headed toward the companionway stairs, tripping along the way over coils of rope and gagging on the fumes from the bubbling whale blubber.

"And just where do you think you're going, girl?" Zeph grabbed her arm with the strength of an inescapable undertow.

How had he gotten there so quickly? she wondered, shivering with a combination of fear and delight at the shocking heat of his hand on her bare arm. Still, she turned to do battle and found herself face to face with a man who seemed more of a god than any elusive image. Oblivious to the noxious odors that burned her eyes until they watered, he possessed a fire as hot as the one beneath the bubbling cauldrons. The orange flames glittered in his unruly hair, flickered in the blue depths of his uncompromising eyes . . . condemning her.

"Let go of me," she blurted out. "You . . . you . . ."

"Go ahead." His eyes flashed with rigid condescension, as if nothing she might say could penetrate his tough exterior. "For what little good it will do you, call me a name if it will make you feel better."

She fought against his restraining hand, as well as against the grip of her own rampant emotions. Neither struggle did her much good. In fact, her outward resistance only served to assist him as he scooped her up into his muscular arms.

"I do not want to go below," she protested, continuing to buck and twist against his unyielding strength.

Effortlessly, he carried her toward the very steps she had earlier sought on her own. Now she didn't wish to go, not if it meant going with him.

"You . . . you . . ." She continued her mental search for something to call him—something that would pierce his impervious attitude. "You savage . . ."

"Savage am I now, girl? Now, that's like the pot calling the kettle black, wouldn't you say?" His throaty chuckle offered anything but reassurance.

And yet, perversely, the closer they drew to the door of the cabin, the faster she found her pulse racing.

There was something barely detectable in the intense way he looked down at her, in the way he held her as if unwilling to let her go. Something unrestrained. Something, indeed, savage and exciting . . . and most desirable. Ceasing her struggle, Malana explored her own feelings, consequently dwelling on his, suddenly realizing that beneath it all, he might not be any more certain of what was happening between them than was she.

With calm calculation, she curled her arms about his neck, placed her head against his chest, and sighed.

Her sudden submission sent such a physical jolt through him that she could actually feel it. It surged through his heart beneath her ear, traveling all the way to the fingertips that gripped her shoulders and thighs. He stopped dead in his tracks.

"What do you think you're doing, girl?" he demanded. "I'll not fall for your tricks again." The frown returned to mar the perfection of his weather-chiseled face.

Now she understood it.

"Doing? Why, nothing, Zeph Westley," she answered with a smile that settled effortlessly on her lips. "And my name is not *girl,*" she scolded sweetly. "It is Malana."

"I know your name, girl," he responded brusquely.

"Then why do you never use it?" She allowed her hand perched in the nape of his neck to explore gently.

First, he tried nonchalantly to shrug off her caress. So, she entwined a finger in his long, curly hair and renewed her smile, her eyes as steadfast as her finger—even when he clamped his jaws tight with obvious annoyance. Finally, using his foot, he kicked open the door, dropping her just inside the entrance. But Malana continued to cling to his neck, causing him to bend toward her.

"Enough of this nonsense, girl," he growled, reaching behind his head to extract her clinging arms.

"What is wrong, Zeph Westley? Do you not like a woman to touch you?" She stared at his hand vigorously fending off hers.

"I like women just fine," he insisted. Still, having freed himself, he let go of her with the speed of a gull diving after fish.

"Then it is my touch that offends you." She looked down and away, feigning embarrassment.

"Tarnation, Malana. It isn't that," Zeph swore vehemently.

She glanced up to discover his gaze roving hungrily over her, as if he couldn't get enough? . . .

As if he wanted more.

Recognizing that meaningful look, Malana smiled confidently, if only to herself. She had often witnessed such wanting on other men's faces, both Hitihitian and *haole*. In the past, whenever such blatant desire had been directed her way, however, her mother had always insisted she go back into the hut.

But her mother was not there now to tell her what to do.

Still, she remembered denying those men's desires had only made them want her more, made them more determined. They had vied for her, calling to her, trying to entice her to come out. Admittedly, she had found such attention enjoyable—just as she would enjoy seeing Zeph Westley dance her attendance.

Deciding on her line of attack, she slipped around him and walked to the far side of the tiny cabin. His gaze, hot and searing, followed her purposefully graceful movements.

"You should leave now," Malana declared simply, turning to face him.

"What?" As if suddenly aware of the naked desire that showed so plainly on his face, Zeph abruptly glanced up, masking his expression until it once more became hard and unreadable. "Aye, and that I should, girl."

To her complete surprise, he turned and, without another word or look, made his way out the door, closing it softly behind him.

Malana stood there alone, in the middle of that tiny cabin, feeling more confused and vulnerable than ever. It seemed Zeph Westley was like no man she had ever encountered.

# Chapter Five

At the captain's orders, all hands, down to the lowliest swab, gathered on deck at dawn to witness the inescapable punishment of their unfortunate mates. Zeph had to give his crew credit. Not one man uttered a word. They stood, spines rigid, in irregular rows framing the mainmast where their fellow shipmates stood helplessly lashed, bare to the waist. The men's faces remained expressionless, even when their leader made his required appearance.

Their eyes burned with hooded resentment, however, as they turned to watch him climb the steps to the quarter-deck—more as if they turned *on* him, or was that merely self-made suspicion that sent chills racing up his spine? Either way, they waited for him to announce the fate of the accused.

From his superior position on the quarterdeck, which made a sweeping half circle around the mast, Zeph stared down, looking each man in the eye until every one of them glanced away. If he could have figured out a way to call off the flogging while preserving his authority, God knows he would have. Instead, he did the best he could.

"Ten strokes for each man," he directed, his voice carrying easily in the wind that, ironically, snapped the sails overhead like angry whips.

The imposed punishment was light compared to what he could have rightfully ordered, yet it was stringent enough to make every man aboard consider carefully before disobeying one of his commands again. Still, Zeph would have preferred avoiding the necessity of it at all. Damn it. It went against the grain to make another man physically suffer.

How many times had James Kilpatrick warned him that such feelings indicated weakness, something to which a successful captain never dared to succumb? In fact, his mentor had always insisted that any display of strong emotion on the part of a ship's master must be avoided at all costs. Otherwise, the men would lose faith in his leadership.

Since Zeph had spent most of his life aboard a whaler in one capacity or another, he inevitably faced all situations with those words of warning in mind. Show no emotion. Better yet, feel no emotion. As a result, he had managed to successfully make no real commitments except for the one he made to the sea.

Malana. Odd that he would think of the girl now, with a rush of emotions better left unexplored. But then again, maybe it wasn't so inappropriate for his thoughts to turn to her. After all, she had necessitated the unpleasant events of this morning. No doubt, more than one man aboard the *Dolphin* was thinking of her now and of what her presence might mean to him. He suspected none of those thoughts ended pleasantly.

That first whoosh of the cat-o'-nine-tails brought Zeph's attention back to where it should have been and kept it there. The other lashes followed quickly enough, yet he consciously counted each one, wincing, if only inwardly, and wondering when the trying ordeal would end. He wondered, too, whether he could remain as quiet and dignified as the first two offenders who received their punishment if he were at the receiving end of those slashing stripes.

Jake Ainsworth was a different matter altogether. The ringleader of the transgressors made no attempt to hold his tongue or hang on to his honor. Not that honor was something the man had ever demonstrated. In hindsight, it had probably been a mistake to hire on such a troublemaker. Jake's extraordinary skill with a harpoon had persuaded Zeph otherwise.

And now, quite shamefully, the man fought the thongs securing him to the mast, his twisting leaving more sensitive areas of his naked back exposed to the slice of the whip's leather tips.

Ignorant fool. He did himself a disservice. By the time it was all over, the sailor hung, sobbing in his bindings, his back bleeding and shredded, a disgrace to every man aboard.

As for Zeph, the disgrace consumed him as surely as if he were the one hanging from the mast. Stiffly, he turned on his heels and moved away from the railing, making his way stern to avoid passing through the gathering of men.

"What do you want me to do with 'em, Cap'n?"

Without emotion, he paused and slowly stared at his first officer. As captain, he could have the offenders keelhauled if he wanted to. Or tossed overboard, or worse, allowed to rot in their bunks and succumb to infection.

"Take them to Snips and see they get proper care."

The sailmaker was the closest thing to a physician that they had aboard. The tailor would see the wounds of the punished were cleaned and properly tended. If any stitching of either canvas or flesh was required, no one could do a finer job than Snips McGreagor. Zeph could personally attest to the sailor's skill with a needle. The old salt had sewed him up on more than one occasion.

Still, even knowing the offenders were in the best of hands did nothing to alleviate the gnawing sense of inadequacy that coursed through him.

Damn it. It had all been so unnecessary. If only he had had the good sense to keep his emotions under control. What had he been thinking when he had taken the girl aboard? Her fate had been none of his business, and certainly not his responsibility. James Kilpatrick had never even acknowledged the girl as his and he still might not. Then what would he do with her?

He should have stuck to his initial reaction and refused to help Le'utu. Hadn't he learned long ago that fate had a way of being fickle? Just when a man thought he had everything figured out in his life, invariably fate stepped in to change it all.

More importantly, Zeph had learned that rarely did it change to his particular liking.

She liked none of it. Not at all. Being buried in the bowels of a ship with no way of knowing for certain what took place overhead both angered and bewildered her.

Malana glanced around, noting the unrelenting darkness of her surroundings, despising it yet helpless to do anything. Day or night, nothing changed. In spite of the meager candle that burned and the even more meager daylight that filtered in through the small, round windows, deep shadows hung like restless spirits in every corner of the cabin, taunting and teasing her. Unwilling to admit it, even to herself, they frightened her.

She wanted to know what went on beyond the barrier of that impenetrable door. Nervously, Malana glanced up again at the thump of erratic footfalls overhead, wanting an explanation for all those strange sounds. Most of all, she wondered what had become of Zeph Westley.

Just why she cared about a man who infuriated her so she couldn't say, except that he offered her the only connection to that mysterious world beyond her prison. Somehow, Malana knew her destiny was intertwined with his.

That knowledge offered little in the way of comfort. In fact, it left her feeling even more frightened of just what the future held in store for her. No doubt, Zeph Westley would be a difficult man to please, as demanding as any island god could ever be. And she had dared to challenge him.

With that thought, Malana set about the task of somehow making amends. What could she offer to appease his anger?

Only one thing came to mind: the strange drawing she had burned. It had held great importance to him. Perhaps, if she was determined, she could give him back what she had wrongfully taken away. And maybe then he would begin to treat her with something less than contempt.

At last with a purpose, Malana took up the lone candlestick, sat down at the writing table, and found paper, quill, and ink. Nibbling on the feathery end, she closed her eyes, conjuring up a replica of the strange markings she had looked at only once before, and rather quickly at that.

After a few moments of concentrated effort, she smiled. It didn't matter that she had gotten only a fleeting glimpse; as usual, once she had seen an image, it appeared with clarity and detail in her mind.

Without knowledge of what she drew, only that she must carefully copy what she saw, Malana began tentatively to stroke the ink onto the paper. The first marks turned into nothing but a big, black blob, forcing her to start anew with a fresh piece of paper.

Finally, using less ink and more caution, the shakily etched lines evolved, growing steadier and cleaner as she concentrated, until every other thought and concern melted away.

Later, the repeated sputter of the candle caused her to pause from her work and look up. With frowning surprise, she noticed the taper that had been newly lit what seemed only moments before had burned to a nub, threatening to become extinguished. Even the light from the windows had turned a dusky hue of sea-green, casting an eerie patina across the worktable. In the uncertain lighting, the paper, which was very close to looking exactly like what she saw in her mind, took on the appearance of undulating water.

Studying her work with a critical eye, Malana added a final touch here and there, making it as near to perfect as her hand could draw. It was then, staring down at the strange configurations, that she came to the awe-inspiring realization that what she had drawn was a map, that she surely viewed the world as Zeph Westley knew it. So many islands. So many she couldn't count them. With a fingertip, she traced the outline of several, none of which she recognized or had ever imagined existed. Were they larger or smaller than her own precious Hitihiti?

A barrage of questions quickly followed the first. On which one did Zeph Westley live? What did his village look like? Did he have a family?

Did he have a woman who awaited his return?

Malana's heart lurched, her hand trembling as she thought that he might have a woman—a *haole* woman, beautiful and knowledgeable in ways she could never hope to be. She tightened both her lips and her resolve. Not that she cared. Not that she had a right to expect anything different. Not that she could hope to change things.

A bewildered sigh escaped her as she set aside her quill and covered the ink bottle. Oh, what a silly little fool she had been to assume a man like Zeph Westley might show interest in someone as unworldly as she.

The scratch at the door sent Malana scurrying to conceal the product of her labor, stuffing paper, quill and inkhorn back into the desk. When Danny, the cabin boy, entered carrying her customary evening meal, she tried to make it appear as if she'd been idle all day, as usual. But his sharp eyes spied the ink stains on the tabletop and on her hands when he set down the tray.

"You been writin' somethin', miss?" he asked, rubbing a still-wet drop of ink between the tip of his thumb and forefinger. "I didn't know you could write."

Attempting to look as innocent as possible, Malana shook her head in denial, which seemed to satisfy the boy's curiosity. That probably would have been the end of it, but the questions she had asked herself earlier pushed their way past her reservations.

"Danny, what do you call the place Zephiran comes from?" she blurted out just before he reached the door.

"You mean Captain Westley?" Turning, he looked at her with a mixture of surprise and wariness.

Malana nodded eagerly. Even as she willed her wayward tongue to lie still, more and more questions formed in her mind, just bursting to get out.

"He comes from a place called Mystic. Mystic, Connecticut," Danny offered.

"M—M—is—tic, Con—et—cut," she repeated slowly, but the name meant nothing to her. "Is that a big island?"

"Island?" He laughed.

At her stupidity, she suspected, but chose to think of it as his instead.

"Mystic's not an island, miss. It's a town."

A town? That word meant nothing to her, either, but the meaning of his foolish grin was only too obvious.

"Then what is the name of the island?" she demanded, annoyed by his evasiveness.

"He ain't from an island, miss."

"He has to be. Everyone is," she insisted, remembering the map she had just finished drawing.

"Well, then, if that be the case," he answered, still grinning, "I suppose you would call it America."

"A—mer—ca," she mimicked, frowning, realizing the name did nothing to satisfy her curiosity. Oh, how she wanted to see where this America was on the map. But did she dare?

She had done such a good job copying the original, he would probably never know the difference.

"Could you show me?" Without hesitation, she lifted the top of the desk and reached inside.

"You mean on a map?" The amusement on his face turned to horror.

Malana nodded again, attempting to extract her drawing.

"Oh, no, miss." The boy nearly jumped at her, his hand slapping down the top of the desk. She removed her hand just in time. "We'd better not touch the cap'n's map. He'd have both our hides."

"But I have my own," she blurted out, not even aware of how she had given away her precious secret until she had pushed his hand aside, opened the top of the desk, and removed the drawing.

The boy frowned down at both her and the paper. But he accepted her offering and opened it carefully, as if he thought it might snap at him. His brows still knit, he stared at the paper, turning it first one way and then another.

"Where did you get this?" he asked.

"I wrote it," she replied, searching for some sign of approval on his youthful countenance.

His only expression was wry-faced amazement.

"You copied this from one of the cap'n's charts, didn't you?" His question took on an air of accusation. "Cap'n Westley ain't gonna like your having done that. What did you do with the original?" Pushing her aside, he began searching inside the desk. "You better tell me where it is," he demanded frantically, turning on her when his search left him empty-handed.

"It is not here. I—I—I burned it."

Before she could go on to explain what had happened, Danny rushed from the cabin, shouting, "How could you have burned the captain's charts?"

Only after he had left did she realize he still hadn't pointed out the island of America on her map.


"So where exactly are we, Cap'n?"

Mr. Kennedy asked the question innocently enough. Still, Zeph looked up from his useless perusal of the incomplete collection of charts and maps, wondering if he'd heard that certain something in his mate's voice or if it had been merely his overly suspicious imagination.

"At sunrise, I suspect, the lookout will spot Easter Island on the horizon," he responded with a confidence he did not necessarily feel. He had been asking himself the same question throughout the night. Now, sunrise was only an hour away, at best.

"Beggin' your pardon, sir, but that's what you said yesterday."

"And if necessary, mister, I'll say it again tomorrow," Zeph retorted testily, before the sailor had a chance to blink.

"Aye, sir. But tomorrow the men will be even more restless than they are today. Cap'n, they know something's not right."

"And did you set them straight, Mr. Kennedy?"

When the first officer failed to reply, Zeph pushed out of his chair and stood up.

"Well, mister, did you?" he demanded.

"Aye, sir, but you should know that somehow they caught wind of the map incident."

Caught completely by surprise, Zeph managed to limit his reaction to a lift of one eyebrow. "Damn," he finally muttered, running his fingers through his unfashionably long hair, which hours before, had fallen loose from its thong. His curse went unanswered, except for the snap of a chart as he let it go. "Only you and I knew about that, so how could they have found out?"

"The girl knew," Mr. Kennedy reminded him, his ever-alert eyes following Zeph as he paced the small cabin.

"Yes, that's true, but she would have had no opportunity to tell them."

"Then, sir, if not her, it had to have been either you or I who let the cat out of the bag."

At that curt comment, Zeph paused, looking Mr. Kennedy in the eye. He knew the unequivocal truth, no matter how preposterous it might seem. "It has to be the girl, doesn't it?"

Not waiting for a response from his subordinate in rank, if not in wisdom, he turned and headed toward the door, cursing the day he had allowed the little troublemaker to set foot on his precious ship.

It was one of his worse nightmares come true. The *Dolphin,* uncompromisingly a man's domain for years on end, had been turned overnight into nothing but a "hen frigate," and he had no one to blame but himself.

Although dawn had not yet arrived, Malana awoke in the darkness to the sound of someone outside the door of her cabin. Her heart quickened, picking up the special rhythm of the all-too-familiar footsteps.

"Zeph Westley," she whispered, reaching for the coverlet she had pushed aside in her restless slumber. He came to her.

Dare she hope to think why?

When he opened the door and let himself in, she sat in

the middle of the bed, the nightstand taper lit in anticipation. Of what, she couldn't be certain, but her heart hammered with the wild passion of an island drum. In her innocence and haste to greet his unexpected arrival, she had never for a moment thought about how she must look occupying his bed—not until his hard gaze settled on her, lingering longer than necessary.

"What are you doing awake, girl?" he demanded, as if his presence there needed no explanation, while hers did.

"I wait for you, Zeph Westley," she replied, using what she quickly discovered to be her advantage. He wanted her as a man wanted a woman. He did, even if he refused to admit it, and even if he did call her "girl." Slowly, intentionally, she allowed the coverlet to slip a little farther off her bare shoulders. The heat from the candle warmed her skin; his look did not.

It did not surprise her that he frowned. She had learned quickly enough that whenever the battle of wills raged within him, his brows met on the field of honor between them. His words were another matter, however.

"Little witch, you knew exactly what you were doing, didn't you? In fact, you did it on purpose." He took a step forward, his fists clenching at his sides as if that might give him more strength. "Did you hope to undermine me and my authority?"

"No. No. That is not true." Bewildered, she scooted to the far end of the bed. Why did he accuse her unfairly? What had she done to stir such resentment in him? Nothing. Nothing that she could think of.

All that came to mind were the long hours she had spent reconstructing the destroyed chart he had considered so important.

The map. Hope sprang to her rescue. Once he saw what she had done for him, surely he would feel differently.

Tossing aside the protection of the covers, Malana scram-

bled from the bed, darting past him in her excitement to
bestow her precious gift.

He must have thought she plotted an escape.

"Oh, no, you don't," Zeph declared, coming after her,
catching her roughly by the arms before she reached the
desk that contained the folded drawing.

The heat of his work-roughened hands gripping her
bare skin, the feel of his powerful, unyielding chest pressing against her ... something ignited, exploding within
her. She wanted to lean into him, and yet ...

She must resist. She must fight for her honor. At all
costs, she must fight for her identity and everything in
which she believed. Fight and win and make him believe
in it, too.

Somehow, by the sheer strength of will perhaps, she
gained her freedom. Predictably, he lunged after her.
Reaching the desk, she scooted behind it, using it as a
barrier between them. Groping blindly, Malana at last
located the map.

"Here." Breathing hard from the effort of her determination, she offered the map to him, actually shoving it at
him in near desperation, one edge of the paper bending
as it met with the resistance of his forward motion.

"What is this?" he asked, glancing down, his brows knit-
ting skeptically as she continued to prod his chest.

Mouth puckered in silent insistence, she offered the
map again.

After a moment of hesitation, his large hand encircled
the folded sheet, then opened it, slowly, carefully, his gaze
never leaving hers. He looked down only to scan her handiwork. His wariness never altered, except in the brief instant
when he glanced back up, his eyes narrowing as they challenged her.

"Is this supposed to be some kind of trick?" he
demanded, never once giving her the benefit of the doubt.
"Or is it your idea of a prank?"

It hurt to think he didn't trust her. Malana stared back at him in silence, her throat clogged by a painful lump of indignation.

Assuming her silence indicated admission of guilt, Zeph wadded up the map, his black look of accusation never wavering. He turned, lifting his hand as if he intended to throw it away.

"No!" she choked, spurred into action by necessity. She grabbed his sleeve, tugging at it with all her might.

He could have shook her off. Easily, she supposed. But he didn't. Instead, he stood there, the crumpled map still clasped in his angry fist.

For the briefest moment, she thought she saw something register in his eyes that renewed her flagging hope.

"Yes, I did it, Zeph Westley," she whispered. "I did it for you." She lowered her lashes then, her face tilted upward, her arms open and relaxed at her sides. An offering. Of what she could not say for certain, but even with her eyes closed, she could feel him gravitate toward her. Closer and closer, so near his warm breath fanned across her flushed cheeks like the welcome heat of the sun. Malana parted her lips with expectation.

"If that be the case, girl, then for your own sake, I suggest you don't do it again."

Her eyes popped open even as her heart plummeted and her hands moved up in a protective gesture.

But he was already gone.

Small consolation—for the moment, anyway. He had taken the map with him.

Inspired by a sudden flash of insight, Malana smiled, wondering if her mother had had as much trouble wooing her *haole* father.

"So, what do you make of it, Mr. Kennedy?"

Zeph frowned down at the fine piece of chicanery—what

else could it be?—comparing it to the charred remains of what had once been his most valued chart. His eyes focused on one, then darted to the other, looking for variance, no matter how insignificant. Back and forth. Finally, blowing the air from his lungs with a mighty huff, he conceded: They were identical in content, if not in style.

But what of the rest of the map, the part he couldn't compare except against his own unreliable memory? God only knew how unreliable that was. Already they were miles from where they should be. What if there was a difference, something small and easily overlooked? All it took was an infinitesimal slip of the pen, whether on purpose or not . . .

"It's crude, but to be honest, Cap'n, given the circumstances, you couldn't have done any better yourself."

Curse his first officer for his unerring honesty. Nonetheless, the man was right. Whoever's handiwork, considering the circumstances, it deserved his attention.

"So, who do you think drew it?" Zeph asked with an outward show of calmness. He had his own conflicting theories, ones he had no desire to share.

"Who's to say?" Kennedy shrugged his wide, capable shoulders. "But whoever did has a damn fine eye for mapmaking, or an extraordinary ability to copy and"—he laughed nervously, picking up the piece of paper and examining it in the candlelight—"access to your supply of writing materials."

Zeph snatched the drawing from his mate's much-too-brazen hand. Even if he wanted to, he couldn't deny the watermark of a spouting whale came from his own private stock. Indeed, someone aboard the *Dolphin* had drawn it.

"Who, then?" he demanded, pacing, the chart clutched in his hand behind his back. "One of the men with mutiny on his mind, no doubt," he muttered. Someone like Jake Ainsworth, a man with a grudge who would like nothing better than to see his captain fail. "By the way," Zeph asked, "how fare the flogged men?"

"They'll make it, even if Jake declares otherwise. But is the crew behind this?" The mate shook his head. "None of them are educated enough to draw such a detailed chart on their own. They might have copied yours, but then they had to have access to your quarters and maps."

"That leaves you, me . . . and Danny. The boy is as loyal as the day is long. So, are you suggesting I should suspect you, Mr. Kennedy?" Zeph asked, not in the least amused by the unexplained riddle.

"Not at all, sir. There's one more person you've forgotten."

"Who?" Zeph demanded, glaring at the sailor with impatience. Then he paused, knowing exactly whom his first officer meant.

Malana.

The name hung in the air, more of a presence than had it been spoken aloud. It was ludicrous, of course, to think she might have such ability. She was merely an ignorant island girl who couldn't even write her name. How in God's name could she have possibly drawn, much less conceived of, the details of such a map without committing an error?

"That's impossible, you know," Zeph insisted, turning and slapping the map down on the table. Impossible, perhaps, but the only ready explanation. He couldn't imagine Danny daring to defy his authority. And Mr. Kennedy had no reason to lie to him.

As for Malana . . . she was a creature of far different stripes. It was in her nature to defy him. Besides, how could he forget that she had claimed to have drawn it? Still . . .

"It's impossible," he repeated.

"I know." Mr. Kennedy unfolded the discarded map. "Just look at the detail. It's incredible."

"And even if she did," Zeph continued, as if the other man had never spoken, "if you discount her lack of ability, what would be her motive to replace the very map she destroyed?''

At that, Mr. Kennedy cocked his head and gave Zeph the strangest look, one that very nearly verged on insubordination. ''Beggin' your pardon, Cap'n. I don't think you give her enough credit. She does have a vested interest in reaching New England safe and sound, the same as you and me. That map could well be her salvation as much as ours.''

Zeph stared unwaveringly at the man. ''Thank you, Mr. Kennedy.'' Reaching out, he demanded the return of the map. ''That will be all.''

The inevitable silent clash of wills ensued. Zeph never doubted for a moment that his trusted mate sized up his worth as closely as he did his in return.

He glanced down at the map in question, now in his own hand. Did he dare take such a gamble and actually use the chart? Did he have any other choice? Already, he'd proven his memory to be flawed. Not that they were lost. He knew they would eventually reach the coast of South America if they kept to an eastward course. From there they had only to sail south to reach Cape Horn. But without true bearings errors could be made, none more threatening than mistaking the false cape at the southernmost point of Hoste Island as the real one. Many a ship had been lost there.

But even if they found the mouth to the right course at Cape Horn, that was no guarantee of success. Navigating the treacherous straits to reach the Atlantic Ocean took an intuitive master. But more importantly, it required good charts and exact plotting to avoid the many hazards. Captains far better than he had lost their way, and subsequently their own and their crew's lives, to the unpredictable waters off the coast of Tierra del Fuego. Only a fool tried to sail it from memory.

But to trust a map drawn by an unknown, inexperienced hand? That, and a woman to boot?

To do so made him more than just a fool. It made him a desperate one.

Desperation, Zeph had learned long ago, had destroyed far better men than he.

*Chapter Six*

Frozen sea mist sparkled on the stiff white sails like diamonds, hanging from the ropes, spars, and masts in delicate, crystalline-like icicles. At long last. Passage around Cape Horn confronted them, miles and miles of sea riddled with unpredictable weather that could go from dead calm to tempest in the blink of an eye, along with hidden rocks and an undertow that could suck down even the most seaworthy ship manned by the most capable crew. Nonetheless, standing at the helm of the *Dolphin,* Zeph faced the temporary cold and nature's gateway home with confidence.

It had not always been that way. Weeks before, after hours of agonizing indecision in the predawn, he had corrected the course setting according to the configurations on the then still-unproven map. The worse that could have happened, he had finally concluded, was that they would deviate even farther off course, no better or worse off than they already were. But God had remained on their side—or had at least lent a guiding hand to the one who had drawn the mysterious map—and they had found themselves only a few degrees north of their intended destination. The ordeal had proven the worth of the chart and his intuition as a navigator.

Such was not the case when it came to his ability to judge human character.

Malana. What a paradox she proved to be in comparison to all that he knew—or thought he knew—about people, especially females. He truly couldn't decide what to make of her. Innocent. Profound. Simplistic, but, oh, so very complicated. He found it impossible to be around her. And yet that was all he wanted to do—be with her. If he didn't watch himself, it could easily become an obsession.

In the long hours of night when he stood on the deck of his ship, alone, unable to sleep, the temperature quickly dropping the farther south they sailed, Zeph tried to figure out what it was about her that made his pulse pound so hard in his veins. Even now he couldn't say, or perhaps he simply didn't want to face the truth or her sweet, upturned face, the glimmer of mystery in her dark eyes begging to be breached.

The fact was, he lost control whenever he was near her. She, just a mere snip of a girl, could make his blood boil, his reason turn to mush. And what of his one redeeming quality, his strength of character that heretofore had never failed him? Around her, even that quickly became nonexistent.

No one should have such power over another. No female, that is. And so, to protect himself and those who depended upon him—the crew of the *Dolphin,* and even Leatrice far away in Mystic—Zeph made it a point to stay completely away from her.

Whenever his volition wavered, he reminded himself that his only responsibility to her was to take her to her father. And even that he did out the goodness of his heart.

Once delivered, he would be done with her. Her lure, no matter how strong, couldn't possibly reach across the miles between New Bedford, where her father resided, and his home in Mystic. And if it did prove too strong . . .

There was always the sea. A man lost all sense of the world beyond the endless water, the shift of the wind, when shipboard.

And so, day and night, the unhealthy war raged within him. Whenever he felt certain honor had claimed the victory, the nasty urge to go to her invariably resurfaced. It would be rough sailing for a few days. So went his unreasonable reasoning. Duty required that he calm her fears. True, perhaps, but that did not mean he must do it personally.

"Danny, boy, I have a task for you," he said, turning to his cabin boy, who stood at his elbow bundled clear to his eyeballs in a sou'wester, holding his glass, ready to give it up at the first indication. Zeph reached out.

"Aye, sir." Without further prompting, the lad responded, placing the brass telescope in the cradle of his captain's open palm.

Putting the instrument to his eye beneath his own wide-brim rain hat, Zeph focused on the distant rocks they quickly approached. Much too quickly, he decided, lowering it and snapping it closed.

"Trim the sheets," he ordered the crew, who immediately began pulling on the ropes. "You there," he shouted to an unidentified sailor, "lend a hand and be quick about it." With them all dressed alike, it was impossible to tell who was who. Then he turned once more to Danny. "Go below, boy, and reassure our passenger that although the seas may be rough for a few days, there's nothing to fear."

"Aye, Cap'n." With the exuberance of youth, the cabin boy scampered toward the companionway stairs.

"Danny," Zeph called over the moaning wind.

"Aye, Cap'n?" The boy came to a halt on the first riser,

looking back expectantly from beneath the brim of his hat.

"Tell her there's nothing to fear as long as her charts prove to be true."

Frowning, the boy nodded. Then, seeing his captain had nothing more to say, he continued on his way.

Why had he made that last statement? Zeph wondered. It had been cruel, but necessary, to remind her that he, Zeph Westley, not she; controlled this ship.

Under no circumstances could he allow her to get the upper hand. If she did, his ship, and just as likely his soul, would surely be lost.

The unexpected knock at the door caught Malana by surprise, as had the gradual, unexplained chill in the air. Everyday it grew colder and bleaker—weather such as she had never known or even suspected existed. On the island of Hitihiti, it was always warm.

"It's me, miss. Daniel Slater," announced the voice on the other side.

"Daniel?" she echoed in astonishment between chattering teeth, rising from her seat beneath the small porthole that let in the small amount of natural light and warmth she received each day. Today it wasn't much.

Wrapped in the colorful quilt from the bed, she padded eagerly toward the door on cold, bare feet to welcome her only outside contact. Why, without the cabin boy, she would surely have gone crazy if not hungry, long before now.

Still, what was he doing here? It was much too early for the evening meal, one of only two she received each day, along with lessons to improve her English and her knowledge of *haole* ways and customs. Oh, how she looked forward to those times she spent with the boy, someone to talk to, to learn every detail about this place to which they journeyed called Mystic, Connecticut. He was even teaching her how to read and write.

She could hardly begin to imagine such a strange place where the trees changed color at will, becoming plumed like the beautiful birds of Hitihiti—orange, red, yellow. Or houses with so many rooms, stacked one on top of another, where a person could get lost in the maze. Surely, Daniel exaggerated about that. Why would anyone need or want such a large place to live? Daniel even claimed that the people there traveled everywhere in wheeled conveyances pulled around by horses.

About that she figured he told the truth. She had seen a horse once. It had arrived in a ship with a *haole* who declared he had been sent from his God to save all the People from something he called sin. He had brought the horse as a means of transportation around the island. What a wild, unpredictable beast the animal had proven to be, large and useless in the thick undergrowth. Rumor had it that a band of raiding flesh-eaters from another island had sacrificed both man and animal. The horse had proven far more difficult to capture than the man, and far less palatable as well.

Perhaps Daniel had come to share more fantastic *haole* stories with her, to share more of his knowledge. His company had a way of warming her heart, if not her body. Still, Malana ignored the chill in the air and smiled in welcome. Then she noticed the unhappy look on his face when he swept off his dripping head covering.

"Is something wrong, Daniel?" she asked when he entered the room, closing the door behind him and shutting out the soft moans that sounded more as if they came from human voices than from the wind.

"I've come with a message from the captain."

"Oh?" she said, presenting her back so the boy couldn't see the undisguised excitement in her eyes. Zeph Westley had thought of her, even if only briefly. Was he concerned for her welfare? "Why did he not come himself?" Malana questioned, trying not to sound too eager.

"The cap'n been kinda busy of late." The shuffle of Daniel's booted feet behind her was a restless sound. "But he wanted you to know that the seas might get a bit rough for a few days, but you're not to worry."

"How very kind of your captain to show such concern for me." Her jaw tightened with frustration; her cold toes curled. If he wanted to reassure her, then why did he refuse to come see her?

"Aye, miss, he just didn't want you to worry none," Danny repeated, his covered feet scuffling indecisively again.

Her bare feet were so frigid she could hardly stand on them for a moment longer. But she must. It must never get back to Zeph Westley that she needed anything from him, not warmth nor company nor comfort.

"Thank you. Tell your captain that I have no intentions of worrying," she announced. Lifting one foot, she rubbed it against the top of the other, hoping the movement went unnoticed.

It didn't.

"Why, miss, it's freezin' cold," the cabin boy declared, "and you've got nothin' on your feet."

"I do not need anything," she insisted. Despite her brave words, Malana could stand it no longer, so she sat down and tucked the traitorous appendages beneath the thin blanket she had wrapped about her.

Not to be deterred, however, Danny reached beneath the quilt, discovering her icy toes. His hands were warm, in contrast. "We can't have this." He clucked his tongue. "Will be the death of ya, miss. I know what I can do," he announced decisively, jumping to his feet and sprinting across the room.

"No, Daniel, wait," she called out to him. "There is no

need." No need whatsoever to let it be known she lacked for anything.

But the boy was out the door and gone before Malana could convince him otherwise.

Moments later Daniel returned, his arms ladened. The chin-high pile consisted of a pair of thick stockings, boots—large, clumsy, and worn at the heels—a gaily colored shirt, and a pair of pants, all of which seemed much too small even for her petite figure. They looked more Daniel's size than hers. Finally, there was an overcoat and a floppy oversized hat.

"For you," he declared, his voice laced with pride as he dumped the bundle on the floor at her feet.

Malana knew neither what to say nor how to react.

"Daniel, are these yours?" she asked, suspecting they were all he owned besides what he wore. "You should not have," she chided gently. What a senseless thing to say, she realized quickly, as he looked at her with such adoring expectation.

"It's all right, miss. I have no need for them."

Still, she refused to concede.

"I know they're not much," he said in way of explanation, hanging his head, the joyous look of giving doused by her thoughtless words. Did he think she didn't want them because they were not good enough?

"Oh, no, Daniel, you are wrong," Malana explained breathlessly. "They are wonderful. Thank you." Smiling, she accepted his generosity with inborn, royal graciousness. But how could she ever hope to repay such a selfless act?

When he left, she wasted no time sorting through the pile of clothing. The long stockings that came clear to her knees were warm and welcomed. Her toes curled in their softness, the cold numbness slowly receding as she checked out the rest of the bundle. The colorful shirt, while a bit snug across her chest, was equally warm, if somewhat scratchy against her bare skin. But the pants were another story altogether. They hugged her hips and thighs like a second skin, flaring widely around her legs and gaping about her middle so much she could have slipped both hands inside if she'd wanted. Although binding in a strange, confining confining way, they nonetheless kept her warm. She would simply have to get used to the discomfort.

As for the hat and coat, they were quite ugly. Well, she simply wouldn't wear them unless she had to.

It was then that Malana began to imagine how *haole* women dressed. Like their men? She wondered. In confining clothes that covered up every bit of them from chin to toe? Frowning, she glanced down at herself, tousled up like a pig readied for the spit. Oh, surely not. But then, when it came to *haole* and their strange ways, nothing they did would surprise her. She would have to ask Daniel about that.

Suddenly frustrated and—dare she admit it?—frightened, Malana dropped back into the chair that served as her one constant companion during the long, lonely days. There was so much she didn't know, so much she needed to learn simply to survive in the strange *haole* world that she would soon enter. For a moment she almost wished they would never reach their destination. Yet the thought of continuing to live her current bleak existence seemed far worse. Only one person offered her hope: Zeph Westley.

Daniel, of course, had shared so much with her, but Malana sensed his youth colored his view of the world, just as her ignorance did hers.

Yes, her future lay with Zeph Westley. Only he offered enlightenment. Only he could give her the necessary knowledge she needed, and yet she had no idea how to

make him see that. How could he if he refused to give her
the chance even to ask him?

She must find him, confront him, somehow make him
understand, make him truly care. But how?

Picking up the strange hat and coat, she donned them,
tucking her hair beneath the collar and the long-contoured
brim to keep it as dry as possible.

The answer came easily enough, perhaps, even if the
execution was not so simple. All she had to do was figure
out how a *haole* woman would go about it.


How quickly the nonthreatening moans of the wind
increased to devastating shrieks. Time was of the essence.
But with the sheets stiff and frozen, the ropes and chains
iced solidly to the block and tackle, the sails fought every
effort to lower them quickly.

Zeph took control of the helm, sending the more than
capable Mr. Kennedy to take charge of the mainsail, which
seemed to be giving the crew the most trouble. The icy
wheel was stiff and unbearably cold against his palms.
Nonetheless, he hung on, determined to salvage as much
of their precious easterly course, as well as of the canvas
and rigging, as he could. To say nothing of the life and
limb of his crew.

He had to give them credit. They gave all, right down
to the last man, the differences between common sailor
and officer put aside, at least for the moment.

It was then that he saw the unidentified figure dart off
on what could only be deemed a fool's errand. It had to
be his cabin boy, of course, judging by the size and clothes.
Who else could it be? And why did he head straight for
the railing? Damn it, the kid knew better. All it would take
was one good wave . . .

"Danny, come back," Zeph cried over the wailing of

the wind, the teeth-clenching squeal of resistant chain, the gut-wrenching sound of ripping sail.

If the boy heard him, which Zeph doubted, he didn't respond, continuing on his way toward the quarterdeck. Was Danny looking for him? Was something wrong with Malana?

The first wave hit so suddenly, washing across the lower decks with such force, it caught even Zeph by surprise. Committed to his position at the helm, all he could do in his frustration was call out the boy's name again and again—all in vain, it seemed, as the icy water receded. Frantically, he glanced about, but could see no sign of the hapless cabin boy.

Where was he? Had he been washed overboard and even now was struggling in the ruthless water to gasp one more precious breath before the undertow claimed him? Then he spied the kid, clinging tenaciously to the windward stairway leading up to the quarterdeck.

"Hang on, Danny boy. I'm coming," Zeph called out, sensing the moment of lull would be over soon enough, the chance to save his cabin boy gone with it. Thank goodness, Mr. Kennedy returned. Zeph grabbed the mate, turning over the helm to his expertise. "Hold her steady, mister, no matter what happens," he ordered without further explanation, confident his instructions would be followed to the letter.

It took forever to make his way across the deck through the scattered debris, the bits of shredded rope and canvas, strewn about both by nature's wrath determined to destroy the ship and by the efficiency of seasoned sailors just as determined to save it. By the time the second wave hit, he hadn't even reached the halfway point.

Clinging to a stanchion, Zeph had no choice but to ride it out and hope the boy managed to do the same, in spite of the almost supernatural strength of the shockingly cold wall of water. The moment the sea rushed back over the rails, he continued on his way, head bent to the howling winds and the slash of the icy rain that accompanied it.

Almost there, he looked up. The spot where he had last seen Danny was now empty. Had he reached the boy too late? Had he lost him to the raging waters? Love and hate for the only constant in his life—the sea—battled within Zeph's mariner's soul. How could it have betrayed him so?

Then he spied a familiar boot poking out from beneath the staircase.

"Danny boy!"

Rushing forward, Zeph dropped down on his knees to reach into the protective cove created by the slant of the stairs and overhead deck. The third wave hit with such force it knocked him down.

Thankfully, the boy's limp body lay beneath his own. Otherwise, it might have been washed out onto the open deck and overboard. Grasping the lowest riser with one arm, the boy with the other, Zeph hung on, riding out the battering of cold seawater, praying that in his determination to save the lad he didn't crush the slight frame beneath his weight.

The icy, suffocating blanket of water seemed eternal. His own lungs near to bursting, Zeph feared Danny's might have already given out. Seeking only to confirm a beating heart, he slid his hand a little higher along the boy's slim body, praying for a miracle.

God in heaven! Zeph's own heart froze in shock when his hand, indeed, encountered more than a miracle. Since when had the boy grown a woman's breasts?

When at last the deck cleared, Zeph rolled away. Far away. In fact, as far away as he could get in those few seconds of shock and surprise. He didn't even notice when, in his rush, he bumped his head on the slant of the staircase.

How could he have made such a gross mistake? Anyone

could see she was much taller than Danny. What was she doing out here and dressed in the boy's clothing?

God, she just lay there, facedown, a heap of baggy, wet clothes, not moving, not even seeming to breathe. Even as he thought it, his own lungs pumped hard, cautioning him: Keep your head and your distance. But the pounding of his heart, as loud as pagan drums, overrode the warning.

Zeph rushed back in and rolled her over, confirming that it was Malana. Her lips, usually so pink, were almost blue. From the cold or from lack of air, he couldn't be certain. Her lowered eyelids, fringed with dark lashes, appeared so fragile they looked like fine china.

"Malana," he called softly, lifting her by the shoulders to shake her gently. Her head rolled back, the ridiculous hat falling off, her long hair tumbling from its protection like dark streamers, framing the sweet curve of her throat. To his relief, the pulse in her neck beat wildly . . . as wildly as his own heart. Feeling helpless, frustrated, and completely responsible, Zeph did the only thing he knew to do: He shook her again. To no avail. And should another wave wash over them . . .

He looked up, frantic to get her to safety, to keep her alive, to make her survive, if only for the sheer force of his own determination. Dare he take the risk of moving her? Dare he not? If he could get up the stairs to the higher elevation offered on the quarterdeck, she had a chance. A slim one, indeed but here in the thundering wake of the water, she had none. Despite the risk to his own safety, he must try.

Sweeping her into his arms, he half dragged, half carried her from beneath the shelter of the staircase. Then he slung her facedown over his shoulder and ran for the stairs. He knew he jostled her unmercifully, her head, chest, and arms pounding against his back. Zeph cursed himself for his roughness, but unable to think of a way to cushion the beating she undoubtedly took, he continued on, silently promising her it would all be over soon.

"One way or another," he murmured, praying he would make it to shelter in time.

The next wave hit just as he cleared the stairway. Staggering beneath the cover of the half deck, he positioned the girl so he held her in his arms, protected against the vulnerability of his heart. With his defiant back to the raging sea, Zeph took the brunt of the onslaught against his own shoulders. His only thought was to stay upright, to keep her nose and mouth above the water. Holding her up as high as he dared, his free hand cupping her face to keep it from falling forward, he pressed his cheek against her cold one and closed his eyes against the inevitable sting of the brine spray.

The battering was over in a matter of seconds, but it seemed like years to every tested muscle and tendon in Zeph's body. He opened his eyes, slowly wondering what to do to make her breathe once more . . . if it wasn't already too late.

*God, please, don't let it be too late.*

Zeph looked down. Her eyes, wide and luminous as midnight moons, stared back at him with an expression of idolization that could melt even the hardest heart, the jostling having forced the breath back into her body. He could have lost himself in their inky depths for a lifetime and never wanted for more.

No, that wasn't true. He wanted more. Much more, but he dared not think of it, much less imagine how her lips would feel against his own.

But they were blue and chattering . . . in such need. Duty demanded he warm them and her. Slowly, Zeph lowered his face, putting his mouth to hers, vowing only to give her vital heat and then pull away.

He should pull away now.

Instead, he felt her mouth open beneath his, warm and

alive, demanding. And he gave. With all of his being. Forgetting who he was, where he was, or why he shouldn't, he surrendered to the pounding of the drums in his head, savoring the taste of her wet lips, salty and yet, oh, so very sweet as they begged for more.

What more could he give? What more dare he give? Or take?

Like a drowning man, he struggled to reach the surface of his sanity. But even as his mind fought for the survival of his honor, his body sought ways to immerse itself even further into the degradation. Her bare breast thrust proudly against the palm of his hand as he cupped it, exploring the taut nipple with his thumb. His tongue explored the heated, heretofore unexplored cavern of her mouth, teaching hers how to respond, how to dance and duel.

Just where the madness would lead him thankfully remained only a fantasy. Reason in the form of icy seawater rushed over him, silencing the fervid drumbeats that had taken control of his very pulse, dousing the raging fires of passion that gripped him.

Zeph pulled back roughly, glaring down at her as if to find fault. Her lifted face, so close, so damned peaceful and innocent with her eyes closed, her lips parted and sanguine from the ruthless pressure of his mouth . . . what blame could be found there? Reproach was his and his alone.

Yes, lust, pure and simple, he insisted, born of his own depravity.

Then she opened her eyes, and her lips, unspeaking but once again blue with cold, trembled.

How could lust, neither pure nor simple, he suddenly realized as the battle raged within him once more, do what it did to his heart? It hammered. It hurt. It felt so achingly empty and unfulfilled.

This was a new and frightening feeling for Zeph Westley,

a man who had always prided himself in needing nothing
and no one. Thrusting aside what could only be the chica-
neries of a poor, depraved soul too long at sea, he gathered
up his honor even as he again took Malana into his arms,
determined to share only of his body heat and nothing
more.

By God, he was a man of principles. A man with a human-
itarian mission. This child had been given over to his care.
Yes, a child, he reminded himself, as he held her slight
form against his still-wretchedly unhappy heart.

It mattered not that her body felt like a woman's or that
her mouth kissed like a woman's, she was nonetheless a
child. He would deliver her safely to her father. In the
meantime, it was his duty to protect her, especially from
himself.

The break in the storm came as quickly as the tempest
had roused itself in the beginning. Dark clouds, still roiling
overhead, threatened more torrential rain, but for the
moment Zeph felt compelled to take her below deck to
the safety of his cabin.

He should have turned her over to Snips's care when
the old salt offered, seeing as the sailmaker came as close
to a physician as they had, but Zeph didn't do it. He
merely shook his head, clutched Malana to his chest, and
continued on.

"Captain?"

Mr. Kennedy's call stopped him at the head of the companionway stairs that led below. Zeph turned. His first
officer, drenched to the bone as they all were, still commanded the helm, but awaited the formality of being
relieved of his duty.

Of course, the helm was where he, the captain, should
have been now and then, when in some false delusion of
heroics he had lost his head and all sense of priority. In
those few moments the ship and its crew could have been

lost for the sake of one, and it would have been nobody's fault but his own.

And now?

"Steady as she goes, Mr. Kennedy. I'll be below only a moment."

"Aye, sir." With ne'er a flicker in his seasoned sailor's eyes, the mate still let his feelings be known. He thought his captain made a grave mistake.

Let him think what he wanted. Yet in the stillness of the companionway, Zeph began to rethink his decision. At that moment had there been someone to relieve him of his burden, he would have gladly turned her over without hesitation. But as luck would have it, they were alone.

"Zephiran?" It was the first she had spoken, her voice, her steady gaze that bore right to his heart, clean and clear of any guilt.

"Just keep still, girl," he ordered, his own voice raw with a gruffness necessary to keep from looking down, from giving in, from making yet another mistake. But he wondered to whom he really spoke—to Malana or to his own, obviously weak, heart?

To his relief she obeyed, saying nothing, making no move as he carried her into the cabin. His cabin. And yet he felt like an intruder into what, by all rights, should be his domain.

What was the beautiful quilt that Leatrice had made for him doing on the floor? Dear Lord, Leatrice. How could he have forgotten about his ever-faithful fiancée even for a moment? Angered—mostly with himself—Zeph searched for other reasons to vent his frustrations on Malana. For what purpose had she moved the desk chair beneath the porthole? And there were other things, insignificant, petty things, but he focused on them anyway.

Frowning, he glared down at the culprit.

There it was again, damn it. That look of incredible innocence and trust. Just when had she begun to trust him? he wanted to know. Didn't she realize he didn't even trust himself?

He released her legs, letting her feet slide to the floor. His composure slipped away with them. Getting angry might well be his only salvation.

"What did you think you were doing? You could have gotten us both killed." Even as he chided, he stripped off her wet coat and placed her in the chair, kneeling at her feet to remove the clumsy boots. She made no effort to resist, no offer to assist. She merely watched his every move with those great, luminous eyes of hers that held such unreasonable power over him.

"Damn," he cursed when water poured from the shoes, soaking the floor and the beautiful Oriental rug that covered it.

"I am sorry," she gasped, cringing at the venom in his voice.

Still frowning, he glanced up, hoping to discover a glimmer of the fault she professed. It was there, unfairly so. What did he expect? His own shoes were sloshing and just as heavy with seawater.

"Don't be," he muttered, needing to look anywhere but into her dark, soulful eyes. "It's not your fault."

Still encased in damp wool stockings, her feet curled about each other, looking self-conscious and small compared to his hands. Quickly, he stripped them, staring at their slender bareness, marveling at their perfection as he gently warmed them. Realizing he found too much pleasure in what he did, he let go. Clearing his throat, Zeph focused on her wet pants, then suddenly wondered how he was going to continue down—or should he say up?—such a dangerous a path.

Not that she would protest whatever he did. The resistance must come from within. Thank God, it was there, that strength of will, or else he would surely be lost. But if he proceeded any further, he couldn't be so sure of it.

Spying the discarded quilt lying on the floor across the room, he reached for it, picking it up and holding it out like a screen between them.

"Get undressed and into that bed," he ordered.

Without question or hesitation, she obeyed.

"Are you there yet?" he asked, when all grew suspiciously quiet.

"Yes."

He glanced around the barrier to make sure.

She lay on the bed stark naked.

"Good God, girl, cover up," he bellowed.

Which he instantly regretted doing. The look on her face was so pitiful and confused. Without waiting for her to comply, Zeph stepped forward and threw the quilt over her. For good measure, he reached down and tucked the coverlet securely around her shoulders.

"You gotta keep warm." He noticed the tears but pretended not to. But, oh God, the image of her lying there in all her glory burned in his brain, never to be forgotten.

Remembering instead his duty as captain of the *Dolphin*, he turned and walked away, his loins afire with a need he dared never to assuage.


Far away on Hitihiti, a low rumble reverberated across the tiny island. Women paused at their work—*tapa* makers' mallets stilled; artist hands trembled; mothers frantically called their children home.

Among the men, the reaction was much the same. Fishermen turned from their nets, ominously empty of catch, to stare at the distant volcano that dominated their island domain, the only home they knew or could ever imagine. Carpenters descended to the ground, abandoning their boats and buildings, gathering to discuss the meaning of it all.

A couple making love on the beach parted without prelude, hurrying back to the village. One young man herding pigs in the undergrowth dropped his stick and then to his knees.

"Te Tuma," he cried, lifting his arms in supplication. "It is too soon for you to awaken. Why? Why?"

The question was repeated on the lips of every islander— every man, woman, and child. Why, when only two moons ago they had offered sacrifice to sate the great god of the volcano's lust? His period of rest should have lasted for at least the circle of the seasons, if not longer. Why had it not? Why did he awaken with such anger?

In response they received another warning rumble . . . one that silenced the flocks of chattering birds and set the trees to trembling.

High above, in the immense gaseous cloud that eternally circled the dome of the great volcano, the god, Te Tuma, stared down at his moral subjects. His eyes burned with the fire of rage, the living flames capping his enormous head, the hot lava forming the floor on which he paced.

Who among them knew of the deception and desecration played on him and the sacred ceremonies devoted to sating his every need? He studied each upturned face in kind, from chieftain to smallest child, but could find no guilt among them. Nonetheless, he roared his frustration, finding their pathetic pleas for forgiveness inadequate.

He wanted back what had been unrightfully taken from him. So the farseeing god turned his gaze across the water, seeking out those responsible. On the wings of a mighty storm he flew, faster and faster, finding at last what he sought. One tiny ship sailing farther and farther away while the deceiver and *haole* thief drew closer and closer together. Had he not seen them with his own eyes in each other's arms?

She was his bride. He would have her and no one else. Vengefully, he thrashed the vessel in the churning seas he created, voicing his vow of revenge to any who could understand the language of the drums. But the *haole*, if he listened, did not comprehend. The drums only seemed to make him more defiant.

Angered now more than ever, Te Tuma returned to his mountain home to make his plans, to plot his revenge, to continue to roar and belch his frustrations at those powerless to right the wrong. Nonetheless, someone must be made to suffer as he did.

Confused, the People turned to their chieftain and his priests for an explanation of their god's behavior. But neither Mao, his dark tattooed face lifted to the mountaintop, nor his holy men had answers for the islanders. The drums spoke falsely. Not even the most sacred *kava* ceremony communicated the truth between them.

In desperation, Mao stood alone at the foot of Te Tuma's throne, his arms lifted heavenward.

"Did not I give you from my own household a female who was like a daughter to me?" he cried. "Malana was beautiful, virginal, and very desirable. Surely her royal blood pleased you. Hear me, oh great Te Tuma. If that is not enough, I have sacrificed even more. Le'utu, the woman I wanted beside me, left without warning, choosing the stinking *haole* over what I offered her. I would have made her a queen, a woman of such power among all the islanders. My great plans of domination are all made in your name, Te Tuma, the most powerful god. Spare me and my people. Tell me how to appease you."

Against his will Te Tuma listened, but he refused to reply, for the answer was only just beginning to formulate in his great, godly head.

"Great Te Tuma," Mao called out again in the face of the god's willful lack of response, "I will make it right between us," he vowed, standing in the sacred circle as preparations for yet another sacrifice were made. "Show me the way, and I will gladly do your every bidding."

Curiosity piqued, the volcano god grew quiet and still,

distracted for the moment by all the attention given him by his loyal subject. Although patience was not in his nature, he decided to give the People a small reprieve . . . until he could figure out a way to expand his power and get back what he really wanted.

# *Chapter Seven*

The *Dolphin* rounded Cape Horn without further incident—of the sea or of the heart.

Malana spent the long days searching for signs of change in both. In the sea the change was readily apparent, the warmth gradually returning, even if the color and brilliance of the water and the beauty of the sandy beaches were never quite the same as in her island home.

Even so, she chose to remain dressed in the drab, ill-fitting clothing Daniel had so unselfishly given her. They afforded her freedom, she discovered quickly enough. Freedom to go topside. Freedom to feel the warmth of the sun directly on her uplifted face, the wind whipping through her unbound hair.

Her heart proved to be much more resistant to change, however, clinging to island tradition. It was not the way of the People to bind one's heart to another. Regardless, she felt something for the fire-haired captain, that she couldn't deny. But what that something was, which created such havoc, such need yet such anguish in her traitorous heart, she could not easily define.

Dependency, perhaps? That might be part of it, Malana admitted, staring out over the rail into the turbulent waters that sucked at the side of the ship. If so, was it because she had no choice and no one else to turn to?

Indebtedness, then? She considered that possibility and couldn't deny she owed him a lot. Her very life, in fact. But that was not enough to explain the way she thought of him constantly, the way she looked for him among the men, the twinge of pride she felt whenever she located him, watched him, wishing he would return the admiration, even if only a little.

It was that part of the unidentified feelings that confused her the most. What did it mean?

Even as she sorted through the possibilities and quickly rejected them as unlikely, Malana spied Zeph emerge from the companionway. His tall frame towered over the other men, his deep voice unmistakable in contrast. If he saw her, he gave no indication, even when he walked right past her.

Blinking back the wounding truth, she pressed her hand to her mouth. Why? she wondered. If she meant so little to him, why even bother to rescue her? Pushing off the rail, she hurried away, seeking out the solitude of her cabin. There no one could see her when she made a fool of herself, victimized by a heart that should have never been breakable.

Zeph saw her the moment he came on deck. How could he have missed her dressed in those ridiculous clothes? She was all he thought of day and night. Equating her to an island fever, she invaded his blood, running rampant, leaving him weakhearted and forever susceptible, he feared.

"Rio de Janeiro, Cap'n?" his first mate suggested.

"Aye, Mr. Kennedy," Zeph replied. "I'll think about it. This close to home there's little risk of the crew jumping ship." Even Jake Ainsworth would probably bide his time, wanting to receive his share of the profits at the end of the voyage. "I admit we could use fresh supplies for our final leg home." What he didn't say . . . what he really had in mind . . .

It was ludicrous, of course, and so unlike him. He had never gone shopping with a woman, much less with one who had no more notion of what to look for than he did.

But he couldn't present her to James Kilpatrick looking like a hoyden or a wild little heathen. She need civilized clothing, something properly feminine to wear to meet her father, to make a good first impression.

What would Malana think of such an adventure? Would it bring the joy back into her face? Or would it simply overwhelm her? His brows puckered in concern. At first maybe, but there wasn't a female born who didn't instinctively enjoy shopping—once she got the hang of it.

Pleased with his plan, Zeph glanced to where he'd seen her moments before standing by the railing, looking so forlorn. Yes, it would be nice to see the sparkle in her eyes once more.

When he discovered her gone, the momentary pleasure degenerated into concern.

"Ran off in a dither, she did, sir."

"What's that, Mr. Kennedy?" he asked distractedly, glancing around the deck before looking back at his mate.

"The girl, sir." The sailor's always-unassuming gaze slid in the direction of the empty railing. "She headed below a few moments ago. Looked most unhappy, sir. You might want to check on her."

Zeph had not meant to be so obvious in his distress. Did his mate suspect how easily the girl undermined his sense of priorities?

"Thank you, mister," he remarked sharply, trying to sound as if he didn't care.

But he did care. By God, for all the proper reasons, he assured himself. Secure in his justification, Zeph made up his mind. It was only proper that he take Malana shopping in Rio de Janeiro.

The day the *Dolphin* arrived in the Brazilian port turned out to be glorious, after several dreary ones that promised rain. The sun shone brightly. Even the sea sparkled with a heretofore unnoticed beauty.

Thinking finally they reached Zeph's home of Mystic, Connecticut, Malana hurried topside and leaned as far out over the railing as she dared, not wanting to miss anything as they entered the bay. She had never seen such a large village. Why, the houses, many like the one Danny had described, went clear up the sides of the mountains, spilling down into the valleys.

Her pulse thudded with excitement, yet her brain raced with uncertainty, anticipating at last the unknown she must face. What should she do? What exactly would Zeph—and her father—expect of her? What should she expect from herself?

At the moment all she wanted to do was to throw off the strange, binding clothing she wore and run along the beach, barefoot and naked again. She wanted back her innocence of the world beyond.

She wanted her mother. Her mother who had stayed behind for reasons she had yet to fully understand. Le'utu deserved to be here, to share the wonder of it all. Perhaps someday that could be arranged.

"Mystic?" she cried out in her excitement, grabbing Daniel's arm as the boy happened by.

"No, no, miss," Daniel quickly explained. In turn, tugging on her arm, he urged her to return to the safety behind the rail. "We haven't reached home. Not yet. Not for a while."

"How long?" Malana demanded, frowning to cover up her embarrassment, suspecting that Daniel might be secretly laughing at her ignorance.

But he wasn't, she decided after a moment of scrutiny. His gentle look offered only sympathy and encouragement.

"Many days yet," he replied. "We stop here only for supplies."

"Oh," she murmured, disappointed that she would not be able to go ashore.

Yet when a few moments later Zephiran sent word for her to prepare to disembark, Malana was struck with renewed panic. Had he decided, then, to be rid of her?

Again, dear Daniel came to her rescue.

"He plans to take you to the marketplace."

"What for?" she asked suspiciously.

"To buy you more clothing."

"Clothing? Why, what more do I need to wear?" she demanded. Then, deciding that perhaps Daniel wanted the ones he had loaned her back, she blushed and stammered, "Oh, I did not mean to say I want to keep yours. . . ."

"Oh, believe me, miss, you can have them, but they will never do for your needs."

"What do you mean? What kind of needs do I have?" she asked, more confused than ever.

"What he means, girl, is that they are not decent for a proper young lady to wear when she goes to meet her father."

"Danny, don't you have something better to do with your time than to constantly bother our passenger?"

Caught off guard, Malana turned to confront what she expected to be contempt on the part of Zeph Westley. Yet, once she faced him, she saw something much more discerning.

His expression was stern, uncompromising, piercing, but

he always looked that way—at least when he focused on her—so she didn't find it all that odd. So, what was it about him that made her pause, that made her heart lurch, touched by something? Was it pity? No. Zeph Westley was not a man to evoke pity. It was that nagging something else she could not, would not, verbalize.

He looked away, then, as if he didn't want her to discover the truth—in him or in herself. But what was the truth? Could it be that he actually cared about her, even a little? If he did, perhaps that would justify her own feelings.

"Are you ready to go, girl?" he asked gruffly, presenting his arm. Once again his look was unreadable, and she decided it had only been her wanting that had made it appear to be something more that it was.

Instinctively, gratefully, Malana accepted his arm, placing her hand in the crook of his elbow the way Daniel had said a woman walked with a man in Mystic, Connecticut. It felt safe there, protected and warm. As did she, in a way no one else had ever made her feel.

Without further ado or comment, he led her down the gangplank. The moment her feet touched the shore she stumbled, her legs possessed by an unexpected heaviness that made it impossible to walk.

"Oh," she cried, grasping his arm to steady herself. Then realizing that she clung shamelessly to him, she released her grip, wishing she could move away, yet unable to so without risking a fall.

At that he actually smiled, if only briefly. "It's just your sea legs, girl." The humor now gone from his face, he took her by the elbow and starting walking. "You'll master land again soon enough."

Uncertain what he meant by that or why he seemed unaffected by whatever malady made her unable to walk unassisted, Malana did her best to forge ahead, determined not to be outdone by him, yet secretively glad for his supportive hand, if not for his smugness.

But soon enough the strangeness of the place—the smells, the people speaking and dressed so differently—made her forget her physical discomfort. She had never seen so many humans in one place.

Malana began to take notice of the other women they passed on the streets. Some were gaily attired, their dresses flounced and as flashy as the multihued birds on Hitihiti. On their heads they wore equally colorful wraps. Shiny metal rings dangled from their earlobes; smiles curved their lips as they chattered happily—or so it seemed to her—among themselves.

Then there were the other ones, the ones she sensed were the proper *haole* women. Their clothing was very different from the happy women's, and most unflattering. Their long, dark skirts seemed even more restricting than what she wore, and they held their bodies so rigid. Why, it was as if they had swallowed spears.

"Are you hungry?"

Fearful that was what Zeph would expect of her, Malana turned, adamant refusal on her lips. She would not eat a spear.

Instead, he handed her the strangest-looking food, wrapped in a piece of white cloth but much too small to contain a spear. Strange-looking or not, it smelled heavenly, the steam curling around her face. It had been so long since she had had something delicious to eat, how could she resist it?

Her mouth began to water. Oh, how she missed the tree-ripened fruits, the freshly caught fish, even the breadfruit. For too long she had survived on the unappetizing fare aboard a *haole* ship, fearing she would have nothing else.

Taking a tentative nibble of the cloth-wrapped food, Malana found it spicy and very tasty. She hesitated only a moment before cramming the rest of it in her mouth.

Hot. Hot. Her eyes watered from the intense pain, her

hands fanning the air in hopes of cooling it down. Yet it tasted so good, she refused to waste even a morsel.

"Slow down, girl," Zeph scolded.

Of course, he glared at her, but she didn't care.

"There's plenty more where that came from."

Ignoring his chiding, Malana shoved an escaped crumb back into her mouth and licked her fingers, just to spite him, she suspected.

"I suppose you want another meat pie."

She nodded eagerly and watched as he exchanged a collection of shiny metal disks for two more of the wrapped treats.

"What is that?" she asked, pointing to the remaining disks in his hand.

He glanced down at them, then gave her the strangest look. "It's money, girl." Then he added, with a sigh, "But then, I suppose you have no idea what that is, do you?"

He looked so serious, she wished she could think of a way to make his smile return.

"It seems we have more than your manners to work on," Zeph finally concluded, offering her one of the meat pies only after he had carefully unwrapped it, allowing it to cool. He kept the other for himself, eating it with disinterest as he watched Malana devour hers. "It would never do to have you attack your food with such vigor at your father's table."

"I care not what my father thinks of me," she said between licking her fingers.

It was a lie, of course. One meant to undermine Zeph's assumed attitude of superiority. And of course, it evoked his instant reaction.

He grabbed her arm tightly, forcing her to turn around and face him.

"Of course you care." His brows knit, his eyes flashing beneath them. "You had better care, girl. Your father is all that you have."

"I have you, Zeph Westley," she replied, lifting her chin with confidence.

"What you have, girl, is a false sense of self-importance. What you are is trouble." As if to emphasize his cutting remarks, he shook her, none too gently. Then before she could answer, he turned her around once more, forcing her to assume the grueling pace he steered from the rear.

The tears welled, unbidden, unwanted, uncontrollable. Struggling to master her wayward emotions, Malana stared straight ahead to keep Zeph from seeing her moment of weakness. But it was only a moment, she swore to herself.

"I believe we'll start with proper clothes," he stated, emphasizing the word *proper*.

"No," she protested, knowing exactly what he meant. "I refuse to look or act like them"—she pointed to a passing group of spear-swallowers. "I want to be like *that*"—Malana indicated a gaily clad woman, laden with packages, standing across the way.

"God's wrath, girl. *That's* a servant."

At a building that resembled all the others, Zeph paused long enough to glance at the display of spear-swallower clothing in the window, before opening the door and shoving her, still under protest, through. Inside, a strange array of sights and smells caught Malana's attention. Bolts of cloth covered all of the empty walls, floor to ceiling. Why, she had never seen so much at one time, in one place, and in so many colors. It must have taken the women of an entire village many seasons to pound that much *tapa* cloth. A cloying odor, like a bunch of flowers filling the too-small room, clung to it all.

Against her will, she sneezed.

Giving her another little shove, Zeph shot her one of his looks of disapproval.

"I could not help it," Malana protested in a venomous whisper, feeling yet another sneeze overcome her.

A woman, a spear-swallower, emerged from a cloth-covered doorway in the rear, hurrying forward to intercept them.

"Welcome, *señors,*" she greeted, somewhat leery as she sized up her prospective customers. "How may I help you this fine morning?"

Zeph swept off Malana's hat, her long hair tumbling down her back in a black mass. She glared back at him silently.

"Indeed, I can see how you need my help, *señor,*" the shopkeeper gasped, not bothering to hid her dismay. She came forward, walked slowly around Malana, studying her from all angles. "And quite a bit of it, I would say," she added, clucking her tongue.

"How quickly can you provide me with two dresses?" Zeph asked. "Nothing fancy or too expensive, but something of quality and station." He shot Malana a look that dared her to contradict him.

"You are Yankee, *señor?*"

Zeph nodded.

"It will take me at least two weeks, and each dress will cost twenty pesos."

"Two weeks?" he protested. "Unacceptable. I need them tomorrow," he commanded, no doubt expecting the same instant obedience from this woman as he did from everyone else.

"Impossible," the shopkeeper insisted, standing her ground as no one else dared.

Except for Malana, herself, or so she would like to think she did.

"One week, and not another day less," the woman continued. "And it will cost you double, *señor.*"

"If that is the best you can do, then good day, madam." Zeph took Malana by the arm and marched her out the door.

"Why must you always be so stubborn, Zeph Westley?" Malana demanded, pulling away from his unbearable grip.

Spinning in the middle of the street to face him, she planted her fists on her hips.

At that, he merely cocked one brow with calculated annoyance, reclaimed her arm, and continued to lead her away, ignoring her protests. "You will learn, girl. Sometimes it's best to keep your mouth shut."

"And someday you will learn you cannot always have your way."

They had taken only a few more steps when a hissing sound caused them both to pause and look.

"F—fst. F—fst. *Monsieur Capitaine.*" Petit and nervous as a frazzled bird, the strange female, not much older than herself, Malana decided, beckoned to them.

Up went Zeph's inevitable brow. For a moment, Malana thought he would simply ignore the page and continue to direct her down the street.

"If you are speaking to me, miss, then step forward," Zeph finally said in his booming captain's voice.

Looking one way and then the other, the woman stepped from the protection of the crates and boxes beside the dressmaker's shop, sidling close to Zeph.

"You are in need of a seamstress, *monsieur. Oui?*" she whispered.

Malana could have told her he was immune to such an approach.

"And what if I am?" Just as she knew he would, Zeph stepped back.

"I am in need of passage."

"To where?" he asked skeptically.

"Where are you going?" There was such desperation in the woman's eyes.

"I don't accept passengers. Come along, girl," he said, taking Malana once more by the arm.

"Please, *monsieur,* I can sew ze dresses you need and many more, if you will simply take me away from here."

"Are you in some kind of trouble, woman?"

How irksome that he would call another not much older
a woman while insisting that she, Malana, was still a girl.

"Oh, no, *monsieur,* no trouble."

"Then some hoaxer looking to part a fool and his
money?"

"No, I swear zat isn't so, *Monsieur Capitaine.* My name
is Honoré de Magney. I am merely a poor working girl
seeking passage out of Rio. From ze back room of *Señora*
Mendez's dress shop, I heard you place your order. I am
her seamstress and would have stitched ze costumes had
you not left so hastily." At that she giggled, the sound
lilting and intriguing.

Then and there, Malana decided she liked Honoré.
What a strange name; how funny she spoke. But more
importantly, she detected a free spirit kindred to her own.
Someone with whom to share. Someone who could understand her.

"Please, Zephiran," Malana pleaded softly.

Even as she said it, silently hoping for his heart to soften
a little toward her, she expected nothing.

"My ship is the *Dolphin.* We sail with the tide, Miss de
Magney."

It took Malana a moment to realize he'd actually agreed
to take Honoré aboard.

Judging from the woman's dejected look, it took her
even longer. Then her face lit up. "What are you saying,
*monsieur?* Zat you will take me along?"

"I'm saying I'll not wait for you or anyone else."

"Oh, Zephiran, thank you." Uncaring who saw or what
they thought, Malana threw her arms around Zeph's neck,
squeezing in gratitude.

The fact that he gruffly extracted himself from her clinging arms, taking charge once more and leading her away,
fooled her only for a moment. Why, she'd detected a smile,
even if only a fleeting one. Whether or not he admitted
it, it pleased him to make her happy. Uncertain just what

to make of her discovery that asking sweetly got her so much more, nor how best to use this new knowledge to her advantage, Malana chose to say nothing—for the moment, anyway. She simply tucked the powerful bit of information away to consider later.

"*Monsieur Capitaine,* I will be zere in an hour."

Honoré's declaration trailed their hasty departure, leaving in its wake a whole new realm of possibilities and promises.

Zeph stood on the deck of his beloved *Dolphin,* rocking on his heels, his hand planted firmly behind his back, regret his only companion. What had gotten into him? What demon had possessed him to take yet another female aboard his ship?

Maybe, if he were lucky, the Frenchwoman would have the good sense not to show up.

Even as he thought it, hoped for it, began to plan what he would tell Malana when she realized she had not gotten her way, he saw the seamstress coming down the wharfside street. Behind her came a small, overladen cart pulled by an even smaller donkey, whose plaintive brays filled the air. Now and again the poor boy in charge of the vehicle had to halt and readjust the ridiculous load to keep it from tumbling into the street.

It was better off there, Zeph thought vehemently. He had neither patience nor room on his ship to store such feminine nonsense.

As luck would have it, the woman and the cart arrived unscathed, if a bit shaky, at the end of the pier where the *Dolphin* lay at anchor.

"*Monsieur Capitaine,*" the Frenchwoman called out in a lyrical lilt, which distinctly brought back childhood memories of his grandmother's singsongy voice. "I am here just as I told you I would be." Lifting her skirts, she stood poised like some kind of shorebird waiting to take flight.

God knew, he wished she would take wing—fly right off the face of the earth and out of his hair. When that didn't happen, he had no choice but to order the plank lowered, the woman and all her paraphernalia escorted aboard.

His purposeful, imposing silence went unnoticed as Honoré, seemingly without ever taking a breath, warbled and fussed over each piece of luggage as if it contained the lost Hope diamond. Then, as if on cue, Malana emerged from the companionway. Such joy radiated from her face that Zeph experienced a moment of pure guilt for having wished away the single source of her happiness.

Forced to accept that he was not that source and never could be, Zeph frowned, caught himself, then justified his reaction as one of a man in a self-made dilemma. He didn't want the responsibility of Malana or her feelings.

Only a fool willing took on such accountability.

"Cap'n, where do you want me to put her?" Mr. Kennedy's question deserved an immediate answer. In the last hour however, he had yet to come up with one.

"With me, Zephiran, please." Malana's dark, steady gaze touched his face like the rays of a warm tropical sun, penetrating clear to his heart.

He couldn't have come up with a better solution himself. So why did he wish to resist it? Why deny her what she so obviously wanted?

"Put her in the hold for all I could care," he declared, disavowing himself of any softening, making his return stare as icy as he could. "Just make sure, girl, that both of you keep out of the way of the running of this ship."

*"Merci, Capitaine,"* the Frenchwoman murmured in appreciation. "I promise, you will never even know we are aboard."

"That, miss, I doubt very seriously."

They could make ne'er a peep, yet he would never forget

the presence of the island enchantress who quickly made a mockery of everything he prided himself on being.

What she liked most about Honoré, Malana decided as she watched the woman bustle about the small cabin, was that she could carry on a conversation all by herself. She asked questions, answered them, then moved on to the next subject all in a single breath.

"You are not American, are you, *cherie*? No, of course not," she answered the question herself, clucking her tongue. "Not with zose exotic eyes. And your hair." Moving around Malana like an ocean undertow, she inspected several dark strands, discarding them just like her subject. "Oh, but zose clothes. *Mon dieu.* Zey are awful. Wherever did you come up with zem?"

"A friend gave them to me," Malana managed to interject. Fascinated, she watched the birdlike woman flit around the room with endless energy, inspecting everything as she moved along.

"Zen you are in need of a new friend, *cherie*. A better friend, someone to teach you everyzing a woman should know. Would you like zat? Would you like Honoré to make you somezing beautiful to wear?"

Before Malana could respond, Honoré fluttered off again, this time her attention settling on the pile of boxes and bags heaped on the floor in the middle of the small cabin.

"Somezing beautiful," the woman repeated, her words muffled as her curl-laden head was buried deep in the bags as she dug through them. Then she paused and looked up at Malana, a mischievous glint in her sea-gray eyes. "I overheard you tell ze *capitaine* you wanted something colorful, no?"

"Colorful, yes," Malana blurted out, uncertain whether,

in her strange way of speaking, the Frenchwoman meant
to agree or disagree.

At that Honoré laughed, a twittering, avian sound. "Zen
colorful zey shall be, *cherie*. Like you." Her thin brows knit.
"Not like ze *capitaine*. He is such a drab man. Oh, well,
we cannot all be perfect, can we, *cherie*?"

With that she whipped out a bundle of the most beautiful
material Malana had ever seen, allowing it to roll out across
the floor like a splash of rainbow. Unable to stop herself,
Malana dropped down beside it, reaching out. The fabric
was so soft and lightweight. It rippled as easily as waves
upon a shore, nothing like the coarser *tapa* fabric made
on Hitihiti. Bending, she put her face against it, rubbing
gently.

Twin tears that seemingly sprang out of nowhere welled
from the curtain of her eyelids. How foolish that a bit of
cloth could evoke such emotion. It was only that it
reminded her of the never-ending tap, tap, tap of the
women's *tapa* mallets, of her sheltered island life . . . of
her mother. More than anything, she supposed, she missed
her mother.

"Oh, *cherie*, what is it?" Without hesitation, Honoré
moved close, putting her arms around Malana's shoulder.
"Is it somezing I said? I did not mean zat remark about
your *capitaine*. He is handsome and will find you irresistible
in ze lovely new dresses I will make you."

"No, he will not," she cried from the depths of her
heart.

"He will," Honoré insisted. "Why, he zinks you are
beautiful dressed even as you are now."

"No." Malana shook her head. "He only wishes I would
go away, that he had never laid eyes on me."

"No, zat is not true."

Honoré's lighthearted laughter caught her so completely by surprise, Malana looked up, curiosity erasing all
evidence of her tears.

"My silly little poppet, surely you can see how badly he wants you."

Malana shook her head in wide-eyed disbelief.

"Tsk. Tsk. He wants you so badly, *cherie*, why, I would bet he even dreams about you."

"No, Honoré. I am sure that you are wrong," Malana protested, wanting so much to believe, but unable to conceive, that such was possible. There had been that one brief moment during the storm when he had rescued her. He had held her in his arms as if he cared. His kiss had taken her breath away, made her glad that death had brushed so closely, for it had given her hope.

But only briefly. Afterwards, he had acted no differently toward her than before. It was as if that glorious moment had never occurred. Yet it had, and she clung to it.

Just as she clung to the hope Honoré offered her even as she denied it.

"Believe me, *cherie,* your *Capitaine* Zeph Westley is a flesh and blood man like any other, even if he tries to deny it. Once I, Honoré de Magney, lady-in-waiting to ze famous Pauline Leclerc, sister to ze Emperor Napoleon . . . once I make you a proper lady and teach you all zat I know about men, your dour *Capitaine* Westley will be reduced to putty in your hands."

Putty in her hands? A most intriguing image. Was it possible?

What harm would it do to listen to what Honoré had to teach her, even if it was the *haole* way?

# Chapter Eight

Like the true, free-spirited lady Zeph knew her to be, the *Dolphin* sailed before the wind without a hitch. Every snap of the billowing sails, creak of wood, whine of winches, spoke of the desire to reach their destination.

Nonetheless, being a man of caution, Zeph plotted their course with care. They crossed the equator, then the tropic of Cancer, avoiding first the Windward Islands, then the Bahamas, both British territories. Peace between the United States and England remained uneasy at best, the fear that yet another conflict would flare between the two countries a real possibility. There were still rumors of entire crews of American whalers suffering impressment at sea, their precious cargoes disappearing as well, their ships left to drift like abandoned ghosts, especially among the many English strongholds that dotted the Caribbean Sea.

So, choosing to take no chances, he steered the *Dolphin* wide of the troubled areas. Out of sight . . . out of mind.

At least, when it came to the industrious British.

Such was not the case with his two female passengers.

True to their word, Zeph saw hide nor hair of them. At first, he assured himself he wanted nothing better than for them to leave him and his crew alone. Then, slowly, it dawned on him that he missed Malana and quite frankly didn't trust the little French seamstress he had so recklessly hired.

What those two, no doubt as industrious as any English sea dog, were up to behind the closed doors of his cabin was anyone's guess.

Danny proved to be his only source of information.

"Sewing up a storm, sir," the cabin boy reported, looking a little too smug for Zeph's comfort.

"A storm, indeed," he muttered. More like brewing trouble, he suspected.

So when the invitation came, asking that he join the "ladies" for a cup of tea, he thought for sure the calm just before the brewing storm had finally struck.

"Tea?" As far as he knew, there was not a single leaf aboard, never had been. Tea was something a man left behind when he went to sea—and gratefully so. Afternoon socials were a landlubber pastime, a feminine one at that, a haven for matrons, spinsters, and debutantes. They had been all the rage when he had departed New England, Leatrice's obsession, while he had avoided them at all cost. And now?

As for now, he supposed he owed it to Malana, as well as to James Kilpatrick, to play along. No doubt, the girl would have plenty of real such functions to attend once she arrived at her father's home in New Bedford. Best the girl made a good first impression. It was bad enough they were showing up unannounced, no sense creating undue scandal for his old and dear friend, at least no more than could be avoided.

Then there was Leatrice waiting for him in Mystic. As always, she would be the first to ever so gently remind him of his own social duty to her, to his family name, pointing out his inadequacies from his many months at sea.

Social graces. At the mere thought, Zeph sighed, then began to plan his next voyage and a quick escape from the unpleasantries of life ashore. Still, for now, pleasant or not, they must be attended to.

God knows, he would much rather confront the largest, most dangerous whale in all of the Pacific, come face to face with death itself, than attend a single, solitary afternoon social.


"Hurry, *cherie,* we have very little time left."

"I am doing my best, Honoré." Sitting in a lace chemise, Malana minded her needle just as Honoré had taught her, making the stitches small and even, keeping the row of tiny buttons down the back of her new dress in a straight line. The Frenchwoman made haste to complete the hemming of the skirt, adding a pretty ribbon and cluster of flowers around the edge in a scallop.

Malana had only halfway completed her assigned task when she again pricked her finger.

"Oh," she cried in frustration, sticking the wounded appendage into her mouth. "I shall never be good at this sewing."

"Let's hope you never have to be, *cherie,*" the seamstress said, giving her a gentle, yet encouraging pat on the hand. Taking the gown, she tackled the task with experience in no time at all.

Malana watched, taking solace in the regular rhythm of the needle moving in and out of the soft blue material. Over the long days cooped up in the cabin together, the two women had unburdened their souls to each other.

Honoré had spun an elaborate tale of life at the French court of the great Napoleon. Her colorful story had left Malana feeling more uncertain than ever before. The seamstress had been the personal maid to the emperor's sister, Pauline. Such goings-on—intrigue, deception, liaisons, even an occasional murder—why, the *haole* were no different than her own people, but they were dishonest about what they did. Was Zeph like that, too? Her father? No, she did not want to believe that to be true.

Still, according to the Frenchwoman, Malana's circumstances were precarious at best. The Frenchwoman's eyes had grown round as saucers as Malana had gone on to explain how Zeph had taken her aboard his ship with the intention of delivering her to her father. A father who had never acknowledged her and might not want her, who might banish her to a life of seclusion, or worse, simply refuse to accept her. What did she hope would become of her should her father deny her his protection? Honoré had demanded to know.

"Then Zephiran will protect me," Malana had answered in all certainty.

"Bah," Honoré had replied. "Have you not listened to anything I have said? He is a man like any other, your *Capitaine* Westley. If it becomes too complicated and he is left to his own devices, he will choose to abandon you, too. Zen what will you do, *cherie?*"

Malana refused to give credence to Honoré's words of spite, even as the woman buttoned her up into the beautiful, colorful gown, a labor of the true affection that had blossomed between them. Zeph was not like other men. He could not be controlled by feminine wiles.

"Do you still believe your *capitaine* is different?"

Stoically, Malana nodded, unable to believe that she was the woman in the looking glass Honoré held up for her.

"We shall see, *cherie.* I will simply have to show you how wrong you are."

\* \* \*

Heeding duty, Zeph knocked on the closed door of the cabin at exactly the appointed time. At first, he received no answer. The sound of shuffling feet that filtered through the door, however, produced a self-satisfied smile.

"Come in, *Capitaine.*"

The Frenchwoman's suspiciously lilting invitation sobered him quickly enough. In fact, it wiped the foolish grin right off his face. Prepared for the worst, he hesitated only a moment before doing as instructed.

What he discovered was far worse than anything he could have imagined. Dumbfounded, he inspected the small cabin that had once been so much . . . him. Without his permission, it had been completely transformed. Female frippery hung everywhere—yards of material, cards of buttons, piles of bows and lace covering the bed, making his rightful domain look like a dockside sporting house.

As for Malana . . .

Zeph's heart stilled at the very sight of her. Could that truly be Malana?

Gone was the pretty little island creature he remembered. Completely obliterated, except for her dark, unfathomable island eyes. In her place sat a . . .

Why, he didn't know what to call her. Surely not a woman. The last thing he must ever willingly label her was a woman. As a woman, he could never hope to resist her. Only by keeping her a child was she safe from him and he from her.

Still, woman, a vision in blue, best described her appearance. The daringly low cut of the gown, the tiny cap sleeves that left her arms totally bare . . . although he knew it to be stylish, on Malana it looked downright indecent.

Until then he had only seen her wearing her long hair down, unadorned, caping her shoulders like black velvet. It swept upward now, piled like a conch shell and held in place with fancy mother-of-pearl combs. In such abundance, it gave the impression of a heavy burden she carried on top of her head, while at the same time exposing and accentuating the elongated curve of her neck.

A woman's neck in every way.

When he realized he had stared overly long at the slender column, contemplating its exotic softness, aching to touch it, Zeph shook his head to dislodge the unseemly images, the drumlike pounding that seemed inevitably to fill his skull to the point of explosion whenever he forgot his place and hers.

*"Monsieur Capitaine,* please, won't you join us?'' chirped the little Frenchwoman.

As annoying as he found the seamstress's grating voice, Zeph nonetheless considered it a blessing. Because of it, he dragged his gaze from Malana's tempting display to stare at Miss de Magney, thinking it best simply to refuse the invitation. But how could he forget the undisguised pleading in Malana's dark eyes—so trusting, so innocent . . . so needy? How could he be so cruel as to dash her girlish hopes?

''I suppose I could for a moment,'' he conceded, certain it was the wrong thing to do, but just as certain it was the only thing he *could* do.

His sea chest had been turned into a low table of sorts, covered with a lace cloth. Three chairs, two of which he had no idea from where they had come, comprised the rather intimate setting. It didn't go unnoticed that the chair left open for him was opposite Malana's. From there she would fill his vision—a vision truly worth contemplating, God help him, no doubt a detriment to his soul.

Although Malana smiled ever so slightly, her gaze settling on him as he sat, she uttered not a word as she set about the intricate task of pouring tea. With surprising expertise that he suspected the little Frenchwoman had worked hours to perfect, the transformed island girl lifted the delicate china pot, positioning it at just the exact height over the three cups in turn, filling each halfway. The only indication that she experienced even the least bit of nervousness was when her hand clasped about the handle shook, not so much that she spilled the tea, but enough that he noticed. Completing the ritual, she deposited the teapot and picked up one set of cups and saucers.

"Captain Westley," she said, her voice soft and pliant as she presented the delicate china to him. Her dark gaze searched his for approval.

He took her offering, of course. What else could he do but accept it, nodding, somewhat stiffly, his acknowledgment of a job well done? Zeph brought the cup to his lips, determined merely to pretend to take a drink, to go through the motions, then excuse himself as quickly as he could.

The distinct smell of brandy brought an end to his plan to escape and the cup to a halt just beneath his nose.

Lifting one brow, he sniffed, then took a sip, thinking surely he'd been mistaken. But it was brandy all right, fine French cognac, the finest he'd ever tasted. Nonetheless, he choked, surprised because the liquor was much too smooth to cause that reaction.

"Where did you get this?"

"Do you like it, *Capitaine?*" Miss de Magney asked ever so demurely.

"It is not a question of whether or not I like it, madam," he stated, staring pointedly at the Frenchwoman. "I asked how it came to be aboard my ship without my knowledge."

"Did you, *monsieur?*" she countered with the coyness of a French courtesan, lifting her own cup and taking a delicate sip.

"Yes, madam, I did." Zeph deposited his cup and saucer with the decisive force of a gavel, then rose. From the corner of his eye he saw Malana jump at his sudden movement, while the seamstress never blinked. "Teaching this . . . this child the vice of drinking spirits is not what I hired you to do, Miss de Magney."

"No, of course you did not. Rest assured, *Capitaine* West-ley, it will not happen again."

To Zeph's utter surprise, the Frenchwoman took a lace handkerchief from the sleeve of her dress, suddenly sniffed, and began dabbing at her eyes.

"I was only trying to help, *monsieur,* to teach ze girl ze manners she will need in her new life. We had no tea." She sniffed again, then sighed, looking at him so forlornly. "I used what I had—my most precious possession, a bottle of cognac General Bonaparte himself gave me for loyal service."

Taken aback by the woman's unexpected concession, her most disturbing show of tears, and the fact that she knew the abdicated French emperor, Zeph sat, the righteous wind knocked out of his sail. Every sailor knew that when that happened, the ship—or in this case, his ire— was left sitting dead in the water.

"Yes, of course, Miss Magney, I didn't mean to accuse you unjustly," he muttered.

"It's all right, *monsieur.*" She sniffed again and smiled up at him ever so bravely. "I forgive you."

It wasn't until he made his excuses and hastily departed that Zeph realized he had been the one to apologize and that Malana had said nothing, merely watching the entire exchange between himself and the Frenchwoman with wide-eyed amazement.

Why, if he wasn't the master of this ship and all that took place on it, he would suspect that he had just been smoothly, expertly manipulated. What he couldn't under-stand were the Frenchwoman's motives.

In the aftermath in what Malana found an extraordinary turn of events, she watched Honoré drink her cup of brandy down to the last drop, then set the cup back in the saucer.

"See, I told you, *cherie,*" the woman said cheerfully, all traces of tears completely gone. "All men are ze same. Zey are brutes who must be led to believe zat zey have won, zen made to feel guilty about it. Only zen will zey do what you want zem to do."

"Is that not unfair?" Malana asked.

"Unfair?" At that the Frenchwoman merely shrugged. "No more so zan a man who takes advantage of a woman much weaker zan he, then casually tosses her aside for another. Is zat not even more unfair?"

Malana thought about that a moment. She had been at the mercy of men all of her life, she supposed. First, there had been her father's desertion of her mother, leaving her at the mercy of Mao, who had decided her only value lay in sacrifice. And now, Zeph Westley thought to control her life without once asking her what she wanted. And should her father truly not want her . . .

Was it not in her own best interest to learn how to get men to do what she wanted them to do?

"Oh, Honoré, how did you get so smart about men?"

"Experience, *cherie.* Lots and lots of experience," the Frenchwoman responded, picking up Zeph's discarded teacup and downing the contents in one swallow.

Picking up her own drink, Malana followed suit, taking a swallow. She had every right to decide for herself what she wanted. Every right . . .

The fiery liquid burned like hot lava as it made its way down her throat. Tears sprang to her eyes. She sputtered and coughed.

"Easy, *cherie,*" Honoré said, taking the cup from her hand and gently patting her on the back. "You need not learn it all in one day."

The scorched feeling in her throat slowly dissipated; the equally raw spot in her heart did not. Malana decided then and there she would give up everything, go to any extent to gain the necessary knowledge to be a great lady in the *haole* world. That way, Zeph Westley would have no choice but to deal with her as such. No matter what else happened, she could not allow him to abandon her.

There was no question that over the next few weeks Malana learned how to wield a fan, to tilt a parasol provocatively, to walk with the stately grace of a young debutante and make the proper gestures, to smile at just the right moment, to flatter even the most seasoned sailor into a babbling fool willing to do her every bidding. How the Frenchwoman managed to teach her all that and even more so quickly and so well, Zeph could only consider amazing. Perhaps the talent lay within Malana herself. Was not the map she had drawn from memory proof of extraordinary ability to learn? Whatever it was, it was a miracle James Kilpatrick would simply have to appreciate.

And hopefully wouldn't see through.

Zeph saw through it. One could dress Malana up in the finest clothing, tame her hair, subdue her manners, even improve her language skills, but nothing would ever take the exciting look out of her dark, exotic eyes. In their depths the island drums still pounded, the hot tropical sun still shone brightly. The lush beauty, the pristine beaches that would forever be Hitihiti, were reflected in those liquid pools of paganism.

Perhaps that was what intrigued him the most about Malana. She presented him with a challenge much like that of the sea, which had given life to her island culture. Unpredictable, yet foreseeably, excitingly so. No man could hope to know her fully or to tame her any more than the vast oceans. And like all sailors addicted to the contest, man against nature, determined to be the one to tame the veritable mistress, Zeph kept taking voyage after voyage.

As for Malana?

God knows, he had all the conflict and challenge he wanted in his life. He didn't need it from a woman. No doubt, that was the reason he'd remained faithful to Leatrice year after year, coming home, if only briefly, to the safe haven she offered in the form of the predictable life that she led. Lovely, composed, conservative, the daughter of a sea captain, Leatrice never changed. She never questioned him or his decisions. Never tried to make him give up the sea or his determination to be successful before they wed. Without a doubt, she would make him a damn fine wife. So why not marry her?

With the conclusion of this voyage, Zeph intended to do just that, take the plunge. Watching Malana make her way toward him, he decided he better do it with all haste.

"Good morning, Zephiran." The pretty pink and yellow parasol Miss de Magney had made to match her dress spun teasingly in Malana's petite gloved hand. The perpetual breeze stirred the ends of her lace shawl as well as the tiny hairs that escaped her careful coiffure. She looked up at him expectantly.

God in heaven, just the way she said his name set his pulse to racing uncontrollably.

Yes, he would definitely marry Leatrice just as soon as he reached Mystic. Thank goodness, that would be only a few days from now. At any time the lookout would spy Nomans Land, the outermost island of Rhode Island Sound. From there they were less than a day's journey to New Bedford.

New Bedford, James Kilpatrick, and blessed salvation. Not a moment too soon.

"You should be below, girl," he directed gruffly.

The smallest frown of uncertainty marred her pretty face, but only temporarily. Quickly enough, she recovered, as any sophisticated young woman would.

"I think not, Captain," she replied impertinently. "I do

not intend to miss anything." Turning away, she twirled the parasol like an annoyed cat switched its tail.

Nonetheless, he had no intention of letting her have her way, much less demand more from him than he wished to give.

It struck him then that if Leatrice had witnessed their exchange, she would assure him that he made much ado about nothing. Let the poor girl stay topside, she would say in that gentle, irreproachable way she used to handle everything and everyone. What possible harm could it do?

What harm indeed? he wondered, even as he formulated a scathing reply. Laying claim to Malana's shawl-covered arm, he spun her around to face him. The parasol clattered to the deck, a frilly splash of yellow and pink against the sea-weathered wood. Such a contrast, just as she contrasted with him and everything he sought to be.

She stiffened, glancing down at her lost possession ever so briefly before lifting those dark pools to meet his steely gaze. Expecting defiance, what he got instead was a look of incredible pain.

He hadn't meant to hurt her. Truly, he had thought only to subdue her, to make her do what he thought best for her.

"I am sorry, Malana," Zeph apologized, bending to retrieve her parasol. Dusting it off, he stuck it into her gloved hand. Then, to be on the safe side, he held her at arm's length, even though she offered no resistance. "Please, just go below, and I promise to call you up the moment land is sighted."

"Thank you. You are very kind, Zephiran. Very kind," she murmured.

Kind? Kindness did not for a moment fit into his plans.


"Land ho!"

The much anticipated cry from the crow's nest came

even as Malana draped her pretty lace-edged pelerine across the back of the chair on which Honoré sat, putting the final touches on yet another beautiful gown. Completely forgetting what she had just said to the Frenchwoman boasting of her accomplishment—she had successfully made Zeph heel to her desire—Malana rushed back toward the door.

At last they had arrived. A mixture of joy and uncertainty gripped her. In turn, she grasped the handle, ready to fly to the deck above to get her first glimpse of this place called New England.

*"Non, non, cherie,"* Honoré chided gently, hurrying across the room to stop Malana's much too eager departure. She placed the flat of her hand against the door, keeping it from opening. *"Capitaine* Westley said he would send someone. We must wait."

But she had waited so long already. Nonetheless, the Frenchwoman was right. Zeph must be made to keep his word.

Oh, why must it take so long?

Finally, much later, much too late as far as Malana was concerned, Daniel arrived at the door with the announcement. A warning look from Honoré kept Malana in her chair and from racing out the door with the cabin boy as he made his departure.

When at last the seamstress deemed it appropriate for them to appear topside, Malana immediately made her way to the railing, determined to miss nothing of her new home.

Her first view of the land of her father, this land of hope and supposed plenty, was a disappointing, desolate one. The coastline offered little in the way of welcome, no trees to speak of, only gray waters lapping equally bleak rocks, dirty sand, and low brush.

As if Honoré knew what she was thinking, as if she

thought it herself, the little Frenchwoman clutched Malana's hand in her own.

"It will get better, *cherie,*" Honoré whispered.

"And if it does not?"

"Zen we will simply make the best of it."

"Oh, Honoré, what would I do without you?" Malana squeezed the other woman's fingers.

*"Non, non.* What would I have done if you had not come along when you did? *Mon dieu,* my previous employer had threatened to fire me because I did not work quickly enough to suit her, yet the faster I stitched, ze more she expected of me. It was only a matter of time before she tossed me into ze streets of Rio de Janeiro, a hapless victim as surely as you."

"I promise you, Honoré, no matter what happens, we will stay together. Should my fortune be good, then so will yours."

"Oh, *cherie,*" Honoré replied, clucking her tongue. "Ze tide of fortune is not somezing we can predict or depend upon." She looked back out at the bleak horizon that hazed over the splendor of the setting sun. "We shall see. We shall simply have to wait and see what fate has in store for both of us."

From his position at the helm, Zeph watched the two, Malana and the de Magney woman, standing at the rail on the deck below. He couldn't begin to make heads nor tails out of his aggravation. Nonetheless, he couldn't banish his irrational feelings.

Those two women ran together like mackerel, he decided. It was no more than he should have expected. They spent day and night together. They were bound to have become friends. Still, he would have liked to have been the one to share this moment with Malana.

Filled with his own sense of anticipation, he gazed out

over the roiling waters of Rhode Island Sound, the cliffs of Gay Head off to windward now, Cuttyhunk Island dead ahead on the horizon. What did Malana think of it all? he wondered, again watching her as she stared straight ahead, unblinking, her hand clasped tightly in the Frenchwoman's. The coastline of the outer New England islands offered nothing as spectacular as that of Hitihiti. Unfriendly best described its initial appearance, and yet he knew it to be otherwise.

Once they reached the mainland, New Bedford had an undeniable bustling charm all its own. But even if Malana did not like it, he had no intention of prolonging her agony. As soon as they docked, he planned to take her straight away to her father's house.

There would be no question of his welcome, even in James's absence. The servants knew him well. Often he stay there when he had business in New Bedford.

As for James Kilpatrick, should his mentor indeed not be at home, which was possible, Zeph knew it would only be a matter of a few days before he returned. Three years ago, just before the *Dolphin* had set sail on her current voyage, the aging sea captain had given up the rigors of whale hunting, investing his resources instead in developing lucrative local trading. When last Zeph had heard, Kilpatrick Shipping had a half-dozen vessels that carried on a profitable trade between the rice and tobacco communities in the southern states and the dry goods merchants up and down the coast of New England.

It was an honorable retirement for a seaman who wanted the best of both worlds, Zeph supposed, even if it was not what he envisioned for himself.

And what did he envision when he thought of his own future?

Like all men, Zeph believed himself immune to the rigors of time. As long as there was a sea, he would sail it. As long as there were whale, he would hunt them.

And as long as there was Leatrice, he would return to her for short, intermittent rests, then begin it all again.

It was then, while deeply engrossed in his own thoughts, that he sensed the eyes upon him, hot and probing, seeking to invade his very soul. Zeph turned to discover Malana, still standing beside the Frenchwoman, looking at him with such longing that it made him momentarily doubt himself and the unwavering path he laid out.

In that ever so brief but intense interplay between them, he caught a glimpse of what he could have. Paradise. Every sailor's dream of an idyllic life filled with a passion so overwhelming it would no doubt dominate his life. He had only to reach out, claim it for himself. In exchange, he had only to be willing to forsake who and what he was.

It was a sacrifice he would never make, not willingly. Somehow, he must garner the strength to resist it—just a little longer. Then the temptation would be gone, no longer dangling before him like a baited hook.

He found instead the rationale to bring him to his senses. And he used it liberally like a bucket of cold seawater. The young daughter of James Kilpatrick was not to be lusted after even if it was what she unknowingly sought.

Lowering protective shades over his emotions, Zeph forced his attention to the task at hand. He had a ship to get into port. With Cuttyhunk Island behind them now, he could see the hazy outline of the mainland. Calling for a little more sail to carry them through this last stretch of open water, he adjusted his course, both as a captain and a man, accordingly.

# Chapter Nine

The clip-clop, clip-clop of the horses' feet on the stone-covered thoroughfare sounded unnatural to Malana's ears. But then so many things seemed strange to her—so many unfamiliar sights, noises, and smells—as they traveled through the crowded streets of New Bedford. Even though Honoré had prepared her, learning about them was not the same as dealing with them firsthand. With overwhelming uncertainty, she approached her father's house. Add that to the trepidation she felt sitting beside Zephiran, who stared moodily out the small window, his unapproachable silence more foreboding and unnerving than all the commotion beyond the carriage window, she wished now that the moment she must face her father would never arrive.

Honoré occupied the opposite seat, facing them, her delicate features, usually so animated, relaxed beneath her stylish hat. Her gloved hands gave her away, though, twisting and picking at the threads of her royal blue dress. The Frenchwoman felt as uneasy as she did, Malana realized.

Knowing she wasn't alone in her apprehension didn't make Malana feel any less anxious, however.

"You *do* know what to say to your father when we get there, don't you, girl?"

Zeph's forthright question boomed in the silence of the carriage so unexpectedly, Malana jumped in her seat, brushing the arm of his jacket. Pulling away, she looked up at him, frowning, the large feather in her jaunty hat bobbing in her eyes in a most annoying way. She felt anything but certain beneath the brooding skepticism in his blue glare.

Something welled in her, rebelled against his lack of confidence, she supposed, even if she felt none herself. Perhaps it was simply her nerves stretched beyond endurance that snapped. Whatever the cause, the need to defend herself burst through the dam of her anxiety. By what right did he question the way she chose to greet her own father?

"I will not act like a savage, if that is what concerns you."

Up went that judgmental brow of his, but his gaze never flickered. But then, it never did. "See that you don't," he retorted. Enough said, he returned to contemplate calmly what she deemed the unfriendly world outside the window.

But it was no more hostile than the atmosphere inside the coach. An unjustified hostility.

"Do not worry, Captain Westley. You'll be rid of me soon enough," she cried. "And then you can happily go back to your ship and . . . and to your slaughter of creatures who never did you any harm."

It was the most hurtful thing she could think to say on the spur of the moment, intended to evoke his anger, she supposed, or at least a little guilt. Something. Any response but that unreadable disinterest capped by a lifted brow.

"Aye, and that I will, girl." His gaze slid to unmercifully pin her once again. "Just as soon as I'm rid of you."

They were her own words, deflected. So why did they hurt her so much while he seemed completely unaffected by them? Against her will, Malana's throat contracted, working over the painful knot of emotion that welled there. Turning away, she pretended to stare out her own window, but her eyes misted over and she saw nothing.

"Then I am glad that we agree, Captain Westley," she murmured.

Uncomfortable silence prevailed once more inside the carriage. It seemed to go on forever, just like the ride. Finally, thankfully, Honoré spoke, asking the question uppermost in Malana's own mind.

"Have we much farther to go, *Capitaine* Westley?"

"Not much farther at all, Miss de Magney," Zeph reassured with a sweeping glance that included both of the women.

Moments later, much to a mixture of relief and trepidation on Malana's part, the carriage halted in front a large, prestigious house. She craned her neck to see as much of the structure as she could through the small window on the opposite side from where she sat, determined not to touch Zeph. It was so hard to believe that soon such a mansion would be her home. Or would it be? Would her father accept her or turn her away?

"Are you ready, girl?"

Zeph stood on the outside, his hand lifted to receive hers, his voice softened by the emotion shining in his eyes that she by choice labeled pity. If he noticed her hesitation, he gave no indication. He merely waited patiently, hand presented to help her descend.

Pressing her fingers as lightly as possible into his, Malana navigated the two steps from the carriage. It was not until her foot caught between two of the uneven stones in the street that she realized how much she depended on Zeph's strength. How very much she would miss it. When she stumbled, he kept her from falling, his other hand reaching out to clasp her arm.

"How clumsy of me," she murmured, quickly disengaging herself from his grasp. Malana glanced up from the corner of her eye to find him watching her with an intense, naked look of longing.

"Zeph," she whispered over that unrelenting knot in her throat that simply refused to go away.

"Come, girl. It's best we get this over with."

Yes, of course it was best—for him at least. Perhaps that was why she dreaded it so much.

Zeph recognized Mrs. Bassett, James's housekeeper, when she opened the door to his summons.

"Why, Captain Westley," the matronly woman welcomed wholeheartedly, stepping aside to allow him entrance into the darkly paneled foyer. "Do come in. Have you come from Mystic?" she asked matter-of-factly, her gaze straying to the two women who stood behind him.

"Actually, I haven't been home yet. I've come to discuss a pressing matter with James." Reaching behind, Zeph gripped Malana's arm, pulling her forward. "Is he here?"

"Oh, my. Oh, dear," the housekeeper mumbled, glancing left and right, then pausing at the foot of the main staircase.

"What is it, Mrs. Bassett?" Zeph demanded.

"Why don't we get you and your"—she looked the two women over with a noncritical, but curious, eye—"lady companions settled first. Then we can talk."

Zeph glanced down at Malana, whose arm he unknowingly held so possessively. Self-consciously, he dropped his hand and stepped back.

"Yes, of course, Mrs. Bassett. You are most thoughtful and quite right. Please see Miss Kilpatrick settled. Her maid, Miss de Magney, will be comfortable in the servants' quarters. No need to show me to my room. I know where it is. So I'll wait here until you return."

"Miss Kilpatrick? Oh, my. Oh, dear," the housekeeper

repeated under her breath, her eyes wide with disbelief at Zeph's unexpected revelation. "Whatever you say, Captain Westley."

Knowing the faithful servant would return quickly, Zeph showed himself into the elegant drawing room to the left to wait for her.

Whatever she had to tell him—no doubt that James would not be returning home soon—he contemplated how best to handle the situation. Perhaps James's absence would make his position more difficult, but not impossible, he assured himself, settling down in a comfortable wing chair.

But no matter what the housekeeper had to tell him, Zeph decided, he simply must leave Malana and be on his way.


Just as soon as the talkative housekeeper left her alone in the magnificent room, having insisted on personally helping "the miss" out of her cape and hat, Malana returned to the door, pressing her ear against it. Clasping the handle, she listened hard, counting the woman's soft footfalls until they faded. Waiting an extra few minutes just to be safe, she finally tested the door. To her relief, she found it unlocked. Without hesitation, Malana slipped out and made her way back to the winding staircase that led below.

She needed to find Zeph . . . to make certain he did not leave her.

Spying Mrs. Bassett making a slow, calculated descent, as if wishing the steps might never end, Malana ducked behind a bronz pedestaled statue to conceal herself. Her eyes focused for only a moment on the glistening figurine just inches from her nose, before returning to their all-important vigilance. She quickly glanced at it again.

From such close quarters, she suddenly realized the

detailed masculine physique was covered in a most vital spot by only a small leaf. Did it represent the *haole* god? It was indeed godlike, reminding Malana of Zeph with a broad chest and a flat stomach and . . .

She forced herself to look beyond the flagrant display to the housekeeper's progress. How could the *haole* accuse her people of being pagans? At least, Hitihitians did not openly display naked statues in their homes, idols or not.

Once Mrs. Bassett reached the floor below and disappeared from view, Malana quickly followed in the woman's footsteps, making her way as noiselessly as possible to the place where she had last seen Zeph near the front entrance.

There, to her dismay, she faced a quandary. Rooms went off in every direction. Glancing around, she panicked, thinking she did not know where Zephiran had gone. He could easily have left through the front door and be far away by now. Then, to her relief, she heard his familiar, reassuring timbre issue from close by. Following the sound of his voice, she moved to a nearby closed door, pausing to place her ear against the barrier to listen, only to reassure herself of his presence, not to pry.

"Ah, there you are, Mrs. Bassett," she heard him say. "Tell me, what is it that has you so distraught?"

"Oh, Captain Westley, apparently you haven't heard the tragic news."

A noise from above momentarily distracted Malana. Thinking she'd been caught spying, when that had not been her intention at all, she pulled away from the door to investigate, looking up guiltily. But after a few seconds, spurred on by the need to find out what was happening, she dropped her head, returning to her eavesdropping. After all, if it had to do with herself and her future, it was only fair that she know.

"When did it happen?" Zeph demanded, his voice foreboding, yet containing a note of emotion she had never before heard.

"What? What has happened?" Malana murmured, realizing that in those few seconds of inattentiveness she had missed vital information.

An unnerving silence followed, disturbed only by the shuffle of feet from the other side of the door.

"It's been nigh on a year now, sir, since we learned."

*Learned? What had they learned?* Malana pressed the side of her head harder against the door, hoping to find out, knowing that, somehow, it affected her.

"To think, for more years than I've been alive, James Kilpatrick sailed some of the most dangerous waters in the world unscathed. How is it possible that Long Island Sound, so tame in comparison, could have bested him?"

Malana struggled to understand the meaning of Zeph's statement. One thing was quite clear: Whatever had happened, it had happened to her father.

Strange, confused feelings stirred within her as the voices continued to converse. The reality of it struck her then. If in truth it turned out that her father was unable to take her in, there was the hope that Zeph might take her with him. Not that she wished something terrible to have happened to her father. Still, she hardly knew him. And more than anything, she wanted to stay with Zephiran.

*"Mademoiselle,"* a voice from behind her hissed in a whisper, "whatever do you zink you are doing?"

The unexpected inquiry caught Malana off guard. With a gasp, she jumped, bumping her head on one of the oak panels of the door.

The voices within ceased abruptly. Determined footsteps started forward, moving quickly, coming toward her faster than she could think. Malana spun on her heels.

"Honoré, what are you doing here?" she demanded, somewhat relieved to discover the Frenchwoman, and not someone else, standing behind her.

"Hurry, *cherie.* Follow me," the seamstress replied, signaling for Malana to join her in what appeared to be a small recess beneath the central staircase where she stood.

Without questioning her companion's motives, Malana moved swiftly, slipping beneath the staircase just as the closed door behind which she'd been standing swung open. Zeph stepped out, his face wrought with a dark, undefined expression. Worry, anger, regret, perhaps? She couldn't be certain. He looked around, then turned back into the room.

"I'm positive, Mrs. Bassett," he said. "I heard someone outside the door." He moved farther into the foyer, coming toward the very spot where they stood watching him.

Knowing they were trapped and would soon be discovered, Malana braced herself for the sure-to-follow interrogation. Zeph would be furious when he found her. But Honoré surprised her again, taking her hand and guiding her toward a small door beneath the staircase.

"What is this place?" Malana asked, ducking in the door frame to follow Honoré's lead into the dark, bare stairwell beyond. It looked as if it belonged in the dank bowels of a ship more than in such an elegant house.

"Ssh!" the Frenchwoman insisted, closing the door behind them and treading swiftly down the steep, winding staircase.

Meanwhile, Malana crept along, feeling her way blindly in the near darkness. Every now and then she paused and lifted her head, listening to the muffled voices above.

"Where are we, Honoré?" she asked in an awed whisper when they finally reached the bottom landing.

"In ze servant's quarters. What did you find out?"

Malana hesitated for just a moment.

"I think something has happened to my father," she finally said. "I think he must be dead."

There. She had said it. The truth, no doubt. Her father was dead. Funny, but she didn't feel any the worse for finally admitting what she knew in her heart. He had died, never acknowledging her, never returning for her mother who loved him and had been willing to wait for him for the rest of her life.

"Oh, *cherie,* I am so sorry you had to find out zis way," Honoré murmured, taking her hand and squeezing it. "You have a cousin, Niles. I have heard ze other servants discussing him. Zey say he is"—she paused for a moment, as if choosing her words carefully—"he is young, single, a welcome guest in ze finest homes in New Bedford. Best of all, zey say he is reasonably tolerant of what goes on in ze household. Chances are—"

"I don't care about any cousin," Malana interrupted. "I've decided we will go with Zephiran."

Honoré's sympathetic look deepened.

"Why do you stare at me that way? Do you still not think Zephiran will take me with him? I have learned the *haole* way to make a man do what I want, just as you taught me." Malana slapped the Frenchwoman's hand away.

"*Cherie,* zere are some zings no woman can make a man like *Capitaine* Westley do if he doesn't really want to."

"And you think he will choose to abandon me. You are wrong, Honoré," she cried. "You are wrong, and I will prove it. Just you wait and see."

Perhaps her own fears—inwardly recognized while outwardly denied—made her lash out so vehemently. Zeph wouldn't desert her. Not now. Had he not rescued her during the violent storm at sea? Then he had kissed her with a passion so strong that it had swept her away as surely as the raging sea would have had he not chosen to risk his own life for hers.

They never spoke of it; they didn't have to. Still, that unbridled kiss hung in the air between them, remembered. Always remembered and relived . . . and yearned for.

It had touched him, too. Of that she felt certain. How could it have not? So, her line of reasoning followed, how could he possibly forsake her now?

"Come, *cherie.*" Honoré spoke softly, reassuringly, with the confidence Malana had come to rely upon over the last few weeks. "If you are so determined, zen we have much to do. But first we must get you back to your room before *Capitaine* Westley discovers you are missing. What he doesn't know zat we know . . . perhaps zere is a way we can use zat information to our advantage."

Two lamps burned brightly in the study when Zeph responded to the late night summons. One sat on the edge of the desk, intended as a reading light. The other, a wall sconce near the door, threw giant shadows across the room and the man who sat waiting for him.

Niles Kilpatrick. James's nephew and closest living relative—acknowledged, that is. Just as he had always bragged that he would, Niles had at last inherited the more than modest Kilpatrick fortune.

It had been years since Zeph had last encountered Niles. Even now, the remembered injustices stung.

Sitting there, a pair of wire-rimmed glasses resting on the end of his long nose, his hands coming together, his spidery fingers clasped in front of him, Niles looked exactly as he remembered, only a little older, a little more conniving, if that were possible. Thin and pale—unhealthy looking, in Zeph's opinion—he still had a head too large for the rest of his body. Large heads were reputed to be a sign of wisdom.

Somehow, nature had missed the boat when it came to Niles.

"My, my. Zephiran Westley. How long has it been?" Niles asked in that well-remembered, over-pronounced whine of his, which still made Zeph grit his teeth in instant dislike. "Four maybe five years?" he continued, looking up, not in the least ruffled by the fact that he sat and Zeph stood advantageously over him.

"More like seven, Niles," Zeph replied, staring, unblinking, across the desk—James's desk—at a man who had no more right to sit behind it than did a cold codfish. Posturing Niles, who hated life at sea, who had never willingly lifted a finger to learn the first thing about shipping or whaling.

Zeph glared at those interlaced fingers now, still templed self-righteously on top of the desk. Kilpatrick Shipping in such inept, unappreciative hands. It made Zeph's stomach churn.

He could still remember the one and only seaboard excursion the little weasel had ever taken, and only because James had insisted. With just a few months' difference in their ages, at eighteen Zeph was already a seasoned sailor, Niles a consummate complainer. They had not even sailed beyond the protection of the bay before Niles had started whining to return to shore.

Zeph had to admit, he had never seen anyone so prone to seasickness. It had gone on for over a week without any indication of letting up. Niles had been as white and limp and useless as hoisted canvas on a windless day. Still, it was unheard of for a captain to succumb to the whims of one of the crew or even a passenger. But finally, breaking the unwritten code of the sea, James had given in to his nephew's unreasonable demands and had changed course. Docking in Wilmington, he had put the still-complaining Niles on a coach back to New Bedford.

True, they had been better off without him, but Zeph had never really forgiven James for coddling "the boy" simply because he was kin. Nor for making him his heir for the same damn reason.

And now, Niles controlled all that James had worked for over his lifetime, and he would no doubt run it aground like an unpiloted ship.

"Ah, yes, seven is it?" Niles replied with a mirthless smile, one Zeph met with stone-faced silence. "My, how the years do fly and circumstances change," Niles mocked, his smile turning devious.

"Oh, really, Niles. I bet you still can't sail worth a damn."

"You'd be surprised how owning the ship makes all the difference in how you feel when you're out to sea. Quite frankly, I find the ocean air does my health good."

"Seasickness. I should have known you were lying all those years ago."

"Even if you had, Uncle James would never have believed you over me," Niles gloated. Then his expression altered, narrowing like that of a stalking ferret. "So, what did you hope to accomplish by bringing that pagan imposer into my home?"

"James's home," Zeph reminded, angered by the cruel name he called Malana. But whether it was the _pagan_ or the _imposer_ that upset him the most, he couldn't say for sure. "He would have welcomed his own daughter."

"His daughter? Odd. He never spoke of having one. Nonetheless, it's my home now, need I remind you? And I decide who is welcome and who is not."

It was obvious who was not. Zeph Westley. Only the lateness of the hour kept him from obliging the more than blunt reminder of his position of outsider.

"True, Niles. It's yours. It's all yours," Zeph conceded willingly enough. It had never been James's possessions that he wanted for himself, only the right to say that he belonged, if not from blood ties, then from loyalty. Loyalty never counted for much when it came to a final reckoning, however.

"As for the girl, if in truth she's my late uncle's illegitimate child, as you say, I suppose I could find it in my heart to let her stay on for a while."

"How kind of you," Zeph muttered, turning away to stare, unseeingly, at the wall James had decorated with scrimshaw collected over his many years at sea.

Then his gaze fell upon the very first figurine he, as a

polliwog, had carved—a small seal. In Zeph's opinion, it wasn't that good, even for a first try yet James had kept it all these years, had been proud to display it among the intricate pieces of his collection. How many times had he said that loyalty among shipmates, taking care of each other, was what life was all about?

Taking care of each other. James had never left him to flounder, had backed him wholeheartedly when Zeph had gone his own way, even coming forward with the money to equip the *Dolphin* on her maiden voyage. After his last voyage, Zeph had paid him back every penny. From that point on, they had met on equal terms, whaling men, captains, nothing expected in return except common respect.

Taking care of each other. That was what Malana represented to him. Taking care of what belonged to James. The last thing he would do with the girl, he vowed, was to leave her in the clutches of Niles Kilpatrick, even if James had been foolish enough to leave everything else he valued to the unappreciative landlubber.

If Niles thought for a moment she represented a legitimate threat to his inheritance, might he not do everything in his power short of murder to prevent her from laying claim to it? Zeph suspected he would.

"Your generosity isn't necessary, Niles. I've made other arrangements for the girl."

In truth, he hadn't a clue as to what he would do with Malana. God knows, he dared not take her home with him. It would be like asking for a disaster to happen. With her under his roof . . .

"I see. Plan to keep the delectable creature all for yourself then, Zeph?" Niles clucked his tongue, then chuckled, as if privy to Zeph's disturbing thoughts. "Yes, indeed. Whatever will dear Leatrice say about that?"

Zeph crossed the room with the stride of a man accustomed to commanding a deck and being obeyed. He dragged the sniveling coward up out of his ill-deserved chair with such speed that his quarry didn't have a chance to escape, merely to whine about it. His own face inches from Niles's, he savored the fear he read in those ferretlike eyes.

"James isn't here anymore to protect you. So, mind your vicious tongue, Niles, or I swear I'll have no qualms about ripping it out by the roots and feeding it to the fish in the bay."

"My, but you have always been so ridiculously serious, Zeph," Niles muttered. "And now it seems I have unwittingly scraped a raw spot on that scaly hide of yours, haven't I?" His eyes darted left and then right, refusing to settle on Zeph's unrelenting glare.

Raw, indeed, damn him. What would Leatrice think, and rightly so, if he arrived home, Malana in tow? His longtime fiancée deserved better than that. He had to figure out what to do with the girl now, before he could even think about returning to Mystic.

Zeph abruptly released his grip. Niles fell back into his chair, his initial gasps changing into an ear-grating snicker that pursued Zeph out the door. That laughter, coming from such an irritating source, stung more than a dousing of salt water on an open wound.


"Zephiran, where are we going?"

Malana didn't protest his sudden appearance at her door first thing in the morning, nor his demands that she begin packing immediately. In fact, when the time came at last to confront her future, her heart beat wildly with excitement and confidence.

Until Honoré, who had just helped her dress for the occasion, unexpectedly made her excuses.

"No, do not leave me alone with him," Malana pleaded

in French, certain that Zeph did not understand what she said.

"You'll do fine, *cherie,*" Honoré responded in kind, glancing at Zeph, a knowing smile curving her lips. "Just remember everyzing we talked about last night," she reminded, then slipped out the door.

Left on her own, no doubt to flounder, Malana nonetheless gathered up her scattered courage and faced Zeph. Why did he stare at her as if she were an odd fish? She looked down at herself. Dressed in a day gown Honoré had promised moments before was her most attractive, despite its relative plainness, she decided that was what held his fascination. Why, he might actually think her pretty. Her confidence climbed a notch.

"I didn't know you could speak French."

Her heart skipped a beat. She lowered her lashes over the apprehension that surely shone in her eyes. Had they misjudged him? If he understood what they had just said in French . . .

*"Oui, monsieur,"* she murmured with cautious sweetness. "Honoré taught me, along with everything else," she added in French, just to test him, her gaze sweeping up to gauge his comprehension.

"Well, yes," he muttered, staring back blankly. "Whatever you said, it does sound pretty enough, I suppose. What did you say?" he asked, his eyes flashing with frustration.

"Only that Honoré had taught me." Relieved, Malana released her pent-up breath and fears and smiled as prettily as she could.

"You are indeed a quick study, then," he said gruffly. "I hope you can pack just as swiftly." He started toward the door.

"Where are we going, Zephiran?" she asked again, feeling the shift of power revert back to him. "Back to the ship?" she persisted when he did not answer.

"No."

No? Just no? She hesitated in her uncertainty, waiting for further explanation. He gave none. And if she did not move quickly, decisively, he would be gone as well, her perfect opportunity forfeited.

His hand grasped the handle. Worrying her bottom lip, Malana watched the door swing wide, wishing with all her heart that Honoré would return to block his way. But the corridor was empty. She had only herself to depend upon.

Her first instincts were to throw herself upon him, physically insist that he stop. Past experience had taught her that that approach did not work with a man like Zeph Westley, however. It simply made him even more determined to get away.

"Wait, Zeph," she blurted out in desperation.

He paused in the doorway and turned, staring at her in expectation. There was so much she wanted to say. She had every right to demand to know his intentions, but demands never worked with him, either. Malana tried to remember everything Honoré had taught her, but now, when she needed it most, her brain simply refused to work.

If she experienced surprise at his easy compliance, then she was even more shocked by what came out of her mouth.

"If you wish me to pack quickly, then you must simply help me out of this dress so I can change into something more suitable for traveling." Heart pounding, she pivoted on her heels, presenting her back and the long row of tiny buttons that spanned its entire length.

His continued silence offered not a clue as to what he thought about her brazen request—and it was quite brazen, if not brilliant, by *haole* standards—nor what he planned to do about it.

"What's wrong with the one you have on now?" Zeph finally asked, stubbornly keeping his distance. At least, he was still there.

"Wrong?" She glanced coyly over her shoulder, just as Honoré had taught her to do, and considered her words carefully. "Why, Zeph, you sound as wary as a cat forced to traverse a bowline." And yes, Malana answered the question posed by that cocked brow of his. She could identify a bowline, a jibstay, and even a halyard. The language of sailors was another she had easily mastered over the months at sea. "Do you see something wrong with me or my dress?" she asked innocently enough, pursing her mouth in the provocative way she had practiced for hours on end in front of a mirror.

In breathless anticipation, she waited for his reaction. Would he truly respond as Honoré had promised?

He studied her intently, his gaze traveling the length of her before settling on her carefully rehearsed, as Honoré liked to call it, boudoir expression.

"No, there's absolutely nothing wrong with you nor what you are wearing."

"Good," Malana offered simply, looking away to hide her victorious smile. She gave her shoulders a little shake. "Then help me out of it so I do not ruin it. Will you, please?"

She thought then he would truly make good his escape. To be honest, she came close to running herself. But then she felt him gravitate in her direction. Slowly, at first. Finally, his steps quickened, coming closer and closer.

Closing her eyes, she swayed toward him. She could not help herself. Always she felt him, the manly heat of him, whenever he approached, whether with caution or anger . . . but soon, she hoped, with desire. The warmth, the security his closeness offered, called to her like a magnet. Still, what she wanted so desperately remained just out of her reach.

And then he touched her, his hands like silken fire as they fumbled with the buttons on the back of her dress. She dreamed he undressed her for a reason far less noble than the one she had led him to believe. If only he could want her, even for a short while, she would never ask for anything more. Truly, it would be enough, she vowed.

Luckily, she caught the volatile sob in her throat just before it erupted. Biting her tongue to keep it under control, Malana dreaded the moment he completed the task and once more moved away.

"There, you're unbuttoned," he informed her soon thereafter, stepping back. "I'll expect you to be ready within the hour. There'll be a carriage sent around for you and Miss de Magney."

He never mentioned if he would be there. Did he simply plan to send her away? Was this his way of saying goodbye? Somehow, she had to figure out a means of stopping him before he left.

"Zeph, wait," Malana cried breathlessly, knowing honesty had worked once before. She turned, her hands instinctively crossing in front of her chest, holding the unfastened bodice of her gown in place.

What was it that held him so spellbound? she wondered. Frantically, she searched for an answer. Then it dawned on her. Could it be her show of modesty, her obvious vulnerability that kept him there, planted in that spot, unwilling or perhaps unable to move?

Fearful of creating the slightest distraction, of doing anything that might unknowingly eradicate the wished-for magic of the moment, Malana held perfectly still. Then, to her chagrin, both shoulders of her gown slid down her arms.

Instinctively, she struggled to drag the heavy sleeves back into place, her efforts only making matters worse. Now she would lose him, she fretted. He would think her too forward, too . . .

With a sudden sense of clarity, she saw the irony of her situation. It was almost as if the shyness became real.

"What's so funny, girl?"

She must have laughed, undoubtedly out of nervousness,

although Malana did not actually recall doing so. Zeph's expression suggested anything but amusement, however, as he started to turn away.

"No, Zephiran. Please. Do not abandon me." She darted forward, uncaring that the bodice of her gown again dipped dangerously low across her chest. What difference did all the learned manners, the acquired sophistication, even the feminine tactics make if Zeph did not appreciate them? Without a doubt, she was about to lose him anyway, so why did it matter if she threw herself at him one last time?

She caught him about the waist and hung on as if her life depended on it. And, indeed, it did.

"Malana, what's gotten into you, girl?" His hands probed her desperate clutch gently yet firmly, seeking its weakness. Finally, Zeph managed to pry her off, and he held her at arm's length in front of him. "What's this all about?" he demanded, shaking her just enough so that she looked up at him.

Honoré would tell her to play coy. Instead, the truth spilled from her lips.

"I know about my father. I was listening at the door while you spoke to that Mrs. Bassett," Malana admitted guiltily. "Oh, Zeph, please," she cried, managing to coil her arms about his neck. "Please, take me with you."

"Malana."

Uncertain whether she heard pity or resignation in his voice, she nonetheless closed her eyes and pressed her mouth against his. Half expecting him to pull away angrily, Malana tensed her arms, prepared to hang on for as long as she could.

"I will be good. I promise, I will do whatever you ask of me," she murmured against his unresponsive lips.

"Malana, stop," he insisted.

Slowly, little by ever so little, she felt him soften. At first his hands, restraining bands at her elbows, dropped away, and he allowed her to kiss him, as if merely tolerating it. Encouraged instead of deterred, she forged ahead. He could not resist her forever. With eager fingers, Malana explored the hair that curled softly about the nape of his neck. Zeph groaned, shaking his head as if trying to dislodge her invading hands, but she would not give up.

Changing her tactics, she pressed against him, opening her mouth beneath his.

*Please, oh, please.*

In answer to her silent plea, his arms returned, wrapping about her so tightly she gasped. Then his fingers skimmed along the gaping back of her gown ever so lightly, as if exploring a taboo. But why? Why did he think her something he should not have? They were meant to be together. Why else would fate have sent him to rescue her? She would prove that to him in the only way she knew how.

First one and then the other, Malana carefully lowered her arms, slipping them out of the voluptuous sleeves that encased them. With nothing but the thin lace of her chemise between them, she drew one leg up, caressing his hip, hoping, praying to every conceivable god, for his returned ardor.

The answer to her prayers came in a rush so strong it nearly took her breath away. His mouth, once still and controlled, turned passionate beneath hers, taking charge. His hands, excitingly rough from a life at sea, began their exploration, one reaching down to grasp her lifted leg at the knee, pulling it higher. The other sought the softness of her breast, the thin silk like nothing between them as his palm molded about her.

She sucked in a deep breath, filling her lungs, filling the cup of his hand as completely as she could with her aching flesh. His thumb brushed against the hard nodule, and an unbelievable thrill rushed through her. In response, she covered his hand with her own, offering, begging for more. Releasing her leg, his other hand moved up, joining in the shared caresses.

Was this not the reason the gods had created man and woman? What she had waited all her life to experience? She would not be denied it now.

Remembering the small reclining couch only a few steps behind them, Malana led him in that direction. He followed willingly enough, allowing her to sink down upon it as he knelt beside her.

Pushing away the bit of cloth, Zeph lowered his head, his mouth claiming what his hands had so freely fondled. Where his palm had been rough and dry, his lips were ever so tender and moist. Mindlessly, she arched against the gentle onslaught, reveling in her long-awaited victory, her own hands clutching at his hair, urging him on.

"Yes, Zephiran, yes," she sighed, truly happy for the first time that she could remember in her life.

The moment she spoke she knew she had made a terrible mistake. His entire body stiffened; his head lifted, his hands jerked away. His gaze, gone cold, collided with hers. Even with tousled hair, lips wet from caressing her, the dreaded hardness had returned to his face.

He stood so suddenly that her fingers, still entwined in his hair, ripped out several fire-kissed strands. If he felt the pain, he did not show it.

"Damn it, Malana," Zeph said instead, his pain one of betrayal. "I should have known what you were about. Can't you see this is wrong, girl?" He took several steps backward.

"No, Zeph. It is not wrong." She reached out for him, her arms and heart aching with emptiness.

In response he shook his head, backing even farther away.

Her heart nearly broke from the pain of his rejection, but it was nothing compared to the pain caused by his parting words.

"I suppose, being who you are, you wouldn't see anything wrong with it."

"What is so wrong with who I am?" she cried.

She would never know if he heard her. The door clicked softly behind his back while the tears flowed freely down her face.

Cool mist curled about the tall volcanic peak at the center of the tiny island of Hitihiti. For many moons Te Tuma rested undisturbed. At the foot of his mountain home, his grateful subjects returned to their idyllic existence, certain their wise chief and his priests had appeased the angry god. Which indeed they had for the moment. The breadfruit trees gave forth in abundance, the islanders' fishing nets filled to overflowing—all with Te Tuma's blessing. It was a time to rejoice, feast, and make love.

It was in the middle of the night, when everyone slept, that the great island god learned, through his magical means, that those who dared defy and deceive him had once again nearly come together in the way of a man and woman. That he would not tolerate. His hot, angry roar shook the island so violently that babies cried. Even the village dogs ran off into the jungle howling in terror.

Mao awoke as terrified as the rest of his people. He stumbled from his hut and turned to the mountain, lifting his arms skyward.

"Te Tuma. Te Tuma," he cried. "How can we satisfy you?"

In response the great volcano god belched great volumes of fire and smoke, brimming lava as a warning.

The priests dropped to their knees. They bowed before his unexplained fury. As quickly as they could, they moved to the *marae,* there in the god-house, to fast, drink *kava,* and pray to the mighty Te Tuma to reveal just what it was that made him so angry.

If he could only tell them, he would. But perhaps there were ways they could right the wrong. There was one *haole* whose greed he had overlooked, thinking him powerless to make a difference. Perhaps he had been wrong. Perhaps that one could be the catalyst to bring his wayward bride back home where she belonged.

# *Chapter Ten*

Even from a distance, the *Dolphin* sat regally in her assigned berth, sail furled, dipping and bobbing with the activity that kept the waters of the busy wharves of New Bedford astir. Her stately grace offered Zeph safe haven. He picked up his pace, wanting nothing more than to go aboard and stay forever in the one place he knew himself to be master, not only of those around him, but of his own emotions.

If ever a man needed a place far from harm's reach at the moment, he undoubtedly qualified. He'd come close, much too close, to making a mistake that would have haunted him to his grave.

What was he going to do with the girl?

Girl? Whom did he think to fool by such a label? It seemed only *he* had refused to see the truth. Even Niles had suspected. As for Malana herself, not even for a moment did he believe her clueless to the power of her womanly charms. And now he could no longer deny them. Like it or not, he possessed firsthand knowledge of them.

An unbidden rush of desire coursed through him, leaving him shaken, angry, and more determined than ever to master it. He liked his life just the way it was. He didn't wish to change it. But like a man prone to drunkenness, Zeph knew he could never resist the lure as long as it remained close at hand.

So what did he plan to do to make things the way they were supposed to be? He only had two choices: conquer his weakness, or be rid of Malana. It seemed as if he didn't have the strength to do the first. As for the latter . . .

He might not think of himself as a hero. Still, he didn't want to be a bounder, either. He simply had to find a socially acceptable solution, a place to keep her where she would be out of danger and, just as importantly, out of his hair.

Remembering only too well the feel of her, he brushed his hand across the top of his head, thinking to eradicate the memory.

But it was not that easy.

To be sure, he had already taken the first necessary steps. Before heading to the wharf, he had gone to several of the local public houses, selected the most reputable of them—which wasn't saying much—and arranged for rooms. One for the lady and her servant, another for himself.

"Adjoining, sir?" the innkeeper had asked, not even bothering to look up from his ledger.

"No," Zeph had replied vehemently. "Give me the one farthest away."

The hosteler had glanced up then. Judging from the look on his face, he had thought his newly acquired guest was indeed an odd fish.

From the foot of the pier, Zeph paused to take a deep breath and canvass what he considered his domain, the one and only place he felt completely in charge. The deck of the *Dolphin* was alive with activity, more than seemed necessary for a ship in harbor. Concerned, he hurried on.

The moment Zeph stepped aboard, he knew for certain something was amiss.

"Where is Mr. Kennedy?" he demanded of the first man he confronted.

Wordlessly, the sailor pointed toward the companionway stairs.

He found his first mate in the forecastle, in a power deadlock with the worthless likes of Jake Ainsworth, the disgruntled harpooner who had attacked Malana and subsequently paid for his actions.

"He says he wants his due now, Cap'n," Mr. Kennedy spoke up first. "I told him he'll get what's comin' to him the same as everyone else when we reach journey's end."

"Aye, and that you will," Zeph agreed, pinning the unscrupulous sailor with a look that had silenced better and braver men.

"And why should I have to wait?" Jake demanded, in spite of the domineering glare. "I earned my salary. I was the finest harpooner you had."

"And the most disagreeable. You signed on for the duration of this voyage, or have you forgotten?"

"I don't want to go back to Mystic. I've decided there's much more opportunity here in New Bedford."

"Opportunity for what, Mr. Ainsworth? Berth or bawd?" Zeph quipped.

"Not all of us had the privilege of bringing our whores along with us."

Spurred by loyalty to his captain, Mr. Kennedy lunged, grabbed the insubordinate sailor by the scruff, and lifted him clear off his feet. Knowing he would be justified in turning the entire matter over to his first officer, Zeph considered it. Indeed, Jake Ainsworth deserved to be severely disciplined for speaking thusly to his captain. But what would that prove? The situation aboard the *Dolphin* was uneasy enough without making matters even worse.

"Put him down, Mr. Kennedy," Zeph instructed.

If he experienced surprise at the curt command, the mate never allowed it to show. He did as he was told, released Jake, and stepped back.

"Very well, Mr. Ainsworth," Zeph said. "If you want out so badly, we can settle up now. Mr. Kennedy, kindly fetch the ship's accounts."

It took only a few moments to reconcile the books and pay off the harpooner the sum of two hundred dollars, after subtracting items purchased from the ship's store and advance pay drawn while on shore leave. The sailor started to argue the point, claiming a share of the rare and precious ambergris—a byproduct of whaling—that had been collected on the hunt while he had been confined to quarters under guard.

Of course, Zeph refused to budge on the issue. As far as he was concerned, the man didn't deserve a share of such profit when he had done nothing toward its recovery. Taking the man by the arm, he personally escorted him off the ship.

"I don't ever want to see you around the *Dolphin* again, Mr. Ainsworth."

"Believe me, Cap'n, you don't have to worry. I know when I've been cheated."

Zeph watched the troublemaker saunter away, wondering if he'd made a mistake by letting him off so easily. He knew the Jake Ainsworth type. The sailor would quickly spend his money on rum and women, and in no time be dead broke, in search of a new berth. At that point, however, he became another captain's problem.

Certain he would hear no more of it, Zeph turned to more pressing problems. If only they could be resolved so easily. If only he could step aboard the *Dolphin* and simply sail away and leave them far behind. As much as he wanted it, he knew that was not to be.

Instead, he made arrangements for Mr. Kennedy to take care of the ship and sail her on to Mystic. He would reunite with them there. Knowing Leatrice would meet the ship the moment it docked, he entrusted his first mate with a message for her as well.

"Tell her only that I had business to attend to here in New Bedford. I'll be along shortly. Oh, and, Mr. Kennedy," he added, "tell her I look forward to seeing her again very much."

That, of course, was an understatement. His uncomplicated life with Leatrice began to look better and better every day.

The carriage came for Malana just as Zeph promised it would. Mrs. Bassett supervised the loading of the luggage and saw Malana and Honoré off.

"I'm sorry that Mr. Niles, your cousin, couldn't be here. He sends his apologies," she offered, looking away when Malana smiled graciously.

"I doubt your cousin even knows, much less cares, when we left or where we are going," Honoré declared as the carriage sped away.

"Where do *you* think we are going?" Malana asked quietly.

Honoré merely looked back at her. A long, shared pause followed. The carriage made several turns, the only words spoken those of the driver calling to his team. Malana stared out the window. The houses became noticeably shabbier compared to the one they had just departed. Her courage lost much of its luster as well.

When they pulled up before a large building, and the driver got out and opened the carriage door for them, Honoré finally spoke.

"A public house. It could be worse," she reassured. "Believe me, it could be a whole lot worse."

To Malana's disappointment, Zeph was not there to greet them. Would he come, or had he, as she feared, abandoned them?

Burdened with a heavy heart and feeling completely out of her element in the strange surroundings, she gratefully followed Honoré up the stairs to the room they were to share.

Niles Kilpatrick stared at the ill-kept, common sailor sitting across the desk from him, wondering why he had bothered to receive the man in the first place.

"I promise you, Mr. Kilpatrick," Jake Ainsworth declared in the face of Niles's skepticism. "I ain't lying to ya, sir, but I just don't know if I can trust you with the proof."

"Proof? If you have proof, Mr. Ainsworth, then show it to me, or get out and quit wasting my time."

After a moment's hesitation, Jake fumbled in an interior pocket of his dirty pea jacket. His hand emerged clamped around something. Moving his arm forward, across the desk, he unfolded his fingers, revealing the largest, most perfect pearl Niles had ever seen.

It glimmered with a fire, a pagan heat. It seemed almost to come alive in the sailor's dirty hand, beckoning to Niles, to the ingrained greed that was his mistress.

"You say you picked this up in the South Seas?" As hard as he tried, Niles couldn't drag his eyes away from the gemstone. "Where?" he asked eagerly, revealing his interest.

That was a mistake, one he instantly realized.

"I'll not say. At least, not yet," Jake replied, sitting back and spreading his lips in a gape-tooth smile that left much to be desired.

Cocky swine, Niles thought, not liking in the least that someone tried to gain the upper hand with him. No one would ever do that to him again.

"Then good day to you, sir," he said, rising.

Jake's mouth dropped open. He stared at Niles for the longest time, as if trying to decide if he merely blustered.

Niles Kilpatrick excelled in the art of intimidation. He stood there, glaring down at the sailor, confident the man would not walk away from him now.

"I swear to God, sir," Jake declared in the whine of the defeated, "there's more where this came from. They're just lyin' around, waitin' to be picked up."

"If that's so, then why has no one else discovered them?" Niles pressed, his suspicious nature urging him to continue to use caution.

"'Cause, like I told you before, not everybody knows where to look."

"But you do, and you're willing to show me. Why?"

"You're a merchant with a ship. You have the means to get us there. I have the knowledge where to find 'em. We'll be partners."

Still, Niles was not convinced.

"But why me?" he demanded.

"Because your name is Kilpatrick. And Cap'n Westley, the stiff-necked bastard, swears by that name."

"Zephiran Westley?" Niles asked quickly, his heart pounding with the thought that at last he might be able to get the best of his old enemy. "What does he know about your discovery?"

"Nothin'." Jake smiled again. "I didn't tell nobody about what I found."

"Good," Niles said, rubbing his hands together. "Keep it that way . . . partner." He stuck out his hand to seal the bargain, an act no more unsavory than touching someone like Jake Ainsworth.

All he needed was one of those pearls, and he would be wealthier than his wildest dreams.

Then it would be just as he wished. He would never have to work another day in his life.


It was on the way back to the inn that the solution to his problem presented itself to Zeph. Of course, he should have thought of it long ago. It made perfect sense, and once again he had Leatrice to thank.

School. He would send Malana off to school.

He thought for the longest moment, trying to recall the name of the female academy Leatrice had attended years ago. He ought to be able to remember it easily enough. His fiancée often spoke of her alma mater in her everyday conversation.

"At . . ., Mistress Honeywell always taught us that the proper way to . . ."

Zeph paused and closed his eyes. Why did the name of the headmistress come to mind but not that of the school itself? A prominent female school in Providence, Rhode Island, it was the reason he had met Leatrice in the first place.

James had taken him, while Zeph was still a man without means, to attend Niles's sister's graduation. Early on he had spotted Leatrice among the alumnae. Actually, it was more like *she* had spied *him* and decided she wanted to make his acquaintance. Still, for all of her progressive ways, Leatrice had been pretty without seeming extravagant, intelligent without treading on a man's toes. Quite frankly, some of the young women Zeph had met that day had made him feel less than intrigued by their overbearing ways. Leatrice, on the other hand, while never shy, had made him feel just right with her natural dignity and grace.

They were admirable qualities in a woman. As he recalled, he had felt just as comfortable with her then as he did now. Yes, the New England School of Female Advancement had molded Leatrice into the agreeable, sophisticated woman she was to this very day. The name. He'd remembered it. The New England School of Female Advancement. He would write to Mrs. Honeywell as soon as he reached the inn.

He wouldn't think about the possibility that the school might not accept Malana. He would simply have to see to it that they did not refuse his request. Along with the letter and the reminder of the other Kilpatrick women who had attended and graduated, he would secure the arrangement by sending the enrollment fee in advance, a hefty sum that no one could turn down.

With a sense of accomplishment, Zeph entered the front door of the Fox and Cock Inn and made his way to the public room, to find a quiet corner where he could compose a letter to the headmistress of the New England School of Female Advancement.

While sitting at a corner table, writing his final draft, he decided the best way to assure that the school did not reject Malana's enrollment was to follow on the heels of the missive, arriving at the doors of the academy before such a decision could be made.

He expressed the letter, containing the hefty sum of four hundred dollars in state banknotes, to Mrs. Honeywell that very afternoon. At the same time, Zeph booked passage for the next morning on the mail coach to Providence. The thirty-odd mile trip over land, while not his first choice of travel, shouldn't take more than a couple of days at most. Once he delivered his ward—and he had to get used to calling her that now, Zeph realized—into the capable hands of the school's faculty, he would take a fast packet to Mystic.

Yes, if all went smoothly, he would be home in less than a week. Then he would return to life as usual.

* * *

"Is there a problem, Mrs. Honeywell?"

Standing outside the closed door, Malana pressed her ear a little closer in order to hear better.

"Quite frankly, Captain Westley, I received Miss Kilpatrick's application just yesterday. I haven't had the proper time to consider it."

Miss Kilpatrick? Why, she was Miss Kilpatrick, Malana realized. What had she applied for?

"What is to consider?" she heard Zeph ask. "The girl comes highly recommended by alumni, both family and friends. I have paid her tuition in advance. Surely you don't mean to suggest that the Kilpatrick name is no longer good enough for your school?"

"No, of course not," the headmistress assured him quickly. "Miss Kilpatrick comes from a highly reputable and very acceptable family. But you have to understand, Captain Westley, we have traditions here at the New England School of Female Advancement that must be strictly adhered to."

"As captain of the *Dolphin,* I understand your need for discipline. But be that as it may, Mrs. Honeywell, the fact is you know as well as I do my ward will be accepted."

A battle of wills ensued between Zeph and the strange woman. Malana gathered that much, if not the reasons behind it. She did understand, however, that whatever those reasons, they involved her and her future.

"Accepted for what?" she whispered to Honoré, who stood beside her in the stark outer room, her ear to the closed door.

"Shh!" the Frenchwoman whispered, waving her hand in Malana's face.

But she was tired of others not bothering to explain what was going on, of people making decisions that affected her life without asking her what *she* wanted to do. Why, she should just march right through that door and demand to be included in the discussion. It was her right to decide for herself what was best.

Glancing down, she contemplated her decision, along with the door latch, as she worked hard at gathering her pluck.

The clearing of a throat caught Malana by surprise. She whirled in place, discovering a most stern-looking woman standing right behind them, fist on hips.

"May I ask what you ladies think you are doing?"

Dumbstruck, Malana stared mutely, praying for Honoré to do something.

But for once the Frenchwoman seemed incapable of speaking. Now it was up to Malana.

"Oh, thank goodness," she blurted out, saying the first outrageous thing that came to mind. "We seem to have lost our way. Is that not true, Honoré? We went to look for"—what could she say that would curb further inquiry?—"the facilities," she said, manufacturing a blush. *Haole* always seemed embarrassed when they spoke of such natural things. "We got turned around and . . . and . . ." she stuttered to a halt, uncertain what to say next.

"Please, *mademoiselle,* can you tell us? Is zis Mrs. Honeywell's office?" Honoré added smoothly in that pert sophistication of hers that few rarely questioned.

"Yes, it is," the woman replied somewhat hesitantly, scrutinizing them closely with a critical eye. "I've not seen you before. Are you a student here?" she persisted.

"Oh, *non,*" Honoré answered honestly, if evasively. "But it is all right to sit right here and wait for Mrs. Honeywell, isn't it?"

"Well, yes, I suppose. That is the purpose of the settee."

"*Merci, mademoiselle.* Come, *cherie,*" Honoré said, taking Malana by the hand and leading her toward the empty bench as if it were the most natural thing, as if they had never been caught listening at the door.

They could hardly contain themselves long enough for the woman to get out of earshot. When at last alone, they broke out in peals of shared laughter.

"You handled that wonderfully," Malana remarked.

*"Non, non.* It was you, *cherie,* who remained so collected under fire. You will do fine, you know. Just fine. No matter what happens."

"Oh, Honoré, what does it all mean?" she asked in sudden seriousness, staring at the closed door in frustration, knowing the answers lay beyond. "What will happen to us?"

"Not to worry, *cherie.* I am convinced now zat *Capitaine* Westley will take care of you."

"And what of you?" Malana questioned.

"I can take care of myself," Honoré replied with a carefree shrug.

Before Malana could reassure her companion that she would never abandon her, the closed door at which they waited swung open. A victoriously smug Zeph emerged, along with a defeated-looking Mrs. Honeywell.

"Zephiran?" Malana stood, seeking answers to her many questions.

"Miss Kilpatrick." He looked down at her then, and she realized he spoke to her. Why did he address her so formally? After the passion between them only yesterday, how could he? His gaze, closed and unreadable, never flickered nor flinched. It never softened. "It has been decided that you will stay here and attend Mrs. Honeywell's school."

School?

"No," Malana cried softly, retreating several steps. Turning, she aimed toward the door that led outside the building. She should have seen this coming, should have realized his intentions.

The word *school* conjured up unpleasant memories for her. Once, when just a little girl, a missionary had come to her village, insisting that all the parents send their children to school. Otherwise, the great *haole* god would punish them all, the stranger had insisted. Of course, the islanders, having no desire to anger any god—be it theirs or anyone else's—had meekly complied.

Nonetheless, few of the children had been spared the *haole* wrath. The teacher, a terrible man clad in a dark, flowing garment, had been unmerciful, beating his students for every transgression, no matter how small. Malana had received more than her fair share.

She would not suffer that degradation again.

A powerful hand caught her by the elbow, staying her flight and forcing her about.

"Just where do you think you are going?" Zeph demanded.

"Not to school," she declared, twisting to escape his painful clutch.

"Not only will you go, girl"—the band of steel tightened on her arm in warning—"but you will be a model student and do exactly as you are told."

"No, I will not," Malana insisted, but she knew that she would if it might gain his approval. "Please, Zephrian." She pressed her hand against his chest, feeling the strength of his steady heartbeat. "Do not make me."

She could only hope that her appeal might touch him where her fingertips rested. But his jaw tightened with a determination to match her own.

"Don't you see it's what's best for you?"

"No," she objected. "Staying with you is what I need."

*Then it is best for me.*

He did not say that aloud, of course, but she knew he thought it—and meant it, as well as every word he *did* say. If she ever hoped for his acceptance, then she must give in to his demands now.

But it was hard, so very hard, to think of him going away

and leaving her. The mere thought of being alone with strangers . . . Alone?

"What of Honoré?" she asked. "She will stay here, too?"

"No. Young ladies in school don't bring their maidservants with them."

"Then what will become of her?" Malana demanded, determined not to cooperate, not until she could be certain of her friend's welfare.

She could have sworn admiration momentarily overrode the stubborn expression on his face. But then the look vanished, replaced with a renewed hardness that sent shivers down her spine.

"So now you're concerned about Honoré, are you? Believe me, you worry unnecessarily about that little minx."

"Still, you will make sure that she is taken care of, won't you?"

"Will you promise to do as you are told?"

Of course, it was not a bargain of her choosing, but what else could she do? Defeated, she conceded, looking away.

"Then it seems, girl, we have struck a deal." Grasping her arm a little tighter, as if to warn her not even to consider reneging, Zeph forced her to walk in front of him back into the school.

"I think you will have no more problems with Miss Kilpatrick," he assured Mrs. Honeywell. "Isn't that so, girl?" he asked, squeezing her arm ever so slightly.

Silently, Malana nodded, closing her eyes on the feeling of defeat that clogged the back of her throat.

Zeph released her and she realized he was leaving then, taking Honoré with him. Feeling like a bit of flotsam swept out to sea, torn away from everything and everyone who mattered to her, she started to protest.

The stern look on Zeph's face soldered her lips. He did not want her, not now, not ever. From the very beginning, she had only been an unwanted burden to him, nothing more.

As for Honoré . . .

The Frenchwoman looked back, her smile of farewell filled with bravery, encouragement, and, more importantly, understanding. Had she not moments before assured Malana that she would be all right?

She had to trust Zeph to keep his side of the bargain and see to the care of her one and only true friend.


With the same fortitude and determination she had displayed that first time Zeph had seen her in the streets of Rio de Janeiro, the Frenchwoman faced him across the table in the tavern. Unwillingly, she'd accepted his offer of a meal.

"So what will you do now, *monsieur?*" Honoré asked.

"What do you think I'm going to do, Miss de Magney?" Zeph tried, unsuccessfully, to keep the amusement from his voice. "Abandon you to the streets? That's what Malana assumed, you know. Now, where do you think she might have gotten an idea like that?"

"How would I know?" the Frenchwoman answered defensively, toying with the bowl of steaming hot chowder he had ordered for her. Zeph suspected she merely toyed with him as well.

He no longer found the situation amusing.

"Eat before it grows cold," he ordered gruffly. "It may very well be your last for a while."

Honoré shot him a wary, wide-eyed look. Picking up her spoon, she began to ladle the thick stew into her mouth without pause.

Zeph watched, his own utensil poised over the dish before him. Could it be that she honestly took him seriously? What had he ever done to Honoré de Magney to make her think so ill of him? Had he not given her passage when she'd asked for it? But more importantly, he had given her, a total stranger, the benefit of the doubt, as well as access to his purse, when she could easily have been out to dupe him.

"I was only joking, Miss de Magney."

She paused with her spoon in midair and gave him a thorough once-over.

"Truly, I'm not an ogre."

"No, of course you are not." In spite of what she said, she did not look all that convinced.

"Have you thought about what you will do now?"

"What choice do I have but to look for another position here in . . ." She thought for a moment. "What is ze name of zis place again?"

"Providence. Providence, Rhode Island. But why stay here? You're welcome to accompany me to Mystic," he proposed generously, an offer he had planned to make all along, even before he had struck that bargain with Malana. "There, with a letter of reference from me, I'm sure you will find something suitable."

"You would do zat for me?" She set down her spoon and stared at him for a moment. Then her thin brows furrowed. "Why? What would you expect in return?"

"Must I expect something in return?"

Her unrelenting expression offered little in the way of encouragement.

"Miss de Magney . . ." Zeph set his spoon down by the side of his bowl. "Do you really find it so difficult to believe that I might do something just because it is the right thing to do?"

Apparently so. Her skepticism never faltered, not even for a moment.

"Very well. Have it your own way." Shrugging, he retrieved his utensil and resumed eating.

"What if I decide I want to stay here? Would you try to stop me, *monsieur*?"

"Stop you?" Zeph paused to stare at her. "You can choose to stay with the devil for all I care." Then he thought about it. There was only one reason the woman would want to stay here. Malana. Just what had the two of them planned? "But why would you?" he demanded.

"For Malana. It won't be easy for her."

"Perhaps, but you will make it even harder for her if you try to interfere."

"Interfere, *Capitaine* Westley? Is zat what you call being a friend? Unlike you, I simply refuse to abandon her."

At the unspoken accusation, Zeph issued a defeated sigh. How could he prove her wrong about him? He hadn't abandoned Malana, he had merely done what he thought best for her. Schooling had never hurt anyone. Undoubtedly, Malana would benefit from it as well. True, it might be in his own best interest too, but that was beside the point. Uncertain why the Frenchwoman's opinion mattered, he only knew that it did. Reaching for his purse, he extracted a good majority of his available cash.

"Then stay, Miss de Magney, with my blessing and support." He placed the wad of bills beside her trencher. "This should see you through for a few months, until you can make other arrangements. I'll also provide you with room and board here at this inn, if you would like. That way you can be as close to the girl as you damn well wish."

"You are very kind, *monsieur*," she said, accepting the money without protest and putting it in the small beaded reticule that dangled from her left wrist. "Much kinder to others zan you are to yourself."

"What do you mean?"

"Simply zat you should allow yourself to have what you really want," she responded, a bit of mystery lacing her voice and tilting her lips. "In my opinion, you deserve it."

"Thank you, Miss de Magney, but I already have everything I need," he replied emphatically.

"If you say so, *Capitaine* Westley." Again that knowing smile.

By damn, the woman knew nothing about him, nothing about his life, his desires, his ambitions. Absolutely nothing at all. Zeph rose, placed money on the table to pay for the meal, then gathered up his hat and coat.

"Good day, Miss de Magney," he announced with finality. "Take care."

"I shall, *monsieur*. Hopefully, someday before it is too late, you will decide to do ze same for yourself."

As he walked away, Zeph felt nothing but relief at being rid of every female who had nothing better to do than to try and interfere in his life.

## *Chapter Eleven*

Two days later Zeph arrived in Mystic via the biweekly packet that ran from Providence, at the top of Narragansett Bay, down the entire length of Long Island Sound and all the way to New York. No one greeted him at the docks, but then, he hadn't expected to be met. He had not sent Leatrice the date of his arrival, so how could she have possibly known?

Still, after an absence of nearly three years, it would have been comforting to discover a familiar face in the crowd. It would have been better yet if the Frenchwoman's parting words didn't haunt him day and night, refusing to give him a moment's peace.

It mattered not that she was wrong. A whole world of difference existed between want and desire. A man could desire something but not really want it; in fact, he could know better than to want it. Desire was a thing of momentary impulse. It knew no consequences. Wanting, on the other hand, left room for reason. And reason told him he should feel damn lucky to have what he already had. He'd be a fool to spoil it.

After a short walk through town from the wharf, Zeph approached Leatrice's house, where she lived with her mother, a sea captain's widow, and a white Persian cat. With his travel bag still in his hand, he wasn't certain just what he expected to find after a three-year absence. To his satisfaction, the same white picket fence, freshly painted, surrounded the front yard. The captain's walk on the rooftop was newly painted, too. The same white lace curtains fluttered in the front windows, which had been thrown open to allow the sea breeze freedom to invade the interior of the house. Zeph paused at the end of the front walk before opening the small gate, so he could take it all in and once again be grateful for what he had.

A feeling of familiarity flooded him. It was a good feeling, to be sure, comforting and yet . . .

"Zephiran Westley?" Leatrice's calm voice floated down from an open window on the second floor, as serene as the rhythm of his heart. "There you are."

He saw her then, standing in the window—tall, slender as a willow rod, her pale blond hair piled high atop her head, Grecian style, a beautiful woman by every standard of the day. She smiled down at him as if she had seen him only the day before and did not find his arrival at her door all that unexpected.

*Yes, here I am,* he thought, smiling back up at her.

"I'll be right down."

*And I'll be right here waiting, my dear, just as you always are.*

A few moments later, the front door swung open and Leatrice emerged, immaculately attired and groomed as always, dressed in a conservative light blue gown he did not remember. But it had been three years, he reminded himself. She came forward at a confident, stately pace, her hand outstretched in welcome as she stepped off the stoop.

He took that proffered hand, of course, across the low

fence that divided them, bringing it to his lips, brushing the knuckles lightly before releasing her fingers again.

"Zephiran, you should have let me know your arrival date. Had you, I would have met you," she admonished, pushing open the gate to allow him entrance. Most people would not have noted the barely discernible change of pitch, her voice indicating her disappointment. After so many years, he recognized it immediately.

"Sorry," he told her, smiling crookedly. "I wasn't sure myself when I would get here."

"I'm glad you came back safely." Her eyes, a blue that matched the paleness of her gown, settled on his face.

Again, he felt the calm familiarity flood through him.

"Did you ever doubt that I would?" he asked.

"No, of course not. Never. Come," she said, indicating the front porch with a sweep of her hand. "You must tell me all about your voyage."

"Leatrice," he murmured, impulsively reaching out and claiming her arm as she turned to go back into the house.

"What is it, Zeph?" Her brows knit together.

He stepped closer, dropped his satchel, and put his arms about her, overcome by the reckless, uncharacteristic urge to kiss her, then and there, in front of her house, in plain sight of the neighbors.

His intention must have shown on his face, for Leatrice matched his step in retreat.

"Captain Westley," she sighed in breathless surprise, her gentle gaze widening. She managed ever so gracefully to escape his embrace. "I think it best if we go inside."

Leatrice led the way. Retrieving his bag, Zeph followed. Once they stepped inside, she turned to face him.

"Now if you wish to kiss me," she declared, glancing about the small front foyer before turning her face up to his, "I have no objection." Leatrice closed her eyes in calm expectation, her lips puckered in a less than seductive manner.

Unfortunately, the spontaneity of the moment had already passed.

Perhaps that was for the best, Zeph thought as he lowered his mouth over hers, pressing his lips against hers only enough to qualify as a kiss.

"Welcome home, Zeph, darling," Leatrice whispered, her lashes lifting to expose the undisguised joy radiating from her eyes.

It struck him then as most odd that after nearly fifteen years with Leatrice, he had taken less liberties with her than he had with Malana in the few short months he had known the island girl.

Guiltily, Zeph put space between them, wondering, as Leatrice took his hand and led him into the front parlor, just how much he would tell her about his ill-fated voyage.

Probably the lack of familiarity was the only thing that restrained Malana's normally curious nature. Her first few days at the New England School of Female Advancement were paralyzing to say the least.

The girl forced to share a room with her never spoke unless prompted and warily eyed her from afar. As for the other students . . .

While their manners could not be faulted, Malana did not consider them overly friendly, either.

The food was awful, the rules impossible, the classes bewildering, if for no other reason than the fact that her reading and writing skills were basic at best.

Malana went to bed at night feeling lost, alone, and abandoned. Her sleep was fitful, her dreams filled with images of Zeph Westley, with the way she wished he would act toward her. Each morning she awoke feeling more exhausted and unhappy than she had the day before.

Her only reprieve came in the form of the few moments she spent alone in the small garden in back of the school building. From there she could watch the shoreline and the distant harbor, always managing to find temporary tranquillity. It was easy to pretend that she awaited Zeph's ship to enter the harbor, that he would, in truth, come back for her, as he had promised, if she was good and did what she was told.

She tried very hard to do that.

It was there in the garden that she met Amy Potter, a quiet, petite girl with hair so fair and wispy it almost looked white. A student also, Amy's passion was the rose conservatory that completed the arboretum, as the teachers called the intriguingly laid-out growing beds.

The friendship blossomed when Malana approached the girl and began asking questions about the beautiful, but fragile-looking, flowers she so carefully tended. Why were they grown in a house of glass instead of outside where it seemed, at least in Malana's opinion, they belonged?

"Where do you come from?" Amy asked in a pleasant voice, the first Malana had heard in days. "Apparently, not from around here."

"No, not from around here," Malana repeated, fearful of revealing her true origins. Fearful that the girl might ostracize her, as did the rest of the students, if she knew the truth.

Amy stood, dusting the particles of black soil from her gloved hands. "Malana Kilpatrick, isn't it?"

Malana nodded.

"Some of the other girls say you're a heathen. But I don't believe that. You seem civil enough to me, which is more than I can say about some of them."

They laughed together then, spontaneously, the first moment of joy Malana had experienced since her arrival, since her abrupt separation from Honoré.

By that afternoon, they had gone to the headmistress and asked to be roommates, a request Mrs. Honeywell had seemed more than happy to grant.

That evening, Malana sat at the foot of her new bed, feeling happy. Perhaps her time at the New England School of Female Advancement would not be so bad after all.

Over a dinner of hot, fresh baked bread, roast beef, and new potatoes, Zeph relayed the ending of his story to the two women, Leatrice and her mother, both who listened in rapt attention.

"And so, given no other choice, I enrolled the girl at the New England School of Female Advancement."

"Oh, Zephiran, I don't know," Leatrice instantly objected. "How very unsettling for the poor, dear child. So young and alone. Perhaps you should have given her a little more time to adjust to her new circumstances before shipping her off to school."

Leatrice's image of Malana was of his own making, of course. She thought the girl much younger than her actual age, which, if the truth be known, was something he tended to do as well. He hadn't really meant to deceive her, but now that it was done, Zeph couldn't foresee what actual harm it would do. At least not now. Malana was safely stashed away—out of sight and, he could only hope, out of mind.

"Letty, dear," Mrs. Whitaker interjected. "It is not your place to tell Captain Westley what he should and should not do." *But* you *should make it her place,* the old woman's steady gaze insisted as it swept over him critically.

"Let's not ruin our first night together worrying about Malana," he said. "Believe me, the girl is better off where she is than if I had left her to her fate or in the hands of her cousin, Niles."

"Of course, you are right," Leatrice conceded in that wonderful way she had that always smoothed an awkward moment and made him feel as if he could do no wrong. "What was I thinking? How very noble of you, Zeph, to accept responsibility for the child. How devastating for you to learn of Captain Kilpatrick's untimely demise. To think, Niles Kilpatrick's in charge of his estate now. I remember Niles. . . ." She shuddered. "A most insipid little man. Even his sister hadn't cared much for him when we were in school together."

"Letty! What an unkind thing to say," her mother chided.

"But accurate, Mrs. Whitaker," Zeph assured her. "His attitude toward the girl was anything but cousinly."

"Just how old did you say the child was?" the astute widow asked.

"I didn't say, Mrs. Whitaker," Zeph answered evasively. "Quite frankly, islanders do not keep track of time in the same matter that you and I do, ma'am, so there is no way of accounting for her exact age."

"I see."

Zeph suspected the wise old woman wasn't fooled, not for a moment. He also surmised she accepted, if not actually approved of, his manner of handling the situation and wouldn't say a word to Leatrice to the contrary.

"There's an afternoon social next Wednesday at Mrs. Leadbetter's," she continued. "How nice it would be if you would accompany Leatrice."

It was blackmail in its purest form. Her silence for his cooperation.

"Of course, Mrs. Whitaker. You will be joining us as well, won't you?"

"Why, how kind of you to ask, Captain Westley. I would be delighted." She stood then, her signal as chaperone that the evening was officially over.

"Then I'll be by for you ladies around two on Wednesday." Zeph scraped back his chair and stood, too.

Leatrice saw him to the door, her serene acceptance of her mother's authority, of her social standing and what it required, something that he could never hope to change. Not that he really wanted to. It kept her busy in his absence.

"Good evening, Leatrice," he murmured over the arc of her wrist as he kissed the back of her hand.

Once more Zeph vowed to marry her before he again headed out to sea.

Malana's amazing ability to remember word for word everything the teachers said got her through those initial few weeks of school. Then came the day of the first written examination.

She stared at the paper blankly, unable to comprehend fully the questions.

"I know the answers, Mrs. Honeywell," she declared a few minutes after she had turned in an empty test paper and had been sent to the headmistress, who demanded an explanation. "If only you would ask them to me aloud."

"Do you mean to say you have never learned to read or write?"

"Only a little," she confessed, feeling most inadequate.

"Just what does Captain Westley expect from us?" the woman mumbled under her breath, taking off her glasses and rubbing the frown that formed between her eyes. "A miracle?"

"Please, Mrs. Honeywell, do not tell Zephiran that I have failed," Malana pleaded. "I promise I will do better, if you will only give me the chance."

Perching her spectacles on the end of her nose, the headmistress proceeded to give Malana the test orally. She answered each question verbatim without stopping to consider her words.

"That's amazing, Miss Kilpatrick. Can you do that every time?"

Malana nodded.

"Very well, my dear. You have passed for the moment.

But I must consider the best way to resolve this problem in the future."

Confident that the matter would be handled appropriately, Malana made her way back to the classroom.

The morning of Mrs. Leadbetter's afternoon social, Zeph received his regular packet of mail. What was unusual about it was the letter from the headmistress of the New England School of Female Advancement.

"It has been brought to my attention that Miss Kilpatrick has only a limited ability to read and write," she wrote. "Quite frankly, these are skills we assume our students have already perfected before enrolling in our prestigious academy. It is unfair to expect us to make an exception in Miss Kilpatrick's case."

"Unfair or unprofitable?" Zeph asked aloud, even though the room was empty.

Withdrawing from his safe a sum more considerable than necessary, he sat back down, picked up a pen, and wrote Mrs. Honeywell a note in return.

"With the enclosed, secure the girl a tutor. I think you will find she learns quickly."

Zeph placed the money inside the folds of the letter before sealing the envelope and sending it out in the afternoon mail. Most importantly, Malana appeared to be behaving, he thought with relief as he called for his carriage to be brought around front. He knew from personal experience just how hard it could be to do what others expected of you.

With the *Dolphin* put in dry dock for scraping and major repairs, what choice did he have? He would be moored for some time to come and could only make the best of the situation.

In the meantime, whether he particularly wanted to or

not, he had an afternoon social to attend with Leatrice and her mother.

In no time at all, Malana honed her reading and writing skills and began to understand the hierarchy of school life. She didn't much care for it and might have balked, if not for the bargain she had struck with Zeph. First, there were those girls of superior social entitlement, as Amy explained, who were at the top. Everyone acknowledged their leadership and strived to be accepted by them.

Then there were the hangers-on—another of Amy's terms. While socially acceptable, they moved just outside the popularity circle and would do almost anything to gain entrance. They were usually the most determined and cruel among the students, the ones who gave Malana the most difficulty.

Unfortunately, the remaining few girls, including Malana and Amy, fell into the last and, undoubtedly, least desirable group. Each outcast was so labeled for her individualism. Malana, because she was obviously not a New Englander and sometimes indulged in strange practices. Amy's ostracism stemmed from the fact that she was not a Protestant.

"I do not understand," Malana persisted. "You believe in the same God as they do, yet they do not accept you for religious reasons?"

Indeed, *haole* were strange people, their ways very difficult to understand. Then she thought of her mother and how Le'utu had hidden her religious beliefs from the other islanders. While accepting her lot that taboos existed in every culture and must be adhered to, Malana was not one to stand by forever and see her friends unjustly mistreated.

Inspiration came in the form of an unexpected visitor.

"Honoré," she cried, spying her long-lost friend and

confidante sitting in the small parlor where the students received occasional guests.

The Frenchwoman came forward, took Malana into her arms, and hugged her with genuine affection. Then she led her to the grouping of chairs, sat her down, and cupped her face with warm hands, studying it for a long time.

"Oh, Honoré. I have thought so much about you. How you were doing. Where you had gone."

"I am right here in Providence, *cherie*, and I am doing just fine. I have found a job as a lady's maid. My mistress demands little of me except zat I keep her looking stylish and ornament her entourage. Being French is very popular among ze Americans. But enough of me. How are you?"

Malana put on her bravest face, not wishing to worry her friend. "Being anything but a New Englander has made me anything but popular."

"I see. Zen you are not happy, *cherie*," Honoré stated matter-of-factly.

Malana merely shrugged.

"Has *Capitaine* Westley been to see you?"

She shook her head and held back a tear that threatened to well. "I do not expect him."

"Still, you look for him, no?"

"Every day," she confessed, the misery she felt finally bubbling to the surface.

"My poor *cherie*," Honoré consoled, taking her hand and patting it with familiarity. "And what of your studies?" she asked after a long silence.

"They go well enough."

"And friends? Have you made many?"

"Some."

It all came pouring out then. Her unhappiness, her frustration. The feelings of injustice—not so much for herself as for Amy—that gnawed at her, that demanded satisfaction.

Smiling, Honoré clucked her tongue. "I remember

school, *cherie,* and people just like ze little witches you describe. Perhaps you should do what I did." She smiled in a way Malana instantly recognized. "Let's give zem a dose of zeir own bitter medicine."

Zeph was at the dock, fortunately having escaped yet another boring afternoon of socializing with the ladies of Mystic. He used the excuse that he needed to supervise the launching of the newly painted *Dolphin.* While at the wharves, he happened to spy the mail packet as it entered the harbor.

He sent Danny, the only member of the crew besides Mr. Kennedy to remain on the ship's payroll, to intercept any incoming correspondence he might receive. More importantly, Zeph asked the cabin boy to post a response to a New York perfumer for an extremely lucrative offer to purchase the precious ambergris collected on the previous voyage. Once that sell was handled, hopefully, few obstacles and obligations would remain to keep him ashore.

Plans were already in the making for Mr. Kennedy, the first mate, to assemble a new, hand-selected crew. No more Jake Ainsworths, if it could be avoided. Regardless, as soon as he married Leatrice, Zeph intended to embark on another voyage, to be out to sea where no one challenged his authority, his right to do whatever he pleased whenever he wished.

By the time Danny returned with the mail, the *Dolphin* was once again afloat. Her clean, sleek lines beckoned to him in a way no woman could, Zeph assured himself.

He accepted the small postal packet with little interest and, without perusing it, tucked it into the inner pocket of his pea jacket to sort later.

"There's a letter from Miss Malana," the boy informed him.

"Malana?" Zeph asked, reaching once more into his pocket. "How do you know that?" he demanded.

"'Cause it's addressed from that fancy school you sent her to," the boy responded sheepishly.

Pulling out the letter in question, Zeph tore open the envelope and read the short note from Mrs. Honeywell.

"Damn," he muttered, folding up the page and stuffing it into his pocket, knowing this time he would have to dig deep into the profits of the ambergris sale to soothe the headmistress's ruffled feathers.

Did the satisfaction of getting revenge truly outweigh the possible consequences?

Malana had more than sufficient time to contemplate that question as she sat in the forced confinement of her room. Then there was Amy's morose silence. It offered little in the way of comfort.

"Honestly, how bad can it be?" Malana asked, watching her friend's halfhearted attempt to appear busy.

The girl paused just long enough for a look of panic to develop in her usually serene eyes.

Mrs. Honeywell's curt summons to come immediately to her office left little doubt as to the seriousness of the situation. Although the other students would no longer harass them, Malana realized she had made a terrible mistake. Her only consolation was that while she might never have the opportunity to benefit from her reckless actions, Amy would.

Malana's knees fairly shook beneath the concealment of her skirt as she slowly made her way to what she assumed would be her immediate dismissal.

Would Zeph be there?

The possibility offered the only glimmer of hope ... very brief glimmer indeed.

If he did come, he would be in anything but a receptive mood. He would be furious.

What he would do with her then? That was anyone's guess.

To her surprise and relief, when she was ushered into the headmistress's office, Malana found they were alone. She sat when told to do so.

Mrs. Honeywell drummed her fingers on her desk and stared across its width at Malana. Her irritation was transparent and quite terrible to behold.

"Miss Kilpatrick, I hope you have had sufficient time to contemplate the error of your ways."

"Oh, yes, Mrs. Honeywell," Malana replied breathlessly, clinging to the tiniest spark of hope because Zeph was not there. Surely, the headmistress would never allow one of her students to be unceremoniously tossed out into the streets. Surely, Zeph would never permit that to happen to her.

Or would he?

"What you did, Miss Kilpatrick, deserves immediate expulsion."

"Yes, ma'am," Malana answered, biting back the urge to justify her actions.

In truth, what she had done was to turn the tables on Miss Cirilla Van Haussen, pulling the arrogant girl down a notch in status, which she richly deserved. Cirilla went out of her way to make life miserable for unpopular students like Malana and Amy. She teased them, taunted them, made them the laughingstock of the school whenever she could, always careful never to leave evidence of her cruelty that could be presented to the faculty.

Unfortunately, still a novice at school pranks, Malana forgot to take every necessary precaution. While the bucket she used came from the arboretum, where anyone could have gotten it, and the green dye from Honoré, an untraceable outside source, she made the mistake of spilling a little on herself while securing the filled pail above the bathroom door after Cirilla had entered for her evening ablutions.

From around the corner, Malana and Amy had watched as the unsuspecting student had pushed open the door, dislodging the overhead bucket of green dye. It landed on her head, dousing her pale blond hair thoroughly, then running in streaks down her equally pale face. It would be weeks before the dye faded from her skin and even longer from her hair.

Meanwhile, Cirilla Van Haussen gave no one further trouble. In fact, it seemed that the other students thought she had gotten her due. Overnight, Malana became the hero of the moment, when rumor confirmed the prank had been her idea. Everyone wanted to be her friend.

Such instant popularity might have easily puffed up another's sense of importance, but not so Malana. Graciously, she accepted her new status, while not taking advantage of it. She even attempted to reconcile with Cirilla, but the humiliated girl declared that as soon as she could prove Malana the culprit, she would see her expelled.

Predictably, Malana's victory was short-lived. The school laundress discovered the telltale green stain on Malana's clothing and brought it to the attention of the headmistress.

"Under normal circumstances, Miss Kilpatrick, that is exactly what I would do," Mrs. Honeywell declared, reminding Malana just where she was and how much trouble she was in. "Expel you."

Uncertain why she had been spared, Malana did not question Mrs. Honeywell's decision to let the matter drop nor the motivation behind it. All she knew was that she still had a chance to do what Zeph demanded of her. If she were lucky, he would never know what she had done.

On the heels of her miraculous reprieve, Malana vowed then and there to stay out of trouble, just as she had promised Zeph. Otherwise, he might never come back for her.

Popularity proved an overwhelming responsibility, however, one she took seriously. At first, in little ways, she found herself compromising her resolution to "be good" by the very difficult standards set by Zeph.

A discussion of what it was like to live on a tropical island led to her giving a demonstration of the sensual island dances. By the time she was done, many of the girls had stripped to their chemises and were dancing along with her. Afterwards, she realized such behavior might well have gotten her into trouble again. She would not repeat her mistake.

Curiosity germinates in fertile, misinformed minds, however.

"Is it really true that South Sea islanders run around naked all the time doing the unmentionable?" one of the girls asked her as they sat around on their beds before curfew one night.

"Unmentionable?" she asked. "What is that?"

No one seemed willing to explain. Then Amy bent and whispered in her ear. "You know. Fornication."

Now that was a word she had heard often enough from the missionary who had come to Hitihiti.

"Is that what you all think?" she demanded, staring at each of her new friends in turn.

"Well, that's what I've always been told," another girl piped up, defending what was apparently an unanimous misconception.

"Then you were told wrong," Malana explained, trying to conceal her agitation. "It is true our clothing is less concealing, but by no means do we go naked, at least not all of the time."

That prompted giggles.

"As for the unmentionable," she went on to explain,

carried away by personal indignation, "that is something I have never done."

It was a confession of sorts, she supposed, one about which she had mixed feelings. It seemed *haole* valued a lack of knowledge of what happened between men and women. But why? Why when it was the most natural thing in the world?

"What does it feel like to be totally naked?" a quiet voice spoke out, breaking into her confusion of thoughts.

The titters melted away, replaced with earnest looks.

"Have none of you ever been naked?" Malana asked in amazement.

It seemed that they had not. Even when bathing—which *haole* did very rarely, as far as she was concerned—women did not take off their chemises. As for the men . . .

Did Zeph leave on his underclothing, too?

*How preposterous,* Malana thought, realizing more than ever how very different she was from those around her, including Zeph. No wonder he had chosen to put her away in a school where he did not have to face those differences.

And so it was that, two nights later, Malana stood at her self-assigned post in the garden, staring out over the shoreline just beyond the school's high wall. A full moon beckoned, a white, living light of beauty and promise that cast its magic over the beach, the water, and her lost soul, so far from home and family and everything familiar. She could no longer resist the need to remember, to touch again and be touched by that part of her that would forever be Hitihitian.

"Where are you going?" Amy asked when they met in the hallway as Malana was heading to the front door, the only way out of the school.

"To cleanse my body and soul," Malana announced, almost in a trance, not bothering to stop until she reached the outer door. She turned, discovering to her surprise, that she had a following.

She did not exactly invite the others to join her, but then she did not discourage them, either, when they trailed out the door after her. As she descended the sharp incline that led down to the beach, she began stripping off her clothes, article by article, uncaring what anyone saw or thought.

By the time she reached the water's edge, Malana stood in the moonlight, naked and free.

When the water began to swirl about her bare knees, she realized the other girls had mimicked her every action. But while she stood unabashed, they seemed so unsure.

Every woman should be proud of who and what she was. She told them so.

Bending, Malana, dipped her hand in the water and splashed Amy. Soon enough, they were all doing so, their nakedness forgotten. They frolicked and laughed in such a carefree way that she knew she had done them no harm. Finally, tired and battered by the waves and the cool water, they began to emerge one by one.

Malana saw the swinging white light coming down the hill, but at first she did not think much of it. Exhausted yet feeling exhilarated from her long solo swim, she threaded through the water, moving toward the beacon. Then several of the other girls already onshore began to squeal and scream, and she knew.

They had been caught.

With the dignity and grace of her royal breeding, she forged on. What else could she do? She emerged from the water, unabashed and proud, beads of saltwater streaming from her golden skin and ebony hair.

"Miss Kilpatrick!"

It was Mrs. Honeywell's dreaded voice, of course. The beam of light from the lantern she carried framed the headmistress's face, contorted in horror and disbelief. Beside her stood Cirilla Van Haussen, a victorious smirk on her stained face that looked greener than usual in the yellow lantern light.

Malana made no protest as a scratchy blanket was tossed about her shoulders and, along with the others, she was marched back up the hill to stand dripping and shivering in the front hall of the school.

"This time, Miss Kilpatrick," the headmistress announced with finality, "you have gone too far."

Zeph received the third letter from Mrs. Honeywell while having a quiet private luncheon in the garden with Leatrice, a rare event these days, it seemed. Of late, old Mrs. Whitaker tagged along wherever they went. Not wishing to spoil the perfect tranquillity of the afternoon, he slipped the envelope beneath his plate and groaned inwardly, having always heard that three was invariably the charmer.

Just how much was this one going to cost him?

"Isn't that a letter from the school?" Leatrice asked sweetly.

"Yes," he answered, not wanting to explain further since he had told his fiancée nothing of the problems he had had to deal with thus far because of Malana.

"Don't you think you should open it?" she insisted with that unflappable logic of hers.

"No," he muttered curtly.

"But it might be important," she persisted. "No doubt the girl received some kind of special recognition for Mrs. Honeywell to correspond with you."

He should be so lucky.

"How thoughtless of you, Zephiran. Here. Give it to me," she offered in obvious exasperation, reaching out to accept the envelope. "I'll do the honors."

*Damn it all to hell,* he thought, his anger at being constantly defied and prodded by women causing him to tear the letter nearly in half as he ripped open the envelope.

"Dear Captain Westley," the letter read. "No amount of money could possibly make me change my mind this time, so do not bother to send it. Instead, come and get your ward immediately. Believe me, I have more than valid reasons for my decision, much too horrid to express herein."

"What is it, Zephiran?" Leatrice asked breathlessly when he frowned darkly. "Has something terrible happened to the poor, dear child?"

"How much better for her if it had," he grumbled, crumpling the accursed letter in his fist.

"Zeph," she admonished. "Now, what kind of attitude is that for a responsible guardian to take?"

"One whose ward is . . ." He groped for an acceptable word to use around a lady, but could find none appropriate to describe Malana Kilpatrick. "One whose ward is a bitch," he declared, slamming his fist against the tabletop.

"Zephiran Westley!" Aghast, Leatrice jumped up out of her chair at his uncustomary show of crassness and temper. "I'll have none of that."

Zeph looked up at her and realized then that after nearly fifteen years together, this was his first show of temper around her. Ironically, it was over a chit of a girl who had made him question every aspect of his life, including his relationship with the woman who defended her.

"Leatrice, I am sorry," he offered, uncertain in his heart just what it was he apologized for—his uncalled-for outburst, or the feelings of confusion churning up the heretofore untouched sanctuary he called his honor?

If Malana was allowed to come here to Mystic, to live in his home, how could he hope ever to resist her? And even if he did, he would be no better than any other lecherous man lusting in his heart after a young girl.

"I accept your apology, Zeph," she said, sitting back down. "Now, tell me what has happened." She reached out and covered his fisted hand with her own. "Or must I read it for myself?"

The less Leatrice knew about his desperate measures, the better for her, Zeph convinced himself.

"After only eight months, it seems Malana has been expelled from the New England School of Female Advancement," he confessed.

"Oh. Oh, my!" Leatrice sighed, sitting back in her chair. "Poor child. No doubt, the stress of adjustment must have simply been too much for her. You must go and get her right away, Zeph. Bring her home. We can take care of her," she pleaded nobly.

"Leatrice, I don't think that is the best thing to do," he warned, feeling anything but noble himself.

"What else can you do?" she insisted.

What else, indeed? To attempt to send Malana to another school would be useless. It would only be a matter of time before she got into trouble there as well.

He looked across the table at Leatrice. She was right, of course. With her help and perhaps that of one other, he could manage to keep his unsavory thoughts under control.

"Very well, Leatrice. That's what we'll do. But first," he said, turning over his hand to encompass hers, "let's finish our meal together in peace."

He suspected it would be the last peace he would have for quite a while.

# Chapter Twelve

Only Zeph's unrelenting silence dampened Malana's joy to be reunited with him. On the trip to Mystic, they never discussed the reason for her dismissal from the New England School of Female Advancement. She suspected Mrs. Honeywell had told him everything in detail however. As much as she wanted to explain her actions, Malana wisely held back, thinking once they reached his home and he came to realize how happy she could make him, Zeph would be more inclined to listen to what she had to say.

In time, he might even agree that her departure from school had not been such a bad thing after all.

Meanwhile, she could only wait patiently, watch Zeph from a distance for a sign, and hope fervently for a reprieve, even a small one.

From the harbor Mystic proved to be much the same as the other *haole* communities she had observed thus far. Debris-littered beaches stretched as far as the eye could see. Ships sailed constantly in and out of the crowded wharves. The dipping and bobbing jungle of masts seemed impenetrable. Still, Malana recognized Zeph's ship the moment she spied it.

"Oh, look, Zephiran. The *Dolphin,*" she cried, pointing it out as they sailing past, hoping to draw him into conversation.

"Amazing that you can remember some things, even if the rules of conduct are not among them."

His curtness did not bother her that much. All that mattered was that she was here in Mystic at last, alone with Zeph.

She saw the woman waving then. The green hue of her gown struck Malana as a color she would someday like to wear. Thinking nothing of her actions, she lifted her hand and waved back. Then she lost sight of the figure in the crowd and turned her attention to Zeph.

Was it just her imagination, or did it seem as if he had seen someone he knew?

She focused on the people on the pier. Wouldn't it be ironic if Zeph knew the woman in green?

Malana brushed aside such a ludicrous thought and, on impulse, threaded her arm through Zeph's, staring up at him, overwhelmed by euphoric feeling of well-being.

He did not rebuke her, although he did not exactly acknowledge her, either. His arm tightened on her hand, but then he pulled her along the rail toward the gangplank without proper consideration, practically dragging her through the crowd of passengers starting to disembark.

"Zephiran. Zephiran Westley. Here I am," called a voice lyrical with excitement. A female voice.

Frowning, Malana glanced about, looking for the source. Why would another female seek out *her* Zeph? Her eyes lit upon the green-clad figure she had seen earlier. Why, the woman was waving, just as she had before, and coming right toward them.

"Leatrice." In response, Zeph moved forward. If Malana had not clung to his arm, he might well have left her behind.

Words could not begin to describe that initial meeting on the docks of Mystic. Instinctively, Malana knew she confronted a rival. The hairs on her arms bristled; her hand tightened possessively on Zeph's coat sleeve. The woman he called Leatrice stared back, her benevolent gaze turning civilly wary as she looked at Malana. Then, unbelievably, her eyes focused on Zeph as if she owned him.

"Who is this, Zeph?" The lyrical quality remained in the woman's voice, even if it was a little less benign. "Where is the girl, Malana?"

"I am Malana Kilpatrick," Malana retorted defensively, latching even tighter on to Zeph's arm. "Zephiran, who is this?" she demanded, mimicking the indignant quality in her adversary's voice.

The woman did not direct her response to Malana. Instead, she looked askance at Zeph. "Pray do tell. Just who am I?" she asked.

"Leatrice, let me explain," he said, stepping forward, attempting to shake free of Malana's clutch.

But she was not about to let go. Not so he could go after some other woman. Besides, this woman called Leatrice was not listening anyway. She had turned and started to walk away.

*Good riddance,* Malana thought.

"Leatrice, wait," he called after her, much to Malana's dismay.

"Let her go, Zephiran," Malana urged.

He shook her off then, with one great thrust of his arm.

"Stay here, girl, and don't you dare move an inch," he commanded, waving a warning finger under her nose as if she were a mindless child.

Which is exactly how he saw her, she reminded herself in frustration. A mindless child. A burden.

"For once in your life, do as I say, or I swear to God, Malana, you will live to regret it," he persisted.

Momentarily cowed, she nodded.

Then he took off, following after the woman in green.

Suddenly feeling very alone and vulnerable standing on the bustling pier, Malana glanced around at her unfamiliar surroundings. Just where did he think she could go in a strange place where she knew no one but him?

It struck her then that she would be lucky indeed if he did not decide to abandon her here, confused and penniless, never to return.

"Leatrice, wait," Zeph called out again to his fiancée's quickly retreating figure. Catching up with her, he grabbed her arm, urging her to look at him. "Please."

"Pray tell. Why should I, Zeph Westley? I trusted you," she choked, staring down at his restraining hand as if willing it and him away. "You told me she was just a child."

"She is a child," he defended. Nonetheless, he let her go. What else could he do? After all, Leatrice was a lady who expected, who *deserved* to be treated like one, not to be manhandled like some dockside whore. Perhaps she deserved much better than he could offer her.

"Then I think you should take a closer look." She glared at him in accusation. "Then again, maybe you'd better not." Her expression took on an air of hurt and mistrust. "Maybe you already have."

As hard as he tried to deny it, to block the unbidden images from his mind, all he could think of was how Malana had looked lying half naked beneath him that last day before he had wisely sequestered her in school. It had been for his own sake, he admitted freely, his and Leatrice's, that he had not brought the girl home in the first place. Did he dare admit that to Leatrice?

Would she believe him if he told her it had meant nothing? Could he convince her when he couldn't convince himself?

So what could he say to her that would make her understand? Or if not understand, at least forgive him and trust him again?

Zeph looked into her disillusioned eyes and knew what it would take. He would ask her again to marry him, then and there. Tomorrow.

He formed the appropriate response, ignoring the impulsiveness of it, an event she had awaited a long time and deserved. . . .

But the words simply refused to come out.

Damn it. What was wrong with him? Why couldn't he simply accept what he knew to be best for him?

His reasons had nothing to do with either Leatrice or Malana, yet had everything to do with both of them—or at least with what each represented in his mind.

His freedom to choose. To make the sensible, correct choice between what he had always taken for granted and what temptation dangled before him. It took courage and discipline to follow the path of honor. Courage and discipline—the very foundations of which he had always thought ruled his life. Zeph had accepted the fact that wanting less meant attaining even more in the long run.

Even so, he couldn't bring himself to make the commitment to Leatrice that he should have made a long time ago.

"Can't we discuss this later?" he asked instead.

Leatrice looked at him then, her great blue eyes brimming with her own unfulfilled longing.

"All right, Zeph. We can talk later, if that is what you wish."

He watched her walk away then, climb into her waiting carriage, and drive away without looking back. A great part of who he was went with her, yet Zeph did nothing to stop Leatrice or the loss of his identity.

The house Zeph lived in looked nothing at all like Malana expected. Modest in comparison to her father's house, it nonetheless made an impression with its picket fence and its great height towering over the beach not far away. From the front steps she could hear the familiar ocean sounds, the plaintive cries of the shorebirds that ran up and down the beach. To the left she could see the harbor, could even pick out the tall, naked mast of what she was certain must be the *Dolphin*.

She thought to point it out to him, then thought better of the idea, remembering only too well the sting of his curt remark at the docks when she had attempted to impress him with her observation.

"You have a nice house," Malana commented instead, smiling brightly. "I like it."

"That's good, I suppose. But then it wouldn't matter that much if you didn't." He led her inside, carrying her assortment of luggage himself.

She stood in the front hall, staring up the main staircase to the floor above. To think, just one person lived here.

That is, until now, she reminded herself. Now there were two of them. She and Zeph, alone.

With an assortment of noise, Zeph deposited her baggage at the foot of the stairs.

"Are you hungry, girl?" he asked.

In truth she was starving, but Malana shook her head, not wanting to give him any reason to leave her again.

"Are you sure? I could have Mrs. Fillmore make you something."

"No. I prefer to wait until you eat." *Who is Mrs. Fillmore?* she wanted to ask, but restrained her curiosity, knowing she would find out soon enough.

"Very well, then. If that is what you wish." He frowned, however, as if finding her refusal unacceptable.

They stood there for a moment, Malana with her back to the stairs, staring awkwardly at each other.

"Are you going to show me my room?" she asked.

"Your room? Yes, of course," he replied, yet he looked around as if in desperation. "Ah, there you are," he said to someone behind her on the stairs.

Mrs. Fillmore, no doubt, Malana decided, turning to discover a familiar figure coming toward her.

"Honoré!" she cried. Forgetting everything else for the moment, she raced halfway up the stairs to meet her friend.

"It's so good to see you again, *cherie.*"

"We are home," Malana whispered, falling into Honoré's welcoming arms. "Can you believe it, Honoré? We have at last made it home."

*"Oui, cherie,"* the Frenchwoman replied laughingly. "And we have *Capitaine* Westley to zank for it."

"Zeph," Malana blurted out, turning on the landing to express her gratitude, finally realizing that no matter his gruff exterior, he did care about her.

But the foyer below was empty. Once again, he had planned well and had managed to escape her.

Not bothering to change out of his traveling clothes, Zeph made his way back to the docks. There he sought out the *Dolphin* and Mr. Kennedy, anxious to check out the progress of acquiring a new crew in his absence.

The ship sat idle in its slip, looking as if it had suddenly been abandoned. Sails were only partially mended. Ropes, still in need of repair, were strewn about the deck, which in itself was in need of a good swabbing. These were all chores he'd expected to find completed upon his return. To his dismay, Zeph found his first officer alone, 'tween decks, inspecting the harpoons and other equipment with a critical eye.

"Mr. Kennedy, where in the blazes is the new crew?" he demanded, nonplussed at the lack of activity on what should have been a busy whaling ship preparing to set sail in the next few weeks.

"Ain't my fault, Cap'n," the first officer declared, looking up guiltily from his task of sharpening a dull spearhead. "We had a fine crew. Everything was going along on schedule. Then one of the men found something in the forecastle that got them all mighty upset. Like wharf rats, they abandon ship."

"What did they find that was so disturbing, Mr. Kennedy? The ship itself is sound."

"Aye, Cap'n, she's sound enough, but the men got in their heads she's cursed."

"Cursed? What nonsense is this?" Zeph demanded.

"I'll show ya." Setting down the harpoon, Mr. Kennedy stepped in front of him and led the way to the forecastle.

The neat rows of berths had been just as hastily abandoned as the work topside. In one of them a stone statue, crudely carved, lay on its side, its blank, leering eye sockets staring straight at Zeph.

"Is this the culprit?" he asked, walking over to the toppled figurine. It looked harmless enough. He picked it up, finding the stone heavy and cold, and turned it over in his hands, inspecting the squatty grotesqueness. "The image of some island god, I would say," he offered offhandedly. "One of the men must have picked it up off a beach."

"Not likely, sir. More likely it was lifted from some native god-house. "See this," he said, turning the stone over in Zeph's hand and pointing out the large indent in the middle of its belly.

"Looks as if it might have once had something embedded in its navel."

"Aye, Cap'n. Most likely a pearl the size of a robin's egg. The eyes as well. My guess is that it's Hitihitian, probably a statue of Te Tuma, the god—"

"—of the volcano," Zeph completed the other man's sentence. "I'm very familiar with him." At the sound of the cursed name, the same one Malana had called him when he had rescued her, Zeph clutched the stone figure a little tighter, remembering only too well the place where he had found Malana. It had contained dozens of such figures. He could swear that it grew warm to the touch, issuing strange pulsations that tingled the palms of his hands.

"A gem that size would be worth a fortune," he murmured. Unnerved by the strange sensations that increased by the second, Zeph set the statue down.

"Aye, and the thief would be a wealthy man."

"Or a cursed one," Zeph added, beginning to understand what might have driven his new crew away. Sailors, one and all, were notoriously superstitious. "Along with the ship to harbor the unsuspecting looter. Who do you think it was?"

"Could have been any of the men, sir." Mr. Kennedy shrugged. "Suppose, only time with tell."

"If we're lucky we'll never know, Mr. Kennedy." Zeph turned to face his first officer, in his own mind such superstition an annoyance at best. "Regardless, we must find us a new crew."

"Believe me, sir, I have tried. I put out the word, but it seems every man in Mystic worth his salt has a good berth already."

"One they consider safe, you mean."

"Aye, sir."

"I see." Zeph sat down on one of the hard berths and again picked up the stone image. He ran his thumb over the spot where one of the pearls had been. "Put the word out up and down the Sound. Tell them Captain Westley of the *Dolphin* is willing to pay double for only the best and the bravest New England has to offer."

"Aye, sir. It might work, but it might take a while. I'll see to it personally first thing tomorrow morning." Mr. Kennedy stood.

Zeph offered him the stone figure.

The sailor lifted his hand and backed away.

"Find us a decent crew, Mr. Kennedy, and I'll double your salary, too," Zeph proposed, suddenly aware that he might even lose his loyal first officer if the stigma of a cursed ship grew any stronger.

The mate turned to Zeph. "Thank you, sir. You can rest at night knowing I'll get us a crew even if I have to go to hell to find it."

Zeph looked back down at the statue. Hell might be the only place to find one, he reasoned.


With great care, Malana dressed for dinner that night, one she planned on sharing with Zephiran. The bright yellow of her gown was striking to say the least, contrasting with the darkness of her hair and eyes. She looked like a delicate songbird, or so Honoré assured her.

"*Capitaine* Westley will no doubt be duly impressed."

Through the Frenchwoman's quizzing of Mrs. Fillmore, the housekeeper, they discovered that the customary time for the evening meal was six o'clock. When the timepiece in the foyer below gonged the appointed hour, Malana carefully made her way downstairs. Anticipation churned

her stomach in such a knot that even if her life depended
on it, she could not have eaten.

In the quiet of the elegant dining room, she waited alone
for Zeph's appearance, her head bent, her hands folded
quietly in her lap. The only movement in the room was
the swaying of the lit tapers in the candelabrum that graced
the center of the table. Regardless of her outward calm,
Malana's heart pounded wildly, adding to her inner turmoil.

Then the door swung open. Her head popped up, her
eyes fastening on the activity there, thinking at last Zeph
joined her.

Instead, Mrs. Fillmore entered and began, in silence, to
serve her.

"I want to wait for Captain Westley," Malana announced
definitively.

"As you wish, miss."

Going in and out of the room several times, the housekeeper finished her task of laying out an assortment of
tureens, platters, and bowls on the sideboard, then simply
disappeared.

Uncertain just what to expect, Malana sat there, staring
at the squeaking, swinging door until it settled on its
hinges.

The candles burned halfway down and the food grew
cold before she finally accepted the truth. Zeph was not
coming.

Tears of disappointment brimmed in her eyes. Valiantly,
she fought to check them amidst the battle she waged with
her turbulent emotions. As much as Zeph's callous action
hurt her, she knew in her heart it was not his intention to
cause her pain. Yet, for reasons she couldn't comprehend,
he refused to accept what she considered inevitable, what
fate had decided was best for both of them. This was one
of the valid lessons island life had taught her, in which she

continued to believe. Once destiny had set its course, there was little point in resisting it.

In that way, Zeph had much to learn. If he would only give her the chance, she would gladly show him how to be free.

She was who she was and where she was now because of Zephiran Westley. In turn, he had become an intricate part of her existence, a part she couldn't imagine being without. Like the brightest beacon in the darkness, he always guided her through the most violent storms. He was, and would always remain, her strength, her calm, her faith. Somehow she must continue to hold on to that truth until he learned to trust her in return.

With dignity, she pushed back her chair, rose, and stumbled blindly from the dining room. Upstairs, she fell into the Frenchwoman's sympathetic arms.

"Oh, Honoré, how can I ever hope to make him love me?" Malana cried in frustration.

"Ssh, ssh, *cherie*," the Frenchwoman comforted in a soothing voice, rocking Malana gently until she had no more tears to shed. "Believe me, he already does," she insisted, patting Malana's head pressed against her bosom. "Stubborn man. He's just too set in his ways to see ze truth."

"Is there no way to show it to him?"

"Maybe zere is," Honoré murmured.

Malana looked up with renewed hope.

"I think I know exactly how to make *Monsieur Capitaine* Westley see ze error of his ways. Here is exactly what we must do."

Zeph made it a point to arrive home late that evening, long after everyone would be asleep. It was something he would do every night if he had to.

Avoidance. On one hand, he considered his actions honorable. On the other . . . well, he suspected they would be labeled thoughtless and cowardly.

Perhaps. But then, gallant heroics had never been his particular forte. It was what had gotten him into this mess in the first place.

Jerking the haphazard knot from his cravat, he made his way to the sideboard in the small office he kept but rarely used, preferring to conduct business from his cabin aboard the *Dolphin*. Drink was not a vice that usually attracted him, but tonight he needed a good stiff one.

The bottle of cognac he found lying on its side in the back of the cabinet had an impressive layer of dust on it. Blowing it clean, he uncorked it and poured himself three fingers. Then he settled in the leather chair by the window and closed his eyes, gulping down half the glass.

The burn of the brandy sliding down his parched throat was real, a reminder that a decision, once made, had to be followed through.

He would talk to Leatrice tomorrow. Zeph could only hope she would accept his explanation. He intended to be more truthful with her than perhaps was wise. But then he had never claimed to be wise, only honest.

*"Capitaine* Westley." The summons came on the heels of a decisive knock on the closed door of his study.

He swallowed down a groan with the rest of the brandy in his glass. Whatever happened to women and their supposed beauty sleep?

"Come back tomorrow," he growled.

*"Non, non, Capitaine* Westley. We must speak tonight."

"Then talk, Miss de Magney," he said, not bothering to get up from his chair and answer the Frenchwoman's call face to face. Instead, he poured himself another glass of blissful forgetfulness and settled in to drink it.

He was not in the least prepared for the whirlwind that swept into the room, invading his domain and upsetting his plans to get rip-roaring drunk. Nonetheless, his foul mood fortified, Zeph rose to meet the storm and its source with the fortitude of his calling.

"Presumptuous wench," he declared in his most captainlike voice, quaffing the amber liquor. "Like all women," he muttered under his breath, slamming the glass down on the edge of the desk. "No one invited you to come in."

"Zat is true, *monsieur*. Nonetheless, you must deal with me, just as you must eventually deal with yourself."

Uncertain just what she meant, he lifted one brow.

"I want to know what your intentions are, *Monsieur Capitaine*, regarding Malana."

"My intentions? Just who do you think you are to make such demands of me? Surely not her mother." At that, he laughed and turned away. "God knows I've had to deal with enough of them lately."

"Like every woman, Malana is entitled to a proper life." Fists on her hips, the Frenchwoman pursued him across the room like an unfavorable wind.

"We'll discuss her womanly entitlements when she's grown up, by damn, and learns to act properly. And not before." Refusing to acknowledge that the impertinent female, a servant no less, stood right behind him making demands, he refilled his glass to the rim.

"She is a woman, *monsieur!*" she exclaimed. "In every way, as you well know."

"No, she is not!" Gritting his teeth, Zeph held his ground. He'd be hanged if he'd give credence to such nonsense. "She is just a child," he insisted.

"If zat is true, zen what does zat make you, *Capitaine?*"

The accusation stung, and rightfully so.

"Get out." He turned so suddenly and furiously that the brandy in his glass sloshed over his hand, running down his wrist and staining his shirtsleeve. Most would have been cowed by his black, threatening look.

Not so Honoré de Magney. She stared back at him,

daring him, making him face what he had refused to see from the moment he had set eyes on Malana Kilpatrick. Call her what he would for whatever his reasons might be, noble or not, he wanted her as a man wanted a woman.

What a mistake he had made by allowing the ungrateful Frenchwoman to come here, to live in his home, to claim privileges far above her station. He should have left her to rot in the hire of that ancient hag in Providence, who constantly demanded to be made to look young and beautiful, a feat beyond even Miss de Magney's many talents. Well, he would not be intimidated by her bluster or insinuations, no matter how much truth they might hold.

"Good night, Miss de Magney," he announced calmly, tossing back the last of the cognac remaining in his glass.

"Tell me zis, *monsieur*. Who are you to decide what is right for Malana? Her guardian or her owner?" she demanded in a voice so quiet and dignified, he had to strain to hear what she said. Yet it afflicted him deeper than had she lashed out in anger.

Zeph swallowed the mouthful of burning liquor, the hot stab of guilt that caught in his throat a much more bitter dose of reality to assimilate. He felt as trapped and floundering as a ship run aground, as deflated as a slack sail in a calm.

As insufferable as the woman was, she had the spunk to speak the truth. He didn't own Malana; he had no claim to her—body, heart, or soul. Never had she asked him to take charge of her life, to rule it with an iron hand. Yet he had given her no other recourse. She was a victim of fickle fate as much as was he.

"Just what do you expect me to do, Miss de Magney?"

"Only what is right, *Capitaine* Westley. Malana must be brought out in a timely manner. Introduced to society so zat she can make a proper match."

"You mean, get married?" His hand gripped the delicate

stem of his glass so hard he feared he would snap it in two.

It was the most logical conclusion, and yet he had never considered that Malana might marry.

"Yes, of course. Is zat not what you, as her guardian, intended for her?"

He had no idea what he'd intended. He only knew what he hadn't. How could he give her over to another man? But how could he deny her if that was her choice?

"Is this what Malana wants?" he asked, uncertain just what he wished to hear.

It seemed she looked at him for the longest time, as if weighing her answer and, ultimately, his reaction.

"She speaks of nothing else, *monsieur,* but ze day she might marry," the Frenchwoman declared.

It hurt, of course. Hearing the truth often did, he had learned over the years. Even so, wisdom did nothing to lessen his pain.

"If that is her wish," Zeph replied, "then you are quite right, Miss de Magney. I will attend to the matter tomorrow."

It wasn't until a few moment later that he realized he was alone again, stripped even of the ability to escape the agony that tossed him about like so much flotsam in a violent sea.

Malana. The thought of some other man, some stranger, or worse yet, some stripling landlubber, touching her as he had ripped at his gut like a dull knife. It left him raw and aching . . . and angry.

But mostly confused.

It was more than he could bear to imagine, and yet to shirk his duty was just as unimaginable.

Perhaps there was something to the curse Mr. Kennedy had told him about. The curse of Te Tuma. Perhaps it lay not upon the *Dolphin,* but on the broad, deserving shoulders of her captain.

*  *  *

The round of weekly afternoon socials began immediately. In fact, the very next morning Malana received written instructions on her breakfast tray, telling her to be properly dressed and ready to depart at two.

"Our plan is working," Honoré assured her, clapping her hands like a willful child as she helped Malana into the most elegant of her afternoon gowns, a pale green dress, high at the waist and flounced at the hem with matching satin ribbons.

"Oh, Honoré, I do not know if I am ready for this."

"Of course you are, *cherie*. Just follow my instructions and everyzing will be just fine."

"And Zeph?"

"He will be just fine, too. Just you wait and see."

But to Malana, it seemed as if Zeph grew even more distant, if that were possible.

Although no mention was ever made of the night he had not returned home and had left her to dine alone, his manners became impeccably faultless from therein. Like the dutiful guardian he claimed to be, Zeph escorted her to every affair, overseeing her introduction to the social circle. But he never looked at her and rarely ever spoke to her. If he did, he did so only in public and in a most formal manner, calling her Miss Kilpatrick.

She met everyone, young and old, of importance in Mystic. Careful to follow the rules of etiquette that Honoré had drilled into her each night, Malana managed to make few mistakes. The younger set took to her easily enough. Apparently, those few months in school had taught her what her peers expected and, in turn, what to expect from them. The matrons who ultimately decided the status of newcomers in their midst were far less abiding, however.

It seemed they found it odd that Captain Westley, an unmarried man, had a marriageable young lady under his guardianship and living in his household. If that wasn't bad enough, they found her ways much too foreign for their taste.

Strangely enough, she had Leatrice Whitaker to thank for her acceptance among them.

The woman unselfishly took Malana under wing, playing the role of sponsor. Uncertain why Leatrice, whom she considered a rival, would go out of her way to be so helpful, Malana found herself slowly beginning to trust the other woman. Begrudgingly, she even acknowledged what it was about Leatrice that surely attracted Zeph, what traits the older woman possessed that she herself did not: unfailing patience, genuine kindness that extended to everyone, and a manner of grace and self-assuredness that never faltered even when put to the test.

And so, with such support from one so well liked and respected in the community, no one questioned Malana's right to social position among them.

As a result, no one questioned the propriety of her living with Captain Westley, her self-proclaimed guardian, undoubtedly a man of honor and distinction to care for the only child of his dearly departed mentor, Captain James Kilpatrick. If Leatrice, his fiancée of fifteen years, was not inclined to show concern, then why should they?

So how could Honoré think, even for a moment, that their plan was working, when in truth Zeph had made it perfectly clear to everyone that he had no interest in her except of a platonic nature?

"Not to worry, *cherie,*" Honoré reassured her, smiling in that furtive way Malana labeled as proof of the Frenchwoman's untold experience when it came to men and how best to deal with them. "Believe me, it is working better zan anyone could suspect. And if you do everyzing I tell you to do, you will soon see for yourself just how right I am."

* * *

Zeph happened to answer the door when the card arrived from Mrs. Leadbetter inviting him and his ward to attend one of Mystic's social affairs of the season. Only those citizens of good standing in Mystic and the surrounding communities attended the Leadbetter's Harvest Ball, thus named for its hostess and not for the fact that her husband, Jeremiah, harvested anything except money at his bank, the only one of substance in the community. Zeph's initial reaction was to ignore it, but then he remembered his responsibility not only to Leatrice, who would expect him to escort both her and her mother, but to Malana, whose burgeoning popularity should have given him great cause to celebrate.

After all, it meant nearing the end of his unsolicited responsibility to her.

Regardless, it didn't make him particularly happy. Instead, it left him wondering how everyone, including the girl and his fiancée, could be having such a wonderful time when he was so miserable.

The next morning, however, he begrudgingly sent his acceptance both for Malana and himself. Then, before setting off for the day, Zeph sent a note to her room, informing her of the event at the end of the following week, leaving it as usual to Miss de Magney to instruct Malana on how to act and to see to it that she had something appropriate to wear.

"What a flurry such nonsense creates," he grumbled as he made his way back home later that afternoon.

Opening the door of his house, he was surprised to find Leatrice there.

"Had I known you were going to be here, dearest, I would have returned earlier," he announced upon meeting her on the staircase coming down from the bedrooms above. Zeph reached out and took her hand.

"That wouldn't have been proper, Zephiran," she stammered, backing away.

"Dare anyone question our propriety after all of our years together?" he asked in a rare, teasing mood. Refusing to release her, he bent to give her a kiss.

"No, Zephiran. I doubt anyone would bother to question it," she replied stiffly, presenting a dutiful cheek to his lips. Then she extracted herself from his clutch and hurried on past him. "But I didn't come to see you. I came to help see Malana properly prepared to attend the Harvest Ball."

"Oh," he murmured, somewhat disappointed by her lack of enthusiasm for his attention. Nonetheless, he took their relationship for granted, just as he accepted her involvement with his ward's welfare in the natural course of things.

"Believe me," she continued, "after tomorrow night, she'll have swains by the dozen. That is what you want, isn't it, Zephiran? For Malana to find a suitable husband to take care of her?"

What an odd look of uncertainty she gave him then, as if somehow she knew the deception that lurked in his heart. But how could she know? Of late, he had been nothing, if not completely attentive to his fiancée's needs. It was only his imagination, combined with the ongoing problem of finding a suitable crew for the *Dolphin*, that made the situation seem worse than it really was.

"Yes, of course. That's what I want," he replied with detachment.

"Zeph," she began, "there is something I need to talk to you about."

"What is it, Leatrice?" he asked when her words stumbled to an abrupt halt, her hand clutched the banister, and her eyes cast about as if looking for something other than his face on which to focus.

"Nothing." She smiled, a perfunctory expression that left him to wonder what was wrong, especially when she continued to avoid looking him in the eye. "Everything is just fine."

"Yes, of course," he concurred. "Everything is perfect."

But if everything was truly so perfect, then why did his heart and soul twist violently at her announcement that Malana would have plenty of suitors by the end of the week?

## *Chapter Thirteen*

The day of the much-talked-about ball arrived after a week-long whirlwind of activity that left all involved exhausted at the end of each day. But the results of both Honoré's and Leatrice's unfailing efforts showed in the transformation that had taken place in Malana.

Leatrice, whom Malana trusted completely, oversaw her instruction. She conducted the dancing lessons, teaching Malana the intricate figures of a quadrille as well as the less demanding, if much more intimate, steps of the latest rage on the dance floor, the waltz.

Waltzing created a protocol all its own. While communication between dance partners during a quadrille had always been limited to looks and smiles, the waltz gave birth to one-on-one conversation, an art unto itself. Quickly enough, Malana learned what was considered proper conversation and how to avoid less appropriate subjects without giving or taking offense.

She learned that an introduction by the hostess was necessary before she could dance with a stranger—not that she hadn't already met most of the younger "set" in Mystic, but there would be guests from surrounding communities who were as yet unfamiliar to her. Then at the conclusion of each dance, the couples would promenade the perimeters of the room. The gentlemen would always inquire if the lady would care for refreshments. If she said yes—and she only said yes to those young men she wished to encourage further—then there was another whole set of rituals that had to be followed at the refreshment tables.

Finally, she was informed what to do and where to go should her dress get torn beneath the feet of a less than adequate dance partner, or should wax drip into her hair from the chandeliers overhead, or where she might obtain a damp, cool cloth to place on her forehead should she feel overwhelmed by the heat and excitement of what would no doubt be a long, fruitful evening that could well extend into the wee hours of the following morning.

Throughout the daily recitation and rehearsals Honoré, seemed happy enough reiterating almost everything Leatrice said without variation. Only on occasion did she add her own twist to the information. Her comments usually began with, "When I was in ze employ of ze Emperor Napoleon's sister, Pauline . . ."

Leatrice seemed quite willing to take to heart anything the Frenchwoman said that followed those particular words.

"How very interesting, Miss de Magney," she would reply. "I shall keep that in mind the next time something like that happens to me."

Although Malana still couldn't quite envision the magnitude of Napoleon's worldly influence, she came to accept that whatever the French emperor and his sister Pauline did was undoubtedly the accepted thing to do, especially since Leatrice seemed willing enough to accept it as well.

Less than an hour before the long-anticipated affair was

to begin, Malana stood patiently before the full-length dressing glass as Honoré, standing on a chair so that her charge wouldn't have to sit and wrinkle her gown, wound a coronet of white flowers through her dark hair.

"*M*allow, *a*lyssum, *l*ily, *a*ster, *n*asturtium, *a*thaea," she explained, pointing to each of the different kinds of blossoms as she named them. "And that, as you can see, *cherie*, spells Malana."

It seemed yet another incomprehensible *haole* ritual, this spelling out the wearer's name with the first letter of the name of each of the flowers in her hair, but Malana had to admit she found the results most appealing. She wondered if Zeph would like them, too. Would he at least see her as beautiful? As a woman in every way?

Honoré assured her that he would, that he *did*, and if Malana promised to follow every instruction that she gave her, by the end of the evening she would be well rewarded for her efforts.

And so it was, in this open frame of mind, that Malana listened to what the French maid had to tell her. Staring down at the bit of sponge Honoré placed in her hand, she was more than familiar with the diversity of its uses.

On Hitihiti, her people had harvested them from the ocean floor. Then as children, they had soaked them in fresh water to take on long forages along the beach to keep from getting thirsty. Mothers had used them drenched in coconut milk to pacify restless babies, and when those infants grew older, they used them to apply protective oils to the girls' fragile skins to keep them as white as possible.

So Malana understood exactly what Honoré wanted her to do, but it struck her as most unseemly. Not that it offended her sense of modesty—for, in truth, Malana had none, at least not by *haole* standards.

As for Zeph's, however, that was another matter altogether.

"I am not sure, Honoré. I do not think Zeph will like that at all."

"Believe me, *cherie*, Pauline Bonaparte used zis ploy to attract ze attention of one of her many lovers. If it worked on her gallant French colonel, what do you zink it will do to *Monsieur Capitaine*? It will make him go wild with jealousy." Her hands flew out in demonstration. "And once any man's green-eyed passion is aroused . . . hah, zey cannot control zemselves," she promised.

And so influenced by sensible Leatrice's earlier undaunted acceptance of Honoré's declaration of the wisdom of Pauline Bonaparte, she took the sponge and the water-filled scent bottle and stuffed them in her reticule, prepared to follow through with Honoré's outrageous plan.

If Malana's happiness was his only consideration, then why, when the girl descended the stairs the night of the cursed affair, did Zeph's heart lurch painfully, his blood pounding in his veins when confronted with her undeniable femininity? How could any man, old or young, possibly resist her? How could he hope to resist her for much longer?

She floated toward him, her dark beauty accented by the cloud of white gossamer silk that clung like jealous hands to her lovely body. If the material had been any lighter, she would have looked indecent. But that was the style of the day, and there was nothing he could do to change it or his reaction.

Had it been purely coincidental, or had she intentionally placed a crown of white blossoms on her head, making her the image, at least in his mind, of the island princess that haunted his nightly dreams?

"Miss Kilpatrick," he said stiffly over the knot of desire

that crowded his throat as he bowed over her gloved hand. "You look very presentable this evening."

He had meant only to compliment her. So why did the silly chit look so crestfallen? Why, to judge by her reaction, one would think he had just insulted her.

"I expect you will be the model of decorum," he added, thinking that, as her guardian, it was the appropriate comment to make.

But that comment garnered no better reaction than his first one.

"Yes, Zephiran," she replied, but she looked almost terrified as her fingers clutched at the strings of her reticule as if it held secrets she did not wish to share.

He didn't bother to say more, knowing somehow that whatever he did manage to get out would probably only make an impossible situation worse. Instead, he took her wrap and placed it about her slender, bare shoulders, careful not to touch her.

To touch her would see the crumbling of every barrier he had so carefully erected to protect himself.

In the carriage, he sat across from her. As usual, silence prevailed between them. He thought he caught her looking at him once, but when he turned his head to verify his assumption, he found her staring quietly out the window.

It wasn't disappointment he felt, Zeph assured himself as he studied her exotic profile, her long neck accented by the heaviness of her dark hair piled high on her head and crowned by the mass of white flowers. It was relief. Sensing she was about to turn her head his way, he averted his gaze to the street beyond, unwilling to be the one caught staring.

Once Leatrice and her mother joined them in the carriage, he mastered the urge to look at his ward. Mrs. Whitaker, sitting next to her, noticed as she watched him closely. It was as if the old dame could read a man's most intimate thoughts. Perhaps it was a gift acquired with moth-

erhood, an instinct nature provided for the protection of
its young. Real or imaginary, he was careful to give her
nothing she could misconstrue as lecherous.

Their arrival at the Leadbetters took matters out of his
hands, at least for the beginning of the evening. After
greetings from their host and hostess, the ladies went in
one direction and he, thankfully, went in another.

Joining the rest of the male attendees for an obligatory
drink and smoke until the actual dancing got under way,
Zeph found the young men most unremarkable, not nearly
good enough for Malana. They reminded him of a school
of silly, colorful fish just waiting to be hauled in by some
scheming mama's net. To be honest, he had never understood the inane protocol of these landlubber affairs.

Of course, all functions required structure. He couldn't
argue that. But rules were intended to serve a logical purpose, not to make for contradiction.

If the main purpose of these otherwise meaningless
dances was for females to go seining for the unattached
men in their fishing grounds, then why go to so much
trouble to keep the bait and the catch apart?

Even as he thought it, the first strains of music filtered
down the hallway. En masse, the more eager young men
rose, puffing the last of their cigars and gulping down the
dregs remaining in their glasses before responding to the
siren's call.

He should have gone along with them, Zeph supposed.
After all, technically, he was still considered an unmarried
man, but his long-standing relationship with Leatrice put
him on the fringes of bachelorhood. He had to admit, he
was quite comfortable there and chose, for the moment,
to remain where he was—a man who claimed the best
of both worlds, as his host, Jeremiah Leadbetter, didn't
hesitate to point out to the rest not nearly so fortunate.

Finally, growing tired of the unremarkable hand of cards
he held and the conversation that inevitably centered on

topics relative to landlubbers, Zeph made his excuses and his way to the activity taking place down the hall.

Just what he expected to find in the ballroom he couldn't say. The room set aside for dancing was packed like a barrel of salted herring with gaily clothed, cavorting bodies, both men and women, in the midst of a quadrille, truly one of the most insipid excuses for entertainment as far as he was concerned.

He immediately spotted Malana, partnered by one of the young bucks he had criticized earlier that evening. Where had she learned the intricate steps of the quadrille? Zeph wondered, but then there was so much she had picked up with ease since he had reluctantly rescued her from the isolated island of Hitihiti. It was hard to believe she was the same frightened, unworldly girl she had been then. She certainly didn't look that frightened and unworldly now. Against his better judgment, he couldn't take his eyes off her.

When it came time for the dancing couple to join hands and move to the center of the quadrille, Zeph stiffened with an emotion he cared not name. It was only a dance, he reminded himself, forcing his hands to relax at his sides, his breathing to even out, his imagination to remain under the iron discipline of his intellect.

Feigning apathy, he ambled away, seeking out Leatrice, certain just where to find her. Undoubtedly, she would be paying her usual attendance on the matrons, many of whom were her friends and peers who had married long before. His gaze drifted from chair to chair, group to group. Odd that he didn't see her anywhere. He looked toward the refreshment table near the back of the room. Still, no sign of his missing fiancée.

Finally, he focused his search on the small sitting room off to the left of the ballroom, a retreat set aside for dancers to cool off. Upon spying his target, he arched one eyebrow in surprise. Whatever was Leatrice doing out there? And who was that talking to her?

More out of curiosity than possessive concern, Zeph navigated his way through the crowd, following the current of movement around the fringes of the room. Spying him before he reached her, Leatrice greeted him with her customary smile, yet it seemed to twitch a little at the edges as if somewhat forced. Or did he simply imagine that?

"There you are, Zephiran," she said, accepting the arm he offered.

Again, was it only his imagination, or did the light touch of her hand on his sleeve convey nervousness? Did he detect a tremble in her voice?

"I thought you might never leave your cards and gentlemen's conversation," she rattled on. "You know Mr. Poole, don't you?" she asked, by way of introduction to the person who stood next to her.

"Amos," Zeph acknowledge with a curt nod, vaguely remembering that the man had left his fellow men at the first sign of dancing. He knew of Amos Poole all right. The owner of a lucrative mercantile there in Mystic, the man had been widowed just before Zeph had left on his last voyage. What did he want with Leatrice?

"Mr. Poole, as he has often done in your absence, has been kind enough to lead me in a couple of turns on the dance floor," Leatrice explained, almost as if she knew what Zeph was thinking. "I know how much you despise dancing, so I didn't think you would mind."

Did he mind? Should he be concerned that another man had spent the evening dancing with his intended? He supposed he should have reservations. Those he did have come at the spur of the moment, not from an undying sense of possessiveness.

"No, of course not," he replied.

Leatrice's look of relief spared him of any guilt.

"Thank you for your attentiveness, Mr. Poole," she said,

turning a smile on him that seemed to blossom with sincerety.

The merchant accepted the dismissal like a gentleman. "Perhaps we could do it again a little later, Miss Whitaker." He looked at Zeph. "With Captain Westley's permission, of course."

"I would like that very much, sir," she remarked in a breathless rush that gave Zeph little opportunity to speak for himself.

Why, if he didn't know better, he would swear he detected a note of excitement in her voice at the prospect of dancing with that bobbling fool again. It had to be his imagination. This was Leatrice after all, the one steady factor in his life, the one person he could count on for no surprises.

Surprises, on the other hand, were Malana's forte, and he hadn't seen the girl for quite some time. More than a little curious as to her whereabouts and what she might be up to, Zeph glanced once more around the ballroom.

The orchestra had taken a short break, leaving the dancers, now milling on the sidelines, to entertain themselves for the moment. His ward had not come past where he stood with Leatrice, so he knew she had not ventured into the retreat set aside for recuperation, nor did he see her in the throng congregated around the refreshment table. He did, however, spy the youngster he had seen dancing with her earlier. The lad was alone, which pleased Zeph to no end.

"What is it, Zeph?" Leatrice asked.

"Malana," he replied, continuing his search. "I can't seem to find her anywhere."

"I'm sure you worry unnecessarily. More than likely she's retired to a closet with some of her friends to freshen up."

Even as Leatrice casually offered her reassurances, the orchestra resumed their places and took up another tune. Still no sign of Malana. Then to his relief, Zeph caught a glimpse of her flower-crowned head through the crowd of accumulating dancers. Odd, that everyone seemed to stop in his tracks to look at her, too. Odder still, that every young man in the room flocked to her side.

Just why had she grown so popular all of a sudden? he wondered. Even as he thought it, his stomach knotted, remembering the strange look she had given him when he'd reminded her to behave herself tonight.

The crowd parted momentarily, just long enough for him to get a good, long look at her.

"Oh, my God," Zeph choked, unable to believe what he saw.

It was the nightmare of the school fiasco all over again, only this time he was there to witness the humiliation of it in person.

Like a golden goddess she stood there, her head lifted proudly without shame. Her lovely gossamer gown, thoroughly dampened from the conservative dip of the neckline to the hem of the skirt, couldn't have been more revealing if she been wearing nothing at all. If anything, the suggestion of the dark crests of her breasts, the dusky shadow of her womanly secrets much lower, was even more alluring and exciting.

It was scandalous.

Zeph forgot everything but the promise of paradise he had experienced firsthand when he held Malana in his arms. All he knew for certain as he forced his way across the room was that Malana had exposed for all the world to see what should only be his to admire. Grabbing the only thing he could find along the way—a linen tablecloth from the refreshment table—he ignored the shatter of expensive glassware as it hit the floor and the indignant cries of protest from their hostess as he pushed through the gawking crowd.

Incensed as much with himself as with her, Zeph said not a word as he wrapped the tablecloth about her, head to foot. In turn, she lifted her chin a little higher, almost as if she dared him to do something he would no doubt regret.

Unthinkable or not, he picked her up like pirate's booty and tossed her over his shoulder.

It was hard enough to ignore the snickers and gasps as he carried her across the length of ballroom to the exit on the other side. But it was harder still to pretend he felt nothing at the soft, unresisting press of her lower body against his chest, the curve of her thighs in the crook of his arm.

"Zephiran, wait. What do you think you are doing?"

It was Leatrice, of course, who followed him from the ballroom, the only one who had the presence of mind to try and stop him.

He swung about, a nonresisting Malana still slung over his shoulder, and met the horror on his fiancée's face head-on.

"I'm doing what should have been done a long time ago. I'm sorry, Leatrice. Perhaps I made a mistake ever bringing her here. Now that I have, though, I cannot let her go. No doubt, I'll make even bigger mistakes in my life. I never intended to hurt you."

"Zeph, what are you saying?" she gasped with quiet dignity.

"Go back to your dancing, Leatrice, and your more-than-accommodating Mr. Poole. Believe me, you're far better off with a man like him than with a cad like me."

"Very well. If that is what you want, then so be it," she replied, the catch in her voice unmistakable. "May you rot in hell, Zeph Westley." Turning, Leatrice hurried away, never once looking back at him.

He marched on then, out the front door, stopping only long enough to call for his carriage. Setting Malana on her feet, he stared down at her for just a moment, wanting to shake her as hard as he could. Damn it, why did she

have to force his hand, especially for the whole world to
see? Instead, he turned her about-face like a top and shoved
her inside the vehicle, jerking off the tablecloth as he did.

"Please give this back to Mrs. Leadbetter, along with my
apologies," he said to the surprised groom, presenting him
with the soiled linen. Then without further explanation, he
stepped into the carriage and closed the door.

Zeph considered the dark interior a blessing of sorts,
giving him the opportunity to clear his mind and decide
just what to do.

The carriage lurched forward, the only sound the driver's
calls to the team, the crack of a whip, and the clip-
clop response of the horses' hooves.

Then he heard another noise, unfamiliar at first, a clatter
that grew louder, emanating from the other side of the
vehicle where Malana sat, otherwise silent.

God in heaven, the girl's teeth chattered so loudly he
couldn't possibly ignore it even if he'd wanted to. If she
was cold, it was her own blasted fault, and yet, somehow,
he felt responsible.

"Damn," Zeph muttered, realizing that in his haste to
escape, he'd forgotten their outer wraps at the Leadbetter
house. "You're cold."

"No," she stuttered between her excessive shivering, "I
am fine."

"No, you're not. The last thing I need is for you to catch
your death by cold." He stripped off his dress coat and
offered it to her in the darkness. "Wouldn't that be the
crowning grace of scandal?"

After a moment's hesitation, a timid tug took it from his
outstretched hand. Then there was the sound of shifting as
she no doubt wrapped the garment about her. Eventually
the chatter slowed, coming in erratic spurts, followed by
telltale sniffs and gulps.

*God, please don't let the girl be crying now.* Anger and frustration, along with an irrepressible feeling of impotency, bub-

bled up from deep inside him with the force of an erupting volcano.

"Just what in the hell did you think you were doing back there?" he demanded, leaning forward on the seat.

The sniffs and gulps turned to breathy little catches in the back of her throat. But she said nothing, gave no explanation, no reason for her actions . . . and no apology.

He sensed then that she had only done what came naturally to her. Her heart was chaste, her motives pure, while he had worked like the devil to change her, to make her something she was not, something he didn't really want her to be, something she could never be even if he had succeeded. And suddenly he was grateful for her stubborn resistance, her childlike innocence, and ashamed of his inability to accept her for who she was.

But most of all, he was stunned to realize he had never really accepted himself for himself, but had always tried to be what others wanted him to be, what he thought he should be in order to gain acceptance.

"Do not be angry, Zephiran."

There was no sign of pleading or broken-spiritedness in her simple statement. Just with whom did she mean? he wondered. Her or himself? It was almost as if she could read his mind in the dark silence of the carriage. In spite of how he thought he should feel, the unyielding pride in her voice touched him as nothing else could. Touched him deeply. Touched him in a way he had no desire to ever experience.

"Malana . . ." Reaching out, he pulled her toward him. She came without resistance.

He said her name only once, uttered on a sigh of confusion and—dare he admit it, especially to himself—of fear. It beckoned in the darkness like a most powerful, unspoken need between them.

He wanted her as he had wanted nothing else in his life, and he would do anything to have her.

Had he possessed even a smidgen of honor—the kind he considered genuine and worthy, the kind he had always prided himself on having—he would have found the strength of character to deny the feelings that coursed through him.

But it wasn't by his own doing that he narrowly escaped committing the unthinkable again. Instead, it was the unexpected halting of the carriage, the expressionless face of his driver as he opened the vehicle door for them to descend, that claimed full responsibility.

"Help the lady out first, Henry," Zeph murmured, releasing her, more than grateful for what had been either divine intervention or pure luck.

The driver offered Malana his hand and she took it.

Remembering her state of indecency, Zeph reached across and made sure his dress coat was still securely about her. Even in such a brief exchange, his pulse accelerated, the heat of a promise he dared not explore cutting through him like a knife.

"Go on," he muttered, snatching back his hand.

Her light step as she descended caused the carriage to sway. She turned expectantly, waiting for him to join her in the drive.

In the pale light issuing from the carriage lamps, he saw once more the perfection of her beauty, the seductive innocence in her eyes. His heart, that traitorous beast, lurched, willing him to succumb.

"See Miss Kilpatrick inside, Henry, and see that her maid, Miss de Magney, is called immediately."

His last instruction was probably not necessary. Knowing Honoré de Magney as he did, Zeph suspected she was behind Malana's actions and would be waiting up for her.

"Zephiran, are you not coming with me?" Malana's voice, a siren's song to tempt even the most tenacious man of the sea, set his blood to pounding.

"Not now," he replied, reaching out to close the carriage door before he changed his mind.

*Not ever,* he vowed, when the driver at last returned, accepted his directions, and set the carriage in motion once more.

It was much later, as he stood on the wharves watching the reflection of the moon sparkle on the living waters, those vast arteries that connected man with fellow man, culture with culture, that Zeph began finally to conceive of what fate held in store for him.

Odd, how the sea could ground him as nothing else in his life could.

Even as he stood there, a late night fog settled in around him. Eight bells rang out from a nearby ship, announcing the midnight hour, startling him. He'd been standing there for hours, and yet time seemed to have stood still.

He glanced back at the carriage that waited patiently for his return. The driver hunched sleepily in his box; the horses hung their heads as well, dozing in their harness.

The time had come to go home, to face what must be faced. The many-layered reason for staying away melted like wax to the flame.

Malana was only a child, his honor told him. If she was old enough to marry another, reason argued, then she was by no means a child, at least not in the eyes of the rest of the world.

She was the daughter of a man who had been like a father to him. James Kilpatrick was dead, and as noble as his attempt to think of Malana as kin, that just wasn't the case.

Then there was Leatrice. But it seemed even that obstacle no longer existed. Tonight at the Leadbetters he had released her and, Zeph suspected, she had released him in turn.

That left one reason, perhaps the only real one, for him to resist what his heart cried out to claim: fear.

Fear of discovering that life lent itself to things far greater than those he pursued. That he would find someone other than who he thought was lurking beneath the facade of man, mariner, and master. But what he feared most was discovering something or someone more important than himself.

How much easier it had been to conceal it all beneath a cry of honor when, in reality, honor had nothing at all to do with it. There was no honor in denying the truth. And the truth was, he had never loved Leatrice as a man should. He had simply used her to shield his heart, to avoid love at all costs.

Turning away from the docks, from their familiar security, Zeph made his way back to the carriage. Reaching up, his gently shook the driver by his knee.

The poor man fairly jumped awake, gathering up the reins, which caused the horses to shift nervously in their harness.

"I'm sorry, sir," Henry mumbled sleepily, looking down guiltily from his perch. "I was only resting my eyes."

"It's all right, Henry. Decent men should be abed." *Indecent ones as well.* But he didn't say that aloud. "Let's go home."

Uncertain just what he would find—salvation or ruination—Zeph set his course to sail the uncharted waters of love against all prevailing winds.

# Chapter Fourteen

From her nightlong vigilance at the windowseat in her room, Malana saw the carriage approach, saw the driver crawl down from his seat and open the door. Zeph descended, head bent, his steps purposeful, however.

"Honoré, he's home," she cried with breathless relief, rising from her knees on bare feet that tingled when they touched the cold floor. "I must apologize." She picked up the oil lamp on the table beside her and aimed for the door.

"Wait, *cherie*. First smooth your hair. And unbutton ze throat of your night jacket."

But Malana was already gone, unmindful of how she looked, Honoré's instructions trailing after her. She paused at the top landing, her heart pounding as she waited.

It seemed to take forever for her to hear his footsteps in the foyer below. They halted as if undecided, then echoed in the direction of the study.

Dare she hope he might change his mind and venture

upstairs? Dare she dream he might welcome her with open arms, not turn her away like all the other times? Tentatively, Malana descended a riser, then another, losing courage on the third, where she paused and clutched the banister as if it were the hand of a supportive friend. Then she heard a door open below. Struck by a wave of self-consciousness, she turned and raced back from where she'd come.

"Malana? What are you doing still up?"

His voice rang out from the darkness below, strong and commanding. She thought to continue on, to pretend she had not heard him, but her feet, governed by the whims of her heart, simply refused to obey.

"I . . . I was worried about you," she offered, fearing to turn around and look at him. Even though it was true, her response sounded lame.

"Worried about me?" He laughed. "Good God, girl, it's not your place to worry about me."

"What is my place, Zeph Westley?" she asked. Spurred by indignation, Malana spun about, staring down at him from her superior position at the top of the stairs. "And I am not a girl, so stop calling me one."

"Not a girl?" he quipped, his lighthearted tone much more irritating than his words. "Then pray tell me, just what are you? Surely not a boy?"

"I am serious, Zephiran. You know as well as I do that I am not a boy—and I am not a girl, either. I am a woman," she declared, determined to stand her ground, face him down if she must, and convince him.

His gaze, always so critical and cold, slowly traveled the length of her, as if he truly saw her for the first time. It lingered on her face, on the curve of her breasts, and suddenly Malana wished she had listened to Honoré and paid more attention to her appearance.

"Yes, Malana, you are a woman. All woman," he conceded easily, clearing his throat. "And quite a one at that."

His expression turned pensive in the illumination of the brass oil lamp he held. So much so that it took her breath away.

Somewhere on the stairs between them the beacons of their respective lights met and merged, along with their unspoken thoughts. Did she interpret his correctly?

She took a step toward him, then paused, her heart pounding painfully in her chest. To her disappointment he remained where he was, staring up, his breathing so even and calm that she feared she had once again made a mistake. With a heartfelt cry, she wheeled about and fled, blinded by tears of lost hope and frustration. What was so wrong with her that he did not want her?

"Wait, Malana. Don't leave."

She stumbled halfway down the gallery, almost to the door of her room, before his request caught up with her. At first she dared not believe that she heard something more, something vulnerable in his voice. It must have only been the roar in her ears, her own desire to make it so, nothing more.

"Please," he added, then, on an unmistakably softer note, "I don't want you to go."

The heat of his hand claimed her arm. It arrested her fears and stilled the uncertainty that regulated her heart.

Readily, eagerly, she turned to him in trust and hope, resting her head upon his chest.

The tempest that had blown so violently and undirected within her only moments before transcended into the gentlest of winds, calm and uplifting, yet the anticipation welled within her like the sweetest island melody. It emulated the sound of the ocean breaking on a sandy shore, the clatter of palm trees in a light tropical breeze. The innocent laughter of her heritage, the playfulness of Hiti-hiti drums at a harvest feast. And she knew then of what those around her had spoken. This thing they called love. It made her feel whole, happy, and peaceful.

Closing her eyes, she gave herself up to such new, wondrous, and most civilized feelings, as well as to the warm lips that breathed life into them.

Zephiran Westley. More than anything, she wanted to be his woman in every way. And she would, Malana vowed, just as quickly as she could.

The calm that had instilled confidence in him earlier, that had convinced him that honor inspired his actions, simply vanished the moment his lips touched hers. It was anything but honor that coursed through his veins at that moment. Instead, something more earthy and primitive, something of the flesh and blood that made him mortal, that destroyed the last vestige of his self-will.

It was a sudden squall, the kind that every sailor feared. The kind that ripped sails and snapped masts, leaving its victims broken and adrift. A siren's song, and yet, like a fool, he held his course, steady as she goes, sailing dead ahead, right into reef-filled waters.

But it was more than that. It was the pulsating madness of island drums, exciting and controllable at first. But then the rhythm took over, drowning out the last vestige of civilized thoughts and civilized intentions.

He only knew that Malana's body, her heart, her very soul, beckoned to him in a way he had never known with another woman. And his responded in return. God help him, he didn't want to turn back, couldn't have even if he'd tried. And he didn't care who knew or disapproved.

Without hesitation, Zeph deposited the oil lamps they both held on a nearby table, unmindful that one of them teetered, threatening to topple. He dragged her into the circle of his arms, reveling in the feel of her sweet, young body pressed tightly against his own. Her mouth, a hot haven of passion, ignited the madness into a flash fire, consuming the last of his self-control.

Zeph scooped her up in his arms then, bending to gather her legs behind the knees and swinging her up against his chest. He marveled at her lightness, at the way her dark, fathomless eyes held his so steadily, so calmly, as if she had waited a lifetime for this moment . . . as if she'd always known it would come.

Dare he confess that he, too, had secretly dreamed of feeling such powerful, uncontrollable emotions, of finding in his heart the same freedom and challenge and, yes, even the risks, that only the sea had offered up until now. With the boldness that made him successful as a whaler, he carried her down the hallway toward his own room and the delights that awaited them there.

*"Mon Dieu."*

He heard the whispered expletive, saw the curious eye staring through the small crack in the door as he walked past it.

"Go to bed, Miss de Magney," he ordered without pause, knowing exactly who spied upon them.

The door closed instantly.

"Do you think we shocked her?" Malana asked, her gaze filled with genuine concern as she glanced back over his shoulder.

"Not likely." Zeph shifted her weight, bringing her face closer. "I suspect that woman has witnessed more than you and I could ever even begin to imagine. Probably even instigated much of it."

"Zeph, how unkind," she murmured, her mouth drawing nearer to his.

"But true. Admit it. It was Honoré de Magney who put you up to that ridiculous stunt tonight."

Their lips were so close that they brushed as they spoke. Their breaths mingled; their hunger merged.

"I admit to nothing. And it was not ridiculous. Pauline Bonaparte used it to . . ." Caught in her own inadvertent admission, she clamped her mouth shut.

"Pauline Bonaparte?" Zeph threw back his head and laughed. "And what do you know of French intrigue that that insufferable Frenchwoman didn't tell you? I should have known she would go out of her way to embarrass me."

How beautiful Malana looked in her confusion, how utterly irresistible in her innocent indignation. With the sudden swiftness of a summer squall, he pulled her to him, laying claim to her mouth with his own. How sweetly it welcomed his exploration.

The island drums beat wildly in his temples, fanning the all-powerful flames of passion that had burned deep in his soul since the moment he had first laid eyes on her.

"Zeph." Malana pulled away, sucking in a breath of fresh oxygen.

Oh, how he envied the air's ability to know her so intimately. To caress her everywhere at once, to be deep inside her perfect woman's body.

"I did not mean to embarrass you tonight," she said.

"Didn't you?" Zeph countered, yet he knew for certain that she spoke the truth. Malana was not capable of deviousness, at least, not on her own.

"No. I swear to you. I wanted only for you to notice me."

"Oh, I noticed you all right, and so did everyone else in Mystic."

A little frown formed between her delicately arched brows. On impulse, he lowered his head and kissed it away. Hers was not a face made for unhappy expressions.

"It doesn't matter now, Malana," he whispered against the soft skin of her forehead. "What they think is unimportant."

"Are you certain?"

"I'm sure."

With the trust of the child he had for so long erroneously labeled her, she accepted what he said, wrapping her arms about his neck and dropping her head against his shoulder. Perhaps that was what he had initially seen in her, an innocence of the world around her, that had made him view her as childlike. It was a part of her he never wanted to change, would go to any extent to preserve. And perhaps, if he were truly lucky, she could instill some of this precious quality in him.

But for now, he would be the teacher, instructing her in all that he knew about the ways of love, both physical and emotional. By no means was he deficient in the physical act. Like every sailor, Zeph had known his fair share of women. Certainly, nothing to be proud of, but in a world where there were only two kinds of women—the good ones who didn't and the bad ones who did—a man rarely had options. Nonetheless, he had always shown discretion, and had treated the unchaste with dignity and humanity, which was more than most men could say.

His limited inexperience in matters of the heart, however, was something altogether different. Forever, it seemed, there had been Leatrice in his life, serving as a convenient shield between his heart's desire and his upbringing. To have treated her with anything but decorum would have been ungentlemanly. To have wanted her in the baser ways a man hungered for a woman would have been simply unthinkable. And so he had accepted the mandates of society, had used them to his own advantage, he supposed, to keep aloof and apart, to never make a commitment. There had never been the urgency. And so, he realized, he had never really loved Leatrice the way a man should love a woman.

Then Malana had come along, wreaking havoc on the comfortable way he had viewed his social position and obligations. Knowing nothing of the puritan rules by which he played, she had openly and honestly expressed her desires, while he, desperate to cling to what was familiar and safe, had conjured up an unsurmountable barrier of reasons not to reciprocate those feelings. In truth, to surrender to love meant facing himself and the emptiness of his existence.

An emptiness he could no longer tolerate.

Reaching the door to his bedroom, he carried Malana inside and laid her on the bed. Malana, the keystone to this in-depth search of his soul. She looked like a white gossamer island in the middle of the dark coverlet and pillows, truly a siren calling to him.

He fumbled at the already-loosened knot of his cravat. One sharp tug and the neck cloth fell away in his hand, to be discarded without thought on the nearby shaving stand. His waistcoat and linen shirt quickly followed, leaving him bare to the waist. At that point, his hand poised on the fasteners of his pants, he paused, considering her reaction.

Although she watched his every move with steady, unfrightened eyes, Zeph felt certain that Malana did not know what to expect. After all, she had been the virginal sacrifice to Te Tuma, that most unworthy pagan god, when first he had seen her. So how could she know?

Instinctively, he sought to protect her. Sitting down on the edge of the bed, he leaned forward and, thinking to spare her embarrassment, cupped his hand about the flame of the lamp with the intention of blowing it out.

"No," she said in a voice heavy with the same passion that made him reckless and bold. "I want to see."

He looked back over his shoulder at her. "Are you sure, Malana? Sometimes it's much easier," he explained, "especially the first time, if it's dark."

"Have you forgotten from where I come? I know what a man looks like, Zeph." She pushed up from the pillows, pulling her legs beneath her so that she could kneel and press herself against his bare back. Her warm breath filled his ear; her arms encircled him. "I know how a man and woman mate." Her fingers boldly explored the sea of manly hair on his chest.

"It's not merely mating, Malana." Zeph turned swiftly, dislodging those brazen hands that sent sizzling bolts of need throughout him. He pushed her down on the mattress, pinning her there with his own passion-racked body. "It's making love."

"Then make love to me," she whispered without hesitation, her hands sliding to caress him once more. Her thighs, bared in the tussle, vised his, and she lifted her hips in invitation, the softness of her body against his hardness almost more than he could bear.

The drums. The wild, pounding pagan drums consumed him, urging him to take her then and there, swiftly and without regard. Determined to master such lustful thoughts—by God, he would love her, not simply mate with her—he spread her arms wide, cuffing her wrists with his own hands as much to control himself as her. His excited breath mingled with hers; his hungry gaze intently watched the rise and fall of her lace-covered bosom, remembering its rose-tipped creaminess.

Like a wild thing captured, she struggled for just a moment against his domination.

"You must trust me, Malana. I will not hurt you," he murmured, kissing her temple, her cheek, then moving on to that little hollow in front of her ear.

Believing him as she always did, she succumbed, lying perfectly still beneath his caresses, anticipation written clearly on her beautiful face.

Releasing his grip, Zeph reached to unfasten the front of her nightdress. When her hands moved to join his, he grasped them, silently commanding that they remain where they were. This was his to do, his alone.

With only a pledge of faith to bind her, she yielded, allowing him to undress her, which he did slowly, meticulously, revealing each of her hidden treasures one at time.

Lying naked beneath him, Malana trusted him when he
wasn't sure he could trust himself. Yet, from somewhere—
dare he label it love?—he found the strength to make each
move, each gesture, one to be remembered and revered.

Still, those insatiable drums continued to beat against
his temples with an overpowering urgency.

"Take her, take her," they seemed to chant, almost as
if they were an active participant in their intimacy.

Foolish, romantic notion, he told himself as he quickly
stripped himself of his remaining clothes. The drums, the
islands, the pagan gods, for that matter, were all far away
now, no longer able to reach them. There was only himself
and Malana ... and the love he wished to unveil and
nurture.

He buried his face in the firm mounds of her breasts,
exploring them, worshiping them with his lips and tongue.
Uninhibited, she arched to meet each of his caresses, yet
her hands remained where he had placed them on the
bed, clutching at the coverlet. He moved lowered, tasting
every inch of her warm, spice-tinged body. It was as if the
scent, the exotic flavor of the South Seas, was permanently
ingrained in the sweet folds of her womanly body as it
opened to him.

Her little cries of ecstasy encouraged him to boldness
in his quest to give her pleasure. He loved her in ways he
had only dreamed of doing before this moment. How easy
it would be to lose himself forever in a world of fleshly
delight, as long as Malana shared it with him.

Wild with want and need, he surrendered to the overpowering rhythm of the drums that filled his head, tainted
his blood, and invaded every fiber of his being, refusing
to give him a moment's peace. Moving up to cover her,
he poised above the cradle of her femininity, suddenly
aware that should he take this final step of consummation,
his life would be forever changed.

There would be no going back, no avoidance of commitment.

"Take her. Take her," the drums demanded.

Not until the deed was done did he realize that it was her hand that guided him, her gentle urging that convinced him there was neither sin nor shame nor regret in what they did. Lost in the sweetness of the moment, in the silkiness of her pristine body as it closed about him, Zeph struggled to master the brute desire that threatened to take over. More than anything he wanted to truly make this, their first coming together, a shared union of both body and soul.

Running his hands beneath her hips, he held her tight, steadying himself as he gently, lovingly broke through that final barrier of her innocence, all the while kissing her impassioned mouth as she cried out to him in virginal astonishment.

"I did not know. I did not know," she gasped, her hand clutching at the taut, quivering muscles in his arms that held him in check.

"Malana. My sweet, beautiful Malana," he whispered in her ear, tracing the pearl-smooth shell with the tip of his tongue. "I promise you. The best has yet to come, but only when you are ready." Even as he assured her, he wondered how long he could hold out. As long as she needed, he vowed.

"Now, Zeph, now," she cried, rising up to take him as deep within her as she could.

So deep, he nearly lost himself in the wave of ecstasy that washed over him.

Attuned to mastering every aspect of his life, he found this, the act of making love to a woman, an almost impossible task of control. The challenge in itself heightened the battery of sensation created by every stroke.

Gently, slowly, he demanded of himself in spite of the hard and fast percussive rhythm that gave him no peace.

He wanted Malana with him every step of the way, but the drums opposed his every good intention.

Finally, he realized that the only way to defy the invasive force was to relinquish control to the one person who mattered.

Gripping Malana by the waist, Zeph rolled over, putting her on top and in command. At first she seemed confused by what he wanted, but soon enough she discovered the advantage of her position. With his hands molded about her hips, he anticipated her every move and countered it with one of his own.

The rise and fall, no longer of his control, was like riding out the unstoppable undulation of a storm at sea. It was exhilarating, thrilling, almost a little frightening, and yet he gave himself up to it and, in the process, discovered a level of intense excitement like none he had ever known before.

And the drums, be damned, they pounded and demanded, impotent in their desperate rage to be obeyed. But it seemed Malana did not hear them, or if she did, she had the strength to ignore them.

And so it came about, his turn to trust, to give himself over to the desires of another—a woman, no less—to consider her needs before his own. He watched her grace, her unfaltering femininity, as she charted a mutual course through the unexplored sea of passion.

On the precipice of fulfillment, he sustained a flash of what could only be described as pure knowledge. He understood why even the most staunch sailor referred to the seven oceans and the vessels that sailed them as "she." Only a woman as pure of heart and soul as the forces of nature could give a man what he experienced now.

Then in those initial moments when the waves of ecstasy began to rush over him, to carry him deep into their overpowering depths like so much flotsam, did he fight not to go it alone. Taking charge once more, he rolled Malana beneath him, riding her, holding out as long as he could, balancing on the crest of release until at last she joined him. Only then did he allow the will of the waves to break over them.

"Malana," Zeph cried out, clinging to her, burying his face in the softness of her breasts as the undulations accompanied by the thunder of the drums claimed his body and soul.

Later—he wasn't sure how much later, as it could have been hours or minutes—he awoke to a calm like a shipwrecked castaway on a pristine beach, surprised to find they had transcended neither time nor place. They still remained in his house, on his bed, the covers twisted all about them the only evidence of the passionate storm that had swept through the room. To his amazement, Malana clung to him just as he clung to her. Her dark gaze, ever alert and intelligent, ever innocent, searched his in wonderment.

He smiled. She reciprocated. Her mouth, ever so sweet in passion or the aftermath thereof, welcomed his with an eagerness he willingly matched. How had he managed to live so long without her?

He kissed her deeply, held her close, wishing only that the magic of that night might never end, that the sun would not come up on the morrow, that the unfriendly, unforgiving world beyond the closed windows and doors no longer existed.

Only a dreamer or, worse yet, a fool dared hope for what could never be. Pulling away, he pillowed Malana's head against his heart and contemplated the consequences of his actions—his, not hers—chiding himself for the belatedness of his concern.

Tomorrow the public events of the night would be a full-blown scandal, one that, in all good conscience, he could not let Leatrice face alone. God only knew how much of what had taken place in the privacy of his own home would become common knowledge with the light of day.

"You should go back to your room."

"Why?" Malana stirred against him, her mouth brushing lightly over his chest.

"Because I say you must," Zeph replied, somewhat sharper than he had intended. But her exploring mouth made it impossible to remember his duty and obligations before . . .

Before he asked her to marry him.

The words formed easily on his tongue, and for once in his life he had to bite them back lest they escape prematurely. Her long hair draped across his bare chest, Malana gazed up at him, her eyes conveying a pain she undoubtedly felt.

"I'm sorry," he said, reaching up to touch her cheek, wanting to explain that he only wished to protect her from gossip or worse.

"No," she replied, pulled away, flinging her long hair as she did. "You do not have to apologize. I understand *haole* ways. Why should you be any different? Remember, Zeph Westley, all of my life I observed how your people treated my people. You are done with me. Now I should leave. Have you a trinket to give me as well?"

"Malana, it's not like that." He reached out, putting his hand over hers in an attempt to calm her down.

She stared down at his flesh covering hers, then looked up, her eyes unrelentingly cold. Then she rose, so glorious in her nakedness that his heart twisted violently in response. Wordlessly, she gathered up her clothes in her arms, making no attempt to don them.

"Malana, wait," he called out, rising from the bed.

Without looking back, she went out the door. He thought to follow, getting as far as the threshold to the outer corridor, then realized his own shocking state of undress.

Frustrated, he watched her sashay the length of the gallery and enter her own room, without once considering what others might think.

But that was Malana, the part of her free-spiritedness he had insisted not so long ago he had absolutely no wish to change. Zeph ground his teeth at the irony of it all. By damn, she infuriated him, but he would have her no other way.

Tomorrow, he must face the consequences of that free-wheeling spirit. Tomorrow, he couldn't put it off. He must confront Leatrice, tell her as gently as he could . . .

Zeph stepped back into the room, closed the door, then fell upon his bed once more, not really tired but uncertain what else to do. Exactly how did one tell a woman like Leatrice Whitaker, who had shown nothing but loyalty and patience for so many years, that he had no intention of marrying her? If he were lucky, Leatrice's mother wouldn't attempt to slap him with some kind of breach of promise suit. It was no less than he deserved, he supposed. Leatrice, however, deserved better. The scandal would be bad enough without adding legal ramifications.

Hours later, as the first fingers of daybreak found their way through the cracks in the shutters, the debate still raged within his head. How in the hell had he gotten himself into this mess? he fumed, flopping once more onto his back.

How? It had been so damn easy and painless. Getting out of it was another matter altogether.

Halfway around the world on the tiny South Seas island of Hitihiti, the native drums beat in wild abandon. The last rays of the dying sun blended into the fiery aura capping the top of the volcano that had given life to the land and could just as easily take it away. The pounding percussion and the answering rumbles from above personified the voice of the pagan god, Te Tuma, to whom the half-clad, half-crazed islander paid homage.

Naked, sweating bodies. They were everywhere, doing everything imaginable and then some. Niles Kilpatrick had never in his life seen anything like it, and he couldn't take his eyes off the barbaric spectacle. One sultry-looking wench danced by so closely, he could have reached out and fondled her bare breasts if he had wanted to.

He had wanted to, and Niles could have kicked himself for hesitating and allowing such a perfect opportunity to pass him by. He was determined not to let it happen again, since he didn't get all that many chances when it came to women.

It was paradise perched on the fringes of hellfire and brimstone, he decided, glancing about nervously, uncertain what to expect from the volcano that dominated the island. It looked ready to explode at any moment. But he was just as concerned about the savages. They could murder him in his sleep, for all he knew. By some accounts he'd even heard that many island tribes were cannibals. What if the purpose of this ritual was to cook him alive?

He shuddered, first in fear. Then when the Polynesian girl gyrated by again, this time pausing and falling to her knees before him, her breasts glistening within reach, lusty tremors racked his body.

"She wants ya, Cap'n."

Niles glanced at Jake Ainsworth, who sat down cross-legged beside him. The experienced sailor leered at him in gape-toothed confirmation.

"Do you really think so?" Niles asked, his gaze coveting the girl's naked body as his hand snaked out to claim the offered prize.

"Hell, Cap'n, she'd gobble you up alive, here and now, if you'd let her."

Gobble him up alive? Niles gulped and jerked his hand back, the phrase stirring up vivid, unnerving images, but undoubtedly not the kind the sailor had intended. Ignoring the overt invitation, he scrambled to his feet, his knees knocking, his heart pounding. Damn, but he wished they would just get what they'd come for and leave.

"Where are you going, Cap'n?" Jake asked with only mild interest, his own gaze fastened on the pretty island girl who had turned to him when Niles rejected her.

"Back to the ship."

"Can't. Not now. Mao, the chief, has agreed to talk with you," Jake said, without once looking in his direction. "He waits in his hut."

"Have you seen them?"

Jake shook his head, but his eyes never left the island girl. "Cain't get close to 'em."

Them, of course, were the reputed pearls. Their inaccessibility was the one hitch in this devil's pact he'd made, which irked Niles to no end. They weren't exactly lying on the beach begging to be picked up the way Jake had first described. Instead, they were in a heavily guarded temple deep in the jungle. A man would foolishly risk his life to go after them. Being a businessman, Niles had decided to try to bargain for some of them.

But he suspected Jake Ainsworth was holding back on him, that perhaps he had plans to get them for himself and leave his "partner" out.

"Come on, Jake," Niles insisted, grabbing at the preoccupied sailor's arm. "You have to come with me. You know I don't speak this island gibberish."

It was yet another aspect of this ill-fated adventure that galled him, having to depend on his partner to act as interpreter. As they walked through the cluster of tiny huts, Niles wondered, as he often did, if Jake repeated everything that was said, or if he kept choice tidbits of information to himself.

Reaching the designated hut, they were met by a woman, who led them inside. Mao, the chief, hideously tattooed on his arms, face, and torso, was sprawled on a woven mat, surrounded by three more females. Wives or concubines or, if the rumors were true, maybe even sisters and nieces, they continued to lavish their attention on their man in spite of the visitors. The garish islander welcomed them inside with a grunt and a curt gesture.

Niles could only begin to imagine what it would be like to have a harem of women to wait on him. Perhaps when this ordeal was over and he was wealthy beyond his dreams, he would find out.

They sat where indicated, took the strange drink offered in a shell, and sipped it to be polite. Niles couldn't control the curl to his upper lip at the bitter taste.

If their host noticed, he gave no immediate indication.

Finally the chieftain spoke, looking at Jake and ignoring Niles. The lengthy exchange, conducted often enough with strange gestures rather than words, made no sense at all to Niles, although he listened and watched intently, hoping to pick up a clue. At one point the islander grew quite agitated. Niles decided that if it came down to it, he wouldn't hesitate to run, leaving his partner to fend for himself.

After all, it was every man for himself, as far as he was concerned.

"What did he say?" Niles demanded as soon as the savage grew silent once more.

"Says there is only one thing we have that he wants."

"Whatever it is, did you promise to give it to him?" He would give the man all the trade goods and trinkets he wanted.

"It ain't what you think, Cap'n."

"Then what?" Niles frowned.

"A woman."

"What woman?" Niles glanced around. Didn't the lecherous heathen already have more women than he could handle?

"When I was here last with Captain Westley, he took off with a girl. . . ."

"Yes, yes, I know all about that." Niles waved his hand in impatience. "Malana. She's supposedly the daughter of my uncle, James Kilpatrick."

"Did you know she was the intended sacrifice to the volcano god when Westley whisked her away?"

"Zeph Westley?" Niles laughed. "How cavalier and so unlike him. So what?" he asked matter-of-factly.

"Well, Mao here didn't know that Malana was who Westley took. He thought her mother—his woman—had sailed off with him. When he learned it was the daughter instead . . . well, he about blew his stack. Claimed that is why the volcano is about to erupt."

"So what are you saying? He'll trade pearls for Malana so he can sacrifice her to some god?"

Jake nodded.

"Tell the old fool that volcano's going to eventually blow its stack no matter what he does or doesn't do."

At that, Jake merely shrugged. "Cain't convince him of that, Cap'n. He wants the girl."

"But that could take a long time and a trip all the way back to New England," Niles whined, but he didn't care. "Surely we have something else he wants. Did you offer him the glass beads, the material, the guns?"

"The girl or nothin', and he insists on going with us. However, there's still my way, Cap'n. I say we just steal 'em and make a break for it."

Perhaps Jake was right. Maybe they should take the risk. It might be their one and only chance, as there was no guarantee that if they went back for Malana and even managed to nab her, the island and its treasure would be there when they returned. Still, was it worth his life to try and steal them? Damn, they had come so far to fail now. Niles looked at the hideous face of the Hitihitian leader.

He suspected that if he didn't agree to give Mao what he wanted, none of them would live to tell about it.

"Tell him he has a deal," Niles said, just to be on the safe side. He gave Jake an unmistakable look when the man started to protest.

"Gotcha, Cap'n." The sailor grinned and did as instructed.

Together they rose and departed the hut.

"We gotta be careful and make it look real," Jake warned as they walked along. "I don't think he trusts us."

"Hopefully, he'll be none the wiser until after we've left. If you're smart, Jake, nobody will see you but that supposed volcano god." Niles laughed at his own witticism.

Was it just his imagination, or did the ground tremble beneath his feet in response?

"Me?" Jake whined. "You expect me to go it alone?"

Yes, that was exactly what he expected. Then, if Jake should fail, Niles had his own plan to fall back on.

Even as he thought to betray his partner, he felt what was unmistakably a tremor, followed by a thunderous boom.

"What the hell?" Niles choked, turning to look over his shoulder.

In the distance, the top of the great volcano belched a fireball with the force of a giant cannon. The lava. He could see it crest the jagged rim and begin to run down the side of the mountain in a fiery trail.

Scared to death, Niles started to run, wondering if any of them would live to see the light of day and the opportunity to leave this cursed island before the volcano spewed forth death and destruction, claiming them all as victims.

# Chapter Fifteen

Zeph woke to a gray, dreary day, his own spirits not much brighter. He dressed to fit his somber mood and left the house without telling anyone, not even Mrs. Fillmore, of his early departure, deciding to walk the short distance.

It was an unseemly hour in the morning when he reached the home Leatrice shared with her mother, but it was an equally unseemly task he had to perform. To be honest, he fretted her reaction, yet outwardly he gave no sign of the inner turmoil as he made his way up the walk.

Leatrice herself met him at the door.

"Zephiran," she said breathlessly, her gaze darting to look beyond him. "What are you doing here?" She seemed genuinely dismayed to find him on her stoop, as if she expected someone else, a close friend, a confidante perhaps. She had several of those, but he couldn't recall their names. After so many years, he should have at least known the names of her best friends. And after what he had said to her last night, he couldn't blame her for her reaction.

"I know it's early, Leatrice, but we need to talk."

"I think you made yourself perfectly clear last night," she replied, chin lifted in uncompromising pride.

"I suppose I deserve that," he conceded, truly admiring Leatrice for the unfailing lady that she was. Nonetheless, Zeph refused to be daunted and stared back, uncompromised.

"Then come in if you must," Leatrice declared when she realized she could not get rid of him that easily. "Better the parlor than to air our differences on my front porch."

"Thank you."

He followed her lead into the small front room, formally decorated, noting the prominent display of many of the items he had given her over the years, exotic gifts brought back from voyages. After today, he wondered if she would still keep those presents, or if she would store them in the attic or, better yet, dispose of them. Zeph stared at a particularly pretty lamp he had picked up in Rio de Janeiro several voyages ago, remembering the day he had given it to Leatrice and how pleased she had been.

"You had something you wanted to say?" she prompted.

"Yes." Clearing his throat, Zeph turned to face her, to confront his own shortcomings. "About last night," he began. "I want to apologize for . . ."

"No, Zeph." Leatrice held up her hand in protest. "Before you begin, I have something I need to tell you first."

Pausing, he looked at her quizzically.

"I suppose I should have told you when first you arrived home," she continued. "But to be honest . . ." She looked down and away, her hands flitting about like unsettled butterflies, a most unusual reaction for Leatrice. "To be honest, I wasn't too sure of my feelings, nor how you would take them."

"What are you trying to say, Leatrice?" Truly perplexed, Zeph frowned down at her.

"It's Mr. Poole."

"Amos Poole? What does that poor milksop have to do with anything?" he demanded.

"Zephiran Westley. I will not have you speak of Amos in that manner. He heard what you said to me last night and thought you quite heartless. It was Amos who stood by and consoled me, Amos who showed me now much he cared about me." Leatrice stood tall and stared back at him in an equally bold way.

"Amos?" Zeph brows furled. "Since when are you on a first name basis with Amos Poole?"

"Since he asked me to marry him last night."

It took Zeph a moment to realize what Leatrice had said to him, that he had just been jilted. And here he had come this morning, filled with guilt and dread, not wishing to hurt her.

Suddenly, he began to laugh. He didn't mean it in an unkind way, it was simply the relief of knowing he didn't have to be the one to break it off officially.

"What's so funny, Zeph?"

"It's nothing, really. I'm extremely happy for you."

"Do you mean that?"

Zeph sobered in deference to the years they had given each other. "Yes, Leatrice, I do mean it," he said in all sincerity. "I want you to be happy. Truly, that is all I ever wanted for you. Amos Poole makes you happy?"

"He is kind, generous . . ." She took a step to emphasize each of his rival's attributes. "But most of all, he is always here. It means a lot to me to know that he will not leave me on my own for years at a time."

"It's odd to hear you say that, Leatrice," he replied reflectively. "I always thought you desired the independent life of a captain's wife."

Leatrice looked at him with an odd mixture of patience and disbelief. "No woman truly wants that, Zeph."

"I guess I never really knew you, did I?"

"I suspect you never really knew yourself until now. So what of you and Malana?" she asked.

Her question came out of the blue.

"What of me and Malana?" he asked.

"Oh, come now, Zeph. I have known you a long time. She ignites a spark in you that I never could. She's good for you, Zephiran. Spirited with a streak of . . . artlessness." At that, Leatrice smiled.

"Artless doesn't begin to describe Malana. She and her artlessness may well be the death of me."

"Oh, no, Zeph," Leatrice declared with conviction. "She will bring out the life in you the way I never could."

It was the truth, of course, the wonderful, soul-releasing truth. Malana made him want to live, to experience all that life had to offer. She made him want to laugh, to pull his hair out in frustration sometimes. But no matter what, she made him feel.

"Thank you, Leatrice," he murmured, choked by the unfamiliar array of emotions that coursed through him.

"And I thank you, Zephiran."

The moment turned awkward then. There was nothing more to say. Since he had never even removed his outer coat, Zeph made his way, unassisted, to the front door and let himself out.

He started home at a slow but steady pace, but by the time he reached the halfway point, he was clipping along like the fastest of ships headed into its home harbor after a long, tiresome voyage.

He couldn't wait to get there, to find Malana, to tell her. No, no. He must ask her to marry him, not tell her.

"Zeph Westley, you're about to embark on the greatest adventure in your life," he said aloud, uncaring who might hear him.

By damn, he was going to get married. It had to be done quickly, unobtrusively, without great fanfare. He did not wish to detract from Leatrice's happiness, nor to lend any more fuel to the gossips' fires.

Strange, this *haole* ritual of marriage. Everyone seemed to be making such a fuss over it and her and what she must do.

First Zeph, who had maintained that getting married was the only thing they could do. Malana contended she didn't need, as he put it, "words spoken over them" to make her love him and, in the *haole* way, spend the rest of her life at his side. She realized now that that was what she had wanted from the very first moment she had seen him, when he had saved her from certain death. Still, he had insisted, having already made arrangements with a friend to take them aboard his merchant ship and marry them at sea.

And now Honoré took up the banner, telling her what she should do. The cramped quarters of the cabin assigned to them to prepare the bride—almost as if she were to be sacrificed again—gave Malana little chance to escape her friend's ranting.

"You should be married in a church before ze eyes of God, not aboard a ship," the Frenchwoman fumed as she helped Malana adjust the traditional bit of netting over her face.

Malana thought about that for a moment before formulating a logical response. To her, aboard a ship certainly seemed the perfect place to marry a sea captain.

"The *haole* God cannot see you when you are on the ocean?" she asked innocently enough. "What good is a god of such limited vision?"

"Ze one and only God can see everywhere," Honoré sputtered, pausing to practically glare at Malana as if she were a disobedient child. "Getting married in church is ze proper way."

"And if we do not marry in the proper way, I will not really be Zeph's wife?" Malana asked, a bit worried, mulling over the strange concept of "wife" in her mind. She liked the sound of it, truly she did. At the same time, the images conjured up by the title frightened her. To be honest, if only with herself, she was not exactly certain what Zeph would expect of her when she finally became his wife.

"Of course, you will be his wife, *cherie,*" the Frenchwoman admitted, smoothing down the intricate lace against the long, unbound strands of her dark hair.

"Then that is all that matters," Malana insisted when it seemed Honoré was about to launch into another tirade.

"*Cherie,* you argue with me?" A pained look crossed the Frenchwoman's face.

"No, Honoré. I have simply made up my own mind, and you must abide by my decision." Without giving the woman a chance to protest, Malana turned to look at herself in the small, oval mirror on one wall. Her only regret was that her mother could not be there to witness their union. Le'utu would certainly be proud of her.

Thankfully, a knock at the cabin door precluded any further discussion.

"Whenever you're ready, Miss Kilpatrick," called an unfamiliar voice from the other side.

Suddenly, Honoré's overprotectiveness did not seem so unbearable. Reaching out, Malana grasped the woman's hand and held on tightly.

"You will do fine, *cherie.* You will make *Capitaine* Westley a wonderful wife," the Frenchwoman assured her. Then her face puckered with a militant look of determination, one with which Malana was only too familiar. "And if he should ever have any doubts about zat . . ."

"No, no, Honoré." Malana squeezed the Frenchwoman's hand. "Zephiran has done nothing wrong. I only wish I could be as certain of my abilities as you are."

"Ah, *oui*. You suffer from a little cold feet, zat is all, *cherie*. Perfectly understandable."

But it was not her feet that felt cold. Instead, it was her knees that shook beneath her long white gown as if struck with the ague.

Nonetheless, Malana's steps held conviction as she went out the door, down the long companionway, and up the stairs. Honoré followed, holding her silence—at least for the moment—and the train of the bridal gown, to keep it from snagging on anything along the way.

When she reached topside, Malana paused, taking in the clean, uncluttered lines of the ship, much smaller in comparison to the *Dolphin*. All around, nothing but ocean could be seen in the distance. Overhead, crisp white canvas snapped in the breeze, which swooped down like a tern to pick up her veil and the scalloped hem of her lace overdress. She pushed them both down, even as her eyes were irresistibly drawn to the quarterdeck.

Zeph. There he stood, resplendent in his formal naval attire, the sunlight glimmering bronze in his hair and on the metal buttons of his jacket. He turned then, aware of her presence, his smile and his eyes brimming with an emotion that gave her courage to continue forward, to climb the last set of steps to the upper deck, and finally, accompanied by Honoré, to join the small group of men that awaited them.

"I thought you would never get here," Zeph whispered, taking her hand, placing it in the crook of his elbow, and covering it with his own strong fingers.

"To tell the truth, neither did I," she whispered back.

In that shared moment of nervousness, Malana realized the importance of getting married. Never in her life had she felt so close to another person as she did to Zeph right now. Never had she felt so frightened yet, at the same time, so sure of what she was doing.

She spoke her vows with conviction, promising to honor

and obey without hesitation. Then, closing her eyes, she listened as Zeph promised, in that deep, resonant voice of his, to honor and protect her always. And once it was over, she turned up her face as he lifted the veil and kissed her not once, but twice, quite passionately, which elicited snickers and comments from the male bystanders.

"Surely, Westley, you can wait until we reach shore."

"Only if I have to," Zeph murmured, bending to kiss her again.

The wait, so unbearably sweet, was well worth it. It took several hours to return to shore, but the minutes traversing the streets of Mystic seemed to take even longer. They reached home—her home now as much as his—and fell into each other's arms the moment the front door closed, completely oblivious to Honoré and her unrelenting chatter that followed them inside.

"I have married your mistress, Miss de Magney. What more do you want of me?" Zeph growled, never once looking at the Frenchwoman. "Now hush, or I swear I will put you out into the streets this instant."

"You wouldn't dare, *monsieur.*"

Ignoring Honoré's sputtering indignation, Zeph swept Malana up into his arms and carried her the full length of the grand stairway without a single misstep. Then he proceeded into his bedroom—their room now, she reminded herself—and shut the door.

At the same moment, they both began to laugh, Malana softly, Zeph so loud that she knew for certain the entire household had to have heard.

"Ssh. Ssh." Malana covered his mouth with her hand. "Honoré will surely hear you."

"So what if she does?" he demanded, not bothering to lower his voice even a notch. "I'm sure she has been amused more than once at my expense."

Releasing Malana and allowing her to stand, so close that he still held her upright, Zeph grasped her restraining hand and kissed the palm, then the fingertips, one at a time.

They were alone at last, in body and heart, husband and wife, with no reason to ever be separated again.

Without a moment's hesitation, Malana slipped out of her wedding gown, allowing the white satin to puddle about her feet. Then her chemise quickly followed.

Completely naked, she gloried in the familiar feeling of freedom. She felt no shyness now, not like she had during the ceremony. To be with Zeph in this way . . . why, it was the most natural thing in the world. If this is what she had to do to be a wife, she would have no trouble at all.

She set about her wifely task with enthusiasm, beginning by undressing him. Then remembering all that the priests had told her, prior to the sacrificial ceremonies to Te Tuma, about the art of pleasing a male, she experimented. Be he God or man, surely it was all the same.

Anything but "the same," his response took her breath away. His touch was masterful, his mouth an instrument of delight as it coaxed her into braver, bolder spontaneity, which in turn heightened his sensitivity. It was as if they soared, kindred free spirits, high above the realm of reality into a world where surely only the gods and those they blessed could ever find their way.

Giddily, Malana strove to stay there, never to come down from the clouds again. She willingly climbed higher and higher into that celestial plane of ecstasy, safe and secure in the knowledge that Zeph was there beside her, always with her, there to love and protect just as he had vowed. Blindly, she flew on, dipping and weaving like a red-tailed *tavake* bird on a tropical wind, laughing all the while.

"Malana, come back."

Why did Zeph sound so distraught? she wondered, even as she soared higher and faster.

"No, Zeph, no," she replied gleefully, turning to glance over her shoulder. "Come with me."

The echo of her own voice followed her reckless ascent.

From somewhere off in the distance—or perhaps it came from above her—Malana heard what she instantly recognized as the pounding of drums. Drums like she had not heard since her days on Hitihiti. Alarmed, she attempted to slow down, but the winds of ecstasy that had lifted her so gently suddenly turned turbulent, whirling all around her, whipping her hair into her eyes, her mouth.

"Zephiran," she cried out, looking about but finding herself alone. Frightened, she tried to turn back, but the current swept her into its whirling midst, dragging her farther and farther away.

"Malana."

She heard someone call her name but knew instinctively the harsh voice did not belong to Zephiran. Zeph? Zeph? Where had he gone? Why had he deserted her? Oh, why had she not listened when he had tried to call her back? Fearfully, she turned toward the thundering voice, uncertain what or whom she would find.

"You are mine." The presence—for that is what it was—loomed over her, flames surrounding his enormous head, issuing from his mouth. Dark eyes stared deep into her soul, stripping away her will, her pride . . . her very essence.

"W-w-who are you?" she asked. "What do you want?"

"I am your destiny." The terror-evoking entity reached out with a hand as large and as powerful as any god's, compelling her to grasp it.

No, no. She did not want to. She only wanted Zeph. Twisting about, Malana tried to dart away, but it was as if strong ropes bound her in place, making it impossible to move.

"Zephiran. Zephiran, please. Where are you?" she cried out in desperation.

She knew not from where he came, but suddenly Zeph was there, putting himself between her and her aggressor. His only defense was one of those terrible barbed harpoons used to spear the giant whales, but it seemed so infinitesimal compared to his opponent. Nonetheless, with seaman's courage, Zeph unblinkingly faced down the unnamed god figure, his harpoon lifted, ready to be thrown.

"She is mine," the god said in that thundering voice she had come so quickly to fear.

"I claimed her first, Te Tuma," Zeph replied, his courage undaunted in the face of his rival's all-powerful wrath.

Te Tuma?

One large hand reached out, picking Zeph up as if he were no more than the palm leaf doll her mother had made her as a child.

"No, Zephiran, no," she screamed, fearing he was lost.

The barbed harpoon left Zeph's hand, sailing straight and true for its target's heart.

The god figure bellowed fire, his flailing arms stirring up a mighty wind. Falling to his knees with a thundering crash, he reached for the harpoon embedded in his chest.

Malana, too, was forced to her knees before the hot tempest, so hot she dared not even look up, fearful that it would blind her.

"Ma-la-na." The desperate cry came from far away, or so it seemed.

"Zephiran," she cried out, lifting her face and struggling to rise, no longer afraid except for the man she loved more than life itself.

"I'm here, my love. I'm always here," Zeph's commanding voice encouraged. Then he was there beside her, taking her hand, lifting her up and leading her away from Te Tuma's angry ranting for revenge. Leading her back to ecstasy. "Come, come quickly."

She followed him without question, racing toward the great precipice and leaping into it at his command. Then she was falling, falling, wrapped in his loving arms of strength and courage.

Malana opened her eyes, finding herself lying on the bed, still cradled in Zeph's loving arms. Confused, she glanced about, seeking evidence of the frightening events she was so certain had been real.

"It's all right, Malana. I'm here, love." His hand brushed back the damp, tousled strands of her dark hair from her face. He kissed the tip of her nose, the hollow of her cheek, the frown between her eyes. "My God, Malana. For a moment I thought I had lost you in the throes of passion." He laughed, the sound unsteady yet relieved. "But you are here, back with me, thank God."

"You saved me from him."

"Him? Him who?" Zeph asked, that ever-active brow of his lifting with mild amusement. "Did I miss something? Was there someone else in our bed I'm not aware of?"

It was on the tip of her tongue to tell him just what she had witnessed, or thought she had seen, the great, decisive battle between him and the god Te Tuma. But would he believe her? Or would he think it only her imagination, the product of some Hitihitian lore? Would it only make him think her a heathen? Yet, it had been real, so very real. And it frightened her to think that the god of her people had arms to reach across the world and find her.

"Zephiran, promise you will never leave me," she whispered, clutching his arms with all of her might.

"So possessive, woman? Since when?" he teased.

But she was serious and refused to relent until he made his pledge.

"Promise me," she insisted.

"Not to worry, sweet Malana. Never worry. I will always be your husband—to love, honor, and protect until death do us part."

It was the same vow he had made at their wedding. She savored it, believed it, hoarded the deeper, private meaning in the cache that was her heart.

"And I will stay beside you always, Zeph," she promised in return.

Yes, he had defeated the horrors that were her past, that stood between her being the wife she had vowed to be. Only she could lay them to rest, however. They could never harm her, never again, she assured herself, not as long as she had Zeph there to protect her.

And so she believed, without question, his promise to be there always.

# Chapter Sixteen

It was only a matter of time, of course, before other obligations demanded Zeph's full attention. Surely, Malana would understand. Their livelihood depended on whaling, the *Dolphin* and its new crew his responsibility. Nonetheless, Leatrice's statement that no woman wanted the life of a captain's wife haunted Zeph continuously, especially at night when he made passionate love to his bride.

It was what, for weeks on end, kept him from bringing up the subject, from telling Malana of his impending departure. Instead, he watched her blossom into the most beautiful, happy, dedicated wife a man could ever want. He didn't want to make her unhappy, but just as importantly, he couldn't bear to witness what seemed inevitable if Leatrice's warning held even a shred of truth.

And so, week after week, whenever he ventured to the wharves, checking on the status of acquiring a crew, the laying in of supplies, and the last-minute mending and repairs to the canvas and lines—all preparations for another long voyage—he never said where he was going. Only out. Business, he told her.

Had she questioned him, he would have undoubtedly told her the truth, but she never asked, and so he didn't have to face that particular dilemma.

At least not right away.

"Cap'n, have you decided on a departure date?" Mr. Kennedy asked, at last forcing Zeph into a decision.

"The crew is all accounted for? The supplies? The repairs?" If he didn't know himself better, he would think he was looking for an excuse to put off finalizing his departure.

Each question he put to his first officer, however, received an immediate affirmative answer.

"The new moon is next week."

"Aye, Cap'n."

"We'll sail then."

Why he chose that particular day Zeph couldn't say for sure, only that it gave him a little time to break the news gently to Malana.

That evening he watched her bustle about the house, from sitting room to dining room then kitchens, directing Mrs. Fillmore and the cook she had insisted they hire now that there were full-time mouths to feed. One would never suspect she was the same barefoot island girl he had rescued from certain death not that long ago.

No one, that is, who didn't share her bed.

Malana made love with uninhibited splendor. She made him experience his masculinity to its fullest, made him forget all that was considered proper and right, but more importantly, she made him laugh and acknowledge that love extended beyond the self.

Now when it came to himself, he threw caution to the wind, but the fear of someday losing this love made him fiercely protective when it came to her. If anything should ever happen to Malana, he wasn't sure what he would do nor how he would survive it.

And so, telling her he must leave would not be an easy task.

She listened graciously, like a lady born to it, never interrupting, letting him speak his piece. How much simpler it would have been if she hadn't sat there in silence, just staring at him.

"Take me with you, Zeph," she said with quiet, dignified sincerity.

He considered her request for a moment. It wasn't unheard of, a whaler's wife accompanying her husband on such a long voyage. But he remembered her reaction the first time she had seen the wholesale slaughter, and Zeph wasn't sure he wanted her to see him in that light again. Besides, the *Dolphin*'s crew—a damn fine one, the best his money could hire—was nervous enough with the hearsay buzzing around that the ship and her captain sailed beneath a mysterious South Seas curse. To bring along Malana, the rumored source and a woman to boot, would only be inviting unnecessary trouble.

He shook his head. "It's better if you stay here and wait for my return."

"But I dare not wait. I want to go with you." Her chin lifted, her lips sealed stoically as if she faced a certain death sentence.

"Goodness, Malana," he groaned. "You act as if I'm leaving you forever. A year, maybe two, and I will return. And if it is a good voyage, perhaps it will be my last."

It was a giant concession on his part to volunteer to give up his whaling life, a true sign of how much he loved her. For Malana, he would do just about anything. In return, he merely expected her to appreciate his sacrifice and be patient, to wait for him just this one time. It was little enough to ask.

That's how he saw it, anyway.

Malana, however, held a different opinion.

"Then go, Zephiran, if that is what you want to do."
She rose, her shoulders straight, her head held regally as
she departed, leaving him alone at the dinner table.

He finished his meal. By damn, no woman would interfere with his appetite. The food, however, usually to his
liking, tasted like mush.

Later, he found her in their room preparing for bed,
and he broached the subject once again.

"Malana, you are being most unreasonable."

She sat at the dressing table he had given her on their
one-month anniversary, brushing her long, dark hair. He
loved to watch her brush her hair. It glimmered like ebony,
felt like silk as he ran his hands through it.

More than anything, Zeph was tempted to reconsider
his position. But vivid memories of how difficult it had
been on her first voyage with him, of how she had looked
during the cutting in and trying out, squelched his moment
of weakness. With brute strength, he turned her, padded
taboret and all, to face him.

"Malana." Staring down at her uplifted face, he was at
a total loss for words.

He kissed her then, relying on the one form of communication that never failed between them.

"Please, Zephiran," she cried out, wrapping her limber
arms about his neck. "You must take me with you."

"Malana, I would if I could," he said with all sincerity.
Then he set about explaining the situation to the best of
his ability.

They made love that night with the usual passion. Nothing more was said about his leaving.

Zeph drifted into sleep, certain that Malana had
accepted the matter and would give him no more trouble.

He was truly a lucky man. He couldn't ask for a more
understanding or obedient wife.

* * *

The day of Zeph's departure arrived with leaden clouds that threatened rain. Malana stared out the window, as unsettled as the weather.

"Do you plan to come with me to the docks?"

She turned, silently watching him pack the last of his clothing and gear in the sea chest that would accompany him where she could not.

"No. I think I will stay here. If you do not mind, that is."

Joining her at the window, he took the curtain from her hand and swept it farther back, so that he could share with her the view of the first rays of sun fingering the watery horizon.

From their bedroom, the dock and the *Dolphin* at anchor were clearly visible. The high, sleek lines of the ship, highlighted in the light from the lanterns, brought on yet another attack of jealousy. How could he love that vessel, that thing of wood and metal, more than he loved her? How could he chose to be with it instead of her?

"I agree. It makes no sense for you to get soaking wet seeing me off on the wharf. It would simply be confusing. We can say our goodbyes quite adequately from here. In fact, I think I prefer it to a public display in the middle of a thunderstorm."

From the corner of her eyes, Malana watched his face crinkle with a pleasant expression meant to reassure her. He seemed to have forgotten who she was, where she had come from, how much nature played a part in her identity. A little rain had never before stopped her from doing what she wanted. Did he really think it would interfere now?

"Yes," Malana agreed, forcing a smile she did not feel. "We can say our goodbyes here."

He took her in his arms then, holding her close, kissing her passionately. A passion she returned with equal fervor.

No matter how he might disappoint her at times, she loved him with all of her heart.

"There is plenty of money with my solicitor. You still have that card I gave you with his address?"

She nodded. They had been through this so many times, she could predict what he would say next.

"Spend however and as much as you please, my dear. I want you to be comfortable and happy while I am gone."

"Thank you," she murmured. How could he possibly think she could be happy with him gone?

"I've already given Mrs. Fillmore more than enough funds to continue the running of the household for quite some time, so there's nothing to concern you on such mundane matters."

"I am not concerned."

"Also, Leatrice has offered to come by the house and check on you periodically," he continued. "Along with Miss de Magney, that should give you plenty of opportunity for female companionship."

"Leatrice?" she asked, surprised.

Leatrice had married her most unremarkable Mr. Poole less than a month after Malana and Zeph had wed, and she seemed quite content. She liked her former rival, truly she did. Still, whenever they met, the moment inevitably became awkward when the conversation turned to Zeph. But that did not matter. Leatrice did not figure into her plans.

"I shall miss you, Malana. More than you know," he declared with finality. Zeph hugged her, then kissed her one last time.

Wrapped in his arms, her heart began to hammer with uncertainty. Was she about to make a mistake? His open display of emotion gave her the courage to stick to her conviction not to be left behind.

A knock at the closed door ended the private moment, but not her determination.

"That's probably my men come for my chest."

"Then you had better not keep them waiting."

"It is my prerogative to keep them waiting as long as I please." That smile again, meant to lighten the moment. *And it is mine to be with my husband.*

The two men entered at Zeph's invitation, shouldering the heavy chest without comment and leaving as quickly as they had come in. Alone once more, Zeph took her hand and led her to the window.

"Watch for the flag to fly as I hoist my sail," he said. "It is my signal to you, my way of telling you that I love you with all of my heart, Malana. Look for it on my return."

His grand, romantic gesture touched her deeply. Reaching out, she stroked his face, praying that her actions would be equally appreciated when the time came.

"Is he gone, *cherie?*"

"Yes, I must hurry or I will be too late."

Dressed in the ragtag trappings of a street urchin, her face smeared with dirt and a tattered hat pulled low over her eyes, Malana was unrecognizable even to herself.

"Perhaps you should reconsider your plans."

Her plans? They were simple and direct, if, perhaps, a little desperate. She had figured out a way to sneak aboard the *Dolphin* without being seen and to hide herself for several days. Only once they were out to sea would she let her presence be known.

"How can you be certain that *Monsieur Capitaine* won't simply turn the ship around when he discovers you?"

"No, no, not Zephiran. I have heard him say many times that nothing short of the plague could make him return to shore once he sets sail."

"I hope you are right, *cherie,* for your sake."

"I am right. I have to be," Malana declared with conviction. She accepted Honoré's generous embrace, reciprocating with one of her own.

"If you zink it would be best, I will gladly set aside my own plans for a month or so ... until we are sure," the Frenchwoman offered.

"No, Honoré. That is not necessary."

It had been agreed that with Malana gone for so long, there was no need for Honoré to remain in Mystic. As a gift for all of the Frenchwoman's devoted servitude, Malana had purchased for her a ticket to France, departing two days after the *Dolphin* set sail. It had been years since Honoré had seen her homeland, the family and friends she had left behind to pursue her New World dream. Admittedly, she was homesick, but had agreed that she would gladly return to America. Malana had only to send word.

"I shall miss you, *cherie*."

"And I you, but if I do not hurry, I will miss the boat altogether."

Their shared laughter made the final moment of separation a little easier.

Malana gathered up the small satchel of clothing and food, wrapped in an oilskin cloth to keep it dry, and hurried out the door. Glancing up at the sky to judge the weather, she knew it did not matter in the least if it rained. She would be wet soon enough.

Her plans to board the ship included swimming to a line secured near the stern. At least it had been there when last she had been aboard the *Dolphin*. She could only hope the rope was still there now. From the water she would climb abroad, with any luck unnoticed. Heavy rains would only offer her better cover as she made her way to one of the secured whaleboat's and crawled beneath the canvas covering, where she would stay for a few days. At night, when no one would see her, she could venture out and stretch her legs for a few moments. Stowaways were rare on whaling ships, so Malana was confident that no one would think to look for one.

Although she said nothing to Honoré or to anyone else for that matter, it bothered her immensely to disobey Zeph. Not that he had actually forbade her from going with him. It went without saying that he expected no less. But once she was abroad and proved to be a helpmate instead of a responsibility on the long voyage, she felt certain he would see things differently. He would be glad for her company, and she, in turn, would be relieved to be in his protective sight.

Reaching the wharves, she made her way beneath the piers and slipped into the water near the pilings. As she swam along guided by the ship's many lanterns, she told herself she was doing the right thing. Not once had she mentioned to Zeph the frightening vision of Te Tuma she had had that night of their wedding. Still, it haunted her, jerking her awake while sleeping, leaving her in a cold, terrified sweat. It was fear that drove her to such desperate measures.

Malana was thoroughly chilled by the time she reached the side of the ship, as the bay off the coast of Connecticut was far colder than the tropical waters of Hitihiti. Shivering in the pale light of dawn, she climbed the line that thankfully was right where she remembered it, then stealthily made her way the few feet across the deck to the whaleboat that would be her home for the next few days.

Lying in the darkness beneath the canvas, she listened to the activity all around her—the cries of the sailors, the sound of sails being hoisted, and finally, what she was certain was the flag being raised. Just for her.

More than ever, she felt guilty. Maybe she should reconsider, go home ... do as Zeph wanted and wait like the obedient wife she had vowed to be. Then the shudder of the ship as it pulled away from its berth took the decision out of her hands. Closing her eyes, she settled in for the duration.

Much later, the rain began to pound heavily upon the canvas above her. Huddled on the bottom of the boat, cold, wet, and miserable, Malana opened her eyes, wondering how long she had been asleep. Minutes, hours, perhaps the entire day? It was hard to tell without taking a peek and risking discovery.

The cramped quarters closed in around her like hands seeking to squeeze the very breath from her body. Her legs ached from inactivity; her shoulder hurt where an unidentified sharp object jabbed her; her stomach growled in hunger. What had made her think she possessed the discipline to lie concealed for hours on end? If she moved, even to stretch her limbs, shift to a more comfortable position, or remove something from her satchel to eat, someone might see her. And she dared not make a sound, not even a peep, or the men working close by would certainly hear and investigate.

All of a sudden, the urge to sneeze swept over her. Trying to fight it, Malana put her finger under her nose and grit her teeth, but it did not help. Finally, she buried her face in her hands and held her breath. . . .

"A-a-a-choo!"

Who would have thought that her well-laid plan could be spoiled by a simple sneeze?

"Cap'n, we have a small problem."

A problem? Already? They had sailed a mere twenty-four hours, barely rounding Montauk Point, making their escape from Long Island Sound and heading out to open sea. Suppressing a sigh, Zeph fixed his attention on Mr. Kennedy, who stood before him holding by the collar a small, dirty stranger, no more than a kid judging his size from beneath the large oilskin rain hat.

"What is this?"

"An unwanted passenger, it seems, sir."

"Nobody in his right mind steals aboard a whaling ship. What are you doing here, boy?" Zeph demanded, but received no answer.

He looked the waif up and down, his eyes settling on the bare feet sticking out of baggy pants. Why, he would know those feet anywhere, the slender, dainty toes, the high instep. He had kissed them on more than one occasion.

Zeph gripped the wheel beneath his hand tightly, but gave no other indication of recognition. What was Malana doing here? She was supposed to be waiting at home like a good wife. He should have known better than to expect her to do as he told her, should have realized that her acquiescence had been much too easily given. How had she gotten aboard without being seen? Where had she been for the last day?

"Found him hidin' in one of the whaleboats," his first officer volunteered, answering the last of Zeph's mental questions.

"Look at me, boy," he commanded, stressing that last word with ridicule. Getting the immediate response he sought, he stared into familiar eyes, realizing Malana had yet to figure out that he was on to her. Did she really think to fool him with such a lame disguise?

Was he angry? Yes, by damn, he was more than mildly irate that she would so readily disobey him, and yet he wanted to gather her up into his arms and welcome her. Of course, he could not do that. Her presence aboard ship was a threat to the very well-being of his authority. It mattered not that it was his wife who disobeyed him. If she got away with it, others would think they could do the same. Zeph had been through that once before. He would not tolerate it again.

"Thank you, Mr. Kennedy." He abruptly handed over

the wheel in exchange for his wife. "Keep her steady as she goes. I'll assume responsibility for our unwanted passenger from here."

"Aye, sir."

Taking Malana by the arm, Zeph steered her below. Once the door to his cabin was secured behind them, he began to pace in front of his unsuspecting wife, deciding on how best to impress upon her the seriousness of her actions.

"So tell me, boy. Have you any idea what I do to those who disobey orders or steal aboard my ship without invitation?"

Her head wobbled back and forth, but her eyes widened, perhaps in memory of the punishment the three sailors who had attacked her had received.

"Speak up, boy, or does a cat have your tongue?"

Predictably, her hands moved up, exploring her mouth. A look of relief crossed her face—what little of it he could see beneath the brim of her hat.

"What am I to do with you?" He moved toward her aggressively, noting with satisfaction that she retreated with equal zest. "Perhaps I should keelhaul you. Do you know what that is, boy?"

She shook her head, taking several more steps backward for safe measure.

"We bind you hand and foot and drag you beneath the hull of the ship. You're lucky if you don't drown."

Her eyes, round in disbelief, followed his every move.

"Or perhaps I should just throw you overboard, period, and be done with it."

"No!" she blurted out, instantly clapping her hand over her wayward mouth.

"No?" He grasped her arm, shaking her none too gently. "And why not? Tell me why I should not feed you to the sharks?"

"I do not believe you would do that to anyone," she cried. "I know you better than that, Zeph Westley."

"As I know you, my dear, deceitful wife." Reaching out, he jerked the hat from her head. Her hair, bundled up inside, tumbled down in wild disarray.

"Why, you knew it was me all along," she declared indignantly, snatching the hat from his hand and turning her back to him.

"Did you really think to fool me, Malana?" he asked, finding her display of temper rather amusing.

"What does it matter now? I have gotten what I want." Her chin lifted pridefully.

His hand snaked out, grabbing her and forcing her around to face him.

"And just what would that be, my love?" He frowned down at her lack of proper wifely demureness.

"I am here, with you, for the duration," she announced with candid hauteur, staring him straight in the eye. Why, she thought she had him over a barrel.

"We will simply have to do something about that, won't we?" He kissed her then, hard, hungrily, and filled with a mixture of determination and regret.

After a short absence, Zeph made love to her that night with such gentle, caring passion, Malana felt confident she had indeed done the right thing by sneaking aboard the *Dolphin*. Once again, Honoré's time-proven assessment of the nature of men held water. Men rarely knew what was best for them. Every now and then they all needed a little push to ensure that they made the right choices.

Malana could not have felt happier or more secure than she did at that moment lying in the arms of her sleeping, loving husband, with the first rays of dawn spilling across the coverlet.

"Land ho."

She heard the cry topside, but thought little of it. She turned on her side to nuzzle up against Zeph's strong, bare shoulder, only to find him wide awake, watching her, a challenge issuing from his blue eyes.

"Get up, Malana. And get dressed."

"Not yet," she murmured sleepily, kissing the muscular bulge of his arm beneath her face.

"Now." The flat of his hand came down hard on the curve of her rump.

"Not now. Later." Judging his action as playful, if a bit rough, she shoved his hand away and rolled over.

"Suit yourself, but you have a long day of travel ahead of you, my love." He rose, gathered his clothes, and began to don them. "Thought you might like the time to get properly dressed."

"Dressed for what?" she asked, without thinking much of it. "I plan on staying abed today and waiting here for you to return," she said with naughty intent.

"No, Malana, you will be going ashore."

She was lying on her side, facing the wall. It took a few moments for his statement and the seriousness of it to penetrate the comfort of her warm, emotional cocoon. When it finally did, her eyes snapped open and she sat up abruptly.

Aware that her firm, young breasts were exposed, that Zeph watched them like a hungry cat follows the movement of a bird it has every intention of attacking, she was not above using every advantage to get her way.

"I cannot believe it," she announced with confidence, allowing her breasts their freedom. "You would never return to Mystic."

"You're right, Malana. I wouldn't. We haven't," he conceded, but the glimmer in his eyes did not lessen. "We'll be in New York harbor in the next hour or so. I plan on putting you personally on the next packet back to Connecticut."

And so that was it. Decision made. He planned to go on without her, without even hearing her out.

"Go to hell, Zeph Westley," she cried, uncertain just where the courage to say that came from, but hoping it would upset him as much as he upset her. She jerked the covers clear up to her chin and fell back against the pillow.

"No doubt, I probably shall, but in the meantime, *you* will go home and stay there."

Zeph watched the packet leave the harbor, reminding himself that life's lessons were never easily learned and abided by. Over the course of the last few weeks, he had discovered that it was best never to criticize another's decision. Inevitably, fate would force the censor to face a similar dilemma, if for no other reason than to prove him a hypocrite. Hastily spoken opinions always came back to haunt the thoughtless, the ill-advised, and the fool.

Long ago, he had criticized James Kilpatrick, calling him weak for putting to shore in order to send his unhappy nephew Niles back home. Now, Zeph freely admitted his mentor had simply done the wise thing by getting rid of a source of contention.

It was exactly what he had had to do with Malana. She was hurt and angry, but then, so was he. Hadn't he promised this would be his last voyage? Couldn't she have found the patience to wait?

The look in Malana's dark eyes had shown anything but patience as she had boarded the packet in the company of the kind matron traveling to New Bedford, who had agreed to take his wayward wife into her entourage and see her safely and properly home. Resignation, perhaps. Betrayal, for sure. Damn it, that wasn't how he wished to remember her.

Nonetheless, it couldn't be helped. God knows how much he would miss Malana, but Zeph firmly believed she was better off remaining at home. He, on the other hand, had a living to earn for both of them.

If it was as simple as that, then why did this nagging feeling of unrest, that somehow he had let her down, continue to dog his every conscious thought?

And why did the thought of chasing after whales leave him with less than an honorable feeling?

To tell the truth, if he had his choice, he would simply turn around and go home now.

But he had yet to decide that he had that choice.

# Chapter Seventeen

Malana arrived home in Mystic without incident, except for the injury done to her heart. Unfortunately, she arrived just hours after the ship taking Honoré to France departed. How much larger, quieter, and more ominous the house seemed in the wake of both Zeph's and Honoré's absence. Quickly enough, she realized how much she depended upon them, each in his own way.

But not one to sit about and bemoan her circumstance, Malana tried her best to keep herself occupied with matters at hand. Since nothing could be considered pressing, she sometimes found that difficult. Then on impulse, she wrote to Amy Potter, her dear friend and previous roommate at the New England School of Female Advancement, inviting her to come and spend a week or two during her upcoming summer vacation. Uncertain what the response would be, it nonetheless gave her something to anticipate in the near future.

While waiting to hear, she spent most of her days in the garden working side by side with Mrs. Fillmore, who she

discovered, quite by accident, shared a love of the earth
and the beauty that grew from it. She doubted that Zeph
would approve of her actions, of her digging in the dirt,
but Malana needed to do something with her hands, something to keep her busy. And it did just that, just as Amy
had shown her in school, giving her more than a minimal
amount of satisfaction. There lurked a weed of unrest
among the carefully tended flowers that comprised her
contentment, however.

The bad feeling—that was all the vision was, nothing
more, Malana assured herself afterward—swept over her
with the force of a gale wind. Frightening, to say the least,
it consisted of a jumble of faces framed in fire. One she
identified as Te Tuma, another as Mao, her stepfather.
Her mother was there, too, only oddly inanimate. And
there was one more person present whose name she did
not know. He was *haole,* of that much she was certain. Still,
somehow she sensed his relationship to her.

Then finally, just outside the circle of flames, she could
see Zeph. But she could not reach him, no matter how
hard she tried. He just kept saying that she had disobeyed
him. How could she expect him to keep his vow to honor
and protect when she had not keep hers to obey?

It was not until she opened her eyes and discovered the
poor housekeeper kneeling over her, muttering worriedly
and fanning her face with a pair of garden gloves, that
Malana realized she had fainted.

"Poor Mrs. Westley," the woman exclaimed. "Must
surely be the heat. You're not . . . in a family way, by any
chance, are you, ma'am?"

No, she was not "in the family way." Once Malana confirmed what the woman meant by the expression, she made
that perfectly clear. And it was not that hot, at least not
by tropical standards. Malana allowed the housekeeper to
think what she wanted along those lines, however. Any-

thing was better than trying to explain what had really happened.

She made an effort to conceal her anxious restlessness from Mrs. Fillmore, whose tendency to worry overly drove Malana to distraction. Sometimes, it seemed she was worse than Zeph.

Zeph. She could not help but wonder if he truly felt that she had betrayed their vows of marriage? Perhaps that was why he had sent her home without a single sign of regret. Did he feel the ties of matrimony no longer bound them . . . that he was no longer obligated to her?

These were all questions she desperately sought to answer, but there was no one to ask. Not Mrs. Fillmore and not Leatrice Poole who, as she promised, came on occasion to visit. Malana, for reasons of pride perhaps, could not bring herself to open up to the one person who had held Zeph's affections for so many years.

Then the letter came from the New England School of Female Advancement. It had to be from Amy, of course. Anxiously, Malana started to tear open the envelope, when she noticed that it was addressed to Zeph, not to her.

Why would someone at her former school send a letter to Zeph? It stood to reason that it had to have something to do with her.

She started to open the letter again, then wondering if Zeph would consider her actions yet another disobedience, Malana paused. But he would be gone for a long time. Was it not her place as his wife to handle the situation?

Undecided as to her best course of action, she set the unopened letter on the top of her dressing table. She would deal with the matter later, once she had had the chance to think it through.

"Mrs. Westley?"

"Yes, Mrs. Fillmore." Malana turned to find the housekeeper standing in her bedroom doorway.

"Those seedlings you ordered last week just arrived. What do you wish me to do with them?"

"Why, help me plant them, of course." Malana rose, gathered up her gardening gloves and basket of implements, and led the way downstairs to the gardens, where she found she always did her best thinking.

To be honest, Zeph didn't know exactly what kept him from giving the *Dolphin* and its mission his undivided attention. Perhaps it was the fact that he was still a newlywed, or that he had sent his wife off in a fit of temper. Or maybe it was the restless, driving drums that pursued him in the darkness, making it impossible to sleep. It was almost as if they mocked him, proclaiming victory in a whisper that reverberated in his head. Or perhaps it was that feeling of dread he felt whenever he thought about the whales. Of late, it seemed he'd been haunted by a lasting memory of that final whale he had killed. Its great weeping eye stared at him in accusation in dream after dream. But whatever it was, he found himself considering the unthinkable.

Six days out, and he wanted to turn the ship around and go home—to make sure that Malana had reached Mystic unharmed, but just as important, to make sure she remained that way. Each day, the farther away he got the stronger the urge grew, as if a lifeline stretched between them, drawing tauter and tauter.

It was the biggest mistake in his career, in his marriage, and in his life, but the following morning he called for a change in course. The crew, silent yet curious, did as instructed. Mr. Kennedy, however, was not so reserved.

"Is there something wrong, Cap'n? Something I should know about?" he asked.

"Only that your captain is a romantic fool."

"Not at all, sir. In fact, since we left New York harbor,

the men have laid wager among themselves on how long
you would hold out.''

''Damn.'' Zeph ground his teeth to give himself strength.
''They'll think I'm weak.''

''Actually, sir, they'll find it reassuring to know you're
human, after all. More than one man aboard swears that
you aren't, that you possess a heart of stone. I assured
them that wasn't the case. I've sailed too many years with
you not to know the truth, no matter how hard you try to
disguise it. To prove my point, I told them that no matter
how long the voyage lasts, they will still get their agreed
pay. I hope I wasn't amiss in saying that.''

''Amiss, Mr. Kennedy? A bit generous with my money
perhaps, but not wrong.''

''Aye, sir,'' the mate replied, turning to leave.

It was a difficult moment of reckoning for Zeph Westley,
master of the *Dolphin* and, until now, of his own life. To
indeed accept his own humanity, that another, especially
a woman, through the power of love, claimed her share
of the control. It was just another one of those humbling
lessons learned, he thought, swallowing the bitter pill fate
forced down his throat.

Under normal circumstances, he would have been glad
his subordinate had the presence of mind to walk away,
and Zeph wrapped himself in the comfort that at least he
had not acknowledged the revealing truth aloud.

''Mr. Kennedy,'' he called out.

The man turned to face him.

''Thank you,'' he offered instead.

The sailor gave him the oddest look before replying.
''No problem, sir. Always glad to be of service.''

''Then take us home, mister,'' Zeph said, turning the
wheel over to his more than competent first officer, and
his eyes and heart toward the northwestern horizon. ''Just
as fast as you can.''

* * *

Malana had just sat down to rest on the small stone
bench outside the French windows off the private back
parlor, when she heard what she was certain must have
been the front door slamming.

"Is that you, Mrs. Fillmore?" she called out in mild
curiosity, thinking the woman had returned with uncanny
efficiency. More likely, she had simply been so busy with
her flowers that she had lost track of the time.

What seemed only moments ago, Malana had sent the
housekeeper to do the shopping alone that morning, wanting to water the last of the new seedlings she had planted
the day before. She did not want them to wilt in the warm
sun. The task was only half done, her watering can in need
of a refill. But she had discovered evidence of some type
of rodent who had taken liberty among her flowers, indis-
criminately gnawing at roots and stems while unearthing
much of the previous day's work.

"Mrs. Fillmore," Malana called out again when she
received no reply. "Did you remember to go and collect
the mail?"

She still anticipated an answer from Amy Potter. When
she came to visit, her friend would undoubtedly appreciate
Malana's efforts in the garden and might even have some
helpful words of advice on how to eradicate the pest that
had invaded the flowerbeds.

Instead, the sound of a crash coming from somewhere
inside the house disturbed the tranquillity.

"Mrs. Fillmore, are you all right?"

Concerned that the older woman might have slipped
and fallen, Malana pulled off her dirty gloves and hurried
through the doors. The bright light of the sun left her
momentarily blinded as she made her way, by memory,
through the back parlor, then behind the front staircase,
her destination the kitchens.

She was breathing hard from exertion in the ill-lit corridor when the hand clamped over her mouth and nose, nearly cutting off her air supply. Instinctively, she began to struggle, striking out with her feet at whoever held her from behind. A grunt of pain from her assailant and she grew bolder, kicking and stomping and flinging her fists.

The cruel hand pinched her nostrils with calculated deliberateness, making her struggle futile. Still, she fought on, until she had neither strength nor breath to continue. Uncertain who would wish to harm her, Malana tried to see behind her.

In the halo of the single wall sconce, a familiar face straight out of her worst nightmare greeted her efforts just before she lost consciousness.

The docking of the *Dolphin* at the Mystic wharves seemed to take forever. Pacing up and down the deck, shouting orders both necessary and unnecessary, Zeph couldn't explain the urgency he felt. The moment he could, he disembarked, leaving Mr. Kennedy to keep the crew in check. Under no circumstances was he to allow them to go ashore.

During the mad dash home, he had come finally to see himself as the rigid, narrow-minded fool that others undoubtedly labeled him. Taking Malana with him on this, his last, voyage had not been on his agenda. Therefore, he had failed to recognize the validity of doing so. How much easier it would have been to deal with a disgruntled crew than to worry constantly about what might have happened to her in his absence.

To Zeph's surprise, as he approached, he found the house a buzz with activity, reminding him of a deck in the wake of a storm. An assortment of unfamiliar carriages lined the walk. The front door stood wide open and neglected. Several groups of men were tramping through the gardens. What were they looking for with such diligence and disregard in the new flowers that had been planted there?

He hurried forward, entering the house unnoticed in the commotion.

"What's going on here?" he demanded, grabbing the first person he saw, a stranger, no less, roaming through his house carte blanche.

"Best talk to the magistrate."

"The magistrate?" A sickening sense of fear ripped through Zeph. "Where can I find him?"

"Upstairs in the bedroom," the man mumbled, returning his attention to his search.

Zeph took the stairs two at a time, unfairly chiding himself for his slowness. Had something happened to Malana? If so, it was all his fault. Reaching the gallery, he discovered Mrs. Fillmore sitting on the wooden settee, oblivious to the flurry going on around her, her face buried in her hands.

"Where is Malana?" he asked, staring down at the weeping housekeeper, couching his own fears in the sternness of his voice and stance.

"Oh, Captain Westley. Thank goodness you're home." The woman practically fell into his unsuspecting arms. She began to wail, quite unlike the normally levelheaded servant that she was.

Zeph couldn't understand a single word the hysterical woman blubbered.

"Calm down, Mrs. Fillmore." His command had no effect at all. In fact, the woman began crying even harder, if that were possible. After a moment's hesitation, and a lifetime of awkwardness in such situations involving females, he cautiously patted her head. "Please, Mrs. Fillmore, you must get a hold of yourself."

"Poor woman. Been like that for two days, since she

arrived on my doorstep claiming something terrible had happened to her mistress."

Zeph looked up to find a man who looked vaguely familiar standing before him, offering an outstretched hand.

"You must be the magistrate." He took the hand and shook it, not bothering to conceal his agitation.

"That I am. And if my reckoning is right, you're Captain Westley. Thought you were out to sea and not due back for quite some time."

"I was," he replied curtly. "Now tell me, where is my wife?"

"Apparently, she disappeared three days ago."

"What do you mean she disappeared? Where did she go?" he persisted.

"Mrs. Fillmore here seems to believe something diabolic took her."

"Diabolic? Please explain."

"She told me the night before that she saw something or someone lurking outside the house looking in the windows. He was all feathered up like an Indian, but he had tattoos covering his face."

"Tattoos?" Hitihitians, especially the men, often tattooed themselves, but it was highly unlikely . . . no, impossible . . . that one of Malana's people who lived thousands of miles away might have been skulking around his house.

"Haven't been Indians around for a long time," the man continued. "Anyway, whatever he was, he scared her half to death."

"Mrs. Fillmore, what exactly did you see?" Zeph demanded, questioning the validity of the woman's story.

"I was closing the draperies like I do every night, when this face—Captain, it was horrible—stared back at me from the other side of the window. He had tattoos all over his face, shells and feathers in his ears and around his neck. I shut the curtains and didn't look again. I was too scared.

The next morning I searched the bushes outside that window but found no sign that anyone had been there."

"Was Malana aware of what you had seen?"

"Oh, no, sir. I didn't tell her. She had been so upset as of late. And I convinced myself I had only imagined it," she went on, as if trying to exonerate herself. "Then later that day, at Mrs. Westley's request, I went out shopping. While I was gone, he took her." She hung her head guiltily. "Captain, I'm sure of it now."

"It's all right, Mrs. Fillmore. You can't blame yourself," Zeph said to comfort her. "Have you checked the dock registries and the passenger lists?" Zeph asked the magistrate with a resigned sigh, dismissing the housekeeper's tale as just a figment of her overactive imagination. Most likely, this was just another scheme Malana and Honoré de Magney had cooked up for reasons yet uncovered. He should have fired that incorrigible Frenchwoman a long time ago.

Zeph didn't want to think that Malana had left him. Not that he could blame her, but that didn't mean he intended to let her go. It would be easy enough to figure out where the two woman had gone.

"That's exactly what we did, Captain Westley, when one of my men came across this on your wife's dressing table." The magistrate held out a piece of paper.

Zeph read the letter addressed to him from Mrs. Honeywell, the headmistress of the school Malana had attended for that short, disastrous time. It seems a person claiming to be her cousin Niles had come looking for Malana.

"Niles Kilpatrick?" he murmured, lifting one brow suspiciously. What would Niles want with Malana?

The letter went on to state that this person had asked a multitude of questions regarding Miss Kilpatrick's whereabouts. Mrs. Honeywell had refused to answer the inquiry, which on afterthought she considered unseemly on her part. If indeed the man was who he claimed to be, she felt it her duty to report the matter to Captain Westley and let him decide whether to contact the man on his ward's behalf.

"Is that where you think she has gone?" If Malana had run to Niles, she wouldn't be there long, of that he was quite certain. At least with Miss de Magney with her, she would be relatively safe.

"Not exactly," the magistrate replied. "The letter was unopened when we found it, but under the circumstances we felt it necessary to see what it said."

"I see. Then my wife never read it."

"No."

"Then what do you think is the connection?" he asked.

"It seems a ship registered to this Niles Kilpatrick docked in the harbor, then departed on the same day your wife disappeared."

A sense of foreboding oozed its way into Zeph's mind, causing him to pause and reconsider. First, someone who resembled an islander had been spotted sneaking around his house. Then, to learn that Niles had been here at the same time . . . It had to be more than a coincidence.

"Oh, sir, you're much too kind. It is all my fault. I should have never left her alone," the housekeeper wailed, reburying her face against the front of his coat.

"Alone? Wasn't Miss de Magney with her?"

"Oh, no." Mrs. Fillmore sniffed and shook her head. "Didn't you know?" She looked up at him in surprise. "Honoré sailed for France right after your ship left."

Malana alone with the likes of Niles Kilpatrick? Fear raised its ugly head one notch higher. What was the bastard up to? Had there truly been an islander lurking around the house?

"Did the dock registries state the destination of Kilpatrick's ship?"

"That's the strange part, sir. The destination was left blank in the logs, but several sailors at a local tavern swear that a Jake Ainsworth bragged they were headed to paradise to claim their fortune in pearls.''

Paradise? Pearls? In Zeph's mind, that could only mean one place. The South Seas ... Hitihiti, in particular. A tattooed islander, Niles, and now Jake Ainsworth, together in one place. It was his worst nightmare. Then he remembered the stone icon that had been found aboard the *Dolphin*, stripped of the precious gems that had once adorned it. Had Jake been the one to steal the statue?

The terrible sinking feeling that had been with Zeph since the moment he arrived home hit the bottom of his stomach with a dull, anxious thud. Whatever Niles and his motley crew were up to, he felt certain that it boded ill for all parties involved—especially Malana.

Malana awoke to total darkness. Disoriented, she tried to move, only to find both her hands and feet securely bound. Fighting down a sense of panic, she focused on her surroundings. The creaking sounds above her, below her, in fact, all around her, were familiar. So was the continuous rolling motion and the acrid smell of tar and sea-soaked wood.

She was aboard a ship, but whose? And going where? But more importantly, why?

Renewing her struggle against her bonds, she fought on until she was exhausted, her muscles aching, her wrists raw from her efforts. As raw and as aching as her throat from fighting back the rising fatalism.

Somehow this all had to do with the visions, the terrible, haunting images that swooped down on her whenever she least expected them. They foretold of her inevitable separation from the man whose love and protection meant her salvation. *Zeph*, her heart cried out, knowing he could not possibly hear her. And even if he could, Malana was not certain he would listen.

The creak of a door opening set her heart to racing. All too soon, it seemed, she would come face to face with the reality of those waking dreams.

"Who's there?" she called out in an unsteady voice, wanting to know and yet, at the same time, fearing what she would discover.

The soft, steady echo of approaching footsteps was her only answer. Then a flame flared with a hiss and the volcanic smell of sulfur a few feet in front of her.

"Hello, cousin." The voice issued from the darkness as a hand carried the flicker of fire to ignite the wick of a lantern hanging from a low beam overhead.

Recognizing the face haloed in the bright illumination as the unnamed one in her visions, Malana bit back a small cry of dismay.

"You must be Niles," she said, certain as to his identity, if not his intent.

"How astute of you, my dear," he replied, snuffing the match between two fingers.

"What do you want? Where are you taking me?" she demanded with more bravery than she felt.

"So many questions?" He made a noise with his tongue, like palm leaves clacking in the wind. "Most unbecoming in a proper young woman. But then, you are not really proper, are you?" He stooped over the small bed on which she lay, bound, bringing him so close she could feel the heat of his breath brush her cheek. "And I suspect you're not really my cousin."

The venom in his voice caught Malana by surprise, but not nearly as much as the cruel hand that clamped like a vise about her jaws, jerking her head backward.

"Just what did you think to gain by pretending?" he asked, a vicious sneer creeping into his demeanor. "My money?"

"No. No. You are wrong," she cried, fighting without success to escape his painful clutches. "I want nothing from you. Please," she pleaded softly but with dignity, "take me home."

"That is exactly what I am doing, dear cousin. Returning you home where you belong." He released her then, with such force that her head slammed against the lumpy mattress. "Where it seems, my dear cousin, you have some unfinished business to attend to."

With a diabolical laugh that trailed him out the door, Niles departed, leaving her bound on that tiny bed, the cabin so small she could have stood in the middle and touched the walls all around her.

But worse, she remained the prisoner of her own fertile imagination. Just what had he meant by unfinished business? And where did he mean by home? The only place that came to mind was Hitihiti.

Zeph took a great risk, this dashing off without confirmation. To be honest, he had no more to go on than a hunch and a lot of circumstantial evidence. No one had actually witnessed Malana boarding Niles's ship, willingly or otherwise. No one but poor, hysterical Mrs. Fillmore had seen the tattooed intruder, and even she couldn't be certain she had. As for the testimony placing Jake Ainsworth back in Mystic, even that was without satisfactory conclusion. The eyewitnesses had left port without notification. No one in the tavern remembered Jake being there, or if they did, they weren't talking.

Zeph made his decision based on speculation and a certainty in his gut. Call it foolishness. The authorities tried to persuade him to see reason and give them a little more time. Call it heroics. Many did, including Leatrice, who came without concern for protocol, offering him her unconditional support, encouraging him to follow his heart. Zeph was glad for such friendship and, for the first time in his life, didn't hesitate to show his appreciation.

Amos Poole had a true gem in Leatrice Whitaker. He hoped the unimaginative merchant appreciated her as he, Zeph, never had.

But whatever others might label his impulsive actions, he considered them those of a desperate man with no alternative.

Zeph left the magistrate's men still stomping in the gardens, with no more to show for their single-minded efforts than a lone glove found in the bushes just outside the front door. Mrs. Fillmore claimed it belonged to Malana, that she had been wearing it, along with its mate, on that afternoon when she had left her mistress working in the gardens out back.

"Clean up after them the best that you can," Zeph instructed the distraught housekeeper as he prepared for a hasty departure.

"You will find her, won't you, sir?" the woman asked in return, her great eyes lifted as if she firmly believed he had the power to make it happen.

"I'll find her, Mrs. Fillmore. I promise, even if it is the last thing I do."

Sounded like fairytale heroics to him, the foolish kind that never produced results, the kind he had scoffed at all his life and swore he would never participate in. Leave it to God to make him eat his hypocritical words yet again.

He sailed then, his crew no doubt questioning his sanity and his authority when he pushed them and the ship to their limits and beyond. The fact was, Niles had five days of good head wind on him. If Zeph had any hope at all of catching up, then he had to take risks.

And he took them. At every turn. Without regard to his own safety or that of the ship he had once considered his all-important mistress. If he found it odd that not one man aboard registered a complaint, he couldn't spare the time to think about it.

Late one night, when they were well past the dangers

of the Strait of Magellan but there was still no sight of their
quarry, and his confidence of ever finding Niles glimmered
dimly even in the pale moonlight, Zeph stood alone at the
wheel of his ship. He listened to those ever-present drums
that pounded in his head. Like the voice of some fire-
breathing, pagan demigod who could take on human form,
they seemed almost to mock him, to warn him to turn
back, to come no farther. Malana was where she belonged.
Zeph had lost, and he would lose even more if he persisted
in his present, destructive course.

Feeling infinitesimal and anything but heroic, he stared
up at the slack sails, wondering if, in truth, he'd made
a big mistake, if God—his God—was trying to tell him
something.

Perhaps Malana wished to return to her native land. If
she did, who was he to try and stop her? Maybe he should
give up this crazy transoceanic chase and go back to what
he knew best. Whaling. The dangers there presented fewer
threats and challenges than the unexplored waters called
love. His heart, however, refused to listen to such reason.

The lone voice accompanied by a strange four-string
musical instrument, the likes of which he had never before
witnessed, drifted from the quarterdeck and filled the
empty crevices of his heart, as a dry sponge soaks up mois-
ture.

The song was romantic drivel, of course, the lament
of an ancient mariner who pursued a beautiful mermaid
around the world, looking for her in every lagoon and
harbor. All for naught, as so many of these foolish tales
ended, with the sailor taking his last, dying breath without
giving up hope. It was something in the refrain that caught
Zeph's attention and bolstered his own flagging optimism.

"Zephiran, Zephiran, oh, god of the west wind, carry
me, cradle me, find me her arms. Then I will die a happy
man."

Malana was out there somewhere. She needed him. He couldn't give up.

*Damn sentimental fool,* he chided himself for allowing the words of a song to affect him so. Determined nevertheless, Zeph turned up the collar of his pea jacket to the sudden westerly wind that took hold of the sheets overhead, billowing them with speed and renewed hope.

He would find her. Bring her home, no matter the cost. Then he would love her as no man had ever loved a woman, and he would never leave her again.

God, let him get there in time, before whatever the persistent drums warned him would happen actually did.

# Chapter Eighteen

The meaning of Niles Kilpatrick's spiteful words became clear quickly enough. Day in and day out, the future hung over Malana's head, a fear-evoking black cloud. She'd discovered that Mao, her stepfather, chief of her people, was also aboard. He had come for her, determined to take her back to Hitihiti, back to the sacrificial fate that awaited her there.

On the long voyage, the chieftain picked his moments to visit her in her dark, cramped prison, always reminding her of the duty she had run away from and the harm it had done the People. She had been promised to the god, Te Tuma, a sacrifice for the sake of all the Hitihitians. To her horror, she learned of her mother's fate. Her mother, who had gladly sacrificed herself for the sake of her daughter's life. The knowledge made Malana weep. It took her sense of self and misshaped it into guilt. So even though the truth might have persuaded Mao to let her go, she did not bother to confess that she was no longer the virgin called for by the ritual.

Not that she believed the reoccurring visions, for Te Tuma told her it did not matter. He wanted her regardless. But would the sacrifice of her life help her island people? Malana doubted it. She put no faith in the pagan gods and their vengeful demands for human sacrifice. Just when she had lost her island innocence, she could not exactly remember, but she wasn't sure she wanted to believe in the *haole* God, either. So what did that leave her?

In the dark silence of her confinement, she desperately clung to the love she felt for Zeph Westley. It was the only truth she had. Without it, she was lost.

Even with it, she doubted her redemption. Who was she to deserve deliverance again?

Finally, once they reached the open waters of the Pacific, where no hope lay in her possibly escaping to land, Malana was given limited freedom to venture topside. The warmth of the remembered South Pacific sun worked like a healing force. Dare she imagine that, in spite of the fact she had disobeyed Zeph, he might still love her, too? And if he did, could she believe that somehow he would know where to find her? How could she hope for that when he did not even know of her plight?

Her one wish, her one prayer to the *haole* God, if she could believe in Him, would be that her logic prove false. That Zeph was on his way. He had defeated Te Tuma in her visions once before. He could do it again. The terrible, taunting waking dreams came more and more often and with such vividness that they left little room for hope. It was as if whatever force was behind them gained strength the closer she drew. Then the day came when the distant horizon glowed red.

Uncertain just what it was she saw, Malana stared at the phenomenon for the longest time. "What is it, Mao?" she asked of her stepfather.

"It is the god's wrath," he announced, his pointed stare reminding her of her part in all this. Then he lifted his arms toward the heavens. "Oh, Te Tuma, I have returned. Just as I promised, I have brought you what you seek." He grabbed her arm, forcing her to her knees, and bound her there on the deck of the ship.

"Mao, listen to me. My death will accomplish nothing." Valiantly, she tried to resist, to struggle to her feet.

"Be quiet, girl. I speak with the god." Filled with his own self-importance, the chieftain roughly shoved her back down to her knees.

Head bent in defeat, Malana saw no choice but to await her fate with the grace and dignity that would have made her mother proud.

Then word of the distant, unidentified red glow spread shipwide.

At last, Niles Kilpatrick's true colors revealed themselves as greed.

"The pearls, Mao. We must get them right away," Niles demanded, clutching one of the islander's uplifted arms. "You promised. The pearls for the girl."

The stout chieftain easily shook off the lightweight man and continued his tirade to the heavens.

The crew's curiosity turned to panic when they realized their captain intended to sail straight for the fiery sky. Their initial reaction verged on mutiny.

"I'll make every man aboard a rich one," Niles promised in his obsession.

But wealth was not enough to convince the basically honest men to risk their lives.

Finally, Jake Ainsworth, the second in command and a pirate at heart, took matters into his own hands, demanding their obedience. His pistols cocked and aimed at the insurrection leaders, he forced them back to their posts.

Their arrival in the normally still, blue-green waters of the natural harbor of Hitihiti was an uneasy one at best. The hot, red glow emanating from the mouth of the volcano reflected in the sea, turning it a violent shade of purple. The beaches were littered with crying babies and other small children, along with the meager possessions of the islanders being loaded in every available canoe, seaworthy or not. Pigs, dogs, and fowl ran helter-skelter, their plaintive calls adding to the confusion.

Malana watched, her heart going out to the People, her people. No matter what else she might become, she was still a Hitihitian princess. Frightened and leaderless, the People had been unsure of what to do, where to turn. Mao's long-anticipated arrival filled them with a resurgence of hope, the kind that she had abandoned long before. Proclaiming their joy, they flocked into the water, some swimming, some in boats, to meet him.

All around the ship, the multitude of vessels and swimmers bobbed. The uneasy crew refused to allow them aboard. Malana voiced no protest, nor did anyone else, when her stepfather dragged her off the ship and into one of the larger, double-hulled canoes, forcing her, hands still bound, to sit where all could see her.

"Te Tuma. Te Tuma." The chant was taken up on every pagan tongue, as the native vessel carrying her made its way to shore.

With the regal grace that was a natural part of her, Malana held her head high even in the face of demise. She was a princess after all. No one could ever take that away from her.

In spite of her brave facade, her heart quaked when the mighty volcano roared and spewed a fireworks of living embers that fell in ash and cinders, sizzling when they struck the water. In the smoke cloud that followed, she could swear she saw a face.

The face of Te Tuma. She recognized it from her vision yet refused to give it credence. Still, it mocked her. It told her of her fate, from which there was no escape.

"Zephiran!"

Only the pain in her arm where Mao gripped her made Malana aware that she had stood up in the canoe and voiced her cry aloud. What her purpose had been—to make herself heard, to defy the god, or to throw herself overboard—she could not be certain, but the gathered natives roared their excitement as she was brought ashore and led up the beach toward the god-house deep in the jungle.

She knew it was futile. Even so, Malana glanced over her shoulder and scanned the vast expanse of sea, hoping. Praying to a God whose name she did not know, Whom she was not even certain existed.

There was nothing but water to be seen clear to the distant horizon.

Zeph was not there. He could not hear her.

He could not help her.

There was nothing on the horizon but the never-ending blueness of the vast ocean that blended with the ceaseless sky.

Glass in hand, Zeph watched it with a diligence that belied the calm expression on his face. He glanced up at the sailor stationed in the crow's nest high above.

"Anything, mister?" he asked for what must have been the hundredth time that morning.

"No, Cap'n. Nothing yet," the man replied.

"Call me as soon as there is." It was undoubtedly the hundredth time he had said that, too.

"Aye, sir," the sailor responded, as if it were the first time.

If ever there was hell, this was it, Zeph decided, renewing his vigilance. He knew his goal was out there, just beyond the horizon, and yet it seemed he never reached it.

Malana. She didn't even know he was coming. But just

as disheartening was the fact that he couldn't be certain he would get there in time.

Staring into his glass, Zeph willed an end to his agony. Then as if in answer, he thought he saw a faint red glow.

Lowering the telescope, he studied the unusual phenomenon with his naked eye. Was it only his imagination?

"Do you see that, mister?" he called up to the watch.

"Aye, sir."

"What do you make of it?"

"Ain't nothin' like I've ever seen before," the sailor admitted, his voice laced with uncertainty. "It's as if the whole world beyond the horizon is on fire."

"Not the whole world," Zeph muttered to himself, "merely paradise."

Paradise at the mercy of hell. Once, long ago, he had witnessed the eruption of a volcano. He knew of the fiery devastation, knew what it meant to those caught in the path of the hot, molten lava.

Zeph closed his glass with a snap of determination. He would have called for more sail, but the ship's rigging was already filled to capacity.

Malana was out there. He must get to her, no matter what it cost him personally. But did he have the right to demand the same from his crew?

He glanced around. All eyes were on him, waiting for orders. These men. Zeph knew their superstitions, their fears, yet he had come to trust them just as they trusted him. In turn, they knew of his mission, as he had kept nothing from them. But would they agree to risk their lives for it?

He could command them. Undoubtedly, as the ship's master, he could make them obey. But was that what he wanted? Was blind obedience enough for him anymore?

"All hands on deck," he ordered.

The crew obeyed, their fears surfacing in the looks they

gave him, the first signs of distrust. He had them gather so all could hear what he had to say.

"I know that you have all seen the red sky. I know what you are thinking . . . that the curse of Hitihiti is, at last, upon us."

His statement received a muttering of response.

"When a volcano erupts, it is not a curse," he insisted, lifting his hand, demanding silence. "It's not some island mumbo jumbo. It's nature. Raw, frightening, uncontrollable nature, to be sure. I won't lie to you. There are risks involved, but I've seen it before and lived to tell about it. A ship in harbor is relatively safe from the lava flow. Waters can get rough, but we have sailed the worst the sea can dish out and survived it."

"Cap'n, I hear hot ash can catch a ship afire."

"That's true. It can. Be we'll go in prepared. We'll douse the sails and the deck with seawater." Was it only his imagination, or were they beginning to soften? "I won't ask any man to go ashore with me, and I will leave instructions with Mr. Kennedy to sail at the first sign of real danger."

"What about you, Cap'n?"

"I'll take my chances," Zeph replied.

It was heroics as its best or at its worst, depending on how one looked at it.

"I can't do this alone," he continued. "Believe me, I would if I could."

In those few moments when minds were being made up in spite of him and what he might want, Zeph saw himself for who and what he really was. A man in love, a man who had found himself outside of himself. He was no longer an island.

With studied calculation, he looked each man in the eye. What would he do if they should all refuse him?

"We didn't come all this way just to turn back now. I'm with ya, Cap'n." The first man stepped forward, followed quickly by each in turn.

"Steady as she goes, Mr. Kennedy," he called out to his first officer at the wheel.

At long last, Zeph Westley knew what it meant to be captain of his crew, captain of his life, and, most importantly, captain of his heart.

Bedecked in island costume and in the traditional feathered cape and headdress of the sacrificial bride, Malana tried once again to warn Mao of the futility of his act.

"We must see the People to safety. We must get them as far away from the island as we can," she tried to reason with the chieftain.

Once again, Mao refused to listen. His eyes, his hopes, were pinned on the distant volcano, glowing red with death and destruction. A dense black cloud encompassed the dome, blotting out the sun. He hauled Malana forth, the chanting priests following, torches lit. They left the thatch god-house filled with its pearl-adorned idol, making their way across the yard of the *marae* and out the stone archway.

Was she the only one in the unnatural darkness to see Niles Kilpatrick slip in behind them, his eyes glazed with obsession?

Malana tried to convey her discovery, to warn them of the rape their culture would suffer at the hands of her greedy cousin, but the sacrificial party had eyes only for their pagan god spewing his hot wrath upon them. Bits of ash, cinder, and spiral-shaped molten rock fell all around them, blackening the palm fronds, the underbrush, the bright yellow feathers of her cape.

They climbed the familiar path leading to the mouth of the volcano, higher and higher, hotter and hotter, until Malana could no longer breathe. To her left a small fire broke out in the underbrush, from the heat or from the hot ash, she could not be certain. Malana stumbled, crying out her pain when Mao roughly pulled her up by her arms bound behind her back, forcing her to take another step and then another. She turned her face away, the hot breath of Te Tuma too much to bear.

"We must go on," Mao bellowed.

But the priests shook their heads, pointing skyward toward the dome of the volcano, their fear as real as her own.

Malana looked up. A river of fire had spilt over the lip of the cone, slowly making its way straight toward them. Lava, she realized. It would destroy everything in its path, be it flesh, wood, or stone.

"Please, Mao, you must listen to me," she cried over the roar of the hot, smoky wind that blanketed the island. "Everyone will die if you do not lead them to safety."

"I will save them. The sacrifice. The sacrifice. It will work. Te Tuma, why do you continue to forsake me?" Grabbing her by the arm, the chieftain brushed past the cowering priest, dragging her blindly in the darkness toward the river of lava still coming at them.

They had traveled only a few more excruciating yards when Malana stumbled again and fell, pitching forward, hitting her cheek against a huge boulder. Mao jerked on her arms, nearly ripping them from their sockets. But her foot, which had slipped between the rock and the side of the mountain, was wedged so firmly that even when Mao squatted down to try and dislodge it, it would not budge.

He looked up then at the top of the volcano, listened to the roar of the wind, the pelting of stones all around them. Then he turned to her.

"It is here that you await your fate, my daughter," he told her. "Remember your duty to the People."

"Mao," she cried, struggling to release her trapped foot, to avoid being struck by the hailstorm of hot cinder, ash, and stone that fell all around them. "Please, do not leave me here like this."

But he was already gone. Only the living river of death slowly making its way toward her would release her now.

Zeph decided he would row himself to shore if he must. To his surprise, almost every member of his crew volunteered to take him and wait for his return. He picked the best, most experienced oarsmen among them. The powerful rowers got him there fast enough. It took him longer to thread his way through the confusion on the beach.

He looked up at the top of the volcano already spewing lava, then out to sea, where Nile Kilpatrick's ship lay at anchor not far from his own. There was no denying the truth. It was just a matter of time before the entire island succumbed to the power of nature's force.

"Start taking these people aboard the *Dolphin*," he instructed his men. He didn't expect Niles to aid in the islanders' plight, but Zeph would do everything in his power to take as many to safety as his ship could hold.

"Cap'n, are you sure?" one of the oarsmen asked. "What if we're not here when you get back?"

"Then I'll wait, or I'll swim if I have to."

He prayed he wouldn't have to.

The mention of Malana's name among the panicked islanders clustered on the beach brought only one response. They pointed where their eyes rolled, upward toward the erupting volcano, where even now the fiery trail of lava spilt over the open wound of the dome and slid slowly down the side.

Malana.

He had no idea just how far up she might have been taken, but he would go to the very top, to the ends of the earth, if he must, to find her.

Remembering his way along the footpath that led to the god-house deep in the jungle, Zeph found himself recalling the events of that night when he had once before rescued her. She had been so young, so helpless and naive. He had been so reluctant. He cringed to think that he had almost refused to help.

What would his life have been like if he had refused? What would it be if he could not find her now?

Reaching the stone archway of the *marae*, he spied the unnatural flickering light emanating from the god-house. If only it were true that Malana was still there. He raced forward, pushing through the door constructed of plaited palm fronds. There, to his dismay, he discovered Niles Kilpatrick.

His old enemy whirled, the knife he held in his hand, intended to dig out the pearls embedded in the icons, pointed straight at Zephiran's heart.

"You can't stop me, Westley," he hissed, lunging forward with the weapon.

Zeph easily avoided it. "I won't have to, Niles. Soon enough, your own greed will take care of you. Where is Malana?" he demanded, caring not that Niles held a fortune in pearls in his hand.

"What do I know or care what happens to some heathen wench?" Turning, Niles resumed his madcap plunder of the temple icons, slipping his rewards into a small leather pouch attached to his wrist.

Zeph left Niles to his own fate, noting that bits of cinder and ash fell on the thatched roof of the hut. Should he try to make Niles see reason? No, there wasn't time. Selecting one of the rush torches to light his way in the eerie darkness, he started up the treacherous path littered with bits of hot cinders and ashes, which made it that much harder to navigate. Nonetheless, he pressed on, knowing his time at best was limited. Partway up, Zeph paused in a bend to assess his progress and to catch his breath.

Just ahead, he spied what looked like a human foot. Fearful that he had found Malana, but much too late, he dashed on, unmindful of the hot volcanic ground cover burning his feet even through the thick leather soles of his boots.

Rounding the corner, Zeph discovered Mao crumbled in the pathway. He took only a few precious moments to decide that the island chieftain was dead, his eyes wide open, staring blankly with a look of betrayal forever etched on his tattooed features. It was undoubtedly a freak accident that a large, hot bit of molten stone had hit him in the head. Or was it an accident? Zeph wondered, looking once more at the dome of the volcano overhead.

No, just as he'd told his men, it was not island mumbo jumbo. Volcanoes did not house pagan gods. They did not seek revenge or human sacrifice. But even if they did, that would not stop him.

Stepping over the fallen figure of the island chieftain, Zeph continued on his way, threading carefully, always conscious of the hot bombs raining down upon his own head from the volcano. The heat grew so intense that he dropped his torch along the wayside, using his arm to shield his face. Confronted with a brush fire to his left, he removed his pea jacket and beat it out, but only enough to get past it. What about his return? He would deal with that when he had to.

How much farther could he hope to go?

He would go until he died or until he found Malana.

The first rivulet of lava oozed across the trail, coming from a small fissure on the side of the volcano. Zeph had no choice but to jump across it. Glancing up, he saw that the thin, shallow stream turned into a wider one coming down the mountainside not far ahead. It was just a matter of time before it grew too large to get across.

Nonetheless, he continued on his way, hoping . . . no, fervently praying, that he found Malana soon.

He saw her then, just up ahead, lying in the pathway. She seemed so still, and remembering the fate of Mao, he

feared the worse for her. Was she already dead? His heart
near to bursting with pain and regret, Zeph cried out her
name.

"Malana!"

The fierce, hot wind carried his voice in the opposite
direction, as if it didn't want him to be heard. If Malana
did hear him, she did not respond. Then, to his relief, he
saw her move ... actually, struggle better described her
actions.

Forging ahead, he tried to understand why she remained
in the path of danger. Why didn't she run? Was she injured?
Had Mao done something to her to keep her from escaping? How could he possibly hope to get her back down
the mountain if that was the case?

It was only after he drew close enough to see what
impeded her escape that she saw him, too. Like a rabbit
caught in a snare, she looked so frightened. Her foot
appeared hopelessly wedged between the boulder and the
mountain.

"Zephiran!" she called out, lifting her arms to greet
him when he cut the rope binding them.

He clung to her then, holding her as if he couldn't
believe that she was real, that he had found her alive and
whole.

"You came," she whispered. "To protect me just as you
vowed."

Her words sounded so calm and confident. If only he
could be as certain of his abilities as she seemed to be.

Dislodging himself from her embrace, Zeph tried valiantly to release her trapped foot, but to no avail.

"Twist it a little to the left, Malana," he instructed.

He could tell from her pained expression that she did
her best. Still, her foot remained steadfastly caught beneath
the heavy boulder.

Zeph looked up. The lava was coming closer and closer
by the moment, picking up speed as it traveled. Thankfully,

the falling missiles of death no longer rained upon them, as the flow must have released enough pressure, at least for the moment. Still, if he did not get her free soon, they would never be able to escape the hot liquid death inching its way toward them. He glanced at her then, trying not to let his worry show, but she, too, had judged the distance and the odds of their making it.

"It's no use," she declared, struggling hard to free herself, beating her fists against the rock that held her like arms of a jealous lover. "You must leave me, Zeph, and save yourself."

"No, never." He grabbed her then, so slender and fragile beneath his sea-weathered hands, shaking her until she looked up at him and once more laid her fear upon his strong shoulders. "You can't give up, my love. I will figure out a way. You have to believe in me."

"I do believe in you," she declared with a calmness that gave him the courage to believe in himself. "No matter what happens, I will always believe in you."

He couldn't let her down, not now.

The boulder was perched precariously on the edge of the pathway. The only way to move so that it didn't crush Malana's leg when he rolled it out of the way—if he could roll it out of the way—was to skirt around behind it. But the ledge he needed to use was so narrow that there was barely enough room to give him a secure foothold. There wasn't time to study it, to think it through, however. At the most, he had only time enough to act.

Throwing the last of his ingrained caution to the wind, Zeph navigated the ledge, thinking at any moment he might lose his balance. He tried to imagine that he made his way among the spars and masts of the *Dolphin,* a place where he always felt at home. Then, without looking back at the precipice that awaited him should he make a mistake, he pitted his weight and all his strength against the mighty stone, willing it to move. It did. Zeph's heart surged with confidence.

Then his foot slipped.

"Zephiran, no!" Malana cried, reaching out and grasping nothing but air, when he nearly lost his balance to plunge backward to certain demise.

Still, the close call with death did not thwart his determination. Once again, he secured as firm a foothold as possible and put his shoulder to the rock. It seemed forever, to the point that his strength was about to give out, when the boulder finally relinquished its ancient hold on the earth with a groan that sounded almost human.

Zeph didn't wait to watch its fatal descent. Instead, he rushed forward even as the giant crashes echoed from below. Kneeling beside Malana and her freed foot, he quickly assessed the damage. Beneath the blood on her ankle—telltale evidence of how hard she had fought to escape—the bones appeared solid, the swelling and bruising minimal. But could she walk?

Taking her arm, he lifted Malana to her feet, aware of the grimace of pain, which she bravely attempted to conceal, that crossed her face. Without asking, he bent to pick her up, uncertain how he would make the descent back down to the beach carrying her, but determined to accomplish it nonetheless.

"No," she murmured, pushing his hands away. "I can do it by myself."

Her first few steps were shaky at best. Then, with the fortitude he recognized as a vital part of her . . . a part he loved so much . . . she pressed on, ignoring any pain. He took her hand, squeezing it to show the pride he felt in her, and set the pace, knowing it was faster than she could probably handle for long, but also knowing it was necessary for their success.

The first real obstacle came in the form of lava. The thin, fiery stream oozing out of the small fissure nearby, which he had been forced to cross on his way up the side of the mountain, had widened, just as he'd predicted, bubbling and hissing with warning as it gobbled up everything it touched. If it were just himself, he might have attempted to jump the shallow ribbon, but Zeph knew without a doubt that with her injury and her bare feet, Malana would never make it across. What was he to do?

Desperate for a solution, he glanced around and spied the thin, bowed palm tree just on the other side of the lava stream, just out of his reach. He stretched, moving as close to the lava as he dared, but still he could not grasp it. Then he saw the rock, a solid island jutting up out of the shallow stream of lava. If he could reach it and could tolerate the heat, he would be able to grab the palm and, with a little luck, bend it enough so Malana could use it to get across.

She clutched his arm when he started to cross, her look filled with trepidation.

"Trust me. I know what I'm doing," he assured her, even as he wondered if he actually did.

Zeph reached the precarious position on the rock without incident. Still, it proved slippery, and seeing the lava flow all around him did not make it any easier to perch there without anything to hang on to, then to stretch out and grab the bent palm. Once he did, he realized he had been holding his breath the entire time. But the palm proved as strong as he'd hoped, and with the agility of a sailor, Zeph managed to make it back to where Malana stood.

She looked at him with uncertainty when he explained his plan.

"You can do it," he told her then, showing her how to grasp the trunk and, by moving hand over hand, pull herself along the arched bridge the palm created across the lava.

Fortunately, the rough frond husks clinging to the trunk

of the tree gave substance to her handholds, which at first were calculated and uncertain.

"You can do it," Zeph assured her again in a quiet voice when she hesitated.

Because she believed him, Malana forged ahead. But then halfway across, she cast her eyes downward.

"No, no, love. Don't look down. Look straight ahead," he insisted, feeling so damn helpless, fearing she would fall while he stood by and watched. If only he could have rushed in to help her, but he couldn't abandon his post steadying the tree on which she clung so precariously.

It seemed a lifetime before she finally reached the safety of the other side. Then, letting go of the tree, which then shot forward, gyrating in the air, Zeph made his way across, joining her.

Once more together, he grasped her hand tightly, thankful that they had made it this far. Nonetheless, time was running short. The wall of lava coming from the main crater had almost reached the place where he had found her trapped beneath the boulder. It was moving faster and faster with each given moment, and undoubtedly there were more obstacles in their way.

The brush fire he had battled on his way up presented the next problem. It had escalated, reaching high into the surrounding palm trees. The heat was intense, while the ground where it had already burned smoldered. Once again, he noted Malana's bare feet, her shoulders also uncovered, as she wore a simple native costume. She would never be able to traverse the path.

Without hesitation, Zeph stripped off his sturdy pea coat, securing it around her head and shoulders like a protective shawl. It was large enough to reach almost to her hips, covering her well enough. Then, ignoring her protests, he scooped her up and made a mad dash across the blackened ground.

He could feel the heat even through the thick soles of

his boots, but he kept on, knowing he had no choice but to continue.

Finally, they reached the spot where Mao's body lay. The fire had swept through. What there was to see, Zeph was determined to shield from her, even if the smell of burnt flesh was inescapable.

As if, with an uncanny second insight, she sensed all was not right.

"Stop," Malana cried out, struggling to push away the lapels of the jacket that covered her face.

"No," Zeph insisted, cupping them back around her like blinders.

"It's Mao, isn't it?"

He nodded curtly.

"Is he dead?"

Again he nodded.

"Are you certain?"

"Without a doubt," he replied, glancing sideways only briefly.

"What will the People do now that they are leaderless?" Her face, so beautiful in her regal concern, looked up to him for an answer.

"Right now all any of us can do is try to reach safety." He set her down on her feet and aimed her in the direction of the beach. With luck on their side, they might make it.

Just ahead he spied the god-house, located only minutes from the boat waiting for them on the beach. The roof of the hut was in flames. As they hurried by, Malana touched his arm.

"I think I saw someone inside," she insisted, pointing, refusing to continue on.

"Niles," Zeph muttered, suspecting whom she had seen. His old enemy had done so much harm to others. Even now he plundered the relics of an innocent society. Did the man warrant Malana's concern or his consideration?

Zeph glanced up at the distant volcano, far behind them.

The lava, that living river of death, flowed closer and closer, however. He grasped her hand, determined to go on, to save her over one not so deserving.

"I know what he has done, but we cannot just leave him," she protested breathlessly, her pleading eyes turning up to him with such reverence.

To be honest, Zeph didn't think Niles would listen to him. He never had. But for Malana's sake, he would try.

"Niles," he called out, running to the door and looking inside. Through the billowing smoke he thought he saw him. Then, when he realized Malana had foolishly followed him, Zeph turned to her. "Go on ahead," he urged. "I'll be right behind you."

"No." Her voice barely carried over the whoosh of the fire, but her conviction was strong. "I will not be separated from you again."

And he refused to lose her, at any cost.

"Niles," he shouted again. "Damn it, man. Give it up. The building's on fire."

"No. No," came the manic refusal. "There's still more to get. I'm rich. I'm rich."

The crack of a timber forced Zeph back. Putting a protective arm about Malana, he dragged her with him just as the center of the roof caved in.

The surprised cries of pain were heart-wrenching, to say the least. Not even Niles deserved such a horrible end.

Zeph ripped aside the door now hanging haphazardly on one lashed hinge. The smoke and the heat were unbelievable. He lifted one arm to shield his face and then he saw Niles, lying on the floor, the burning beam pinning him.

"Zeph, help me," the man cried out, his hand lifting, reaching, begging.

Recklessly, Zeph entered the burning building, Malana's cries of distress following him. He managed, though unsure how he did, to locate Niles's outstretched hand.

"Hang on. I've got you." Grasping the clutching fingers, he pulled and, to his relief, felt the man move toward him. For a brief moment the smoke cleared and he could see Niles, his face blackened, his eyes terrorized. Then the smoke billowed about them again.

Zeph kept pulling, dragging his burden closer and closer to the door, thinking he had at last succeeded, when the roof snapped right over his head.

He stumbled backward, in the melee losing his grip on Niles's hand. But he still held on to something, a leather pouch attached to the man's wrist. The blaze ignited. It seemed everywhere, and yet he kept pulling, hoping, in spite of the fire and smoke that made it impossible to see, that he still had Niles.

Then, suddenly, the pouch gave way, the thong that held it breaking. In the doorway, Zeph fell backward. The flames engulfed everything he had left behind.

Knowing it was too late for Niles, he grabbed Malana's arm and forced her to continue on down the path in front of him. By the time they reached the beach, the lava had claimed the *marae* and everything inside it.

On the beach the small boat waited for them. He noted then that Niles's ship was already gone. His disloyal crew had left him behind. Mutiny, no doubt. Zeph could well imagine what had happened to whomever Niles had left in charge. Dead or worse, forced to swim to shore to meet his fate.

It wasn't until later, when exhausted and dazed he sat in the whaleboat, Malana beside him, the steady slap, slap, slap of the oars bringing him back to reality, that Zeph realized he clutched something in his fist.

Perplexed, he looked down to discover that he still held the leather pouch that had belonged to Niles. Automatically, he opened it and peered inside.

"Oh, my God," he murmured.

"What is it, Zephiran?" Malana asked in her sweet, unpretentious innocence.

He took her hand, smoothed out the palm, and poured the contents of the pouch into it.

It was a fortune in pearls, enough to see them more than comfortable for a lifetime and longer.

Wealth? It was what he had worked so hard for all of his life. Was that what he wanted? Was that what he needed to be truly happy? The questions he asked himself were reflected in Malana's dark, trusting eyes.

He glanced down at the pearls, even now beginning to spill from her hand, that did little if anything to prevent their escape. These pearls, these gems of the sea. Zeph suspected they carried the last remaining vestige of the power of Te Tuma. If the god was real, most likely he might survive in the soul of any man who succumbed to the lure of such riches.

Taking Malana's small hand in his much larger one, Zeph guided it out over the side of the boat and turned it over. Soundlessly, the pearls slipped away, returning to their source, forever disempowering their master.

"I love you, Zephiran Westley."

Malana's fervently spoken vow made him the wealthiest man in the world.

# Epilogue

The flotilla, a hodgepodge of vessels led by the *Dolphin*, plowed its way through the open sea. Malana stood at the rail of the whaling ship, her eyes cast first to the islanders crowding the deck, then to those in every sailable double-hulled canoe that had been on the island of Hitihiti.The island. She looked up into the distant horizon. A red haze was all that was left of what had once been her home, the land of her people for as long as they could remember, for as long as the stories had been passed down from generation to generation.

What would become of the People now that Hitihiti was no more? The island, even as they had sailed away, had literally exploded, vanishing as if it had never existed. With it had gone Te Tuma's long reign of terror. With it had disappeared Mao, the last of the royal line. All that is, except for herself.

Her gaze turned then to the man who was her husband in the eyes of the *haole* God in whom she now firmly believed. Zeph Westley. He stood at the helm of his ship, master of all that surrounded him. Master of her heart. What would his reaction be if he knew what she was thinking? Would he declare her negligent in her wifely duties? But what about her duties to that part of her that would always be Hitihitian?

It was as if something cleaved her in two, the divided factions of her heart, spirit, and soul battling for supremacy. If she were forced to choose, there was no question who would win. Zeph. She loved him. She could not live without him.

But why must she choose?

Her gaze turned once more to the desperate, fearful islanders. Even though the choice was clear cut in her mind, she would always feel a pang of guilt if forced to leave them.

But first, she would trust in Zeph to find them a new home.

She was with him when he and his loyal mate, Mr. Kennedy, pored over the navigational charts. In fact, she easily memorized them, each one in turn. Malana smiled sadly to think how simple that task was compared to every other aspect of her life. Finally, Zeph's finger bore down on a tiny spot, no more that a pinpoint on the map, reminding her how small they were in the scope of humanity.

"Here. By my calculations, this island is only a few days away. If memory serves me right, it is uninhabited and there's no volcano there."

The people rejoiced when she made the announcement that they had a new home, safe from the ever-present danger of destruction by a vengeful god. They danced like uninhibited children on the deck of the *Dolphin*. Even the sailors joined in the laughing and singing. Finally, after much encouragement, Malana too added her own agile interpretation of the joy shared by one and all.

Aware only of the music, she looked up to find Zeph standing on the quarterdeck, watching her, his face an

unreadable mask except for the pulse in his left temple.
It pounded in rhythm to the native drums.

Uncertain what inspired her, Malana made her way
across the deck and up the stairs, still dancing with the
abandon of the islands, until she stood right in front of
him. She whirled, her hips gyrating to the drumbeats, her
dark eyes fastened on his blue ones.

She whirled again, her waist-length hair flying out all
around her, and came to a sudden halt, finding herself
face to face with the man who never seemed tolerant of
that free-spirited Hitihitian part of her. But it was who she
was, and no matter how hard she might try to change,
Malana did not think it possible.

She started to move away, only to find that his hand had
laid claim to her arm. He pulled her up against him, his
body uncompromisingly rigid, his eyes steadfastly leveled
on her.

"It seems you're going native on me, Malana."

"Would that be so bad, Zephiran?" she asked, undulating her hips in a teasing way.

"I don't want to lose you." His hand moved down, still-
ing her movement. "Not ever again."

There was such depth of emotion, such vulnerability in
the inflection of his voice, it gave her pause. Reaching up,
she cupped his sea-sculpted face in her hand.

"As I want never to be without you. Not for one day or
one single night."

"Ah, Malana, my love. You speak of a perfect world,
paradise on earth where there are no responsibilities
except making love to my wife. I don't believe it exists."

"You are wrong, Zeph. It does exist." She placed the
flat of her hand against his heart, feeling its wild beating
beneath her palm. "It exists here." Then she turned and
swept her hand in the direction of the ongoing celebration.
"And here, if you will just let it."

"What are you suggesting? That I go native, too?" He

frowned, his brows nearly meeting on the bridge of his nose, an earnest expression that was as familiar to her as his touch.

"Would that be so bad?" she asked.

"What of my life as a whaler?"

He stood so rigidly that it caused her some doubt.

"Killing the noble creatures of the sea? Is that what you really want to continue to do?"

"No. To be honest, I don't think I have the heart of a whaler anymore."

He gave his answer so quickly that Malana smiled, knowing his heart was now a kind and benevolent one.

*"Pu'uwai o Kini."* She turned her gaze to the People dancing below.

*"Pu'uwai o Kini.* What does that mean, Malana?" His arm slipped about her waist.

"It seems you have much to learn, my husband. It means the heart of a king. They need you, Zeph, as much as they need me. You have promised them *lani* . . . paradise. What more could any chieftain provide for his people?" She looked up into his face, seeing the confusion, knowing she had only to find the right words, the right gesture, and he would believe. "Paradise can be ours, too."

"Paradise," he murmured, smiling with longing. "I would give anything if only that were possible."

"It is possible. It is already happening. Why do you fight it so?" she asked, taking his hands and picking up the rhythm of the drums in her steps, leading him across the deck and down the stairs to the celebration below.

At first he moved so stiffly that she had to smile, knowing him quite capable of agile movement when the circumstances called for it. Placing her hands upon his hips, Malana let the natural rhythm of the drums radiate from her fingers as she taught him, as he had once taught her, the rhythms of love. Soon enough, he had it, to the delight of everyone aboard, from islander to sailor. Even young

Daniel laughed and pointed and urged him on. Yes, that island fever that set the heart to racing, the spirit to soaring, the soul on its chosen path, had found its way inside him.

Paradise.

Malana stepped back and watched him with pride. Zeph Westley had at last found what he had been seeking all his life, she suspected. He had found it in the arms of a woman . . . the last place he had thought to look.

In the Zeph Westley upon whom she had come to depend, Malana felt confident that once he discovered what he wanted, he would never let it go.

# TODAY'S HOTTEST READS
# ARE TOMORROW'S SUPERSTARS

# DON'T MISS THESE ROMANCES FROM BEST-SELLING AUTHOR KATHERINE DEAUXVILLE!

THE CRYSTAL HEART       (0-8217-4928-5, $5.99)

Emmeline gave herself to a sensual stranger in a night aglow with candlelight and mystery. Then she sent him away. Wed by arrangement, Emmeline desperately needed to provide her aged husband with an heir. But her lover awakened a passion she kept secret in her heart . . . until he returned and rocked her world with his demands and his desire.

THE AMETHYST CROWN       (0-8217-4555-7, $5.99)

She is Constance, England's richest heiress. A radiant, silver-eyed beauty, she is a player in the ruthless power games of King Henry I. Now, a desperate gambit takes her back to Wales where she falls prey to a ragged prisoner who escapes his chains, enters her bedchamber . . . and enslaves her with his touch. He is a bronzed, blond Adonis whose dangerous past has forced him to wander Britain in disguise. He will escape an enemy's shackles—only to discover a woman whose kisses fire his tormented soul. His birthright is a secret, but his wild, burning love is his destiny . . .

*Available wherever paperbacks are sold, or order direct from the Publisher. Send cover price plus 50¢ per copy for mailing and handling to Penguin USA, P.O. Box 999, c/o Dept. 17109, Bergenfield, NJ 07621. Residents of New York and Tennessee must include sales tax. DO NOT SEND CASH.*

# FROM AWARD-WINNING AUTHOR
## JO BEVERLEY

DANGEROUS JOY                    (0-8217-5129-8, $5.99)

Felicity is a beautiful, rebellious heiress with a terrible secret.
Miles is her reluctant guardian—a man of seductive power and
dangerous sensuality. What begins as a charade borne of desperation soon becomes an illicit liaison of passionate abandon
and forbidden love. One man stands between them: a cruel
landowner sworn to possess the wealth he craves and the
woman he desires. His dark treachery will drive the lovers to
dare the unknowable and risk the unthinkable, determined to
hold on to their joy.


FORBIDDEN                        (0-8217-4488-7, $4.99)

While fleeing from her brothers, who are attempting to sell
her into a loveless marriage, Serena Riverton accepts a carriage
ride from a stranger—who is the handsomest man she has ever
seen. Lord Middlethorpe, himself, is actually contemplating
marriage to a dull daughter of the aristocracy, when he encounters the breathtaking Serena. She arouses him as no
woman ever has. And after a night of thrilling intimacy—a
forbidden liaison—Serena must choose between a lady's place
and a woman's passion!


TEMPTING FORTUNE                 (0-8217-4858-0, $4.99)

In a night shimmering with destiny, Portia St. Claire discovers
that her brother's debts have made him a prisoner of dangerous
men. The price of his life is her virtue—about to be auctioned
off in London's most notorious brothel. However, handsome
Bryght Malloreen has other ideas for Portia, opening her heart
to a sensuality that tempts her to madness.

*Available wherever paperbacks are sold, or order direct from the
Publisher. Send cover price plus 50¢ per copy for mailing and handling to Penguin USA, P.O. Box 999, c/o Dept. 17109, Bergenfield, NJ 07621. Residents of New York and Tennessee must
include sales tax. DO NOT SEND CASH.*

## YOU WON'T WANT TO READ
## JUST ONE—KATHERINE STONE